978-1-7773423-5-7

Also by Krista Wallace

Gatekeeper's Deception I - Deceiver
Gatekeeper's Deception II - Deceived

Coming Soon

Gatekeeper's Crucible
and
Gatekeeper's Revelation

Fantasy Romantic Comedy

Griffin and the Spurious Correlations

Audioshorts

The Inner Light
To Serve and Protect

In Memory of Da and Mumsey, who wondered,
"Where did *that* come from??" Wish you were here.

.

Gatekeeper's Key

One

One Way to Be Noticed

Another town, another gem of a man who wanted to dazzle her with his "broadsword." All she had done was sit next to him, on one of only two empty stools at the bar. Hadn't even looked at him. Kyer set her beer mug on the bar with a clunk and eyed the cocky bastard as if he were a squashed slug. "What did you say?" *Full tavern. About forty. One third elven. Males and females.*

He nodded at the empty counter before her. "If you're hungry, I got plenty you can feast on. Let's go spend the evening up in my bed." He rested his elbow on the counter, displaying the thickness of his upper arm for her to be roused by.

Kyer wished she could vomit on cue. She stared at him blankly. "Why would I do that?" *Door to the corridor about five paces; exit door about twenty, between tables. Two goblins at the booth behind.*

He shrugged and blinked slowly in that way that was meant to be alluring but wasn't. "No sense you paying for your own room, honey, when Jack and I already took my gear up to my regular room."

"Wow." She nodded, feigning awe. "First-name basis with the stable boy. You've taken my breath away." *Door to the kitchen to the left. Tricky to leap the bar without taking someone out.*

"I'll do more than that, beautiful, given the chance," he said, oblivious to her sarcasm.

"I'll pass." She took another large swallow of beer.

He repeated his fingers-through-the-dark-curls gesture that hadn't impressed her earlier.

After three weeks on the road and two days without food, she didn't have the energy for this. She ignored him with as much threat as she could muster. Honestly, why had Brendow sent her here?

"Name's Simon. Simon Diduck," he said—as if she cared. He edged closer with a salacious sidelong smile. "I'm at your service, darlin'."

"Funny, you seem to think I'm at *yours*."

A low chuckle burst from a black-cloaked man two barstools down. She'd noticed him right away upon entering the tavern at the Burnished Blade. One of those types who is always watching.

Her would-be lover remained unaffected. "Oh, come on. You're such a treasure; only a fool'd let you slip through his fingers." He reached to stroke her cheek, and that was where Kyer drew the line.

She stood up, bristling, itching with the desire to scratch his eyes out. A serving girl stepped in through the door from the corridor and hesitated next to the fireplace. She gestured to someone and a large man joined her, leaning his only arm on the door frame. The silence of the crowded tavern was interrupted by only the crackling of the fire and the jabbering argument of the two goblins behind her. Kyer's shoulders stiffened with the gaze of human and elf alike, some with curiosity, some poised to flee. Diduck was a regular here. Had they seen his tactics before? Nobody seemed eager to offer any assistance. She was on her own. As usual. *Fine.*

"Men like you," she said, "are boring." Her muscles tingled to life, dispelling weariness and hunger. "And you're everywhere. Like rats and cockroaches."

He laughed. "Now that's just plain mean-spirited. Come say, 'sorry.'" His hand stretched out to touch her again but halted because the tip of her stiletto pricked the underside of his chin.

"Can't. I wouldn't want to lie to you." The threat tactic usually worked against bullies; this one was particularly persistent. "Now why don't you go and sit somewhere else, and we'll forget all about this."

The cockroach pushed her weapon aside. "Because rejection doesn't suit me."

Especially in front of an audience. The heat of anger climbing her neck, she raised the knife again. "Brace yourself for disappointment."

His lip curled in a sneer. Apparently he still believed—or was willing to pretend—she was bluffing. "You'd better put that away, darlin'; you might hurt yourself." He sought a favourable reaction from the patrons nearby and found none.

A calm, cold fury draped over her. She couldn't back down now. "Let's settle it."

Though the tightness in his lip betrayed a sudden doubt, he laughed.

Her eyebrows shot up. "So not only are you a boor; you're also a coward," she clarified.

His flash of anger told her she might have struck a nerve. "I'd have thought it cowardly of me to challenge a *girl* to a duel! Hardly honourable." He folded his arms on his chest.

Kyer couldn't help but chuckle. "Isn't it a little late to think about preserving your honour? Besides, I challenged you, not the other way around."

"I must insist we do it properly." He patted the hilt of his broadsword.

With an innocent look as if she were dealing with a child, she sheathed her knife. "Naturally." She brushed back her cloak. Murmurs undulated throughout the tavern. Diduck took one glance at her sullied leather armour and the long sheath of the bastard sword at her belt. His face paled then took on a purplish hue, as if he were angry at her, as if she'd somehow misrepresented herself.

Kyer sighed with frustration. "You can't have thought I'd challenged you to a dagger toss." She gave a quick nod to the publican, who reached under the counter and drew out a book. "With respect to our esteemed proprietor, shall we take this outside? Then he won't have to mop your blood up off his floor." Laughter erupted from many of the patrons. The man in the black cloak two seats away snorted.

"That sounds fine with me," Diduck said.

"If you please." The bartender held the book open with one hand, and a quill in the other.

At the top of the page was written the word *Duel*. Below it was a list of named pairs and dates. Next to one name in each pair was the word *Victor*, and the result, everything ranging from "first blood" to "weapon arm severed." Of the four duels listed on the page, none said, "death," which reflected Kyer's opinion that a dispute between civilized people could be decided without loss of life. She took the quill and signed her name under the date, as written by her host. She passed it back to the publican.

"Kire?" he asked, as he gestured to the one-armed man in the doorway.

"No, it's Kee-Air."

"Most unusual."

The one-armed man loomed over her.

"This is Bill," the publican said. "He will be Arbiter." He turned the book around again for Simon to sign. "And the terms?"

Kyer said, "Loss of weapon. If I win, you take your sorry ass to the other inn and I never see you again." She gave him her back and stalked to the door.

"And if *I* win?" Simon called.

She flung the challenge over her shoulder. "If I lose, I'm yours for the night."

"Either way, you're in trouble, boy," a gruff voice said from a nearby table.

Kyer stepped outside into the crisp, late-winter air, shaking tension from her hands. She drew fresh, chilly breaths scented with greenery, filling her lungs, annoyed that it had come to this. When she left home on the advice of her trainer, she was looking for allies, not adversaries. In her three weeks of travelling, she'd had to put up with similar propositions more than once, but usually a few firm words were all that was necessary. Here, she had sat quietly, kept her cloak wrapped about her, her braid pulled around front, minded her own business. Was she supposed to cut her hair off and wear a floppy hat to be left alone? She embraced the sharp chill in her lungs and focussed her concentration.

At the edge of the veranda, she surveyed the yard. Pond to her left, oak tree out front by the road with a bench surrounding it, driveway from the road to the inn's stable at the right. A delineated fighting space. How many times had the area been used this way? Enough that no grass grew. The sun hung just behind the oak tree, casting mottled shade over the area, but it was by no means dim. She crossed the porch and stepped lightly down to the hard-packed dirt ground. The rest of the patrons spilled out the doors and prepared to watch from the veranda and the driveway as if it were a marketplace cock fight.

Bill planted his heavily-booted feet at the top of the stairs. "Before witnesses, Kyer Halidan and Simon Diduck, to the loss of weapon."

The man in black from the bar stood at the end of the veranda, grey eyes piercing from behind shoulder-length black hair. The other patrons gave him his space as they placed wagers with murmurs and shuffling of hands. They became a mere mass of rippling colour in Kyer's vision as she dismissed them.

She circled the yard, scanning the ground for uneven spots or rocks, a meditative procedure, part of her routine that settled her into inner calm.

Damn Simon Diduck couldn't possibly have waited to harass her until after she'd eaten. But never mind. She flexed and stretched her hands and arms and focussed on breathing life into all the travel-weary muscles she was about to call on. The clean scent of wood chips and water lilies on the pond seeped in and awakened her senses. The process took no more than a few moments, but when she turned her attention back to her opponent, she wasn't nervous anymore. He approached, watching her uncertainly.

She removed her cloak to lay it on the ground. In that brief moment, she sensed a quick movement behind her and heard a stifled gasp from the crowd. She spun around. The coward had already drawn and was coming at her. Outraged, she tossed her cloak at him, entangling him and buying herself time to back out of his reach.

In one flowing, swift motion, she let her fingers curl around the hilt of her bastard sword and drew. *Okay, you cheat, you just changed the rules.*

One-handed, she automatically parried the level slash flying at her left shoulder. The yard echoed with a ring of steel. Her left hand now joining her right on the hilt she feinted a thrust at his face, and he flinched, and when he overparried from his right to left, she turned her wrist over in a crossing cut to his sword arm. Again steel clashed as he stopped it, barely. He countered with a weak thrust, and she easily stepped out of his line, sending his sword down and out of the way.

Sensing her advantage, she lunged at him, feet dancing forward, and forced him back across the yard toward the pond. He yielded to her thrust, and with a quick flip of his blade, nicked her left shoulder as he passed her.

She winced. The sharp pain vibrated down to her hand, but she dared not react further. *One to him.* But only one. Angry at her carelessness, she regrouped with a deep breath, not taking her eyes off him. His self-congratulatory smile signalled his over-confidence, and she took advantage of his lack of focus to step closer. She charged forward and slashed at his legs, forcing him to stumble to one side in his effort to avoid her blade.

A thrill rushed through her. *This* was what all those arduous hours of training were for. She kept at him, varying her rhythm, tiring him. She parried his every move calmly and precisely, while he became more careless, and fell behind her increasing tempo. Kyer parried a desperate slash with ease and pivoted to the side. Her blade slid along his with a ringing sound. She disengaged and dropped low, slicing into the muscle over his right knee.

With a yell, he clutched his leg and went down. His face twisted with agony from his wound and his humiliating defeat. Instantly she stood over him. A flick of her foot sent his sword flying a few feet away. Blood dribbled through his clenched fingers to pool into a thick, spreading puddle at her feet.

Kyer nodded, satisfied. "Loss of weapon. I'll get a healer over here for you. Have a good sleep . . . somewhere else." She turned to retrieve her cloak.

A shuffling sound and a gasp from the crowd startled her. She whirled around as Simon, on his feet with his boot dagger in hand, flew at her. His dagger bit the flesh of her upper arm. She plunged her blade into his chest, feeling it grind along his ribs, and as he fell, it stopped in the ground underneath him.

Shock in his eyes, his body convulsed and was still. As his blood stirred up the dirt and trickled away in a muddy whorl, so did the red haze lift from around her vision. The magnitude of what she had done hit like a gust of wind and she staggered. *By Guerrin, I killed him.* It was what she had trained to do, and yet she could not have prepared for *this*.

Trembling overtook her from head to toe, and this time it was not from lack of food. Kyer let her sword take some of her weight and gritted her teeth to stop them from chattering. Her rage depleted, exhaustion replaced it. Her knees wobbled and she knelt down next to her victim's body, gulping air to counteract the nausea. Her breath came out in puffs. *I killed him.* Quivering like an aspen leaf, she hissed with pain as she drew his knife out of her arm and let it drop. The flow of blood striped her sleeve.

Bill shrugged. The outcome was too obvious to declare. Murmurs rose like a flock of birds as the spectators filtered back indoors. Some who'd been watching in the yard stepped over and spat on the cheater's body before returning to what they'd been doing. Kyer fought with her conscience. *I didn't mean to k—* No, wait. That kind of thinking had to stop. She was a swordfighter; trained for years. He cheated in a publicly recognized duel. He hadn't waited for the opening salute. She'd bested him in fair combat, and he'd come at her back with a knife. If she'd let him live, what would he have tried later? No, mid-battle was not the time to waver. Diduck had forced her to make a quick decision, and she'd done it.

The difference between this and her last fight, a week before she left home, was not lost on her. This duel had at least been her choice, albeit one she had been forced to make. Better than the surprise attack in an alley by people she knew, with eight-to-one odds. She shook her head, dismissing the memory and the anger it would rekindle.

In the stillness of the yard, she pushed herself up. She braced her feet and yanked her weapon out of its resting place. With trembling hands, she wiped the blood off the blade on his shirt and sheathed it, allowing the steady, automatic movement to restore her equanimity. She unbuttoned his waistcoat and tore a strip of cloth from his sweat-soaked tunic. She fashioned a bandage and tied it, with the help of her teeth, around the arm that had met Simon's dagger. An inspection of her left shoulder showed her only a small amount of blood seeping; that wound could wait.

Kyer steeled herself, uncomfortable with the thought of performing the customary search. But she had killed him, and it had to be done. Bill watched from the top of the stairs. She slipped a tentative hand inside his bloodied waistcoat and found a purse. Her jaw dropped when she found it contained about thirty hexagonal gold nobles. More money than she'd ever seen. Her own depleted purse would be gratefully replenished and then some. In a breast pocket, she found a piece of cloth folded around a tiny key. She transferred it to her pouch. His dagger was nothing special. Even his sword, though serviceable, was not as good as her own. She left it for the benefit of the cleanup crew. He had nothing else she needed. The job done, she washed the blood off her hands in the pond with a shudder, glad to be rid of the metallic smell. She picked up her cloak, dusty from where Diduck had flung it aside. It had a new tear in it thanks to the louse's sword. *Great.*

She stood in the silent yard and stared at the aftermath—the scuffed dirt, the blood, the body—and the responsibility of having begun her life as a fighter settled its weight on her shoulders. One last deep breath, long and slow. She'd made a decision; she'd acted on it. It was time to live with it.

She took three steps back toward the inn and stopped, a flicker of annoyance tingling in her brow. The man in black stood on the veranda, watching her, even though everyone else, including Bill, had gone back inside. He leaned against the railing, cloak wrapped around his shoulders, the worn heel of one scuffed riding boot hooked over the lower rung. His long, stringy hair curtained his profile.

She continued up the steps and regarded him evenly. "If you're the local reeve, I hope that wasn't a personal guest of the magistrate." She walked by him with deliberate, steady steps. Part of her desired to ask the barkeep for the key to Diduck's room—now hers—and go to sleep for three days. The other part had something to prove. The patrons of the Burnished Blade didn't need to know he was the first man she'd killed. She returned to her seat at the bar, laying her cloak on the counter next to her. A few people overtly whispered. One man raised his mug to her. She felt their scrutiny like darts on her back and sat straighter. Her belly was in knots.

Despite the choice of free seats, the man in black sat next to her. Her arm muscles contracted, and her hairs stood up. She was *not* ready for another Simon Diduck.

She opened her mouth to make a snarky remark, but the bartender set a fresh pint before her. "I figure you could use that."

Kyer's dry throat accepted the long, cool drink with gratitude, and her nostrils appreciated the ale's earthy aroma. The liquid calmed the tremor in her hands and began to settle the disquiet in her belly. Her mouth watered, and suddenly she was so hungry a bucketful of dirt might taste good. She finally ordered some food.

She raised her mug again, and the man in black raised his glass of wine at the same time. Was he trying to be funny? The bartender winked at her as he went to the kitchen, and she wondered if there were some sort of joke she was missing. Still, in no mood to be friendly to eccentric strangers, she drank her beer, watching the man in black out of the corner of her eye as he sipped his wine. She was determined to keep her mug to her lips longer and ignore his game of mirroring her actions. But the annoying man seemed bent on his amusement and kept drinking. She kept drinking too. He drained his wine glass and at last placed it on the wood countertop. Kyer set her mug down and also noticed that her knee was bouncing with residual nerves. Sensing a comment from her neighbour approaching, she clenched her teeth and breathed through her nose; she was not inclined to let him draw her into another fight. She turned her torso to close herself off from him and likewise shifted her attention. Maybe the odd man would go away.

Why had Brendow directed her here? After the attack in the alley, he had at last said it was time. She'd asked the old man where she should go.

"Wanaka," he'd said unequivocally. "To an inn called the Burnished Blade. It's in the southwest corner of Shae duchy and should take you about three weeks. Get yourself a job there in the village."

He was right about the timeframe, but he never told her why this was the best place to start her new life and search for answers. All he had added was, "It's a hub of sorts. Things happen there." What was special about Wanaka? *Apparently not its high class of people.* Kyer drank again.

The bartender burst through the door wearing thick gloves and holding a dish of game pie, which he placed before her. He tucked the gloves into his apron and handed her a steaming, wet towel to clean her hands. He also refilled her beer glass, which made him her favourite person. "I confess I was hoping you would return without the, uh, gentleman."

The delicious aroma of the pie assailed her. Her mouth watered again and she felt weak. But another thought struck her, and it ought to be addressed. "Had the 'gentleman' already paid for his 'regular' room?"

"Yes." The publican wiped his hands on his towel and reached under the counter, pulling out a leather-bound book. "Breakfast is included."

Wary of the man next to her repeating Simon's offer, she said, "Perfect."

"Splendid!" He slid the log book over to her--not the same book as the duel list--and she filled in her name underneath Diduck's. His name had already been crossed off.

He replaced the book under the counter. "I'm Maginn Medlicott, here to take care of your every need. Here's the key. I imagine you'll want to, uh, go through . . . things. I'll have Jack take your belongings from the stable up to the room."

Any second now, the Man in Black would offer to join her in her room . . .

At last, she picked up her spoon and caved in the flaky crust of pie, drawing out an enormous scoop. A puff of steam issued from beneath the pastry, carrying with it a heavenly aroma of meat and vegetables. She burned her tongue on the first bite and had to hiss cool air through her teeth, but she still ate so fast, the pie was three quarters gone by the time Maginn came back with her neighbour's dinner. She set down her spoon so she could breathe. Her neighbour stabbed a piece of meat with his knife.

Maginn smiled. "I guess you like it."

She sighed deeply.

But something was wrong. Unfinished. Brendow's presence was vivid in the back of her mind. Sitting together in his front room after a training session, a bottle and two glasses before them. She needed wine. But not just any wine, not for Simon Diduck. Her first.

Drawing Simon's purse into her hand, she opened it and discreetly counted. It was a veritable fortune. And this was the right choice. It mattered. She got Maginn's attention. Just above a whisper, she said, "Do you have any elvish wine in stock?"

His eyebrows went up. "Why, absolutely." He did not move right away but kept his eyes on her with a thoughtful gaze. Then with an almost imperceptible nod, as if in approval of some unvoiced suggestion, he disappeared for about five minutes and returned with a dusty bottle and a glass. He opened it for her and said in a low voice, "I can tell that you're a woman of good taste. That's ten rydals." Kyer observed the depth of his fingerprints in the dust that clung to the bottle. She counted five nobles out of Simon's purse. She still had plenty to get by on for weeks.

Maginn poured a small amount into her glass. It tasted of an ancient melody, plucked delicately on an unfamiliar instrument. It trickled down her throat like a stream from a mountain spring. Ten rydals was a bargain. She'd drunk plenty of elvish wine before, but this was of a whole new quality. Unable to adequately express her appreciation for it, Kyer said, "That will do nicely." Maybe *that* would show the Man in Black she had some sophistication. But whether it did or not, she needed to carry on. She held the bottle in both hands and closed her eyes.

"Is there another bottle like that, Medlicott?" The Man in Black had a warm voice.

"You bet, my lord." The little man trundled off again.

Kyer frowned (he'd been drinking wine before, so surely he wasn't just copying her again). She focussed, mouthing the name of the man whose life she had taken. She poured to fill the glass and set the bottle down. Nonchalantly, in an effort to be inconspicuous, she dipped the fourth finger of her left hand (the weakest finger on her non-dominant hand) into the rich, red wine and traced the rim of the glass, not quite completing a full circle. *Life cut short.* She raised the glass with her right hand, just a bit, not so much as to make a big show of it, and spoke Simon's name to herself again. She took a sip. Dipped the finger and once more around the rim in the opposite direction, a full circle this time. *Completion.* One more raise followed by a sip. She set the glass down and removed her hands.

There. Now things felt right. Like washing dirt from her hands, the tension melted away, leaving her wiped out. Every training session had ended with a glass of wine, always elvish. Brendow had taught her the ritual, and she had run through it countless times. This was the first time she had done it for real, and she finally grasped its import. She picked up her spoon again.

The Man cleared his throat. Kyer refused to acknowledge him. She twisted in her seat, showing more of her back to him, and gazed around the room.

Most people had gone back to their meals and beverages. Some sets of eyes darted at her nervously; that she had intimidated a few people was a lovely reminder of home. Others expressed a less familiar emotion: admiration. They looked at her and smiled a little as they spoke to their neighbours. She turned away, unused to approval. The goblins in the corner booth appeared not to have let the excitement interrupt their argument. They were snatching a gold coin back and forth between them. The servers had gone back to carrying trays of ale and food. The chatter was as it had been. It was all very pleasant, but *damn it.* Why in hell had Brendow sent her here? And why had he sounded overly relaxed about it?

Maginn returned with the second ancient, dusty bottle and opened it, pouring a taste for the one who'd ordered it. The Man picked up the glass with a heavily scarred hand and sipped, licking his lips in unsophisticated satisfaction. "Marvellous, as always."

Kyer rolled her eyes. *Pretentious git.* She lifted her glass and swirled a sip around her tongue. The Man in Black did the same. Annoyed, she plunked her glass down and spooned up a bite of food.

"Well, Kyer," said the man, "I am impressed by your taste in wine."

So he thought he had the right to use her first name? She chuckled with a scoffing tone. "Too bad I'm not interested in *impressing* you."

He looked surprised. "I certainly wouldn't want to be your enemy." He indicated the door. Was he mocking her?

She did not look at him. "Then I'd advise you not to piss me off."

"Fair enough."

Damn fellow still sounded like he was laughing at her.

"Those were some interesting techniques you were using," he said. "If I'm not mistaken, I recognize some of the more subtle moves."

Nice try. Kyer wasn't about to fall for his bait. He wanted to get her talking to him, but anyone could lie about such a thing. Nobody could truly recognize her *wæpnian* techniques but someone who'd trained with Brendow, and he'd been in Hreth longer than Kyer could remember. Hiding. Anybody who knew Brendow would be someone from his past who did not have his best interests in mind. If this man wanted to avoid being her enemy . . .

"Trained by a stocky short fellow, nasty limp from a bad left knee, has an unusual interest in languages? He taught you the *wasp* manoeuvre."

Kyer leapt from her seat, hand on her hilt. The tension in her throat squeezed so her voice was barely above a whisper. "Why do you know Brendow?" *Shit.* She should never have said his name aloud. And she wouldn't have if this character hadn't tricked her.

Instead of answering, he side-eyed her quizzically and swirled his wine. "Brendow, is it? That's interesting."

"Why?"

His grey eyes pierced her, full of laughter.

Kyer loosened her sword and didn't let go. "Who the hell do you think you are, the bloody Duke of Equart?"

His face lost all expression. Then the corners of his mouth twitched. His left hand eased back along his belt. His movement opened his cloak just enough for her to see his armour, the breast plate intricately enamelled with the rowan tree of Equart over the chest and a tiny sprig of foxglove beneath its left side.

"Shit," she whispered, and the ground fell out from under her. Drowning in embarrassment, she sat down hard on her stool. Mind racing, she connected a profusion of details: the long black hair and moustache, the scars on his hand and the one down the left side of his face, the cloak made of quality fabric . . . He was the only other person in the room drinking *wine,* for the love of Farro, and further—how could she have been so *thick* to have missed it—Maginn had called him *my lord.* She'd heard all the stories countless times; she ought to have at least had a suspicion of who he was, even though his hair concealed his ears. If there was a single person in the entire continent of Rydris she *would* have wanted to impress, this was him. *Shit.* Her heart plummeted to the bottom of her gut.

She drained her glass and tried to think of something to say.

He graciously did not smirk as he said, "Pleased to meet you."

"Kyer." She tentatively put out a hand, which he shook. "Halidan," she added, knowing it wouldn't mean anything to him. "Do you dress in black just to be intimidating?"

"Naw, it's only because my white suit's being cleaned." He did smile then.

She laughed a little but felt slightly sick. He was a dark elf, and about four hundred fifty years old. Stories had been told of this hero since she was a child. Songs in his praise had been sung since the first time she'd stepped into a tavern. And here was she, a nobody from a nowhere place like Hreth, being unforgivably rude to him. Guerrin's fire, she'd killed a man while Valrayker, the Duke of Equart, watched her.

She turned her head to hide her enormous sigh. Following it with a resigned shrug, she poured another glass of wine. For the second time in the space of half an hour, she had a choice to make: If she could have had a second chance at a first encounter with her greatest hero, without a doubt, she would have behaved with aplomb. But as it was, she'd treated him abominably, and whatever his first impression of her was, it was carved in stone. Now she could either slink away to her room and leave town first thing in the morning or she could carry on. Slinking away was not her style. Besides, even if all he gave her was five minutes of his time, she would take it. She'd acted; it was time to live with it.

"Well, now I'm really glad I won that fight." She had a faint hope that he'd tell her she had done the right thing in killing Simon.

"Quite handily too."

"You can't say I didn't warn him."

"No, indeed."

Not reassured by his response, she finished the last few bites of her meal, the whole time aware of Valrayker observing her. She'd been judged and found wanting countless times by people she could easily disregard. Brendow, and her parents of course, she respected. But this time—for the first time—she was being sized up by someone outside her circle whose opinion actually mattered.

"So you trained with . . . Brendow, did you say? Where are you from?"

Well, this answer certainly wouldn't be impressive. "Hreth," she said, biting back a "sorry." "It's a rather backward little village in northwestern Heath." She could tell Valrayker about Brendow's location; Brendow himself would confirm there was probably no one more trustworthy in all of Rydris.

The silence that followed was deeply thoughtful. After a time, he asked, "And what brings you all the way from Hreth to Wanaka?"

"Brendow recommended I look for work here. Didn't seem to be any point in being a swordswoman in a place like Hreth." Even now that she knew his identity, was there a use in telling him she didn't know her own? *I walked out of a cornfield when I was three, and I'd kind of like to know what that was all about* was not likely to raise her in his esteem. Nor was *It's not much fun living in a village where everyone thinks you're a witch.* Instead, she said, "So how do you know Brendow?"

"Knew him," Valrayker corrected. "It was a long time ago."

She wanted to probe further, get him to elaborate, to ask him to explain why he seemed familiar, yet unfamiliar with Brendow's name. But the dark elf's tone had implied finality, and she decided to respect it rather than persist.

Still a bit shaky, she drank more wine to steady her nerves. She knew her reaction wasn't just about making a fool of herself to Valrayker. She had killed a man, and it was not something she could brush off with ease. She drained the bottle into her glass and regretfully set it on the counter. All good things had to come to an end.

Maginn approached and picked up her and Valrayker's dishes. "Will that be all, my lord?"

"For now, thank you." He glanced sidelong at Kyer. "So." Valrayker swirled his wine. "It's . . . lucky I happened to run into you here. I have to be at a meeting in a short time. Would you care to join me?"

Kyer choked on her wine. Could he be serious after she'd shown him how unseasoned she was? When her cough stopped she tried to sound sophisticated and just mildly curious. "What sort of a meeting?"

"All in good time," he said. In spite of the angle, she could still perceive the twinkle in his eye. "You coming or not?"

She hesitated for a fleeting moment. But surely this was what she had been hoping for when she left home. Was this why Brendow— *But how could he have known?* Kyer could not turn down an evening with Valrayker of

Equart. With a passing thought of a few people in Hreth and what their reactions would be to this development, she gave him a casual half smile, trying to hide her eagerness. "I have nothing better to do. Do you mind if I go up to my room and take care of this cut first?" Her shoulder still oozed a little.

"I would mind if you didn't."

Kyer grabbed her cloak, brushing the wine glass off the counter where it landed in Valrayker's lap, and he caught it deftly before it could fall to the floor. Her face enflamed, her gaze leapt to his, fearful that he would see her discomposure and change his mind. But instead she was startled at what she saw. His grey eyes smiled softly and showed the wisdom that only four and a half centuries of life experience can bring. As the last remaining dark elf in the known world, there would be no fooling him. The corners of his mouth turned up gently.

"It takes a while to recover after the first one. And unfortunately, it gets easier."

Two

Indelible First Impressions

Up in Simon's—now her—room, Kyer took a cursory glance at his belongings and dismissed them for later. For now, the duke of Equart himself took precedence. She quickly dealt with her cut and carefully locked the room before descending the stairs. Maginn caught her as she headed out the front door. She handed him the key to her room for safekeeping and he spoke confidentially.

"I don't know what you did to impress him, lass, but this is rare."

"I can't imagine I did anything that impressed him, but . . . I believe you're right."

Valrayker waited for her on the veranda, and together they descended the front steps. In the light from the recently departed sun, Kyer saw that the body had been removed from the front yard. The job had been done thoroughly and efficiently, for there were no traces of the skirmish. He didn't mention it, so neither did she.

Side by side, they headed south along the main road, back the way Kyer had come into town less than two hours before. Valrayker's straight back and long stride suggested a comfort with the world. He had no affectation or pretentiousness, and if she felt a bit inferior, she didn't get a sense that the feeling stemmed from him. She was in awe because of who he was, not what he was. He came across as much more . . . ordinary than she'd envisioned.

Ordinary in an extraordinary kind of way. Still, she did not wish to embarrass herself again, or he would change his mind about this invitation. She wrestled a wave of jitters under control; she had to be ready for anything.

She glanced up at him. Dark elves were, on average, the shortest of the four types of elves; her companion was about six feet. "I always thought the duke of Equart would be taller."

"Oh," he said. "I've always been quite satisfied with my height. I hope you aren't terribly disappointed?"

"Your legs go all the way to the ground. That's good enough for me."

About ten minutes south of the village, Valrayker took an abrupt left turn, leading her into a dense cedar grove. There was a path, but the amount of undergrowth suggested it wasn't well used. The cedars opened into a stand of black cottonwoods. The dark elf's long black hair draped around cloaked shoulders, and his booted feet made hardly a sound. The cottonwoods shivered around them, their leaves fluttering and flashing their silvery undersides to the twilight. A myriad of questions danced around her thoughts, but Valrayker's silence seemed to have taken on a new depth; she was reluctant to disturb it.

Kyer's skin prickled. She always listened to that instinct. Her sword was in her hand instantly, her knees bent in the ready position, as her eyes darted about for the target she knew was out there.

Valrayker had stopped and was looking at her with eyebrows peaked in surprise, but she didn't relax her stance. She felt uncertain. Was he laughing at her?

"Jumpy, are we?"

The heat of a blush flooded her face and neck. She straightened and looked away. If Valrayker himself wasn't unnerved, why should she be? But her shoulders and core remained taut, and she didn't sheathe her sword.

Out of the wooded blackness came a low whistle that could have been an evening bird, only it wasn't, which she knew because she was listening, not just hearing, and was prepared for anything. Valrayker glanced at her—was that a frown?—and replied with a similar call. When a tall, hooded figure stepped like a shadow out of the woods, Valrayker wasn't alarmed. The newcomer was not unexpected. Kyer swiftly sheathed her sword.

"Well, it's about time, Val. What took you so long? Derry sent me to find you. If I'd known you were going to be so late, I'd've stayed back and had another bowl of soup. Where've you—?"

"Slow down there, chum," Valrayker said. "I was enjoying a glass of wine; these things can't be rushed."

Her newest companion pulled down his hood. He had typical elven ears, but his fair complexion, the white-blond hair (which he wore long enough to be scruffy), and his height compared to Valrayker's identified him as a wood elf. Even in the twilight, his flame-blue eyes glowed with an intensity she wanted to look at for a long time. He looked down at Kyer, appealing to her sympathy. "*He's* late because he's drinking wine, while I skipped *dessert!*"

"Good gracious, say it isn't so," Valrayker said. "Shall we go?" Valrayker stepped by the wood elf then stopped and sniffed. "Phennil, when did you last bathe?"

"Uh, I can't remember. A couple of weeks ago."

"Great." He plunged into the woods. "Kyer, I hope you're not prone to fainting spells."

The blond elf gestured for Kyer to precede him. She caught a whiff as she passed him and understood what Valrayker had meant.

"Phennil is our living science experiment."

"I just don't like it."

"The only reason we can stand having him around is that he's so damned handsome."

"Oh, shut up."

Kyer stiffened, watching Valrayker for a sign of his notorious temper. But to her surprise, he was chuckling. "Kyer, do you need to hold on to my arm in the dark?"

"No, I'm all right, thanks." Her eyes had adjusted quickly.

"Phennil, this is Kyer. Watch what you say, or she might kill you."

A shocked laugh escaped Kyer as she paused to acknowledge the introduction. Switching to the Wood Elvish tongue, she said to Phennil, *"Does he always let people tell him to shut up?"*

A smile spread across his face. *"I'd like to think it's because he likes me, but he's pretty easy going that way."* He examined her, lifting her hair from her ears. Changing back to Rydrish, he said, "I can see your ears, but that's all. What kind of elf are you?"

"I'm not. Human through and through." She hurried to catch up with Valrayker.

Phennil's long strides didn't fall behind. "Where'd you learn to speak Elvish, then?"

"My trainer. I was exasperatingly persistent until he agreed to teach me."

"That's nice for me," Phennil said.

Valrayker held a branch so it wouldn't slap Kyer upside the head and spoke around her at Phennil. "The others are all there, then?"

"Yeah, Jesqellan wasn't sure he would make it to Wanaka by this evening, but he made better time than he expected."

"Good. That's good." Valrayker's voice sounded suddenly tired and introspective.

The forest became more and more dense, the canopy closing in and allowing little help from the waning Asp Moon, the final moon of the Rydris year. The thickening clouds already obscured its light, and only the occasional shaft penetrated to the ground. Kyer was thankful to be with Valrayker because she was completely lost.

When Kyer smelled wood smoke, she knew they were nearing their destination. Soon a tiny flicker of flame flashed through the forest, and Kyer's anticipation flared. She followed Valrayker into the clearing. Three individuals stared at her, their arms and hands tightening reflexively at the appearance of a stranger.

"Gentlemen," Valrayker said. "Sorry to have kept you waiting. I assure you it was unavoidable. This is Kyer. Kyer, this is my captain, Derry Moraunt, as well as Jesqellan and Janak. Please be seated."

The captain was a tall human with blond hair, not as white blond as Phennil's, more golden, and close cropped. He wore a few pieces of plate mail, which glinted redly in the light of the small fire. He bowed, a stiff, formal bending of his waist, and he did not smile at the introduction. Although he wasn't unpleasant to look at, he did not have the striking good looks of one or two of the men Kyer had come across (and had become better acquainted with, as it happened). Kyer's quick assessment summed him up as dignified, even haughty, in complete contrast with his lord.

Jesqellan was human, short, black, and bald, wearing dark brown robes and carrying the inevitable staff—a shaman, likely. The other, Janak, was a dwarf who eyed Kyer with as much distaste as he might a dish of maggot-riddled meat. She did not miss the look on the dwarf's face when he saw the sheath of her sword stretch out beyond the hem of her cloak on the ground behind her. Phennil flopped down at the feet of Derry, who sat upright on a deadfall log. Kyer wanted desperately to say, *An elf, a dwarf, and a shaman walk into a bar . . .* But she held her tongue.

Not even a murmur rippled through the group as Valrayker seated himself at the bole of a pine tree. Kyer's eyes followed the trunk of the tree up to where it split in two and those trunks twisted around each other as they reached to the sky.

Valrayker pulled out a knife and began picking at dirt underneath his fingernails. His legs stretched out and ankles crossed as casually as if he were about to have a nap. His brow, however, was knit tight, giving Kyer the impression that he wanted to *appear* less worried than he was.

"I have received bizarre tidings from the north," Valrayker began. "My duchy may be overrun by Dregor's forces, but I don't see this as a reason to neglect my people." Kyer figured this must be for her benefit as his men would already know it. "For this reason, I maintain a selection of scouts who travel around Equart, report to each other and to me. It took some time for my scout to finish his route and return to Shael, and then some more time for me to track you all down and send a summons." He cast a tired-looking grin around the group, absently rubbing the scar that connected his eyebrow to his jaw. "All in all it has been about two months since he was there. Though darkness hangs over all of Equart, there are some pockets that are more or less free to carry on as before. Perhaps Dregor has yet to decide how to make use of them?" He let out a short, mirthless laugh. "My scout reports some disquieting and puzzling behaviour in the village of Nennia, just a few days over the Shae-Equart border.

"He tells me that the villagers' behaviour is unnatural, to say the least. They walk about as if in a trance. If spoken to, they are pleasant enough, but their emotions have been . . . flattened. They appear false, as if in a daze."

"Is that not expected from villagers living under oppression?" the shaman suggested.

Valrayker shook his head. "The scout said it was different. Even people living under oppression have passion. There is anger at the circumstances, vows to fight the enemy. There are underground movements to communicate with other villages, efforts to boost morale. I would even be relieved to hear that people are angry with me for 'deserting' them. Besides, even in the direst situations, people find ways to be happy, in defiance of their oppressors. It is impossible to keep children from inventing ways to play. But no, this is a village full of people, young to old, who would not care if a demon entered the village and stole their children.

"One woman even reported that her husband had gone missing, but when Dev pressed her, she'd forgotten she'd even said it."

The dwarf snorted. "She'd probably offed him 'cause she was dissatisfied."

The captain shot him a look of reprimand. "Janak."

Janak rolled his eyes. "*Human* women are notoriously fickle."

"Dwarf women are lucky to find *one* male worth their time," Kyer said.

Phennil laughed then instantly sobered. The dwarf shot her a dirty look, and the captain's eyes widened in his otherwise expressionless face. The shaman didn't react at all.

Kyer kicked herself. *First impressions count, halfwit.*

Valrayker coughed and there was a general shifting of positions.

"Now, I have asked you all here because I need you to go to Nennia and find out what is going on. Eradicate the problem if necessary. Dev said there was a man by the name of Carver who seemed less affected than the rest. See if you can find him. I am asking you to cross enemy lines, which is why we need to keep the party small. I will go with you as far as Shael but no farther as I have two other task parties meeting me there. Will you go?"

There was a general murmuring of, "Yes, of course." The captain asked the shaman to be his second, and Kyer watched the men interact with each other, reflecting on what it must be like to be part of a group such as this. These men knew one another, had worked together before, and leapt at the opportunity to step up and undertake a task for Valrayker. She'd never given much thought to what she intended to do with all her training, but she'd left Hreth to find out.

"How can you abandon Hreth like this?" Tarqan had said.

"I'm not *abandoning* Hreth. I don't think I was ever meant to be here in the first place!"

"Kyer?" The voice brought her back from the hilltop in Hreth to the clearing.

She turned to Valrayker. What she saw in his eyes surprised her. It was a question.

"Are you in?"

He was asking her to join the mission. She couldn't have been more surprised if he'd asked for her hand in marriage.

"Yes. I am."

He nodded once and got to his feet. Astonished, she remained where she sat and gripped her knees with her hands. Three weeks she'd travelled from a tiny village in a remote corner of the duchy of Heath, waiting for something to happen that would guide her. After three weeks of nothing, she was beginning to despair that she'd have to return home and concede their small-minded suspicions that she was nothing but a troublemaker with a skewed sense of self-importance. *Cymrion spawn!* Kyer thought she ought to feel like her head was spinning. But she felt oddly in control, as if this were meant to be. Brendow had told her to find work . . .

"Hello."

The knight looked down at her with blue eyes that were not unfriendly. He stood back an extra pace or two, politely attempting to not tower over her. She scrambled to her feet. The others prepared to leave. The clearing darkened as Jesqellan doused the fire, waving his fingers over it.

"Captain Derry Moraunt, I think?" She stuck out a hand.

He bowed. *My, aren't we formal?* "Kyer Halidan." His firm handshake matched hers. He indicated that she should precede him into the trees behind the others, and soon the forest closed in around them.

"You must have done something impressive for Valrayker to ask you to join us," Derry said to her back. "He chooses his people very carefully."

Kyer said nothing, unsure if it was a compliment or a warning.

Flora hummed "My Laddie's Coming Home" as she trod up the steps to the second floor of the inn. She was weighed down by her burden but repeated to herself what she'd said to Mr. Medlicott: the yoke *was* ungainly, and doin' it by hand was easier. Martha could keep her opinions to hersel', the lit'le so-and-so. Flora turned left at the top and set the first pail down on the floor by room three, a bit of water sloshing out of it. *Dang, I'll need a rag for that.* Proceeding to room four, she looked to the end of the corridor. A man hovered over the door handle of the last room on the left.

"You there!" she called. "What yer doin'?" She set her pail down on the floor by room four and stood up straight, assuming as much authority as a lowly maid could do.

The man backed away from the door, flushing, and surreptitiously thrust something into his pocket. Seeing her, he pushed his cap back and adopted a jaunty grin. "Have no fear, m'lady." He bobbed his head, walking toward her. "It's only that my key's not workin' t' open this door. Maybe you could send up someone t' help me?"

Not taken in by his charm, she put a hand on her hip. "Perhaps it's not workin' 'cause that's not yer door."

He stopped abruptly and had the decency to look nonplussed. He looked back the way he'd come and chuckled at himself, shaking his head. "I can't believe I made such a mistake. I—"

"You're not foolin' anyone. I know whose room that was, and ye've no business there." She pointed back toward the staircase. "Away with ye or I'll call Bill." She reached up, threatening to yank the rope on the call bell that hung on the wall.

The man blanched at the name, apparently familiar with the one-armed bouncer. He fairly scurried past her.

"I'll be gettin' Bill to set a watch in this corridor now," she told him as he bolted down the stairs. Flora knew what was what. The girl with the sword was the only one with leave to enter the dead man's room. Anybody else was up to no good.

When they reached the edge of the woods, Valrayker grabbed her arm. Kyer stopped, curious, as Derry passed into the road. Then she understood. Derry's long strides took him northbound on the road, and beyond him, the others dispersed with no acknowledgement of each other, their shadows melting into the village. Finally Valrayker let go of her arm and they proceeded. Kyer and Valrayker reentered the tavern at the Burnished Blade, where Derry sat at the bar, already sipping from a tankard of ale. The duke introduced her as if they hadn't met before. Maginn gave them each a pint of ale and expressed his pleasure at seeing Kyer again. Then he rested an elbow on the counter before her.

"These are yours." He handed her two keys. One she recognized as her room key. "This other one is for a shed at the back of the stable. Your friend of this afternoon paid several gold to see that his cart of belongings was kept secure. He also owned the light chestnut mare; Jack will point her out to you. When you have finished looking through his belongings in your room, leave 'em on the floor outside and someone will take 'em away."

Kyer turned the first key around in her fingers.

"Who is this 'friend' who leaves you a key to a shed?" Derry asked.

"The word 'friend' isn't accurate; though I expect you know that. He . . . wanted *company* for the night. When the word 'no' repeated several times didn't get through, we had to have a meeting in the yard."

The knight's upper body retracted ever so slightly. "And this had to lead to his death?"

Resentment shot through her like a bee sting; was he scolding her? "Indirectly. He cheated. Twice."

"The animal," said Derry. "You were right to defend yourself."

She looked at him sardonically. "I'm delighted you approve."

Derry fully exemplified every folktale description she had heard of a typical knight: the pride, the formality, the indignation at a cad's treatment of a woman. At the same time, she was aware of his eyes on her; her story-- and maybe her attitude--had surprised him.

"Would you gentlemen care to accompany me for the unveiling?" she said with a vague hope that the knight would decline. Both men responded in the same fashion: they picked up their mugs and got to their feet.

The late-winter air embraced her, summoning goose bumps on her arms. A thick blanket of clouds had completely obscured the glow of the Asp Moon. The new Swan Moon would bring spring with it in just over a week. Valrayker waited in the doorway of the stable, his puff of breath silhouetted in the light from within. Kyer and Derry passed him to enter the warmth, and Kyer breathed in the horse and hay smells. Jack looked up from pouring oats into a bucket, and showed his toothy grin. With his hair sticking out all over like knives in a practice target, he was the happiest stable boy Kyer had ever seen. He chattered merrily to the resident horses and mules as he topped up their feed for the night, asking them about their days and introducing them to each other as if they were his dinner guests. Kyer checked Trig, who was in good spirits, freshly rubbed down and brushed since his arrival. He was gobbling down the last of a few carrots that had been tossed in with his oats. *I must give that young fellow a generous tip.* Jack trotted over and patted the nose of the mare in the stall across from Trig.

"This one belonged to that Mr. Diduck, if you'd care to look her over, miss. Trig missing anything?"

"No, he's obviously in good hands." She looked at the other animal then back at the boy. "Say, Jack," she said impulsively, "I really have no use for that mare right now. Do you suppose you'd be able to look after her until I come back? Make sure she gets exercise and all?"

The boy nearly burst with pleasure. "For *me*, miss? Really?"

"Just a loan, you understand." She frowned but smiled with her eyes.

Jack's broad grin told her he understood perfectly. "I'll take real good care of her until you come back."

"What's her name?"

Jack looked into the horse's eyes a moment. "Concorde," he announced.

Kyer left the boy talking to the animal, something about lupines. Some rough, low snorting startled her. She turned to see Derry rubbing the nose of the hugest animal she had ever seen. It suited Derry's grandeur that he should ride such a majestic animal as a warhorse. She ambled over.

"Don't worry, he won't hurt you," Derry said gently.

Did he think she was six? "A destrier that's well-trained? Shocking."

Derry's hand stopped. "That was patronizing. I apologize."

His courtesy in response to her defensive outburst was generous, and she flushed guiltily.

"I suppose it would be unwise for you to assume I was comfortable. This is the first one I've seen, but I do know what they're trained for."

"Come on now." Valrayker drummed his fingers on the door frame. "I want to see what's in that cart before the morning."

Kyer couldn't disappoint the duke's youthful enthusiasm. She borrowed a lantern from Jack, and they went out the back door of the stable to a large lean-to shed against the rear of the building.

Derry held the lantern high so Kyer could see to fit the key into the lock. With barely concealed excitement, she pulled the door open, and the stench of mould and mildew puffed out like skunk spray. The light flooded in to reveal a lumpy, boxy shape covered with a sheet of canvas. Kyer banged her shin on the tongue of the cart as she stepped into the shed. She placed a hand on the top; it was damp, though it hadn't rained for a week. Derry lowered the lantern as Kyer gripped the edge of the canvas and flipped back the corner. A leather-gripped sword hilt jutted out.

Valrayker stepped to the far side and helped her to pull the cover back. She gaped at several wooden crates, a dozen or more swords wrapped in oilcloth and a collection of unstrung longbows of a fine, golden wood.

"Hunh," Valrayker said.

Kyer ran appreciative fingers down the length of the smooth shaft. "Yew. These are beautiful. And expensive." She looked up to see Valrayker eyeing her curiously. "And not well looked after." She indicated the dampness of the canvas. Something told Kyer that Simon Diduck had been more than a typical lecherous wayfarer. "What do you suppose he was doing with these?"

"An ordinary shipment, maybe," Derry suggested. "Could be for an outlying town that's worried about conflict."

"Longbows?" Kyer shook her head. "Not a chance." With a dagger, Kyer pried open a crate amid creaks and groans of wood. She reached in and grasped the cold metal of a narrow rod. Amongst *clinks* of iron, she pulled it out. The case was full of crossbow bolts.

The captain kept watch at the door while Valrayker helped Kyer open the rest of the crates. More bolts, sheaf arrows with nasty-looking triple-edged tips, and large-tined throwing stars. Kyer glanced at Derry. "I hardly think average townsfolk would even know what this stuff is, let alone have the skills to use them." Nothing suggested an intended recipient. Whoever expected the shipment was preparing for something and would be disappointed when neither the delivery man nor the items arrived. "Maybe Maginn knows where he was going; Simon has—I mean, *had*—been here before and maybe told him something when he asked to use the shed."

"Possibly," Valrayker said. "But in any event, Kyer, I think it's fair of me to assume that this weaponry is a greater problem than you need to deal with. I would suggest it ought to be given over to the local sheriff to put to his own good use."

Kyer agreed with him and handed over the responsibility of the cart to the duke. They locked up and returned to the entrance hall. "I want to go through Simon's belongings before I turn in, so I'll say good night," Kyer said.

Derry touched her arm. "I would be happy to help you, if you would like it."

He meant well and he was no Simon Diduck, but he was so overly serious, she couldn't help herself. She adopted a shocked expression and put her hand on his. "Why, Derry! Are you asking to accompany me to my room? Usually a man at least buys me a drink first."

Valrayker snorted.

Derry's face went a deep scarlet, and he pulled his hand away. "That is not what I meant! I—"

"I know." She relented with a sigh. Had he no sense of humour? "Your help won't be necessary, thanks. I'm only looking through his stuff. I should be able to handle it. Good night."

She showed the key to the man guarding the second-floor corridor. He waved her past with his one arm.

She opened the door of the room and closed it behind herself. The room was as she'd left it in her haste: her own belongings by the door, the dead man's pack open on the floor next to the bed, and a soiled tunic hung on a chair in the corner alongside his grey cloak. It smelled of pipe tobacco and soap. Kyer remembered his saying he'd been up to the room already upon his arrival. Apparently she'd killed him in his clean tunic. *Pity.* She rifled through his pack amid a rush of mixed emotions. He might still be alive if he hadn't demanded to share this bed with her. But without the duel, would Valrayker have invited her to the meeting? Still, to have killed him was not a thing she could be glad about.

She found nothing interesting among the spare trousers, undergarments, and sundry items in the pack. He must have done his laundry in a stagnant pond if scent was anything to go by. A shaving kit sat on the washstand. A set of saddlebags leaning against the wall contained some cooking implements and a few food items, which she took out to keep for herself. A mildewy woollen bedroll hung airing on the hook next to the door. There was just one more place to check while she was being thorough. Putting the lamp on the floor, she got down on her knees and peered under the bed. *Aha!* Up against the wall at the head of the bed, the flickering flame illuminated a small box. She stretched out on her belly and reached for it. Once in better light, she could see that it was not merely a box, but a chest made of dark wood with a silver lock on the front.

After removing Simon's unwanted items out to the corridor for the bouncer to deal with, she sat cross-legged on the bed, the chest in front of her. Her nerves quivered with excitement. In her fingertips, she held the tiny key she had found in Simon's pouch. With breath held, she inserted the key and gave it a firm twist. The lock clicked open.

She lifted the lid, revealing the aroma of cedar, and a frisson of energy on her face like opening an oven door. A red velvet cushion cradled a three-finger wide piece of pewter with a green gem recessed in the front. Etched with straight, angular lines of varying thickness, the item was curved and nestled in its soft pillow. An armband? Kyer hovered her fingertips over it and a buzzing feeling intensified to a vibration that moved up each finger to her palm. With a shudder, she drew her hand away. Her throat tight with alarm, she closed the lid of the chest, abruptly cutting off the flow of energy. She snapped the lock into place, and it took her a moment to shake the tremors from her hand. Whatever the device was, Simon Diduck had paid a lot for it. No wonder it was hidden under the bed. She set the chest on the floor by her pack. She would show it to Valrayker in the morning or take it to an alchemist in the capital.

Kyer stuck her head out the window into the dark night and took a deep breath of the clean, cool, moist air. The rushing stream suffused the silence. *Rain tomorrow,* she mused. Light from the kitchen spilled out into the yard, but it failed to brighten more than a tiny area, though the moon seeped between clouds and peeked through the trees. Reluctant to end the day but too tired to let it go on, Kyer grasped the handles on the two leaded glass window panes and pulled them to. She fastened the latch with a firm *click*. The crisscross pattern, reminiscent of Brendow's house, made her smile. Kyer latched the shutters and pulled the bar down across them out of habit. She extricated herself from her weapons and leather armour and pulled her tunic over her head.

The medallion that lay against her chest normally went unnoticed. It had been there for so many years that it was as familiar to her as her own face. She had shown it to very few people; only her closest friends. Even Brendow had seen it for the first time not long before she left the village. The runes etched into the strange metal on the front and back were completely foreign to him, he said. She brushed the smooth facets of the violet jewel inlaid in its centre, surrounded by markings and symbols that made no sense to her.

Her childhood had been clouded by whispers of adults, taunts of children. The child who'd shown up in Hreth, "Speaking in tongues," the villagers said. She wasn't born in Hreth, so where had she come from? She was the product of some wizard's mistake; she was abandoned by a whore; she was hatched after a giant rook had mated with a greln. When she was eight, the popular girl at school, Sheska Bolen, set the other girls into fits and giggles with her rumour that Kyer was a Cymrion witch, a tale to which Kyer responded with a knife to the other girl's throat, prompting the schoolmistress to gleefully take a rod to Kyer's palms until they bled while Sheska laughed—

What enraged Kyer was that she couldn't prove Sheska's claim false.

Most recent of all was the attack on her way home, which left Kyer bruised, but left eight men bleeding.

"Stop it," she told herself, and shoved that memory back in its box.

She soaked a washrag in warm water and scrubbed herself, working around the medallion that was the only clue to who she was. The cloth washed away the many days of accumulated grime, and as she rinsed, she also rid herself of the emotions she did not need to visit right now.

Soon, hair still wet and feeling overall refreshed, she nestled among the soft blankets—a luxurious contrast to the bole of a tree she'd have faced had she not met Simon. Fatigue enveloped her. As she reached to put out the lamp, she remembered something. She threw back the blankets. Climbing back in, she turned out the lamp and fell into a peaceful slumber . . . with her sword at her side.

Kyer had no idea how long she had been asleep, though it seemed a very short time. But suddenly she was upright, body rigid with expectation, hand on her hilt. Her ears strained into the stillness for a repeat of the sound that had awakened her. Again. Creaking. But not from the hallway. Nor from her neighbour in the next room. From outside. Could it be—? Someone was climbing a ladder. Up to her window? She was sure of it. In the darkness, she slipped noiselessly out of bed and faced the window, her sword gripped with both hands. Her heart pounded in her throat. The prowler was trying to open the latch holding the windows closed. A little click told her he was successful. How much farther should she allow him to get? A soft squeak informed her that the panes were open and the intruder would soon discover she'd barred the shutters. She hated not being able to see out. *Why'd they have to go and make shutters with the louvres pointing the wrong way?*

She readied her sword tip at the opening between the shutters, below the bar. A dagger tip appeared and flipped off the latch. Then one shutter moved gently in, only to come up against the bar. Kyer heard a whispered curse. That was her moment. The angle was awkward but she thrust her sword straight through the gap, shaving a slice off the wooden shutter and catching the unwelcome guest completely off guard. She heard a stifled cry, a rasping sound as the ladder grated against the siding, and a thud as he hit the ground.

Kyer tried to pull out her sword, but it was stuck between the shutters. "Damn!" She furiously wrenched it upwards, effectively throwing up the bar. A yank on the sword pulled the shutters open with a clatter and freed the weapon. She stuck her head out the window, but all she saw was a shadow disappearing around the corner of the building.

"Damn it!" She sat down on the bed and sucked in breaths to slow the trembling in her limbs. She took a couple of deep breaths to calm herself. *Who in hell was that?* She flopped down on the bed, the answer to the question all too obvious. She doubted the man would come back for more that night, but now she was wide awake and annoyed, both at him and at herself for forgetting that Simon might have had friends in Wanaka. *Anyway, I can't go back to sleep until I do something about that ladder.* After barring the window again, she pulled on her trousers and boots and locked the door behind herself. She slipped down the hall with her unsheathed sword grasped firmly in her hand.

The corridor was dark, but a faint glow from the entrance hall below filtered up the stairs, enough for her to see her way. The lingering smells of ale and evening meals gave evidence that this was a lively establishment during the day, in contrast to the current relative stillness. A small choir of snoring reminded her to descend the stairs as quietly as possible, mindful of the travellers asleep in the common room. She went out the front door, eyes darting all around, looking for any trace of her assailant. If a surprise attack were launched, she was ill prepared, but she relied on the unlikelihood of the man's making a second attempt so soon after his first debacle.

Kyer followed the drive around the building to the right and was thankful for even the limited amount of light from the tavern and the kitchen. A sound from the stable startled her. She stopped and gripped her sword in readiness. Out of the shadows appeared Jack, his perpetual grin ghostly in the flicker of his lantern. Kyer lowered her weapon and sighed in relief.

"Don't you ever sleep?"

"Oh, don't worry about me. I get plenty," Jack responded brightly. "Why are you outside at this time of the night?"

Kyer hesitated then decided this remarkable boy might be able to assist her. Yes, he had seen someone running away, holding his shoulder as if hurt. No, he hadn't seen where he came from.

Jack followed Kyer around to the river-side of the building, to her window where she examined the footprints: large enough to be male, separate heel indicating that it wasn't a flat boot, trail of them leading off toward the river, and . . . that was all. The two carried the ladder to store it in the barn. She thanked Jack for his help and went indoors, pausing at the entrance to the common room.

The warmth from the fire was most welcome, and she shivered off the chill of the damp night air. The room was by no means full, but snores and peaceful breathing rose from nine or ten shadowy bodies on cots or on thick rugs on the plank floor. The fire in the huge stone fireplace that dominated the far end of the room would keep them all warm with or without blankets. It was one of the nicer common rooms she had seen. Across the hall, through the archway into the tavern, she saw no trace of anyone else up and about. *Very late, then.*

She had climbed a couple of steps up when she heard a low voice. "Hello." Derry stood in the doorway of the common room.

"Oh," she said. "Hello. You having trouble sleeping?"

He continued to wordlessly contemplate her.

This is a strange conversation for the middle of the night. The captain suddenly recovered from his momentary lapse, casting his gaze around the entrance hall before becoming the courteous knight once more.

"I awoke at the sound of someone going outside. I was concerned when I saw that it was you. Is everything all right?"

"Yes," Kyer said quickly. "I had something to take care of; that's all."

"Ah. Well, as long as you are all right . . ."

"I'm fine." Then she added, "Thanks. I really just want to go back to bed now."

"Of course." He raised his hand apologetically. "Good night."

Kyer gave him a nod and continued up the stairs.

***

Derry watched her for a few seconds then returned to the common room and lay awake for a while, picturing the young woman standing on the stairs, the lamp on the table lighting her from below. It deepened her alert green eyes, and he had a fleeting thought that nothing would escape her notice, including things about him that he may not want to share. And it shone on her long hair, a little wild from being slept on when it was wet. He marked the way she held her bastard sword, her grip light but confident on the hilt. Not overly tall but attractively muscled from years of wielding such a weapon. Even without armour, she clearly was someone to be reckoned with.

Her continued refusal of his offers of aid puzzled him, but in spite of this, he was strangely pleased that this young woman was to be a member of their party.

***

Ronav paced around his small chamber as he waited for Con to respond to his call. The mind-speaker gem was pressed against his temple. Finally he felt Con's words in his head. Ronav stopped next to his fireplace. *Did he get it?*

No, he didn't get it. He got a bloody great slit in his shoulder for his trouble.

Ronav swallowed and steadied himself on the mantel. *I need it.*

What's in the damn chest that's so important?

Nothing. Ronav snapped to attention. *It's for me. It's . . . a project I'm working on. Nothing important.* He wiped one sweaty palm at a time on his trousers, his heart sinking.

Well, Chief, if it's not that important, you're goin' to 'ave to make up your mind which you want more: the girl or the box.

If it's in her possession, I do not see why you cannot bring me both.

Can't guarantee it. Which d'you want most?

Ronav leaned against the mantel, his left knuckles white as he clutched it. Losing the weaponry was bad enough. But he could get more, and it was only for the current "study." The armlet, on the other hand, was vital to his plan. *The larger scheme . . . my future!*

What?

Nothing. What have you learned about this girl?

I don't know nothin' more about 'er.

Ronav sighed. He'd have to explain to Golgathaur why some girl had killed one of his best men. He'd want to know what *else* she knew about the study. If Ronav didn't have answers, well . . . another trip to the far north—

Chief?

Ronav took a deep breath. It did nothing for his heart rate. He closed his eyes regretfully. What he wanted was quite separate from what he needed.

He made his choice.

Con's flat-tipped fingers massaged the hideous scar that ran along the right side of his jaw. The muscles would never reawaken, and he could not feel his own touch along the scar. He glanced over at Jet, who sat moodily on the bed while one of the others bound his wound. With the mind-speaker gem back in his pouch, spoke to the little group. "Better find out where she's headed."

Three
Dominoes

Kyer sat up and peeked out her window at the misery that fell in torrents. Her encounter in the middle of the night had wiped her out. She groaned and dragged herself out of bed, despite an overwhelming desire to crawl back and bury her head beneath the blankets.

Upon hearing about Kyer's intruder, Valrayker agreed that it was likely an accomplice of Simon's. If it was the weapons they were after, they'd have simply broken into the shed to retrieve them. Clearly they wanted the chest. Rather than give his company the day to prepare, Valrayker decided on an urgent departure. He divided the group into what he called "suitable pairings" and directed Jesqellan and Janak to leave that very afternoon. Kyer and Derry were to wait until sundown, and Valrayker and Phennil would leave later still. Staggering their departure would, with any luck, confound anyone inclined to follow them. And Kyer gave the chest to Valrayker, who buried it in the bottom of his pack. Someone would have a tough time finding it in Kyer's possession.

✦

"Valrayker said we'd have two more nights," Janak grumbled down at Jesqellan. "I call that *one*. One night."

"We have experienced changes of plans before," the mage replied.

"I should be drinking in the Morningstar with a warm bed waiting for me, not lumbering along in the pouring rain." Janak stood up in his stirrups and sat again.

Jesqellan didn't respond. He strode barefoot alongside Janak's horse with an easy grip on his staff. He'd tucked the waist of his Moabi robes into his belt, so they did not drag through the puddles. A hood protected his bald head from the raindrops pelting against it. He seemed altogether too contented to suit Janak's mood.

"Leaving a day early," the dwarf muttered. "And I notice *we're* the lucky ones who are shoved out in this downpour *first*. Isn't this what you humans do to dogs who crap on the floor?"

"I hardly think Valrayker compares us to ill-behaved pets," Jesqellan said.

"Then let him explain to my face why we have to be out in this longer than anyone else."

"You know very well why," the mage said. "If you're cross, blame me, not him."

"We're all used to you being on foot all the time."

Jesqellan looked up at him. "Then this is not about us having to leave first."

It was Janak's turn to say nothing.

Apart from a coach headed toward Wanaka, the two companions met no one on the road. Janak's temper descended into glowering anger. His soaked hat stuck to his head. Water clung to his beard as it would in a sponge. When that was saturated, it ran down each fork of hair and joined the water that trickled down the side of the horse and into his boots. Between emptying his boots, wringing out his beard, and trying to keep the latter flung over his shoulder to prevent the trickling effect, Janak was the personification of cantankerousness by the time the pair stopped for a bit of supper.

Jesqellan found an area under a thick grove of conifers where the ground was merely wet, not muddy. They sat on large roots jutting out of the ground. Janak pried his hat off his head, gave it a good shake, and rubbed his hair and beard with a rag.

Jesqellan laughed at him. "You'd be better off walking," he said. "Look at me. My head may be damp, but I am benefiting from my cloak much more than you are, my friend." He dug into his pack and pulled out bread and cheese.

Janak glared at him. "Shut up." He yanked off a boot and pulled his toe back through the hole in his wool sock, squeezing out moisture as best he could.

Jesqellan broke off a bit of cheese. "Perhaps it will be fine tomorrow and the rest of our journey will be more pleasant." He popped the cheese in his mouth.

Janak dumped the water out of his boot and pointed it at the mage. "If it's fine tomorrow, I'll have that girl's head for making us leave today!"

"It was hardly her fault." The mage broke off another morsel of cheese with his fingertips. "It was Valrayker who resolved that we ought to leave early."

"It was because of her. If she hadn't killed that vole of a man, we wouldn't be running from his friends. As I see it, her quarrel with them has nothing to do with us, leastwise not me."

"It does now since Valrayker asked her to join us."

"That's another thing." Janak shook his finger at his companion. "Why in all levels of hell was a *girl* so vital to the completion of this mission?"

"Valrayker does not handpick unworthy individuals to work for him. Even you were not chosen in haste, although sometimes it appears that way. He chose her for a reason."

"I'm dying to find out what it is. As long as she doesn't get us all killed in the meantime."

They finished their meal in brooding silence.

Janak decided his legs needed a stretch. He did not mount his horse, but continued the journey on foot, and ignored Jesqellan's smug smirk.

***

"Valrayker sure knows how to pick a good time of year to travel." Kyer peered up at the gloomy trees from under her hood. She had to speak loudly to be heard over the drumming downpour.

"Hmph," Derry said. He seemed unaware that she was joking. *Oh yeah, the sense of humour thing.* Maybe he thought she was insulting his lord or something.

"In truth," he pointed out, "this weather is not so bad for travelling. It makes us more difficult to track."

"Really? I'd no idea."

"Indeed."

Her sarcasm was lost on him. Derry couldn't possibly have been more than a couple of years older than she, yet he had an irksome need to educate her.

"Back at home, this would be perfect weather for mud-sparring. The winner is the one with the least mud on him at the end; he has to buy beer."

"I see." It was a wonder his nose wasn't up in the air.

"Gee, are you going to be this much fun all the way to Nennia?"

The young knight didn't reply. *How does Valrayker put up with Mr. Jolly for a captain?* Kyer couldn't figure out why Valrayker would think that she and this solemn, self-righteous caricature would be a good pairing. He rode staring ahead, back straight, in a very dignified manner; the same way he seemed to approach everything. Did he do anything for fun? *Maybe he's worried bits of him will fall off if he laughs.*

They had headed off at sundown in the direction of a tavern on the outskirts of town, hoping to fool any observers into thinking it was their destination. They rode for an hour or so, changing direction several times. Eventually they would backtrack to join the north road to Paterak. They had kept a close eye behind them and were confident they had not been followed.

Kyer took another stab at conversation. "So how come they don't call you Sir Derry?"

"Why would they?"

"I dunno, being a *knight* and all."

"I'm not a knight yet."

"Oh. I thought you were. You certainly . . . behave like one."

"And so I should."

Kyer half expected him to lecture her about her own behaviour. "So when will you be knighted?"

"When I have proven myself worthy."

She clamped down on her tongue before patiently asking, "And how does one *do* that?"

"I have been Dunvehran's captain of the guard for three years. I have devoted my life to serving my lord, the duke, and someday he will recognize my loyalty."

Kyer raised her eyebrows at the mention of the dark elf's formal name but didn't question it. Derry would not have used the name had his relationship with the duke been a simple one of employer and employee. The captain's fealty was without question; Kyer didn't think him capable of feigning the conviction with which he spoke. Why anyone would devote his life to serving someone else was beyond her.

"I've been working for Valrayker less than a day and I've already caused all this trouble. I hope he doesn't wind up wishing he hadn't asked me along."

"He knows you're new to this sort of thing and inexperienced. He wanted you in the party for some reason, or else he wouldn't have asked you. Whatever trouble has been caused, you'll have a chance to make it right, and he'll be watching for it."

Kyer wished she'd kept her mouth shut. *I bet you will be too.*

They rode eastward along the edge of the woods where there were fewer trees and little shelter. Kyer wasn't looking forward to being exposed to the full brunt of the storm when they turned onto the plain.

Trig's ears flicked. Kyer looked back and saw movement in the thick darkness. "Someone's coming."

No sooner had the words escaped her lips than Derry's warhorse started. Derry wheeled around just as an arrow hissed out of the gloom and narrowly missed his shoulder.

Four horsemen galloped out of the black toward them. Kyer reached for her bow, fumbling with the strap and cursing her weakness: fighting on horseback was not a skill she'd mastered. *I'd be better off trying to outrun them.* As she wrestled with that option, Derry hastily brought up his kite shield just in time for the bowman to aim at him again. The missile shattered, sending splinters flying into Kyer's mount. Trig reared in panic, and Kyer, still reaching for her bow, was thrown, landing heavily in the mud. Her breath knocked out of her, she watched Trig tear off into the woods.

There seemed to be horsemen everywhere, and Kyer scrambled to her feet, plotting how to use the trees as protective obstacles now that she was at such a tremendous disadvantage. Her sword was at the ready as the archer drew up. The other three horsemen went for Derry. Her attacker dropped his bow and drew a leaf-bladed short sword. Kyer prepared to duck, but to her surprise, he dismounted and headed for her. She flung off her drenched cloak and bent her knees in the ready position.

He came at her, his sword drawn but held open to the side. She saw her opportunity but hesitated, watching his cloaked form suspiciously. Both hands gripped her weapon as she tried to distinguish his features in the dark. "If you want the little chest, don't think I'm going to make it easy on you."

"The chief isn't after the chest anymore. He wants a word with you." His voice came eerily from nowhere, thin and insubstantial in the murky, rain-drenched woods.

Kyer didn't relax her position. "And is he here?"

"No. You'll have to come with us."

"Not bloody likely. I'm very busy right now." She circled, her boots splashing in pools of water that connected in muddy rivulets.

"Then I'll have to take you."

Kyer was not inclined to listen to threats. He finally swung his weapon, but she blocked it, pushing it out of line. She released and darted a couple of thrusts, testing his reaction time, and planting the notion that she was unsure of herself. She feinted a clumsy stab toward his chest, anticipating his parry, and rotated her blade against his to slash horizontally at his neck. It sliced through his cloak and made contact with his hauberk as she swept back.

He was taller, but she was quicker, and it did not take her long to analyse his skill. She advanced with another quick thrust, allowing him to dodge, and retreated. She repeated the movement, each time drawing him closer. He finally lunged toward her middle, but she had seen him lift his foot and was able to step aside. She feinted a cut to his shoulder, and as he blocked it, she slashed at his upper arm.

With a cry he poked back but she slipped in the mud down to one knee, and his sword met empty space, which threw him off balance. Seizing the chance, she swept her hand-and-a-half upward into his armpit. With a yelp of pain, he retreated, desperately switching his weapon to the other hand, even as his attention shifted. Kyer risked a glance over her shoulder. One of his friends was approaching to back him up, mud smeared down one side where he'd landed after being unseated from his mount.

Kyer positioned herself with her back to a tree, keeping one eye on the still wobbly first fighter. She wiped the water from her brow and levelled her blade at the oncoming attacker.

"Drop your weapon," the man ordered. "You *will* come with us sooner —" *Clang!* He deflected her overhead slash. "Or later."

"It'll have to be later," she snarled back. His next attack was strangely tentative, and she parried it easily. It dawned on her: they were under orders not to kill her. *That works in my favour.* She had no scruples about killing anyone who attacked her in the woods. Grinning wickedly with this wisdom, she lunged at his collarbone.

They all scrambled to keep their footing in the muck, and the light was poor, but they continued to swing. The wounded man wavered but still attacked, and the other timed his hits well. She struggled now, fatigued with maintaining her footing, and preventing either of her opponents from getting behind her. Number Two went for her right shoulder, and she partially blocked it but still felt the tip slice into her upper arm. Blood oozed down to her elbow, but she held on tight with both hands and jabbed low at him, cutting deep into his thigh.

She had to dodge another jab at her shoulder. *Damn it, I'm defending too much!* Water flowed off her bent elbows, and the stream down her face half blinded her. Sweat trickled down the small of her back. Her body was tiring of the fight, and her calves ached from trying not to slip. Giving her head a shake, she hastily wiped hair out of her eyes. Number One staggered to manoeuvre in behind her, his sword raised. But he was in bad shape and couldn't wield it properly. Drawing energy from somewhere deep inside, she faked a stab at Two to delay him then, pivoting in the slick mud to face One, drove her sword into his stomach.

Two's weapon whipped toward her, but her sword had penetrated deeply into the dead man; it took her an instant too long to pull it out. She didn't have time to block, and with the momentum from the release of her sword, she lost her balance. Pain shot through her rib cage as his weapon slashed into her left side. He drew back a half step, sensing victory.

It was an error that would cost him. Brendow's teachings were second nature to Kyer, rooted like an old-growth cedar. *The battle isn't over until the last enemy has fallen.* Gasping and furious, she regained her footing, screamed in rage, and cut down ferociously onto his weapon arm, severing it. In shock, he didn't even try to stop her. With one hand, she ploughed her blade into his chest and pulled it out again. He fell to his knees, his remaining hand futilely attempting to stem the red flow. His look of surprise froze as he fell facedown in the mud.

Blood streamed down Kyer's side, and she swayed, leaning heavily on her sword. She reeled with pain, and a roar had begun in her ears as though she stood behind a waterfall. Each breath sent sharp pains shooting into her. Trying to clear her head and think what to do next, she pushed hair away from her forehead once again. With no warning, a hand grabbed her under her left arm and swung her up, belly down, onto a horse. The motion tortured the gash in her ribs and she screamed. Her weapon fell from her hand and bounced on the sopping ground with a muted *clang*. They galloped out of the woods and headed into the open plain.

"Ronav'll be pleased to meet you," her captor said.

Derry's turn had saved him from catching the arrow in the back. He split away from Kyer, pleased that three of the pursuers stayed with him.

Surely Kyer could handle the one on her own. His opponents attempted to outflank him, though the trees were a hindrance. recognizing this, Derry cut around a large fir, using it to protect his left side. Then he let go the reins and allowed his warhorse to take over. Donnagill slammed into the shoulder of the lighter horse, driving the beast to its knees. Its rider was sent cartwheeling into the mud, where he grabbed his fallen broadsword out of the muck and ran to join his partner. At the same time, Derry swept forcefully at the second rider, who took the blow on his buckler and was nearly unseated. The third horseman entered the scene from Derry's right as the riders turned around and charged again.

Suddenly the second assailant tossed his riven shield away and galloped off in Kyer's direction. Derry had no time to look over at his comrade; his challenger did not let up. They came together with a screech of metal and a scream of horses. Derry's mount won the contest again, and the falling rider had to leap clear from his dying black as it collapsed.

Derry heard a cry but kneed his charger forward, intent on riding his last enemy down. The man dodged the huge animal but, in his haste, wasn't able to get his sword in position. Down went Derry's blade to cleave the man's neck. He felt the Equart-forged steel sheer through tissue and bone, and the head sailed through the air. It splashed down in the mud with its eyes wide open, unblinking and glossy with the rain.

Alarmed by the pounding of hooves, Derry wheeled Donnagill around and saw a horse racing away into the night. He reined Donnagill in, and whispered calming words as he directed the animal toward where he last saw Kyer. There was no one but two unmoving forms in the mud, neither of which was the girl. He muttered an oath of dismay and gave chase, bursting out of the woods to rescue his helpless companion.

In the dim distance, Derry couldn't make out much, but he thought he saw Kyer wriggling in the man's lap. He saw a sudden flinging motion with her arm and the next thing he knew, Kyer had fallen to the ground, flat on her back. The horseman swore a steady stream as he reined in to come back and retrieve her. When he caught sight of Derry thundering toward him, he spurred his horse in the opposite direction. Derry gave a fleeting thought to pursuing the attacker but couldn't hope to catch the lighter mounted man. Nor was there any need. What mattered was that the attempt to take Kyer had failed. Derry reined in Donnagill near Kyer where she lay gasping in the muck. In her right hand was a stiletto knife, a couple of inches missing off its tip.

He dismounted, hurrying to her aid, but she climbed haltingly to her feet. He stopped short. Her left hand clutched her rib cage. Blood seeped out from between her fingers and at the bottom of her leather cuirass. Each breath came short and sharp. Her face was pinched, but she did not cry out. Dropping her broken knife in a puddle, she lifted a foot and placed it down in the soggy grass in front of the other. *Step. Step.* She seemed to be willing herself not to stagger. Derry walked with her, anxiously aware of the deep red stain spreading on her side.

"Come, why don't you ride—?"

Kyer raised her hand and kept walking. Surprised she had turned him down, Derry stayed close in case she collapsed.

By the time they reached the scene of the battle, the rain had abated to a mere drizzle. Kyer's horse had returned to sniff the area near her trampled cloak. Derry rummaged through his belongings for his kit bag. When he turned back to Kyer, she had dug out her own small kit and was bracing herself with a hand on a tree trunk to lower herself to the ground. Derry hesitated as he approached. Her eyes were closed as she rested against the bole, yielding to the exhaustion that would overcome her completely if she gave in.

He knelt down next to her. "Let me," he said quietly and began to unbuckle the side of her leather corslet. Startled, she sat up suddenly, winced, and leaned back again.

"Do you actually know what you're doing, or do you make it up as you go?" Her voice was barely above a whisper.

"The former," he replied. "I may not be a knight yet, but I *am* a physicker-adept."

He removed her armour and lifted her tunic to uncover her wounds, awkwardly averting his eyes from her bare torso. But he couldn't see properly and still keep both breasts covered. He *ahemed* lightly. "I apologize. It seems I must—" Taking her grunt as assent, he adjusted her tunic over her shoulder, and shifted her jewelled pendant aside. In spite of gentlemanly effort, he flushed at the smooth curve of her breast and scolded his embarrassment and lack of professional detachment. Forcing his gaze downward, he corrected the focus of his attentions and hoped Kyer was too incapacitated to notice.

"Interesting," she murmured. "Killer knight who can physick his enemies."

Derry considered. "I don't tend to physick my enemies," he corrected her tactfully.

After a moment or two, she went on. "Anyway, it's handy."

He moved her left arm to access the gash between her ribs. "Hmm," he murmured, assessing the damage. It wasn't pretty. He prepared a cloth, and she flinched as he cleaned the wound. A ragged-looking slice, no broken rib to go along with it, luckily.

"This way, we can fight, I can get really hurt, and you're around to fix me up. Perfect." She smiled weakly. Derry guessed from her pallor and apparent dizziness that she had lost a fair amount of blood.

"In spite of all this, you manage to remain cheerful," he said.

"What's to be all grim about? We won, didn't we?"

He wondered how serious a situation had to be before her good spirit slipped. "I am amazed that you were able to overpower two men on your own."

"Oh, you are, are you?" She closed her eyes again. "You and everyone else."

Derry instantly realized his error and reproached himself. This girl had defeated two men and escaped from a third. Besides that, she had shown stoic endurance of tremendous pain. It suddenly struck Derry that he would not have made the comment if he had been speaking to Janak or even that garrulous elf. Kyer must frequently suffer the indignity of having to prove herself time and again, in spite of her obvious skill.

"I apologize," he said. "I intended it to be a compliment, but I see how you would interpret it otherwise." Admonishing himself for doubting his lord, the captain straightened. "Dunvehran himself asked you to join us; naturally he would have chosen wisely."

"It's all right," Kyer said. "Anyhow, I'm not so sure he wasn't mistaken."

"How so?"

"Well, for starters, we were just attacked by four men, which isn't exactly healthy for our mission. Secondly, we allowed one of them to get away. Thirdly, turns out they don't want the armband; they want me. And because they didn't get me, I doubt we've seen the last of them." She took a deep breath and slurred a few more words. "I have to stop talking now."

Derry said nothing but put a salve he'd made of healing herbs on her wound and bound it. The patient's sigh told him she could already feel its healing warmth. As he tended her arm, he noticed another cut just above it and gently touched it, frowning. It was only a day old.

"Do you know anyone called Ronav?" she whispered.

Derry stopped. "Where did you hear that?"

She gestured. "The one who got away. He said Ronav'll be pleased to see me."

Derry frowned and murmured, "Damn."

"What is it?"

"Ronav Malachite. Haven't you heard of him?"

Kyer shook her head, winced, and shut her eyes.

Derry started applying bandages. "He began as a simple merchant, but he has a faulty sense of ambition. He has his own views on the way the duchies are structured, and the last I heard, he had designs on overthrowing both Dunvehran and Kien Bartheylen." Derry scoffed at the ludicrousness of the idea, but his tone remained grave. "He holds secret meetings and has developed quite a following, which of course only feeds his desire to achieve greatness. His power has grown so that we must no longer trivialise the threat he poses. He could do much to distract us in our fight against Dregor; not to mention the rumour that the two may be linked somehow. Our enemy has many agents."

"And the fact that he was expecting the shipment confirms that he's planning something."

"Probably. Simon must not have been a mere lackey to have been given such an important charge: the chest and the weapons. If that is the case, it would explain why Ronav might be unhappy that you killed Simon and took his property."

"If he's heard Simon is dead, you'd think he'd also know why I killed him."

"I hope so," Derry said emotionlessly. This girl had unwittingly made herself a target for an enemy who must not be underestimated. Did she realize how serious the situation was now?

"Maybe I should have just gone with them," she said. "At least that would have kept them from interfering with the rest of you."

"That would *not* have been acceptable," Derry said unequivocally. He paused. "Are you still worried that Valrayker will be ... disappointed in you?"

"Yes, I suppose so." Her lids closed.

Derry sat back on his heels. "Look at it this way. This all started because you killed a man who insulted you, right?" She hadn't told him the details, but that was the crux of it.

"Well, yeah. I challenged him because he insulted me. I killed him because he cheated."

"Still, do you regret killing him?"

She screwed up her face in what he thought was pain until he realized she was pondering his question. "No," she finally decided. "He was a cheat and would have stabbed me in the back first chance he got."

"Would you do it again under similar circumstances?"

"Yes. He was a scoundrel."

"I concur. And obviously so does Valrayker. You cannot have known what the consequences would be. You simply acted because you knew it was the right thing to do. And that is why he asked you to be a part of this. Valrayker will only be disappointed if you do not do what you feel is right."

Derry finished the job and helped her pull her tunic back down. "Is that all right?"

"Yes," she replied. "Thanks."

He nodded. "Now," he said, pushing himself up. "I will search the bodies for anything of value." Kyer struggled to move, but Derry laid a hand on her arm. "Trust me." He guided her back down. "I will give you everything that is rightfully yours."

Kyer couldn't possibly doubt his word. The man may not have a sense of humour, but he was absolutely honourable. She shut her eyes, and a moment later, she felt him cover her with her cloak. In spite of its dampness, it did help the chill. Soon after, she felt him lay something on the ground next to her: her sword. She reached out and rested her hand on the reassuring and familiar cold steel.

———

"There is nothing more I can teach you," Brendow said. "It is time you were on your way." He'd lowered his weapon and let the tip just barely touch the hard-packed, dusty ground.

After all the times the *Wæmniar* had said, "Not yet," she was finally ready?

Her throat suddenly went dry. "I don't think you're right. I haven't mastered—"

"Are you mocking me? You just trounced me four in a row."

"That doesn't mean I'm ready. It was a lucky br—"

"For the eleventh time in a fortnight."

Okay. She admitted that. "But what do *I* know about—?"

"Everything you need to." He put his hand on her shoulder in a fatherly way, as he had so many times before. "You aren't perfect. But what you need now is experience. You won't find that here in my back garden. I have taught you *everything* I know, which is much. You need now to go out in the world and find the knowledge you seek. And you will find it, my dear, though it will not be easy or pleasant for you. And it will almost always come from the most unexpected places."

"When should I go?"

"As soon as possible, I think." He gazed out toward the barley fields. "Don't be too quick to share with others the reasons for your journey. Don't show--" He pointed his index finger, as if for emphasis, then closed his fist and pocketed it. Kyer's hand rose instinctively to her medallion against her chest. "Be wary," he went on, "but you will recognize the trustworthy ones when you meet them." He paused again, as if there were something he wanted to say but was unsure of whether to say it. "You will have some difficult choices. More weighty than whether to plant corn or beans. Of greater consequence than who you will marry and whether you will have children." His face darkened. "I pray that you will choose wisely."

Kyer took in a deep breath and let it out slowly as she sought from his kindly brown eyes every last fragment of knowledge, of wisdom, of comfort.

"So do I, Brendow." She wanted him to know that she would recall his words every time she faced one of those decisions.

"Now I have something for you." He beckoned her to follow him inside the cottage. While he disappeared into his chamber, she waited in the front room and itemized every inch of it for the sake of her memory. The two ancient armchairs by the fire. The burgundy one on the right had always been hers. The view of his perpetually blooming garden out of the cross-hatched front windows, the only glass windows in all of Hreth. The dining table and two chairs under the window. How many cups of tea and how many biscuits had she consumed in the eleven years she had been friends with this man? The walls that were barely visible because they were covered by crammed bookshelves. The braided rag rugs that they'd had to roll back out of the way to practice when the rain fell too hard. She clenched her teeth to quell the emotion in her throat. It was a good room.

Hearing his "ahem" from the doorway, she turned around. Laid across his palms was a sheathed bastard sword.

Kyer stared at him.

Brendow gestured with his head. "Come on. Take a look at least."

Kyer took the carved leather sheath from him and examined its curved parallel lines and tiny trefoils. The hilt was leather-bound steel with a tiny green gem at the tip and spiral patterns on the ends of the cross guard. She drew the weapon silently, and the sheen of it caught her breath. The blade was unblemished, not a notch in sight. The edges could have split a blade of grass. She held it upright and took a few slow-motion swings, careful not to hit the ceiling.

"It is much more suited to your needs now. A sword worthy of one who has studied the *Wæpnian.*" He grinned, unable to hide his eagerness. "You should easily get used to the length and greater weight. And I think you'll find that the balance is excellent. Do you like it?"

"Like it? It's fantastic!" She had practiced with other weapons, but the only sword she owned was the one she had bought when she was twelve. This was the most perfect gift she could imagine.

"This was my first sword," he added quietly. "My mentor gave it to me."

Kyer just stared at it in awe. Unable to think of anything to say that wouldn't bring on embarrassed tears, she hugged him: her teacher, her mentor, her friend.

The last time she saw Brendow, he looked at her gravely, kissed her on the forehead, and whispered in Dark Elvish, *"Nevellish bena doth huerian effa gandil benith an fraemur."* Go always with courage and the will to do what is right.

Janak and Jesqellan found a suitable location to camp and watch for the others. The cedar boughs provided adequate shelter from the storm, and they could still see the road clearly from where they now sat. Janak volunteered to take the first watch.

Jesqellan arranged himself comfortably to begin his evening meditation. The dwarf moved away and found a willow tree under which to sit near the road, where he would have an almost invisible vantage point. The clouds had thinned, and through the gaps, Janak glimpsed the stars that invariably suffused him with comfort and wonder. He spent the next hour gazing skyward, using the twinkling warriors, chariots, and creatures that filled the skies to make up stories. A lone rider whisked by, in the direction of Paterak, but Janak paid no attention.

Kyer awoke from her doze when Derry returned.

"I have moved the bodies side by side and covered them with their cloaks. Not exactly proper funeral rites, but the best I could do under the circumstances." He held out his hand. "Just a few coins each. Their weapons were nothing to hand down to our children." Kyer eased her way upright, pausing in a squatting position until the dizziness subsided. Her fingers scooped the square silvers out of his palm and placed them in her own pleasantly bulging pouch. She could hardly believe that only yesterday this very pouch had held barely enough coin to get her through the night.

"Thanks." The light-headedness lingered. "We'd better get moving."

He did not offer to help her rise, but she detected the way he discreetly observed to be sure she was all right. Kyer clung to the saddle and clenched her teeth against the pain as she hauled herself up. She glanced at Derry, but he was looking down; if he'd noticed her extra effort, he hid it well. Not many would be as sensitive to another's pride.

Derry roped the enemies' horses to their own, and they rode into the night. Travel was quicker in the open plain. Still, they were more than an hour behind schedule and felt they had better push hard for the road to Paterak. The rain had finally stopped and the moon fought to break through the clouds. A brisk wind grew now, so it seemed the moon would win.

The Burnished Blade was awash with music and merriment, and Phennil climbed regretfully onto Leoht's back beneath the clearing sky. "At least we didn't get stuck riding in the rain," he said genially. He couldn't believe his good fortune, getting to ride alone with Valrayker. Or, it suddenly occurred to him, had the dark elf chosen to ride with him because he simply didn't fit anywhere else?

In an effort to throw off any pursuers, they rode west until they reached the river then turned north to the road.

"If all has gone well, Derry and Kyer will be settled in the camp by now," Valrayker said.

Phennil leapt on the opportunity to chat. "So who is Kyer? Where did she come from?"

"I hardly know anything about her. She came from a small village in northwestern Heath. Beyond that, you'll have to ask her."

Phennil frowned, opened his mouth to speak, and closed it again. His chest had tightened with a combination of curiosity and envy. "You just met her yesterday?" The girl must have done something remarkable to get the duke's attention. *That* didn't happen every day. Three years Phennil had worked to prove himself to Val before being asked to join him, and he'd struggled to defend the duke's choice every day since. "You mean, all you know is that she killed this Simon fellow and now people are after her?"

Valrayker said, "Yup."

Phennil said, "Hmph." What was the duke keeping to himself about what had taken place between him and the young woman? The wood elf stared into the darkness that swallowed the road. "I wonder why a girl from such a remote place learned to speak Elvish."

"Hmph."

Phennil thought it sounded like a *hmph* of agreement. *See? I can be shrewd.* "Shame she's gotten herself into such a pickle."

"At least she doesn't have to deal with it on her own now."

"Can't say that I'm sorry about it," Phennil said, watching for the duke's reaction. "It'll be darn nice to have a good-looking woman in the group. Even if she *is* a human."

For the third time in their conversation, Valrayker agreed with him. Phennil considered it progress.

We can't be far from the road. They had ridden northwest for nearly two hours, and not only were the horses tiring, but Kyer's breath pierced her side like thorns. She had endured the pain for the past couple of leagues and was near the end of her tolerance, but they were behind their time. To stop and rest was out of the question. Her breaths came harder.

Derry reined in and moved alongside her. "I think the road is just beyond those trees. Let's slow down when we get there."

At the road, they slowed to a walk but didn't stop. The sky had cleared, save for a few scattered clouds, but with the breeze and her wet clothes, she shivered. Derry removed his cloak and draped it over her shoulders.

She adjusted it and indicated his plate mail. "Are you going to rust?"

He looked at her blankly and said nothing. She made up her mind to give up on his sense of humour.

Derry checked the position of the moon. "I am sure Dunvehran has met with the others by now and will begin to be concerned for us." He seemed to be defending the decision to keep moving.

"I know. I'll be all right." To reassure him of it, she went on. "You call him Dunvehran?"

"Yes," Derry said. "It is his name."

"But most people call him Valrayker."

"True. 'Dunvehran' is his formal name, used only by those who are close to him." Derry spoke without a hint of arrogance or pride. It was a point of fact. "I have known him for half my life, and he has seen me through many troublesome times. I owe much to him. Yet he would never hold me indebted." He changed to a brighter tone. "Dunvehran is the only one left in Rydris who can speak Dark Elvish—"

Kyer stiffened then winced at the resulting twinge of pain.

"—but he did share some knowledge with me." If Derry was trying not to sound smug, he'd failed. "He told me that 'Valrayker' is a Dark Elvish name meaning both *dangerous*, as in fearful to his enemies, and *impregnable*, like a fortress. His people gave him the name, I suppose because he is their protector. It suits him, I think."

Kyer couldn't very well tell him she already knew the meaning of her employer's name. She figured she probably also ought to avoid telling him that "Dunvehran" meant *The Ancient* and was intended to bestow wisdom upon him when he was given the name at birth. To feign ignorance, she answered with a simple, "Yes," but went on. "He's a remarkable man. It's no wonder the people of Equart love him." She spoke between sharp breaths. "I only met him yesterday. But I understand how they feel."

Kyer clutched the reins and shut her weary eyes, forcing her breaths to come slower. She tried to ease her shoulders and unclench her knees.

"So," Derry said. "Where are you from?"

Well, well, well, Mr. Droll makes small talk. "Hreth."

"I have never heard of that."

"It's a crummy farming village. Not at all like Wanaka."

"Why did you come to Wanaka?"

"The road led there," she said lightly, putting up her guard again, though she had started to feel a sensation very like trust for this young knight-to-be. The feeling was unfamiliar, a vague recollection of friendship. "There wasn't much more for a person like me to accomplish in a farming village."

"You're very—" Derry began. "You appear very young ... to be so ... adept at your craft."

"I'm twenty-three." *Why did it have to matter?*

"Oh," he said. "That fits better; I estimated about eighteen."

"I get that a lot." *Which doesn't make it easier to swallow.* "How old are you?"

There was the subtlest hesitation. "I am twenty-six."

"You're very young to be captain of the guard."

In silence he reached forward and stroked Donnagill's neck. Raising his chin, he said, "I get that a lot."

I imagine you do. She wondered if the others in the party had trouble accepting the young man's authority. Derry must excel at his duties, or Valrayker would never have given him such responsibility. He'd devoted his life to the duke; she'd have thought Derry would deserve to be knighted for that alone. But only Valrayker knew his criteria. Clearly the duke was looking for more. "Where are you from?"

"Equart City," he said proudly. "Well, near it, anyway. I grew up not far from there and helped to defend it when Dregor attacked. Dunvehran and I managed to get away when it was sacked," he finished gravely.

"Did any of your family escape with you?" Kyer asked gently.

"No." In the tone of this single word, Kyer heard Derry sit up straighter. "I lost my family to a pestilence a year after I joined the Equart Guard. At least, I am certain about my parents, but I never learned for sure what became of my sisters. Most of the town was wiped out, and there was no way of keeping track of everyone. No one was able to tell me about them." Derry stopped as if the memory had caused him physical pain. "How are you managing?" It was the captain, not the physicker speaking.

"I can go faster if that's what you mean."

They picked up the pace to a faster walk.

Derry looked over at her. "I will polish it with an oiled rag," he said.

She shook her head. "What?"

"My armour. So it won't rust."

When they sensed someone approaching for the second time that long evening, Kyer could hardly bear it. But within seconds, they were off the road, anxiously soothing the horses to keep quiet. Kyer, nearly faint with stabbing pains, fervently hoped they weren't about to be attacked again. *Let it be friend, not foe!* The rider was nearly upon them by the time she finally recognized the fair head. Derry stepped out and hailed Phennil.

Kyer heaved a sigh and slumped in the saddle.

The elf led them north to the camp. After midnight, they were hailed by Jesqellan, more than three hours later than they had been expected.

A barrage of questions followed, but Derry hushed them and insisted on getting Kyer settled before giving his report. Kyer didn't balk when Derry assisted her out of her saddle and onto her bedroll. Only once she was comfortable did he begin the story, applying a new dose of salve as he spoke. The cool burning soothed her, and she breathed more easily. Kyer recounted her escape from the horseman, including Simon's connection with Ronav Malachite.

Valrayker's grey eyes were grave. After a moment, he smiled at her. "What's life without a good balance of friends and enemies?" She accepted his congratulations.

He rummaged in his saddlebag, and a moment later produced a bottle and small goblet. He poured the equivalent of a few mouthfuls of dark liquid and held the goblet out to Kyer. "You'll want that."

She smiled uncertainly. Did he simply know she liked a glass of wine, or —no, of course. The dark elf had sat next to her as she went through the Dark Elvish wine ritual.

He plugged the bottle with the stopper and grinned. Evidently he was not offended that she had adopted the ritual of his people.

"Thank you." She propped herself up on one elbow. Valrayker asked questions of the others, providing her with a modicum of privacy for the few moments it took her to drink to her nameless worthy opponents. She handed the empty goblet back and lay down.

"Derry?" Jesqellan spoke quietly.

"Yes?"

Kyer did not hear the mage's response, but Derry's voice came a moment later. "Kyer, Jesqellan has offered to perform a Heal."

She took up her propped position again. "What does that consist of?"

Jesqellan sat wordless, apparently preferring that the physicker explain.

"It's a spell, which speeds the patient's healing by degrees, depending on the level of energy the mage commits to the spell."

The idea was not unappealing to Kyer, and she said so.

"There is a cost, however," Derry went on. "The spell requires pain transference. The mage essentially taking on patient pain."

Kyer had trained as a swordfighter; she knew basically nothing about magic and what a Battlemage might be capable of. That a person would be willing to sacrifice his own physical comfort to help someone impressed her. She looked at the mage, his dark skin shining in the firelight. The scent of cedar mingled with the wood smoke.

"How long would that last? Wouldn't that make it harder for you to travel?"

"Hard to say exactly," Jesqellan said. "It depends on the intensity of the patient pain, and how I control the energy and transference." The mage shrugged as if it were nothing. Kyer took a split second to determine she did not agree. She shook her head.

"No. Thank you, Jesqellan, but this . . ." She indicated her wounded side with her chin. "This is on me. I'll be all right."

Jesqellan gave a little nod, and Kyer lay back down, breathing deeply from the exertion.

Fatigue descended on her now that the pain had eased, and she listened to the sound of the stream rushing along a few paces away, reminding her of the swishing sound of wind through the trees. She soon fell asleep.

The greenery swishes like the wind as I step through it. Surrounded by it with blue sky far above between the long leaves. A forest with no path. Mama said be brave. Hands move the stalks apart so I can step through. Stumble. Get up and brush loose hair from my face. Reaching the edge of the forest, step through the last of the stalks and see . . . a little house across the yard. I hear hammering in the distance. Walk forward, toward the house, toward the woman out front who is wiping her wet hands. She has been washing something mucky in a tub. I go closer. It's wool. Mama said be brave. The woman speaks. She is kind, and I am safe.

Kyer awoke with a start and sat up, her breaths quick and shallow. Derry was at her side immediately.

"Is everything all right?" he whispered, a hand on her shoulder.

She nodded. "I'm fine. It was just a dream."

Derry insisted on checking her dressings before she lay back down. Then he left her. She turned her face to the warmth of the fire.

The dream was never frightening, yet she always felt bewildered afterward. She didn't know whether she dreamt it because it had actually happened or because Della and Gareth Halidan, the kind couple who became her parents, had told the story so many times. The dream was a reminder that she knew how she got out of the cornfield but had no recollection of how she got in. No real memories, just formless images. No idea what her first language was, though, oddly enough, she still knew it fluently. Brendow had told her that was near to impossible. She'd been only three when she'd arrived. What three-year-old can fluently speak any language, let alone remember it for twenty years? Yet when Kyer was able to point out the differences between her language and Dark Elvish, down to the slightest variation in inflexion, Brendow looked at her quizzically and didn't question it further.

Gareth, Della, and Brendow remained the only ones who knew about it. Kyer didn't even trust her friends well enough. Tarqan, Adric, and Bianca, her fellow trainees, were the only peers who'd bothered to get to know her. She and Tarqan worked up a sweat, both on the field and in bed. She put up with taunts and scorn from villagers who lauded Tarqan and Adric for their ability to defend the village; derision was flung at Kyer, even while Bianca was fawned over for her plan to become the next magistrate. Kyer alone was spurned, in spite of her superior skill.

Kyer shifted and flinched as she strained the wound on her left side. Life couldn't have been easy for Gareth and Della, either, what with the sidelong glances and whispers that followed them wherever they went. Sheska Bolen said the Halidans had accepted Kyer only because they had no "real" children. Kyer's blood simmered at the memory of the pretty, cruel face laughing at her. But she knew it wasn't true. Kyer still felt Della's and Gareth's sorrow piercing her in the back as she rode out of town. She struck Sheska's face out of her mind. After all, if she'd liked everyone in Hreth, she wouldn't be here now.

Drowsiness crept up on her. Phennil's magnetic eyes *and terrific odour.* Derry, the noble captain, who stood just on the other side of the fire, his back to it. Nice to look at. *Proud, professional . . . and more?* And Valrayker . . . She already felt a bond with him. A hero, a man she'd dreamed of, in every way desirable but thoroughly out of range. Kyer melted into sleep picturing how their relationship might be different if they'd met three hundred years earlier.

Four
The Folly of Shopping

Kyer awoke to Dima, the sun god, brushing her face with his, and to the sound of voices.

"Janak, will you fetch some water?" Phennil asked.

"Now?" The dwarf stopped in the middle of rolling his bed.

The elf stared at him momentarily with a puzzled grimace. "Of course. Val doesn't have quite enough water for the porridge, and I'm not sure how much you know about cooking, Janak, my friend, but water does take time to come to a boil, and I am not drinking any tea that's made with water that hasn't been properly boiled first. The flavour's all wrong."

"And what are you doing that you can't walk to the stream?" Janak snapped.

Phennil's six-foot-four-inch height towered over Janak, and he said proudly, "I am on a mission for our employer, I'll have you know." He gave a sweeping bow to the dark elf who sat on a rock by the fire. "I have been expressly asked to fetch certain herbs which I know to be available in this environment, and if you wish to have flavour in your meals rather than mere variations of bland, you'd better go get the water so I have time to do as I have been requested."

Janak snatched up the pail. "All right, all right! If it means you'll shut the hell up, I'm off." He stomped through the trees.

Kyer smirked.

"They're right over there, Phennil," Valrayker murmured, waving his hand in the direction of some wild parsley and onion about ten paces away.

"I know," Phennil said cheerfully.

Kyer stood up, moving a little more slowly than usual. She snatched up a cloth and towel and followed Janak to the stream to give her wounds a proper bath.

"Morning." She set her things down. He did not reply. She knelt down and whipped her bloodstained tunic over her head, and as he turned to rise with his full bucket, she saw his eyes fall on her bare torso, her medallion, and down to the gash in her ribs. He looked startled but quickly turned his mouth into a sneer and said, "Bloody humans."

Derry, in his physicker persona, watched Kyer's progress to the stream out of the corner of his eye. She moved with a slight stiffness but generally appeared to be healing up well. When she removed her tunic, he felt heat brush his cheeks. Confused, he sat down to sort through his physicking kit.

Janak stomped through the trees.

"What's wrong, Janak?" asked Valrayker. "You look pale. Did you see a fearful sight?"

Janak was about to bark a retort when he saw the dark elf's laughing eyes. Evidently Valrayker had also witnessed the exchange at the stream.

The dwarf set the pail down next to him. "My day started off poorly; it needs no worsening by the sight of female human skin."

Valrayker poured a bit of water into the pot.

"I'm sure she doesn't see herself that way," said Derry as he rearranged out-of-place items in his kit. "She's a fighter, with a fighter's body. I'm sure it won't be the last time it is wounded and I have to treat it the same way I do yours."

"Yes," said Jesqellan, "and I've seen the way Derry shudders when he is forced to scrutinise your leathern skin. It is not a pretty sight."

Phennil rose and peered through the willows. "Damn, she's a looker, though."

Derry sighed. "Phennil, it is hardly courteous to watch her."

"What? You just said she has a fighter's body."

"And do you spy through the trees when I'm bathing too?"

Phennil put the teakettle on the fire. "I notice you're sitting with your back to her."

Derry ignored the remark, but his voice was impatient. "Think of her as a fellow warrior. I'm sure she'll be thankful when we get used to having her around."

Janak grunted as he tied his bedroll to his pack.

"And I'm sure she'll let us know if she gets tired of us . . . appreciating her presence in the meantime," said Valrayker, sifting oatmeal into the water. "Trust me, she can be quite assertive." Derry glanced at his lord and saw a curl of amusement on his lips.

"I do not recall if we allocate this much time, as a rule, to discussing each new person who joins us," put in Jesqellan quietly.

"Not everyone is this much worth talking about," Phennil retorted. "I think she adds a touch of class."

Kyer left her now-clean tunic spread out on the rocks to dry and unbraided her brown hair as she returned to her saddlebags. Valrayker was serving up the porridge.

"Morning." She put on her other tunic then began yanking a brush through the tangles the rain had tied.

"And you," Valrayker returned. "How's the wound?"

"Much better, thanks to our friendly local physicker." She stretched from side to side. "But it'll take a few more days before I can bend normally." Her brush caught an unusually stubborn tangle and she frowned.

"I will put some more of the salve on it before we depart," Derry said.

"If you're ready, come and have some of this," Valrayker said.

"Sounds great; I'm hungry." She returned the brush to her bag. She remembered something else and drew a small knife from her saddlebag to put in her boot sheath as a temporary replacement for the one she'd used on her captor.

"It's only fair to warn you that this won't likely be quite as mouth-watering as your meal at the Blade." His grey eyes twinkled.

She laughed, recalling her slurps during last night's dinner. "And I suppose there's no wine to go along with it."

"You'd only choke on it every time I speak." He grinned, slopping porridge into a cup.

"I was hoping you wouldn't notice that."

He handed her the cup of porridge and said, "At your service, darlin'," in such an accurate imitation of Simon that she snorted and almost dropped the cup. Suddenly she became aware that the rest of the group was quietly observing the interchange. Her face flushed a little, and Valrayker winked at her. He held her gaze for a moment. She knew she was being appraised and that, so far, she was okay in Valrayker's books.

"Is this some kind of an inside joke?" Phennil broke in. "Are you going to share with the rest of us?" He scooped another spoonful of porridge into his mouth.

"Certainly not," Valrayker said haughtily.

"By definition, Phennil," said Jesqellan, "an inside joke is not meant to be shared."

Kyer caught Derry looking at her thoughtfully before he lowered his head to his breakfast.

Valrayker changed the subject and spoke to Kyer again. "Perhaps when the wound is fully healed, you could describe for me, in detail, how it happened." He lifted the kettle from the grate and filled another tin cup.

"I suppose," Kyer replied, not quite sure what Valrayker was getting at.

"Good," he nodded. "I may know a trick or two that could prevent you from giving your blood to our cause so freely. Tea?" He handed her the steaming brew. She nodded in understanding.

"Just let me know when it's a good time for you," Valrayker said.

"I will." She moved over to sit next to Janak and Phennil on the cedar log they shared. Janak grunted and moved to the other side of the fire. She stared after him, open mouthed. *What a jackass.* "Get over it," she said. "I'm not going away."

The others pointedly stared at their food, except for Valrayker, who smirked at Janak.

At length, after some discussion with his mage and captain, Valrayker spoke to the group.

"We should be in Paterak by mid-afternoon. We'll stop there overnight then carry on to Shael. I believe Kien is there, and I have business with him. Let's be off as soon as possible."

Kyer looked up at the mention of her own duke. Of course. Lord Kien Bartheylen and Valrayker were best friends. Travelling with the one great hero almost certainly meant encountering the other.

Kyer rode next to Phennil as the party headed north to Paterak. They chatted, or rather, he chatted and she listened. Although his prattle was probably irritating at times, he was quite likeable. But she was glad to be upwind. The babbling blond elf didn't seem to mind that she wasn't paying close attention to him. Or it could be he was unaware that her attention was on the conversation between Valrayker and Janak, who spoke behind her. No one could accuse her of eavesdropping; she was unmistakably *supposed* to hear every word the dwarf said.

The dark elf asked Janak for his thoughts on their mission to Nennia, what approach he believed they ought to take to find out the circumstances in the village.

"Well, for one thing, we need to keep quiet," the dwarf began with the tone of an expert. "And that is what leads me to believe that our party is just too big. How can all five of us enter the village with no one becoming aware and getting suspicious? No, the smaller party of four was a much better idea. Five is just too many."

"Ah." The duke considered the recommendation. "You feel we need to reduce our number. I won't be there, so that leaves just one more to cut from the group. I suppose it ought to be the one who most obviously does not fit in?"

"Exactly."

"Perhaps Derry, with his plate armour and warhorse. He's certainly not inconspicuous. Or Phennil, who talks incessantly and smells bad. The villagers would know of your arrival three days beforehand."

"Oh no, that isn't what I meant." Janak shook his head vehemently. "No, for such a serious mission as this, on the other side of enemy lines, I think it unquestionably ought to be the one who is the least experienced. The one we are most likely to have to bail out of trouble. We won't have time for that sort of nonsense."

Valrayker said, "Hmm," and nodded wisely.

Kyer had a much better idea. She pivoted in her saddle to speak to the duke.

"If you don't mind my saying so, Valrayker, it seems to me that since Nennia is a *human* village, we ought to be rid of the members of our party that would find it next to impossible to disguise themselves as humans." She looked at the dwarf pointedly, and he gave her a glare.

"These are all very useful considerations." The dark elf winked at Kyer. "I will ponder your ideas and let you know what conclusion I reach."

Janak glowered.

They took care to enter Paterak in small groups, the way they had left Wanaka, and took lodgings at an inn called Aidan's Haven. Kyer thought it in bad taste to name an inn after the goddess of life and fertility, but then Derry explained that the proprietor herself was named for the goddess. Derry dismounted as the stable boys ran out. Unlike young Jack at the Burnished Blade, these lads appeared to be in awe of the warhorse and gratefully accepted Derry's offer to help stable him. Kyer, amused, interpreted his offer as a diplomatic way of saying, "I would not dare trust you with him, and I prefer to groom him myself." She handed off Trig as well as the two extra horses that had belonged to the dead men in the woods.

After an unremarkable meal, in an establishment that reeked of boiling tripe, Jesqellan and Kyer decided to go to the marketplace. The mage was looking out for a pair of gloves, and the warrior needed a new stiletto, one that did not break so easily when thrust between links of chain mail.

Phennil challenged Derry to a sparring match. The elf had told her he was an excellent bowman but always welcomed an opportunity to improve his sword skills. Jesqellan and Kyer left them in the yard and headed off. The main road took them past some shops, including a baker and a weaver, as well as a few guildhouses. The sign above one doorway showed the chisel and trowel of the masons' guild. In the archway of the coopers' guild, a young man in a dark blue cloak leaned against the door frame, reading a pamphlet.

Paterak was larger than Wanaka, enough to be called a town. It was nestled in the foothills at the southernmost tip of the Tarmigon range and did fairly good trade with the dwarves who lived within those mountains.

The marketplace was set up in the centre of town in a square framed by shops and houses. Today's sunshine had not done much to dry up the muddy ground. Kyer's boots squelched and mud oozed up between Jesqellan's toes. Even in the mid-afternoon, the market was a bustle of people. Booths lined all sides of the square for vendors of fruits and vegetables, leather products, and arms. Stalls housed carpenters' tables and chairs and other handicrafts, a fletcher, a chandler, tables of baked goods, hats and bonnets, rag dolls, toys. Musicians had strategically placed themselves to effectively compete for the attention of the crowd. A man standing on a crate expounded his philosophic views on the creation of the world, and another fellow cried out an emphatic warning that the end of said world was nigh. The clamour of all these in counterpoint with the cries of vendors was the music of the market that always sent ripples up Kyer's back.

"I bought my first short sword in a place like this," she commented as they dodged in and around all the people and looked over the wares. "Of course, the market in Hreth is about half this size, but the feeling is the same."

"When was that?" the mage asked.

"I was twelve." Kyer smiled to herself as she remembered proudly showing her purchase to her parents. "Take that, you worm! You dog!" She'd pretended to attack Gareth, who played along by falling to the ground and crying for mercy. Brandishing the sword, she said, "I am going to be a great warrior. I am going to help Duke Kien send Dregor fleeing from Rydris for his very life." And just a few days later, she was approached by Brendow and started training with him. *The old man's timing was impeccable!*

Jesqellan was speaking. They had stopped at an herbalist's booth. "I don't like these places." He placed a bottle back on a display shelf. "I do not like the smell, for one thing, and I will never get used to the noise and the large crowds. I'm from the northern steppe! The peace and solitude become a part of one, and there's no turning away from it."

Kyer didn't bother reminding him that in a few days' time, he would be entering the second largest city in all of Rydris.

"In these markets I never know whether to trust that I'm getting a quality product," Jesqellan went on. "And with all the noise and the people, I feel pressured and ill at ease. There's so much rubbish; you have to be careful what you spend your money on."

A nearby booth displayed weaponry, including a collection of fine-looking daggers. Kyer stopped to look them over. Jesqellan noticed a glover farther on and went to see his wares.

Kyer looked up briefly from a knife with a carved bone handle. The mage drifted away. Kyer could find nothing to suit her among the hand weapons on display and wished to ask the dwarf managing the stall if there were any more in her wagon. She was occupied with another customer, so Kyer waited patiently, glad of the entertainment of the street performers. Her right hand rested on the counter, and she craned her neck to catch glimpses of the sword swallower through the gaps in the thinning crowd. A sharp pain suddenly pierced the back of her hand.

Yanking it away from the table, she spun around in surprise. Her hand had a three inch cut across it, and blood oozed from it. Clutching it, she looked around to see who could have done such a thing. A tall young man stood very near her with his hand tucked inside his dark blue cloak. He watched her casually. No one else was nearby. It had to have been him. "What did you do that for?" He did not speak but the corner of his mouth turned up slightly as she felt a numbing warmth travel up her right arm.

What's he done? She flung her head around to find Jesqellan, but he was completely engrossed in his glove search. The numbness spread across her shoulders. Something took her left arm and gently pulled. Her legs faltered forward, and she knew she was being led by the blue-cloaked man. Had she seen him before? Did she know him? Her vision blurred and the world started to spin. Her knees weakened. Perhaps she was mistaken and this was Jesqellan. He had seen that she was ill and was taking her back to the inn.

The muddy ground swooped up to meet her and she gasped. She was down on one knee. The market whirled about her. She fought panic and pressed her hand against her forehead. An arm was around her, and she was upright and shuffling along again. Images rushed by but they were not focussed. Faces and figures and dark shapes, which she tried in vain to identify. Her legs stumbled along. She could hear what she knew were voices but could not make out words.

"No, thank you." The nearby voice was strangely clear. "My wife is with child and is ill. I am taking her home."

Jesqellan, what are you saying? She frantically tried to cry out but only succeeded in moaning.

"Keep walking!" the same voice hissed in her ear. All other sounds faded. She turned but could not see who had spoken. Blurred vision had become total darkness. Her legs gave out altogether and she crumpled. She was barely aware of being lifted.

⊂━┼━━━⊃

Jesqellan walked a few steps away from Kyer before having to slow down for a group of people who had stopped to watch a fellow swallowing his sword. Growing impatient, he ploughed his way past a woman whose child was dragging his feet crossly and whining that he "really *wanted* the taffy!" and sighed in relief at having finally reached the glover's table. He sifted through gloves to find some that would fit over his long, delicate mage's fingers, and scowled.

He searched through every pair of gloves on that table, and not a single one fit. They were either too large in the palms or too short in the fingers. The poor tradesman had tried his best to find just the right pair and seemed sincerely dismayed that he had been unable to help his customer. Jesqellan had almost resigned himself to the fact that he would have to have a pair custom made once they got to Shael when the glover pulled out a canvas sack from under a shelf behind him.

"These are each flawed in some minute way," he explained apologetically, and Jesqellan thought, *That's not surprising!* "But you may wish to look through them all the same." He laid the sack in front of the mage and untied the drawstring. Jesqellan glanced at him doubtfully but shuffled through the mass. String tied around the thumbs kept the pairs together. He was about to give up when he came across a black pair with oddly shaped fingers. His attitude took an abrupt turn for the better.

"These are exquisite!" he said. "Why did you not show me these right away?" Indeed they were finely crafted of the softest leather yet appeared to be very durable. He slid his hand in and was delighted that they fit perfectly. "Just what I have been looking for." He grinned broadly and held up his hand, looking over in hopes of catching Kyer's eye to show her how successful he had been.

She was not where he had left her. Curious, he hoisted himself onto a nearby crate and felt a slight anxiety when he could not find her. Then as his gaze scanned the crowd, he saw a strange sight. There was Kyer but a man in a deep blue cloak had her by the arm. Was that not the same young man he had seen in the doorway of the guildhouse on their way here? A bad feeling seized him, and he dropped the gloves. Mumbling a quick, "I'll have to come back later," he moved away and vaguely heard the glover mutter, "Damned northerners."

The mage's methodical mind raced. Was it one of Ronav's men again? But why would she go with him so willingly? It occurred to him that he would need help, in the event that she was being taken to a place where there would be more foes than he could handle on his own. As Jesqellan darted in and out around marketplace patrons, he cursed himself for not heeding Valrayker's direction to keep his eyes open for the girl's pursuers.

He had to send a message to one of the others. Any more than one would tire him and take up too much time. He would have to stop to concentrate and could lose her. Which one? Certainly not Janak. The dwarf would ignore the message, thinking that Ronav was welcome to the girl and she could just rot as far as he was concerned.

Up ahead, Jesqellan saw Kyer in her dark green cloak drop to one knee. The man hauled her up again and supported her as they increased their pace and disappeared behind a baker's stall. *He's drugged her.* They wanted her alive, or else he would have just killed her. *I will call Derry.* Derry was at the inn, which was only a short distance away. If she was poisoned, Derry would be needed. Besides, Phennil had been with him. They would both come.

Jesqellan rounded the corner and caught a glimpse, through the throng, of Kyer's escort making a beeline for a narrow road that headed into the western quadrant of the town. Trusting to chance that their direction would not change, the mage stopped short. Vaguely aware of someone swearing at him for nearly causing a collision, Jesqellan drew his staff toward himself, bowed his head, and closed his eyes.

His shaman-trained mind took only a moment to focus in the trance. Darkness surrounded him and his deep breathing made the only sound as he concentrated.

Derry. Marketplace. West side. Your kit and Phennil.

He came out into the light again, hoping the message would suffice, and shook off the light-headedness brought on by the spell. The fleeing pair was nowhere in sight. Jesqellan ran, his bare feet getting little traction in the mud.

Surely the crowd could see he was in a hurry. Why did they impede him? As in a bad dream, every person in the market seemed to have chosen that moment to head in the opposite direction from Jesqellan. He wove in and out, murmuring apologies to the obstacles with whom he made contact. A stray hog darted out in front of him, nearly bowling him over, but the mage regained his footing and pressed on.

At last he reached the edge of the square and went down the road he was sure the two had taken. He ran alongside a three-story building until he came to the corner at the rear. He looked up and down the alleyway. In the dim light, he saw the kidnapper stumbling, close to the north end. Kyer's legs must have given out because the man was now carrying her, armour, weapons, and all—no small feat for a man his size. He did not look steady. Jesqellan kept running and found he was gaining on them, but he had to do something before the two reached the end of the alley and could turn one way or the other and be out of his sight again. He extended his hand with a flinging motion and threw a spell: a direct hit. Her captor suddenly slowed to half speed. He turned to see what had caused it. Seeing Jesqellan, his face broke into a look of panic, and he tried to run. But now it was he whose progress was impeded.

"Put her down!" Jesqellan dashed toward them.

The man halted and practically flung Kyer in the mud. The mage was glad Kyer was unconscious, or that would have hurt. The half-speed spell already wearing off, the rogue reached into his cloak. From only ten paces away, Jesqellan whispered in the arcane tongue, casting a fist-sized ball of magical fire at his chest. The man raised his arm to block the blow, but the flames engulfed him. His scream echoed down the alley as his charred form crumpled to the earth. The mage blinked in surprise. He had expected at least some attempt at defence. How wasteful to use such a good spell on such a sorry excuse for a kidnapper.

Sighing, Jesqellan scanned the area around the corner to see if he could determine the man's intended destination. There was no one in sight but a few dwarves on their way to the smithy in the open area beyond where he stood. No further clues. The alley was flanked by two three-story buildings, and if the wet laundry hanging out the windows was anything to go by, at least one was a hostel. Looking up, Jesqellan saw an anxious face peeking out of a second-floor window. He waved and she hastily withdrew, closing her shutters. The commotion was nothing for her to worry about. Jesqellan poked through the still-glowing heap of carbon with his staff to see what he could find of value that was not flammable.

"There you are!" an exasperated voice called, and Phennil sprinted up. "It took me ages to find you. I'm sorry. Derry sent me on ahead because I can run faster than he can. He told me to find you on the west side of the square, but he didn't say anything about running up and down alleyways. I hope I'm not too late. Dear Goddess, what has happened?" He finally noticed the prone body of their comrade and the smoking remains of another.

"We had a brief adventure, Kyer and I, during our visit to the market. That is to say, we each had an adventure. They were rather separate." The mage felt his staff butt against a hard object. With a closer look, he picked it out with a handkerchief and slipped it inside his robe.

Derry appeared around the corner and jogged along the alley, carrying his physicker's kit immediately to Kyer's side.

"Is she dead?" Phennil asked, his brow creasing.

"No," Jesqellan said before Derry could speak, "but I believe she's been drugged." He removed the dead man's boots, which were only a bit blackened.

"I don't suppose it occurred to you *not* to kill him, so you could find out for certain who he was?" Derry checked Kyer's pulse and breathing.

Jesqellan pursed his lips at the rebuke but carried on with his examination of the body. "It was a fair assumption," he said stubbornly, tossing the boots aside, "because the assassin disabled her, rather than killing her. I presume he brought her down here to meet somebody." He removed a small cloth sack from the man's pocket and hefted it in his palm. Upon hearing the clinking of coins, he drew it open and examined its contents. "I do believe this would be an appropriate down payment for her capture. Who paid him, I wonder?"

"Did you elicit *any* information from him, such as where he was headed?" Derry asked.

"No. I did not really expect him to be as disappointing an opponent," the mage replied. "Phennil is lighter of foot than I; perhaps he could run a search." The elf trotted off around the corner to see if he could learn anything more.

Jesqellan propped Kyer up so Derry could force a brightly coloured liquid between her lips. She coughed and sputtered, but most of it went down her throat. Something else caught the mage's attention, being so close to Kyer. An . . . aroma. Jesqellan searched her face for something that could account for it, but shook his head, dismissing it.

"How did you happen to become separated?" Derry asked.

"We were looking for different things and thought it would save time," Jesqellan said, leaning on his staff.

"Jesqellan, you were asked—"

"I didn't intend to take more than a few minutes. Who would have thought it would take that long to find a pair of gloves that fit?" The mage thought wistfully about the fine pair he had left behind and wondered if the glover would still be there.

"Well, what's done is done," Derry said just as Phennil returned.

"There was a horseman a couple of blocks down," the elf panted. "He bolted when he saw me, so my guess is he was the destination. I couldn't hope to catch him up on foot."

"There's nothing much more we can do about it, I'm afraid," Derry said. "Phennil, please carry my kit and Kyer's sword. We must get her back to the inn."

Derry had far less difficulty bearing the weight of their friend than her captor had. Jesqellan watched his long stride, steady and sure beneath his burden, an image not inconsistent with the young captain's natural, albeit subdued, gallantry. He would be a fine knight someday . . . if he would stop trying so hard. It was well that Kyer, on the other hand, was unconscious, for though he had met her a mere two nights ago, he had a feeling that the "helpless damsel" image would not sit well with her at all.

Derry rounded the corner, Phennil alongside him. Jesqellan's part over, he went to retrieve his gloves.

⊶┈┉┈⊷

The crowds parted for Derry, and he reached the inn in a matter of moments.

Kyer's pulse was faint but detectable. She had a slight fever, but Derry was not concerned; it indicated that her body fought the drug. He had also located the point of entry, namely the scratch on her hand, and cleaned it well with alcohol. The physicker believed that the drug had been a mild poison, so it would wear off in a while, but the low-grade antidote would help her come out of it more quickly and with fewer side effects. The potion would also counteract the detrimental effect the poison could have on her wounds of last night. *She's had more than her share of woe these last two days.*

Phennil held the door open, and Derry carried Kyer's limp body into the foyer of Aidan's Haven. Their hostess popped through the doorway from the dining room.

"Oh, my goodness!" she exclaimed. "The poor dear! What happened? Is she ill? What can I do?"

Derry endeavoured to negotiate the stairs without knocking Kyer's head against the railing. "I would suggest that the most useful thing at the moment would be for you to open her room so I can put her down."

The large woman hustled up the stairs behind him, pulling out a ring of keys and flipping through them. "Oh yes, of course. My goodness, the poor thing. How dreadful to have taken ill. It was the heat that did it, you know. These slender women are apt to faint on warm days like this." Derry waited for her to unlock the door then brushed past her to lay Kyer on the bed. He removed her muddy cloak and tossed it on a chair. "I'll get her some nice chicken soup I have on the stove right now. That will help the poor dear. I told you, she's far too thin. Thin women—"

"Good lady, our friend is not ill, and she did not faint," Derry interrupted, as close to impatient as he'd ever been. "She has been poisoned. Chicken soup would be much less useful than a poultice of comfrey, poppy, and adder's tongue. And, no, madam, she is not a helpless maiden but a fighter who has had a run-in with some enemies."

The innkeeper stared at him, at the armoured woman on the bed, then at Phennil, who emphatically nodded his confirmation of Derry's words.

"What are you on about?" said a weak voice. They all looked down at Kyer, whose pale face was bewildered. "Why's it cloudy?"

Derry knelt down next to the bed, checking her fever, which was abating. "The blurred vision is caused by the poison," he explained.

Aidan, clearly uncomfortable with this new development, bolted out the door to retreat to the kitchen.

"Oh, is *that* what it was," Kyer said softly.

"We presume your captor was hired by Ronav. He's dead now."

"The man in blue."

Just then Jesqellan entered the room. "She's back, is she?" he said pleasantly. "I had quite a time catching up with you, but I made it. And I even managed to go back and get these gloves." He held up his hands, displaying his purchase.

"The poison was not extremely potent and won't take long to work through your system," Derry said. "You should feel better by morning." He left to assist the innkeeper with preparing the poultice.

Jesqellan lingered behind and cocked his head to one side. "Do you by any chance have any . . . magical items on you?"

"No, why do you ask?"

Jesqellan leaned on his staff. "It's just I sensed something on you earlier."

"I'd been stabbed with poison," she suggested.

He shook his head. "I don't think it was that. But I suppose it might have been the residuals from my own spell. Never mind. By the way, did you find a dagger?"

"No," Kyer said irritably, glancing down at her bandaged hand. "I never got to finish that before the bastard slashed me." The mage approached the bed with hushed excitement.

"I saved this for you." From inside his robe, he revealed a shiny knife. "It is the very one he used, so that may repulse you, but I retrieved it, and I thought you might like to have it, for it appears very well made. The fire will have cleaned off any traces of poison. I also checked it for unfavourable magic, and it is completely benign."

Made of fine steel, it had a silver-chased grip and a six-inch, needle-point blade with a narrow, V-shaped fuller. Kyer grinned. *This* one would be suitable against chain mail. "No, I'm not repulsed at all. There's a delightful irony about my keeping this. Thanks, Jesqellan."

Sometime later, Derry brought the poultice and applied it to the scratch on Kyer's hand. "This will help draw out the poison. Now rest."

The next morning, they headed out on the five-day journey to Shael.

Ronav drummed his fingers on the arm of his chair. "You are empty-handed?"

Con stood before him, his body half turned away. "Waste of gold on that bloody sorry excuse for an assassin."

Ronav's knuckles whitened. "Why didn't you do it yourself?"

"I thought it would be easier this way, no chance of her recognizing me."

The feeling that crept over the chief was not dissimilar to the panic that had stifled him when he first was getting used to the darkness of Dregor's dungeon. *Breathe. Just breathe. There's still time.* "Any more idea of who she is?"

Con grunted and scratched the back of his head. Ronav watched his right-hand man's eyes wander the hall to gaze at the others lolling about in various stages of drunkenness. The serving wenches, finished with one type of serving, had moved on to the next. One was curled up among the legs of someone Ronav couldn't identify because the fellow's head was already buried inside her open bodice, one hand up her skirt and the other pinching a reddened, erect nipple. Her head hung back, and she looked intensely bored. If it had been Ronav, he'd have backhanded her by now for not even pretending to enjoy it. On the other hand, there was that crow-haired slut swinging her hips beckoningly to Gyles, and unlacing her bodice. Gyles watched apathetically, but he would soon ladle her up like the evening meal and haul her to the privacy of his room to consume her. Ronav gazed with pride. *I give my men everything they want. Happy in their work.*

"Dunno who she is," Con said finally. "But I think it might ha' been a setup."

"What makes you say that?" the chief said sharply.

"She was seen talking pretty close with a bloke in black after she killed Simon, and left with 'im. Also, she took nothing from the cart of goods but went straight for the chest. It was gone by the time Jet got there. He tried to get in her window, but she was ready for 'im."

"That doesn't mean anything, necessarily." Ronav was hopeful.

"She killed Jet and Rory single-'andedly." Con glared at him. "She ain't an ordinary girl. And one other thing. The fella in black, turns out—I watched them arrive at Paterak—it's Valrayker."

Ronav felt the blood drain from his face. He swallowed hard, trying to collect himself. *Of course. It would have to be Valrayker.* This changed everything. "You must . . . I want to know who she is. I want her. Do you hear me?"

Con looked him fully in the eye, and his face slowly broke into his grotesque half grin, the left side overcompensating for the paralysed right. He rubbed his chest where the girl's dagger had pierced him. "This time, I'll get her myself."

"See that you do."

Five
A New Friend or Two

Kyer's first encounter with Valrayker, exiled duke of Equart, complete surprise as it was, had not allowed her time to prepare. Given the chance to create and present an excellent first impression, she would certainly have come up with a plan that did not involve making an idiot of herself. As they approached Shael, the capital city of Shae Duchy, she realized that the preparation time had its disadvantages. The trouble was, whereas Valrayker had been amused by Kyer's ill-advised insult, Kien Bartheylen was notoriously impatient and unforgiving. Had he been on the barstool next to her in Wanaka, he would likely have just as soon sliced her head off. Preparation seemed the wise choice in this case. But in spite of several days of travel to plan the first impression she wanted to present to the duke of her own home duchy, she felt less and less confident as the moment drew closer.

Derry's advice was to tread carefully. "Lord Kien has a deep appreciation for formality. He prefers to begin a relationship from a position of clear boundaries and clear delineation of status. Once he knows—and therefore *you* know—where you stand with each other, both can relax and proceed."

Kyer swallowed and cleared her throat to ease the sudden tightness in her jaw. In an effort to sound intrepid, she said, "He sounds arrogant."

Derry frowned reproachfully. "He may be but is it truly arrogance if he, in fact, *is* the greatest man on the continent?"

Kyer let the conversation end there and fought down her hackles. Obsequiousness might come naturally to Derry, but to Kyer, it would be as artificial as wearing a dress and playing a lute. Perhaps she could manage a simple "Pleased to meet you."

Shael Castle was enormous, its russet-coloured structure an ominous presence looming over the city walls. The highest tower shot skyward like the arm of a triumphant warrior returning from battle. Two flags flew from the tower, easily recognizable with the wind pinning them stiffly to the east. The lower was the banner of the duchy of Shae, and above it, the flag of Kien Bartheylen, signifying that the duke himself was in residence at the castle.

Lord Bartheylen was thrice a duke: of Shae, of Koral, and of Heath, where Kyer had lived all her life. And she would meet him this very day. Her stomach fluttered like the flags. *Just bow and keep your mouth shut,* she decided.

A light jab on her arm startled her, and she looked over and up at Derry who sat erect on his warhorse, eyes straight ahead with his usual sober expression, and sheathing his sword.

"What did you do that for?" Her face broke into a smile.

"I don't know what you're talking about," was the deadpan reply, though he threw her a sidelong glance from a gleaming eye.

Kyer would never have thought it possible that the ever-serious Derry Moraunt would shed his grim exterior long enough to tease someone. His half smile disappeared in short order. They rode abreast at the rear of the party; otherwise she was certain he would not have done it.

"You are in awe." His voice was deliberately low, so Janak and Jesqellan, a few paces ahead, could not hear. "Can it be that we have found something to subdue the dauntless Kyer?"

She smirked, staring before her at the avenue and the approaching gates. "I'm amazed at the size of this place."

"As capital cities go, it is second in size to your Heatha, but it is a wondrous sight nonetheless." After a beat, he added, "Equart City was once like this."

She looked up at him expectantly, but he was frowning. His eyes looked not at what lay ahead but at the past. An insight struck her in that moment: it was the face of a man who desperately wanted a second chance. Valrayker had named Derry captain of the guard only a short time before Lord Dregor's final attack on Equart City. Under the guidance of the previous captain, the city had managed to withstand two quick assaults by the enemy, though the captain himself had fallen. Under Derry's command, the city was finally taken. He must feel that much of the blame for Equart City's ravagement by Dregor had to lie with him.

All this had happened three years prior, when Derry was her own age. There was no way she felt wise and experienced enough to be in a position of such responsibility. *No wonder he can't relax.*

She wanted to remind him that Valrayker had not stripped him of his position after the fall of Equart. Clearly the duke did not lay the blame with him. The way Brendow told it, Valrayker would never have escaped the siege of Equart City without his captain's initiative. She wanted to assure Derry that he would always be worthy of everyone's respect and that he shouldn't reproach himself. But she could say nothing, for they had reached the city gates.

The two-story iron gate itself was open, but the towers were flanked by a squad of well-armed sentries in dress uniforms. "Why the formality? Doesn't Valrayker come here all the time?" Kyer asked.

Derry nodded. "I'm not sure. They don't usually use the honour guard. It's been a while since we've been here, though. Maybe it's just a good excuse for some pomp and ceremony." The soldiers stood at attention, though their halberds were not at the ready. The party was stopped, and the captain of the guard removed his scarlet-winged helm to hail the duke of Equart.

"Lord Valrayker, welcome!" he called in an authoritative voice. "When my men told me it was you approaching, I came to greet you myself."

Derry emitted a sound, and Kyer glanced at him sharply. It was the closest he'd ever come to open disdain. "The captain is Sir Fredric Heyland." Derry spoke politely, but there was a forced quality to it. "He has been captain for seven or eight years and was knighted three years ago." If it had been anyone but Derry speaking, Kyer would have called it sarcasm. Beneath his pride, was Derry jealous?

"And Phennil, Jesqellan, all of you, it is a pleasure to see you again," Sir Fredric continued, adjusting his helm under his arm. "Governor Lyndon and my lord, the duke, would like you to join them at the castle. I have brought the honour guard to escort you through the city." He gestured to the dozen scarlet-clad men behind him.

Valrayker assured him it was not necessary but thanked him for his thoughtfulness.

Derry whispered something that sounded like "bootlicker," but Kyer couldn't be sure. She looked at him quizzically, but he kept his eyes on his lord.

The redheaded captain glanced her way.

"There is one member of your party with whom I am unfamiliar, and as you know, it is my duty to be informed of all names of my lord's guests."

"Suffice it to say that she is my newest companion," Valrayker returned with the inherent authority that only another duke could assume in the capital city of his best friend's duchy. "She has been with us only a week, and it would not do at all for me to introduce her to you before she meets with Kien. So you will just have to content yourself with being introduced later."

Sir Fredric bowed with an acquiescent smile. "If it were anyone but yourself, my lord, I would not be content with such an answer!" He aimed his smile at Kyer. "I look forward to that moment with eagerness. Now let us proceed. Preparations are even now underway for a banquet in honour of your arrival, and I do not wish to delay anyone's enjoyment of it."

The soldiers parted to allow the guests to ride through their ranks. As Kyer rode forward, cloak back behind her shoulders, she was aware of several sets of eyes on her.

Sir Fredric gave a short bow to Derry, who nodded stiffly in response, breaking eye contact as soon as his code of decorum would allow. Kyer scanned Derry's face for an explanation and found none. She was puzzled and mildly irritated but not consumed enough to miss the extra attention the other captain was paying her. She met Sir Fredric's gaze and held it, approving of the bright, playful eyes that sparkled at her. He wore a neatly trimmed beard and had fringes of grey in his short red hair. She judged him to be in his mid to late thirties. *Very nice.* She gave him a short nod and carried on past him. She, too, looked forward to the introduction.

Derry frowned.

Kyer gave him a cheeky smile. "Does Captain Derry disapprove, or is he jealous?"

Derry flinched and an opaque curtain fell across his face. Once inside the gates, some shuffling allowed for the honour guard escort. Derry made no comment as he nudged Donnagill to position himself up ahead with his lord. *Damn it.* She'd just taken a step backwards in her progress with him.

Her humour didn't recover at the appearance of Janak, adjusting to ride alongside her. Half of the honour guard remained at the front with their captain, and the others closed in behind Janak and Kyer to bring up the rear. With Sir Fredric upon his black-as-night charger at the head of the procession next to the Bartheylen standard bearer, the guards in dress uniforms of scarlet and gold, shining swords on hangers at their sides, they made an impressive parade up the main street of Shael.

The roads crawled with people who stopped and gazed at the cavalcade as it passed. Kyer, unused to such pageantry, straightened her back, doubtful that she fit in with the others to appear worthy of such a welcome.

With a glance at Janak, Kyer noted a release of stiffness in the dwarf's rigid form. It was as if being suddenly surrounded by immense walls of granite had made him feel more free. His grunt in her direction, although still forcibly unfriendly, could not be described as abusive. *Whatever.*

Craning her neck to observe the castle, Kyer saw at once the trick that had been played on her. The one and only hill could not be seen outside the city, hidden behind the massive walls. Shael Castle sat atop this hill, with the result that from outside, the castle appeared twice as large as its true size. It was built up against the easternmost wall of the city and towered over the expanse of buildings like a god surveying his people, its great russet spire stretching up proudly. The late afternoon sun drew out the reddish tones from the stone, giving the immense structure a deep orange glow.

The rumble of carts and buggies on the cobblestone road vibrated in her chest, the clamour of horses' clopping hooves assailed her ears, while the general hubbub of a large population made her head swing like a saloon door. The thick mixture of smells that wafted in waves was occasionally rank enough to bring tears to her eyes: smoke from fuels and cooking and manure swapped by turns with cherry and plum blossoms from the trees that lined many of the side streets. One road led to a bridge over the river, and Kyer had a desire to explore it, to find out what sort of dwelling had the ill luck to be perpetually shadowed by the south wall. She stood a bit in her stirrups to see, but her attention was called back by the shrieks of children, whose play area the riders invaded on the edge of the city square. The children dodged the grasp of a blindfolded boy, who tripped on a cobblestone and was sent sprawling. He cried out but whipped off the blindfold only to find himself staring right up into Jesqellan's round black face. The child was abruptly quelled, and he and all his friends stared in awe as the party passed. Then they broke into excited whispers.

Shael College opened onto the far side of the square, and a few dark-robed students sat or lay in rumpled groups, taking advantage of the warmth to study or converse outdoors. Kyer's mouth watered to read the words carved into the building next to the college: *Shael Library*. Brendow had told her of its existence. The only one of its kind in all of Rydris, the library was yet another reason the capital was such a popular destination.

Finally, beyond the square, the horses ascended the switchbacking path up to the castle.

Captain Heyland announced them at the castle's outer gatehouse, and they were permitted to move through under watchful eyes. Riding by the heavy oak doors into the narrow corridor, Kyer felt like an easy target and wanted to shrink out of sight of the watchers. Inquisitive faces peered at them through the murder holes in the stone ceiling and the arrow loops every few feet on both sides. It was with relief that she emerged from the tiny passage and found herself in the outer ward. Kyer observed the clever defensive design of the castle. The inner gatehouse was not directly in line with the outer one, forcing an enemy to cross the bailey diagonally and be open to attack from all sides as well as above. In the incredible event that foes should survive the passage of the first gate, it was still less likely they would live through to the second.

The procession came to a standstill at the entrance to the inner gatehouse. The guards at the head went into formation, dividing themselves on either side of Valrayker's company, like a sort of passageway of riders. The formal display thrilled her, and she tried to keep back a grin of excitement. Even Janak had an air of appreciation until he caught Kyer's eye, at which point he turned away, a determined frown on his brow. She was too enthralled to care.

A young woman stood at the inner gatehouse, flanked by two guards. She looked to be about Kyer's age. Sir Fredric Heyland dismounted and spoke quietly to her. The woman nodded and Kyer detected an air of impatience in the movement. Sir Fredric moved aside, and she stepped forward. She wore a simple, long-sleeved gown of a deep rust colour. It complemented her blonde hair, which was held back from her face by two combs and hung down her back to just below her shoulder blades. On her feet were leather boots with a low heel, and the gold chain about her waist held a ring of keys. Her face was narrow, with an elegantly straight nose and cheeks that were tinged with just enough colour so her fair skin did not look pale. She reminded Kyer of Hreth's Sheska Bolen, only this woman did not share Sheska's nastiness, arrogance, and superiority. The woman spoke in a clear, confident voice.

"Welcome, Lord Dunvehran," she said with a bow, "and all of you. For those of you with whom I am not acquainted, I am Acadia Heyland, steward of Shael Castle."

Heyland, Kyer noted. Well, isn't she lucky. Kyer wondered what Sir Fredric had said to shake her. Her smile was amiable, but her eyes weren't involved, and to Kyer, it seemed forced, as if she had been shaken by whatever her husband had said.

Valrayker breathed a deep sigh as he dismounted. He caught her eye, and his smile was peaceful, as if he were finally home. Kyer supposed that so long as Dregor occupied Equart, this probably was the closest the exiled duke had to a home. He grasped Acadia's hand, and this time her eyes joined in her smile.

Acadia spoke to the group again. "The livery warden will handle all your horses. Your belongings will be taken to your quarters, so just bring along anything you require immediately." A middle-aged man and several younger stable boys stepped forward. Derry passed Donnagill's reins to the livery warden.

"You won't go with them?" Kyer asked him as she slipped down off Trig's back.

"No need to," Derry replied. "I trust their skill level without question."

"Unlike the boys in Paterak."

Derry smiled. "Not the same level of expertise, no."

A stable girl approached Kyer. "Both of the extra horses are mine," she added, unsure if it mattered or not. The girl smiled and nodded, seemingly pleased that Kyer had spoken to her. "Thank you," Kyer said, handing Trig over. The reins caught briefly on her sword hilt, and as she disentangled them, she looked over her shoulder at her comrades.

She had assumed they'd be asked to relinquish their weapons, on account of entering a duke's castle, but since nobody else appeared to be removing weapon belts, she made no move to do so.

"Derry!" Valrayker called.

"Yes?" Derry clapped a lad on the shoulder as the youngster hefted the captain's saddlebags, and he stepped in Valrayker's direction.

"I hope you'll be up for a drink while we're here."

Derry chuckled. "Is that a euphemism for a game of dice?"

"Can you blame me? I need to win back my fifty rydals."

"Sure, Val. You just keep telling yourself that."

Acadia beamed. "Please follow me." She headed through the gatehouse, Valrayker and the rest of the company following. Sir Fredric gave a warm look to Kyer as she brought up the rear. Though his attention was pleasant, she wondered if he shouldn't save it for his wife. She heard the captain dismiss the honour guard as the gatehouse door closed behind her.

This was Kyer's first visit to a castle; she had expected something more . . . military. More stone and less green. Not a courtyard with a lush lawn divided by a flagstone path, nor well-tended flower beds, nor benches nestled beneath clusters of trees. Stables with barracks above, and the blacksmith near the gates, those made sense. But the pleasant myriad of sweet and savoury smells that drifted through the air and the newly sprouting vegetable garden? There were even a half dozen children playing in the corner near the large entrance doors.

Acadia waved to them as she climbed the steps to the thick, copper-plated oak doors, in which had been etched the Bartheylen coat of arms. A pair of doormen, one on either side, pulled the heavy doors open—without so much as a squeak. The steward stood to one side.

The guests passed her into the foyer and gathered at the bottom of the wide staircase. Acadia nodded pleasantly to Kyer, who had half expected the steward to flinch as she passed. Kyer was used to making other women nervous; Acadia was obviously more worldly than Sheska. Kyer glanced back over her shoulder as the doors closed. Instantly her attention was seized by the wall hanging above the door, and she stopped short.

Breathless and without taking her eyes off it, she took a few steps up the stairs so she could look at it squarely. It was a well-chosen focal point of the foyer. The woman captured in it was the most beautiful Kyer had ever seen. Tall and graceful, her deep sea-blue eyes penetrated into Kyer's heart like a stiletto. Thick, wavy hair fell about her elven ears and tumbled over her shoulders in an unidentifiable colour—reds, golds, light browns, dark browns, and blacks, too complex to be defined. What genius of a painter had managed to find just the right blend of shades to reproduce it?

The woman stood next to her midnight-black horse, the sunlight glinting off his glorious coat. Behind them were rolling foothills with mountains in the distance. But what made Kyer's heart pound was the way the woman was dressed. She wore, not a gown, but a beautifully embroidered leather cuirass, in a design much like Kyer's own, and the enormous sword on which she casually rested her hand clearly found its home in the sheath that was strapped at her waist. With the muscles that corded in the wrists, Kyer did not need convincing that she was capable of using it. There was no doubt about the identity of the woman above the doorway.

Without ever seeing Kien's wife, Kyer recognized the Lady Alon Maer. Despite all the stories of Kien's shrewd, impatient, and fearsome nature as a ruler, there was one thing that went without question: he was devotedly in love with his wife. Only profound emotion could possibly demand the creation of such a likeness as this.

The young swordfighter looked down at her own arms. She grasped her right forearm with her left hand and slowly flexed the muscles in her wrist, admiring the strength she had taken years to build. A thrill shivered through her at having this one thing in common with the woman in the portrait. All doubt fled.

It had been worth it: every slur, every sneer, every backhanded comment and glance from Sheska Bolen and her ilk. Every malicious assertion about her parentage, her desires, her pastimes. Terms such as "freak," often used right to her face, to say nothing of "bitch" and "whore," had been bilious memories. In this moment, even they melted away like so much candle wax.

The portrait of the Lady Alon Maer etched itself into her mind and obliterated the effect those people had had on her despite her attempts to convince herself she didn't care. The bitterness dissolved with a shudder and choke of emotion that she quickly repressed. The wife of Lord Kien Bartheylen was a swordfighter. Kyer Halidan could follow her footsteps with pride.

"Kyer!" It was Phennil, yanking her back to the foyer with a low voice. She dragged her gaze away from the lady and saw that the others had carried on through to the rear of the foyer. Reluctantly she descended the steps and hastened to catch up with the elf. He smiled at her and gestured back to Alon Maer. "She's really something, isn't she?" Still spellbound by the portrait, Kyer had no response.

Acadia stopped outside a door, almost directly underneath the staircase. "This is Lord Kien's meeting room," she told Kyer, the only one among them who had not been here before. In all her internal reaction to the portrait, Kyer had forgotten to be anxious about the imminent introduction. Their hostess opened the door and announced them then stepped aside to allow them to pass her into the room. She called to a servant to fetch ale. A tiny older woman in a red dress with a white overtunic nodded her capped head and dashed off around the corner. Kyer held back while her comrades moved through the informal parlour to greet their hosts. Two men rose from armchairs before the granite-faced fireplace.

Kyer had lived in the duchy of Heath all her life, but she had never laid eyes on her duke until this moment. She knew him instantly. Whereas Governor Lyndon was human, stocky, and greying, Kien Bartheylen, like his wife, was a high elf, and the reports Kyer had heard were justified. He was huge, a full head taller than Valrayker, and well over two hundred fifty pounds. From years of almost constant work as a warrior, he had built up more muscle than most humans possessed, let alone elves, who were typically slender. He was reportedly the best swordsman in all of Rydris. Kyer had a hard time doubting it, even though rumour had it that Kien himself had begun the circulation of that report. To her knowledge, no one had proven him wrong.

A formidable ruler, stories of his unforgiving nature and his lack of patience for foolishness had made their way into the far reaches of the continent. Woe betide the one who tried to take advantage of Kien's occasional generosity. Kyer would never dream of trifling with him. Yet she had a feeling the stories were overblown. His joy at seeing his friend again was like sunshine on his face. Not only that, but Acadia's bearing had relaxed slightly, as if the steward did not require the same businesslike manner now that she'd entered Kien's meeting room. Acadia was not overawed by him.

His hair was grey. Not the grey of old age like that of the governor, but opaque grey, like a thundercloud, like the stone from which the fireplace was built, as if it had been painted that way. His complexion was milky white, with no markings apart from a thin scar that ran straight along his squarish jaw. His pointed ears were more pronounced than Phennil's, perhaps a high elven trait. Kyer did not know whether she found him handsome or not, but the energy radiating from his presence was potent. *Good thing he's on our side.*

Kien and Valrayker embraced, and Kyer was surprised by the display of warmth.

"Alon didn't come with you?" Valrayker was plainly disappointed at not seeing the lady.

"No, not this time, but she sent her regards," Kien replied in a tone that suggested to Kyer that he had more to say on this subject but it was not for all present.

The guests waited patiently to be greeted, though Kyer hung back a bit as she was the only one who would have to be formally introduced. *Just bow and keep your mouth shut.*

Derry shook the duke's hand with exactly the correct decorum. Janak was not impolite, Kyer noted, and figured the duke was somebody that even the dwarf couldn't talk back to. Kien gave Jesqellan a warm welcome but did not make contact. The mage bowed politely. Phennil said hello with his usual amiable grin, and when Kien commented on his distinct lack of offensive odour, the younger elf replied, "They made me bathe a mere three days ago, Lord." He winked at his companions. "In your honour, so of course I obliged them."

Kien laughed. It was good to hear him laugh. The sound was clear and rich, and the idea struck Kyer that he must have a lovely singing voice. The lines of care that had been incised in the duke's forehead over time shallowed somewhat, and Kyer let out a breath she had not been aware of holding. Just then the servant returned with a large tray bearing several chilled flagons of ale as well as a pewter decanter which turned out to contain elvish wine. The servant passed them around to all the guests. But before the drinks reached her, Valrayker drew Kyer forward. If he could hear the pounding of her heart, he made no show of it.

She sensed an eagerness in his voice as he spoke to Kien. "This is the only one you haven't yet met. She joined us just a week ago and has already forced us all to keep on our toes. From your own home duchy, Kien, this is Kyer Halidan."

Amused that the thought should come to her, Kyer remembered her schoolteacher's pronouncement years ago, that Kyer would "stand in judgement before Lord Bartheylen himself one day." These were hardly the circumstances the woman had in mind.

Kyer took the hand that was offered and matched its firm but politely measured grip. She tipped her head and upper body in a bow then looked way up to meet his eyes. His gaze was pleasant and welcoming, but she felt the calculated appraisal behind them. *He's going to test me at every possible chance.* She returned his gaze just as steadily as he regarded her. And she suspected that Valrayker would demand an account of Kien's impressions of her. After a beat, without taking his penetrating eyes off her, Kien spoke.

"Well, Val, you've finally taken my advice and refined your methods of choosing companions. Hopefully, Kyer, you will have some influence over my friend and the rest of the rabble he seems to like having around himself." He smiled as he indicated the others, but he still gripped her hand.

"Not much can change in only a week, but Phennil did bathe," Kyer replied. Formidable or not, it was not in her nature to let him think she was cowed.

"Where are you from in Heath, Kyer?"

"Hreth."

"So far north! What brought you southeast to join up with this lot?"

She hesitated, peering into Kien's eyes. Her mouth turned up in a crooked smile.

"My horse, actually."

Shocked silence seized the chamber. One of the duke's eyebrows shot upward. He pursed his lips.

Oh shit. Too far?

His steel-grey eyes appraised her, unblinking. His lip twitched. "Ah yes. I have one of those, also."

As if a breeze had wafted through the room, people shifted like rustling leaves. "Well met, Kyer," he said with a bow. "I hope you enjoy your stay in Shael." He finally released her hand. "And now, which beverage would you prefer?"

She gestured to the tray. "After such a long ride to get into the city, you're making me choose between my two favourite liquids?"

"A thousand pardons, good lady!" He laughed and handed her both a pint of ale and a glass of wine.

"Welcome, all," Kien said heartily, "old friends and new." Kyer's mouth watered as she savoured the richness of the wine that was so dark, it could hardly be described as red. And the ale was equalled by only that at the Burnished Blade. Derry sat next to Valrayker as the two dukes spoke genially of each other's news. The captain said nothing, and though Kyer tried to catch his attention, he didn't turn her way. When she was finally successful, it seemed accidental. She gave him a half grin, to share her excitement at being here. His expression didn't change, and he abruptly turned away.

Kyer's brow creased. He was annoyed with her for some reason known to only him. She felt like an admonished child. Her small celebration had been crushed as if it were a fruit fly buzzing round his head. She drained her mug.

Adopting his "captain to his lord" tone, thereby dismissing her, Derry asked, "How long will we stay in the city, sir?"

"I'm waiting for scouts to return to tell me the status of the borders," Valrayker said. "You will have at least three days, perhaps longer. Enjoy yourselves while you can, but be prepared to leave instantly upon their arrival."

Acadia offered to show them to their rooms so they could refresh themselves and dress for dinner.

Kyer looked at the steward with a flash of panic. *Dress?* What could she wear that was appropriate for a banquet at Shael Castle? The governor and the two dukes remained seated, but Kyer walked next to Acadia, with Derry and the others close behind.

"You've just joined Valrayker recently?" Acadia asked.

"A week ago."

Acadia pushed open another wooden door through which they all passed single file, Derry and Phennil ducking their heads. "He's wonderful, isn't he?" Acadia said, with a glance down at Kyer as they started up a stone circular staircase.

"Valrayker? Oh, yes, he is," Kyer agreed, running her hand along the wooden banister that wound around up the smooth walls. Acadia was so dissimilar in character to Kyer's old nemesis, Sheska, that Kyer already found this new person supplanting the other girl's prominence.

"Of course you wouldn't dare say otherwise with his captain only two steps behind, now would you?" The steward smiled down at Derry.

"I have no doubt that Kyer would be honest, even if Val himself were here," the captain replied. Acadia laughed but Kyer couldn't tell if Derry was joking.

"In any event, I must say I'm glad you've joined him," Acadia said and lowered her voice conspiratorially. "Most of the women who visit tend to be a bit stuffy."

Kyer smirked. The steward had an overall professionalism but was clearly relieved to have a friendly conversation with another woman her age.

Round and round the stairs curled, carrying them Kyer had no idea how high. The occasional window gave the only clue as the plains below appeared farther and farther down. She'd started out counting doors as they passed them but lost track of which ones went into corridors and which were tower rooms as Acadia pointed them out. How the steward could possibly remember which was which was beyond Kyer. Acadia opened yet another oak door.

"This is the south wing third floor," Acadia told her. "The guest apartments." Kyer followed her along the woven grass mat that warmed the stone of the dim corridor. Tapestries and wall hangings between torch brackets dampened the ghostly echo of footfalls and doors closing as, one by one, her companions disappeared into their rooms. Derry stopped a few paces ahead and turned the handle of his door with the confident air of someone who knows where he belongs in this place. He shut the door without a backward glance.

"Lord Valrayker's suite is this one across from Derry's," Acadia said. Kyer turned to look behind her, and Janak brushed past her to head to his room. No one else was left. Bewildered by the length of the corridor, Kyer cursed herself for not counting chamber doors.

As if in answer to her thoughts, Acadia said, "Your room is next to Derry's. The third from the far end. This one with Telleman Bartheylen opposite." With a smile, she indicated the wall hanging of Kien's father beside Valrayker's door. Kyer exhaled gratefully and liked the steward all the more for recognizing her discomfort and not embarrassing her.

Acadia opened the door and stepped aside. "I hope this suits you."

Kyer stepped into her tiny room and felt instantly at home. In the nearest corner on the right was a low bed with wool blankets, an extra one folded at the foot. And here was also the answer to Kyer's query about attire. To her surprise, special garments in subdued Bartheylen colours lay on the bed. She cast a curious glance over her shoulder.

Acadia stood back from the door, a smile twinkling in her eyes. "Our tower guards see great distances and use their power for good."

Kyer grinned. "Neat."

On the left wall was a tiny fireplace with a coal scuttle and a washstand beside it. Below the little window, a pine chest was crammed at the end of the bed. There was barely room to step between bed and chest. Lifting the lid, she saw all her belongings inside. A familiar sound from the window drew Kyer's attention, and she stepped up on top of the chest.

Through the wavy glass in her third-story window Kyer looked out over the southern battlements to—oh joy!—the practice field. Several groups of soldiers were hard at work jousting, sparring, or firing at archery targets. Kyer unlatched the window to luxuriate in the faint rings of steel and thuds of wood against shield that echoed from far below.

"Do you like it?"

Kyer had forgotten Acadia was there. Tearing herself away from the view, she stepped down. "It's perfect."

Acadia grinned. "Yes, you can use the practice field anytime. Ask Toby or Russ for any equipment."

"You have me figured out, haven't you?"

Laughing, the steward told her to leave any clothing items she'd like laundered in a pile outside her door, assured Kyer that a servant would fetch them all for dinner, and left to attend to her duties. Kyer changed into the insightfully supplied trousers and tunic.

Freshly scrubbed, brushed, and braided, she lay on the tansy-scented bed to analyse more of Shael Castle's hospitality. The bed at least as comfortable as those in most inns, but the blankets were thicker and softer, including one made of some kind of fur. Though she was travel-worn and weary, the thrill at being a personal guest to Kien Bartheylen and relaxing in a room in Shael Castle, of all places, overshadowed her need for sleep.

If only she could speak to Brendow right now! Is this what he'd hoped for her? And Bianca, Adric, and Tarqan, what would they say if they knew? Kyer leaped up, exhilarated and restless. She watched the fighters below gather up their equipment and imagined how green Tarqan would be if he saw her sparring on that field.

Or would he? It had been a while since she'd known if he was truly on her side. Kyer had to admit that it had been a long time since she had really seen eye to eye with her best friend. It was also the last time their lovemaking had been truly unadulterated. One training session with Brendow a year ago had been particularly heated, and she'd dragged Tarqan to the top of Daks Hill and made love to him under the stars. She recalled allowing him to be on top a few times, just so he could fancy for those brief moments that it hadn't all been her idea. And afterward, as they lay in the tall grass, hands clasped loosely, she told him she planned to leave. He'd been less than encouraging. His exact words were, "You're whacked."

"I have too many questions I won't find answers to if I stay here." She'd fingered the chain of her medallion and stared up into the infinity of stars.

"What are you talking about?" he said in a low voice.

She rolled onto her side and ran her hand absently along his tanned, muscular torso. "I mean, I had to have come from somewhere, right? And I just can't think that I've studied—" she just stopped herself from saying Dark Elvish, "—Elvish and the *wæpnian* and all if only to stay in Hreth." She felt his muscles tighten beneath her palm.

"I learned the *wæpnian* too."

She pulled her hand away. "Don't be obtuse."

He sat up, brushing her off, and put his tunic back on, though she could tell he wasn't cold. "Some of us just want to be ready and do our part to defend the village if Lord Dregor comes this far."

Kyer sat up and faced him squarely. "You don't get it, do you?" She stood up and joined him in tugging breeches on. "I don't know where I came from! I'm not *ditching* Hreth; I simply don't belong here!"

He showed her his back and tucked in his tunic. "You're too good for us, I suppose."

"You bastard." She felt hot in spite of the evening breeze that brushed the hilltop.

He finally turned around and looked into her dark eyes with his bright ones. "Hreth is going to need you, Kyer."

"Lord *Kien* doesn't even pay attention to Hreth. Why would Dregor?"

The practice field was empty now. Kyer moved away from the window and pulled the lightweight, burgundy waistcoat over her deep green linen tunic, lacing it loosely up the front. She recognized that what Tarqan really meant was *I need you.*

⊷⊱══════⊰⊶

With the door shut behind him, Derry could relax into the comfort he always felt when he was in his room. He didn't know if anyone else ever slept here, but it was his room whenever he visited Shael, with or without Valrayker. He opened the window and took a deep breath to cleanse his irritation.

Frustration always crept up on him when he came across Fredric Heyland. He could tell Kyer admired the older man and even that she had noticed his own aloofness. Explaining to her, however, would be gossip. Let it not be said that Derry Moraunt was no better than a rumour-monger. Kyer was an adult and more than capable of forming her own opinions about people.

He poured fresh water from the jug on the washstand into the basin. He took off his tunic and, with a wet cloth, scrubbed the dust off his face and out of the week's growth of beard, a little more roughly than it called for. An extra-large splash sent cold water running down his chest; he went rigid as he gasped. Scowling, he shook out the cloth and started again. What was with Kyer, anyhow? *My horse, actually,* indeed! Derry'd nearly leaped to his feet. And to ask for more than one beverage? Absolutely unprecedented.

He scratched his whiskers and contemplated growing a beard. Perhaps it would give him an air of distinction? Derry decided to treat himself to a visit with Cor the barber tomorrow. He hung the cloth on the washstand and picked up his Bartheylen tunic and pulled it over his head.

As he tied the laces at the neck, Derry reminded himself that she had grown up in a small village, which had to account for much of her rural demeanour. If Kien could so graciously accept her, well, so could Derry. He decided, though, to speak to Val about giving her some training in diplomacy before she learned it the hard way. She would probably appreciate it.

Derry slipped his arm through his vest sleeve and stopped. Had Kyer been equally familiar with Valrayker in her first meeting with him? He wondered how his lord would have reacted in that situation. Valrayker had seen a good many people fight duels but did not ask them all to join him, so what else about Kyer had grasped his attention?

The knock on his door startled him, and when he saw Kyer standing outside, he flushed guiltily, as if she had somehow read his thoughts. The dark brown trousers and jade tunic she wore flattered her shape and kindled an emerald glow in her eyes.

"This may sound like a silly question," she said in a low voice, "but do we carry weapons into the banquet?"

"If you have a dress sword, you are welcome to carry it, or a dagger, perhaps, but that is all," he answered, pleased to offer his assistance with her education.

She nodded her thanks.

"Oh! While you're here," Derry turned to the tidy pile of belongings on his bed. "Valrayker asked me to give you this." He handed her Simon's chest.

"Thanks. Say, I had a look out at the practice field . . ." She gave him one of those half grins that unnerved him more than he cared to admit. "What do you think? Shall I nail you to the ground in the morning?"

He took a deep breath. "I accept the challenge." He bowed. "Although we'll just have to wait and see who does the nailing."

Six

Nothing Like a Party

Valrayker stayed with Kien and Governor Jon Lyndon in the meeting room after Derry and the others had gone. His need to refresh himself after a long day's journey was superseded by a desire for conversation with his friend.

The governor took a carrot stick. "What I still don't understand is why Dregor went for Equart first when he could have gone directly south from his own stronghold and taken the Guarded Realm. Why skirt round it?"

"I've asked myself that question more than once," Valrayker said. "Equart has a smaller population spread over a larger area. I wonder if he hopes that having taken us with apparent ease, he will influence Kien's opinion of me on a personal level."

"How would he do that?" Kien scoffed.

Valrayker grimaced. "Does it really sound so far fetched? Come, my friend. Your disdain for those things considered 'weak' is common knowledge. And it's also well known that the only reason we held out as long as we did was because of the extra deployments you sent us more than once." He popped his last bite of carrot into his mouth.

Kien cocked his head. "It's also common knowledge that Dregor attacked you a third time only days after his second massive onslaught. To finally succumb under that kind of pressure does not signify weakness—"

"I'll remember that," Val put in.

"—it shows only that Dregor is willing to spend his countless minions like they are mere grains of sand. *We* value our soldiers more highly." Kien dunked a carrot in the onion dip.

Valrayker smiled. "Does this mean our friendship is intact?"

"Could it be that he has another plan for the Guarded Realm?" the governor said. "I wonder if he's making allies there."

"With a mostly elven population, that would be hard to believe," Val said, "but certainly not impossible."

Kien's chin tipped upward. "The *human* population of the Guarded Realm might be corruptible but not the elves." He raised his palm to his governor. "No offence meant, Jon. I'm speaking generally and it has been proven time and again that humans tend to be more susceptible to negative influence; that is all."

Governor Lyndon half shrugged, half bowed. "That could say more about the human capacity for independent thought."

Val smirked. "He's got you there, Kien. Anyway, it could be as simple as a desire to use Equart's port to deploy armies in all directions. And it is without question that Dregor has some plan for the Tree of Life. Infiltrating the Guarded Realm might further his plans more effectively than an attack." He stroked his cheek with the back of his scarred hand. "It's been an awfully long time since he made a move."

"One begins to feel anxious and expectant," Governor Lyndon agreed. "We have heard rumblings in the northeast, but our spies have not been able to disclose anything that gives us cause to act just yet. Tannis Malfi is preparing Ballin's armies for an invasion."

Kien rose and indicated his three duchies on the working map that covered the wall opposite the fireplace. Duchy boundaries were clearly marked with troop positions noted in charcoal. "Koral is the smallest duchy, which would theoretically make it an easier mark, but it is mine. Koral's well protected between Shae and Heath. Dregor would be foolish to try to split me down the middle." He slid his finger across the map eastward. "Ballin, however, is the eastern flank of the continent and is all too close to that port in Equart. Duchess Malfi does well to feel vulnerable."

"Even though I stationed the remainder of my armies in Ballin?" Valrayker said.

The governor spoke firmly. "Tannis Malfi is shrewd and won't panic. She is preparing because she is wise. But she also trusts that she isn't alone in this war."

Valrayker swirled his wine glass. "We will not sit back and let Dregor pick us off one at a time."

Soon after, Governor Lyndon left to greet the guests. The door closed and a hush fell upon the room as Kien chewed and swallowed. Then he asked the question Val had been waiting for. "So who is Kyer?"

"I haven't the foggiest idea." The dark elf sipped his wine. He had looked forward to discussing Kyer with Kien since he met her. He had some ideas of his own and wanted to see if his friend's intuitive sense came up with anything similar.

"She's the most unusual person you've picked up in a long time. Where did you meet her?"

"In Wanaka. Where else does one meet fascinating people these days? But in this case, it was . . . a fluke. I happened to be nearby when a dispute broke out between a rather arrogant man and this young woman. The way she spoke to him caught my interest, but then she challenged him to a duel and turned out to be hiding armour and a very serviceable bastard sword under her cloak. I was ready to help if necessary, but I wasn't needed." He paused to savour his wine. "She fought very well. He didn't expect her to be as skilled as she is, yet she wasn't overconfident. She beat him quickly and cleanly with only one misread of a feint. No showy blade work, just skill and economy."

"Clearly you were impressed."

"Yes! She was efficient, no wasted effort. More importantly, though, the man cheated: he attacked her from behind before the duel had been declared open and then went at her with a knife after she'd bested him squarely. So she took him out. A greener fighter might have backed down. And the last thing one needs is a fighter who turns soft when it matters most. She showed mature battlefield judgement." He took a carrot and dipped it. There was only one left.

"So you asked her to join you? Based on one fight."

"It wasn't quite that simple." Val hesitated, swallowing and gently pulling on the hairs of his moustache. "I may have asked her solely on the basis of her fighting, but I was struck by several things during our conversation while we were still at the Burnished Blade. Remember how I said our meeting was a fluke? First of all, she ordered elvish wine."

"Excellent! Good way to make a good first impression on you."

"She didn't know who I was at that point, so how would she know that?" Valrayker went on, knitting his eyebrows. "But let me ask you, Kien. You've never seen her fight. What was your *first* reaction when you spoke to her just now?"

"You mean, apart from her sense of humour?"

Valrayker smirked.

Kien swirled the rich, black wine in his goblet. "She is very *aware*. She knows I will want to see what she's made of, and she . . . well, she's absolutely resolute that she will not fail." His brow furrowed as he sipped. "She did not tell me why she came to Shae, which in itself is not unusual; I completely understand her reservations. But she was not *pressured* into telling me, which I do not often experience when people meet me for the first time."

"And what did that tell you?" Val said.

"That she has confidence and strength of character."

"Yes, but it's more than that, isn't it?" Valrayker's eyes glittered intently. "She's far more . . . *perceptive* than is normal for someone her age. I watched her when we entered this room. She sized you up I dare say more thoroughly than anyone else has had the nerve to. And do you know, the evening we met, I took her to the Twisting Pine, and we met Phennil in the woods along the way." Valrayker tapped the arm of his chair with his palm for emphasis. "I tell you, she sensed Phennil's presence before I did. And I was expecting him."

Kien grunted.

Valrayker went on. "That's rare. She has an inner quality that I can't define. There's a whole lot more to this one."

"I see what you mean." Kien's fingertips played with the carved grooves on the arm of his chair. "I did get the sense that she was reading me just as much as I was trying to read her."

Valrayker nodded slowly, encouraging his friend.

"She is very guarded as well," Kien added.

"As are many people who travel the world." Valrayker leaned forward, resting his elbows on his knees, and locked Kien's eyes eagerly. "But, Kien, tell me, do most farm girls in your duchies have a taste for elvish wine? How familiar are they, usually, with the Dark Elvish Toast to the Dead?"

Kien pursed his lips with thoughtful scepticism.

Valrayker continued. "How many of them have a desire to travel outside their village, let alone through two other duchies? How many of them have detailed knowledge of weaponry, right down to the proper use and care of the yew longbow? How many learn to speak Elvish?"

Kien did a double-take. "She speaks *Elvish*?"

"Wood Elvish, to be precise."

Kien shrugged. "I suppose she's a bit of an anomaly but so what? For the sake of argument, let me point out that lots of people like to push their boundaries, improve themselves."

"What is Hreth like?" Val leaned back in his chair.

"I don't know. I've never been there," Kien admitted. "Small."

Valrayker casually swirled his wine. "Have many farm girls in your outlying villages studied the *wæpnian?*"

"The *wæpnian?* You can't be serious."

"The focus, the footwork and positions, the unfailing balance, the agility of the moves," Valrayker said, "those little wrist twists that take years to master. That is how she killed him."

"But how would she—? Who could have . . . ?" Kien trailed off in disbelief.

"I recognized her sword hilt immediately, though it took me a while to place it. Can you guess who has lived in Hreth for the last twenty-odd years, that we all thought had disappeared from Rydris, never to be seen again?"

"No, I cannot possibly guess, Valrayker."

"Does the name *Brendow* strike a chord, Kien?"

Kien carefully set his wine down. "Bren d'Athlan has been in *Hreth* all this time?"

"Training farm girls to be swordfighters," Val finished with satisfaction.

"It's certainly a good place to go if you want to disappear."

"And that serviceable bastard sword I mentioned? It was mine."

Kien's jaw dropped. He frowned thoughtfully. "Who is her family?"

"We've not had that conversation," the dark elf said.

Kien poured again in silence.

"That's interesting, you know," he said casually, "that Bren d'Athlan is in Hreth. That might explain something." He put down the bottle.

"Explain what?" He reached for the last carrot.

"Only two days ago, a messenger informed me that Hreth had been attacked by Dregor's men."

"What!" Valrayker sat forward in his armchair, forgetting the vegetable. "When?"

"Well, it would have been a few weeks ago now," the high elf said. "I have to admit I was sceptical when I was told. Why would Dregor bother to sneak through the lines and attack one of my tiniest, northernmost villages? Except perhaps to goad me into some rash response. I sent a group of scouts to learn more before taking greater action. But if Dregor knew that Bren d'Athlan was there . . ."

Valrayker cocked his head doubtfully. "Why would Dregor bother that much with Bren d'Athlan? He's a *Wæmniar* but not really important politically—"

A knock on the door stopped him. Kien motioned for Valrayker to hold that thought and called out, "Yes?"

Acadia opened the door. "I apologize for the interruption, gentlemen, but you did wish me to inform you when dinner was ten minutes away."

"Thank you," Kien said, rising. "We'll talk more later."

The last carrot went untouched.

Kyer followed Derry back down the circular staircase and into the foyer of the castle. It was the first time she'd seen the captain without his armour. His well-built, muscular form was appealingly visible under his rich burgundy tunic and jade jacket. He'd relaxed his captain role for the evening, though the dignity with which he carried himself was not so easily discarded. There was more than one type of armour.

Led by a guide who seemed far from put out by Phennil's friendly chatter, the group headed past the main staircase around to a pair of large doors on the far side of the foyer. The sounds of music and raucous laughter coming through the open doors made Kyer pick up her pace. Their guide led them into the great hall.

The hall could hold far more than the thirty guests who had been invited from among Shael's higher-ranking citizens. A large square of tables took up half of the hall, occupied by officers wearing the colours of the castle guard, the city guard, and the Shael army, as well as civilians. They indulged in the abundance of ale and wine, welcoming any excuse for a celebration, regardless of the short notice. A fire danced feverishly in the centre of the room, surrounded by acrobats and jugglers. Musicians playing pipes, lutes, fiddles, flutes, and drums were accompanied by dancers and singers. The music, talking, and laughing echoed around the high ceilings, amplified to a delightful dissonance that consorted with the smoky haze from the fire and the smell of roasting meat from the kitchen. The torches that hung on the high walls between the tapestries and paintings cast flickering light onto the crowd. The servant led Kyer and her friends around the perimeter of the activity to seats nearest the high table.

No sooner had Kyer sat down between Derry and Phennil than a horn sounded and everyone rose to acknowledge the entrance of the dukes. The juggler caught his props, the acrobat righted herself from her inverted position, and the musicians struck up a lively air. Kien, Valrayker, and Governor Lyndon with his wife passed through the centre of the square. Acadia brought up the rear of the party.

Kien had altered his attire by simply adding a deep red, calf-length mantle, clasped at the shoulder with a brooch. His long, rich blue tunic with gold embroidered edging showed beneath it, belted in black. He wore grey trousers and tall black boots. The governor wore a burgundy waistcoat and necktie over his gold tunic, and his wife was lovely in a long jade green gown with a bright red sleeveless surcoat. Her long, full skirt trailed along the floor at the back. Grey-black plaits were knotted loosely at the back of her head, and she wore a little hat with a plume. Acadia had changed from the rust-coloured dress into one in a similar style but fuller in the skirt and of a royal blue that dramatically increased the brightness of her eyes and hair. Kyer glanced at Derry, whose eyes followed the young steward closely.

But it was Valrayker whom Kyer regarded fixedly. The dark elf had removed his black cloak, so the lustrous, enamelled breastplate that identified him as the duke of Equart was unconcealed. The belt around his waist shone like a flame, and all the metal armour he wore was a spectacular contrast to his black tunic, breeches, and boots. He fairly glowed in the firelight. His slightly pointed ears showed for the first time, with his long black hair tied back. Kyer stared at him, her sense of awe rekindled. At four hundred fifty years old, he still had such a youthful appearance. He had been through so much in that time, fought so many battles, defeated countless foes . . . Kyer had no idea what other experiences life had brought him. *All I know is it's an honour and a privilege to ser— to work for him.*

The dignitaries reached the high table, and Acadia placed herself at the table directly opposite Kyer's, in the spot closest to the governor should he need her. Kyer's eyes travelled along Acadia's table and noticed Sir Fredric with another man between himself and his pretty young wife. Kyer started to ask Derry about this but stopped as Governor Lyndon spoke.

"Good evening, friends. Welcome to this hastily arranged, albeit special dinner. I hope we did not destroy any of your plans for the evening." Laughter rang throughout the hall. Evidently this was a much more enjoyable way to spend their time than whatever they had planned. "I give you Lord Bartheylen."

Kien rose. "Thank you, Jon, and thank you all for coming to help me welcome my friend and colleague, Lord Valrayker, the duke of Equart." The gathering applauded. "And also his travelling companions, over to my right." More light applause. "I don't wish to frustrate everyone's appetites further, so let us be served!"

The servants brought out the first course, thick broth with barley, as well as more ale and wine. Goblets were filled, toasts were made at each table, and the musicians struck up some lively background tunes. The servants displayed great agility, mostly not dropping or spilling anything as they wove in and out of the chaos to and from the kitchen. Other servants busily removed the occasional mess from the stone floor.

Kyer feasted on lightly spiced roast mutton and pork, and though the meat was a touch dry, the gravy more than compensated for it. And of course, the wine enhanced the flavour of everything. Kyer remembered the question she had wanted to ask Derry. "So why isn't Sir Fredric sitting next to Acadia?" She jabbed a bit of glazed turnip with her knife.

Derry knit his brow in confusion as he swallowed a mouthful of potato. "I don't know. I suppose he could if he wanted to. Why would he?"

"I thought a man might like to sit next to his wife. Or don't they do that in this duchy?"

Derry looked puzzled. Then his face cleared. "No, Sir Fredric is Acadia's brother, not her husband. And though he is more than twelve years her senior, she does not rely on him as her chaperone. Contrary to what some believe, she was awarded her position on her own merit, and I can think of no one better for the stewardship."

"I don't doubt it," Kyer said. Derry had spoken with more exuberance of conviction than Kyer had thought necessary. She remembered the way her friend had watched the steward enter the hall, as well as their conversation while climbing the stairs, and she thought there might be more to his admiration of Acadia's qualities than his dignified manner expressed.

Now that she knew he was not married, Kyer allowed herself to more openly view the redheaded captain across the room. Once again, she was pleased by what she saw. He happened to look up and catch her gaze. Holding it, he raised his goblet and nodded to her. She drank from her cup without turning away.

"Who are the others at that table?" She set her cup down, broke a slice of bread into pieces and slopped up gravy with it.

"I do not know them all, but the heavyset one next to Acadia is General Ilsley, who is responsible for Shael's armies. Then Fredric, of course, and Usher Tompkin, another of the Shael Guard. Perhaps he has been promoted since I last met him, as he is sitting at that table. And the last one in the red jacket is Fynn Tolstoy, the mayor of Shael."

A servant came around with offers of more food. Kyer gladly accepted.

"Tell me more about Kien," she said, catching the attention of both her neighbours. "What do you think about this Greatest Swordsman in Rydris title? Has he come by it honestly?"

"Who knows?" Phennil said. "Technically he'd have to duel every other swordfighter."

Derry put down a bone he'd been chewing on. "But there is that one story from decades ago," he said, wiping his mouth. "A young man--"

"Nobody remembers where he came from," Phennil put in.

"So this young man challenges Kien to a duel, claiming he can best him. It should come as no surprise that Kien beat him handily."

"And as recompense for wasting his time," Phennil said, "Kien demanded a token from the challenger."

"The upstart, more like," Derry said. "But that's right."

"What did he want?" Kyer asked.

Phennil was nearly bursting. "His trousers!"

"Oh no!" Kyer laughed in spite of herself.

"But that isn't the end of it," Derry said.

"This fellow doesn't know when he's beat," Phennil said.

"This young man goes away--"

"Who knows where to?" Phennil said rhetorically.

Derry frowned at him and proceeded. "He comes back several years later, and says he's been training, and wants to get his own back."

"Oh no!" Kyer said, in sympathy with the young stranger. "Let me guess."

"Exactly," said Derry. "Kien doesn't even have to think about it. In front of a crowd of people he doesn't even break a sweat as he toys with the lad. Makes him work til he's red in the face, but doesn't hurt him. Not even a scratch. But finally, Kien has had enough."

Phennil cut in. "He has the cheek to point out the position of the sun, and say he's hungry!"

"The arrogance, you mean," Kyer said.

Derry waved her off impatiently. "The young man, on the other hand, looks panic-stricken, and Kien taunts him by saying, 'Is your Mama going to be cross with you being late for supper?' or some such thing. 'Never mind then.' And he does this fancy twist thing and knocks the lad's weapon out of his hand."

"Clearly something he could have done ages before, but wanted to make a point," Phennil added.

Derry leaned forward. "Then he takes his sword and cuts the fellow across the cheek, and gives him permission to brag about it and say, 'You should have seen the other man,' to all his friends."

"Not very gentlemanly," Kyer said, thinking of Derry's code of ethics.

Derry shook his head gravely.

"Did he demand a token this time?" Kyer asked.

"He did," Phennil said. "He took his boots. Which was all the more humiliating for the boy because they looked new, and it wasn't as if they would fit a high elf."

Kyer couldn't help but laugh, but her heart ached for the young man. "What happened to him?"

"The story goes he slunk away," Derry said. "Far as I know nobody ever saw him again."

Kyer scooped up her last bite of meat. "Forgive me, but I'm not convinced that makes him the best swordsman in Rydris."

Derry, his part in telling the story over, fell silent.

Phennil said, "Bet if you asked Kien about him he wouldn't even remember, it was so beneath him." The elf stuffed bread into his mouth, and began chattering about previous visits to Shael Castle. Not listening too intently, Kyer absorbed his words along with the din from the hall. *I wonder what Phennil's like if he has sugar?* Murmuring politely in response to the elf's tale of being bitten once by a hedgehog, she observed the guests, amazed and amused by the brightly coloured clothes they wore, the amount of food they ate, and the variety of responses to alcohol consumption. Every once in a while, her gaze stopped on Sir Fredric.

She made quick observations then moved her glance along. Unlike Derry, Fredric's mood was evenly balanced between seriousness and humour; she liked that. He and his sister didn't speak much, but that may have been because they weren't adjacent to each other. Fredric talked and laughed with his companions and came across as a genial person. Kyer was all the more curious to know why Derry was so ill at ease around the knight.

She was pleased to notice that Sir Fredric glanced her way frequently. But she was not a blushing schoolgirl, and she remained distant, her own attention to him not overt.

The meal finished, her belly was full and she felt supremely content. Kyer and her companions savoured yet another nectareous selection from Kien's supply of elvish wine. Kyer drained her cup and offered to pour for Derry. He placed his palm over his cup.

"I've had two, thank you. Any more and I won't be able to stand."

"That's it?" She poured a little for Phennil then refilled her own cup for the sixth time.

"I find elvish wine quite potent. Will you not need to be carried up the stairs?"

She laughed. "Not at all. I'm barely tipsy."

"How are you enjoying yourself so far?" Derry said, and she smiled at him hesitantly. Apart from the story about Kien, he had said little since their exchange of words at the beginning of the meal. Perhaps the wine was helping him get past the fit of pique that had come over him earlier.

"I'm having a wonderful time. Definitely glad I came along."

"Perhaps I could take you on a tour of the city at some point and show you around."

"I'd love that."

"Perhaps tomorrow or the next day, then, depending on Valrayker's plans."

She agreed. Derry did not appear to have anything to add, and her attention was soon drawn elsewhere. The guests had begun to mill about, some venturing to the head table to pay respects to the dukes, and others gathered nearer the performers for a better view. Kyer was mildly disappointed to see that Sir Fredric's chair was empty. *He knows where to find me.*

She was right. Within moments, the knight appeared before them.

"Derry, a pleasure to see you again." Sir Fredric extended his hand.

Derry rose to grasp it. "The pleasure is mine, as usual, Sir Fredric." Derry's reply was extra formal, it seemed to Kyer. She did not believe for a second that there was pleasure there at all.

"I continue to admire you for your dedication to the cause of your lord, in spite of his state of exile." The knight spoke sincerely, but Kyer noticed a slight upward turn to the corner of his mouth.

"Our state of exile is the very reason that we must continue to fight for our cause," Derry said with controlled passion. "We must never give up until we have regained the freedom of Equart, and all of Rydris."

The older man nodded gravely. "May Dregor soon meet his end."

It struck Kyer she was now in the real world and no longer falsely protected by isolation and ignorance. She had been more aware than most of her peers, thanks to her education with Brendow, but this was her first encounter with men who had actually been in the thick of the battle for years. She was gladder than ever that she'd chosen to leave Hreth.

Apparently through with formalities, Sir Fredric changed to a brighter tone. "So, Derry, have you fulfilled your dream yet?"

Derry's face elongated and redness crept up his neck. "It seems to be more your dream than mine," he said with quiet restraint. "But it is my own affair, and I am not inclined to discuss it, sir, one way or the other."

"Affair, indeed!" Sir Fredric winked down at Phennil, who smiled wanly. "We shall continue to await the joyous celebration, then."

Kyer heeded her first instinct. Rising swiftly to her feet, she drained her goblet and extended her hand. "I'm Kyer," she announced, looking hard at Sir Fredric.

He turned to her with a gallant smile. "I was wondering when Derry planned to introduce me to Valrayker's newest addition."

"Why trouble Derry when I'm perfectly capable of introducing myself?"

Sir Fredric's eyebrows went up, but he quickly recovered. "I am Sir Fredric Heyland, Kien's captain of the guard here in Shael."

"I know."

"Ah, someone has kept you well informed."

"Derry's been making me feel at home as a guest in a strange city."

"Always the gentleman, is our young Derry. So have these rogues gone easy on you?"

"You should be asking whether *she's* gone easy on *us*," Phennil interjected, a mild slur in his voice. "Things have been altogether too interesting since she came along."

"Oh? In what way?"

"Nonsense." Kyer gave the elf a warning look. "He only thinks that because he has someone new to blether to. Everyone else is tired of him and tells him to shut up." She grinned and Phennil blushed, reacting to both the ribbing and the rebuke. The last thing she needed was for people to talk behind their hands about the girl who killed a man in Wanaka. It wasn't something she was proud of.

They were spared any more awkward moments by the announcement of the evening's entertainment.

"More entertainment?" she said. "Shael certainly has its share of talented performers."

She invited Fredric to sit down in the seat Jesqellan had just vacated on Phennil's other side. The mage had gone to check in at the guildhouse in the city. Janak had also left them to join the fellow Derry had identified as Usher Tompkin at the table opposite. To Kyer's amazement, the young man actually looked happy to have the dwarf's company.

A handsome young bard hushed the room with a few strums on his lute. The neck of the instrument was ornately carved of some pale wood in the shape of a swan's head. He plucked its strings lovingly, and the notes floated gently upward to fill the entire hall and envelop everyone present, drawing them into the music. He began with a tale of the county alliance that formed the Guarded Realm. The ballad painted melodic portraits of unusual people and sketched scenic landscapes in Kyer's imagination. She all but lost herself in the magical strains that flowed around them but remained acutely aware of a barely disguised sullenness from Derry.

"What's the matter with you?" she asked quietly.

"Nothing is the matter with me." He spoke too quickly and with too much determination for her to believe him.

"At least *pretend* to have a good time"—she lowered her voice even further—"even though you don't care for Sir Fredric."

Derry sank into moodiness. She shrugged him off. She intended to become more acquainted with a certain somewhat arrogant but good-looking man who was not married to Acadia, and she refused to allow this tiresomely stone-faced fellow to dampen her pleasure.

In a voice that spoke as melodically as it sang, the bard introduced himself as Becklan Arterian and expressed his honour to be the entertainer for such noble guests. "I hope to see some dancing now!" he cried and his fingers hopped along the strings to a spirited two-step. The lyrics were amusing and, without mentioning names, described the friendship between Kien and Valrayker in spite of the historical animosity between high and dark elves. The two subjects took the song with good humour. Becklan's lean frame was elastic and his short, dark hair bounced around his youthful face as he danced.

Kyer felt a hand on her shoulder. It was Derry.

"Would you like to dance, Kyer?"

She stared at him. "Derry Moraunt, did I hear you correctly? You enjoy dancing?"

"Yes, I do. Do you?"

Kyer shook her head. "No, sorry, I don't. I trip so much, you'd think I had five feet. But thanks anyway."

"Very well, then." Derry bowed politely before moving off to find a partner elsewhere, and Kyer's surprised gaze followed him across the room.

She would have guessed that Derry wouldn't draw attention to himself, yet she admired his ability as he whirled about the floor with Acadia. He steered his partner with grace and elegance, contradicting his rough style as a warrior. He didn't laugh but he did smile—Kyer was pleased to see he was capable of it—and she thought he might actually be having fun, of sorts. Acadia, of course, was beautiful, and followed his lead expertly. It seemed to Kyer that they must have danced together before. More than once. It occurred to her that maybe she should learn to dance, to be a part of— *Oh, don't be silly.*

"You never learned to dance when you were growing up?" Sir Fredric moved to the seat next to her, which Phennil had vacated to join the dancers.

"Who had time? I was too busy practising a different kind of footwork." She didn't miss his doubtful reaction but chose to ignore it. "Besides, if anyone had asked if I ever planned to keep company with the duke of Equart at Shael Castle, I'd have thought it unimaginable."

"It's still not as unimaginable as a girl wanting to practice fighting instead of dancing. Why in the world would you want to learn swordwork?"

Kyer's skin crawled with irritation. "It seemed like a good idea." She watched Phennil float on his elven feet, and his partner laughed as she hopped and twirled, trying to keep up. She nearly blurted that she'd studied the *wæpnian* but didn't think it would shut him up. It wasn't a clandestine art, but those who studied it generally didn't publicise the information.

"You must have had some specific purpose in mind."

"No, as a matter of fact, I didn't," Kyer said with forced politeness.

"What made you decide to come to this part of the world and join up with Lord Valrayker?" He may simply have been making conversation, but she had the impression that he wanted the answer for reasons of his own. And his persistence was annoying.

"I lived in a village. I was bored, okay?" She drank from her refilled goblet.

"Well, all right."

Phennil and his partner sailed by again, the girl smiling gaily into his eyes.

"Besides, no one 'decides' to join up with Valrayker," Kyer continued. "He chooses them, not the other way around."

"I stand corrected." Sir Fredric placed his goblet deliberately on the table.

Aidan's blood! The man was eye catching, but that was where the attraction ended. Somewhat disappointed, Kyer closed the subject by turning her head and body to watch the handsome bard again, who had switched to a sea chantey. She chastised herself for her questionable decorum. As a guest, she ought to be less argumentative or she'd make herself unwelcome. *He works for Kien; he can't be that bad.* Perhaps fatigue was simply wearing her patience thin.

"I'm going to turn in," Kyer said. "It's been a very long day." She plastered on a pleasant countenance and said good night to Sir Fredric. "I'm sure I'll see you later."

Jesqellan moved silently down the alley and found the door he sought. He passed his hand over the latch and whispered the cantrip to open it. He peered cautiously around before stepping all the way in, dark eyes searching the hazy, smoke-filled room for anyone he needed to avoid. Too late, he saw one such person in a far corner; that fellow had spotted him first. Unable to escape what he knew would be an uncomfortable encounter, Jesqellan nodded and reluctantly wended his way between tables and chairs that were too close together. He glanced furtively about the room for any other familiar faces to whom he could retreat once the Diviner was through with him. The smoke billowed as he passed through it and closed in around him, eerily reflecting the red firelight.

"Evening, Trevile. I had hoped not to see you."

"Jesqellan, sit, sit!" the wizened, wiry old man gestured enthusiastically. "I have such fascinating things to impart to you."

Trevile pronounced every syllable so precisely in his high-pitched, nasal drone that it made Jesqellan think of a mosquito with hiccups, and he wanted very much to swat it. Of course, it could have been the things Trevile said that bothered him, not so much the old Diviner's voice. He hoped it would be a short encounter, but politeness mixed with a morbid curiosity held him in place.

The ever-present fine silver chain was rolled into a ball, and using both hands, Trevile held it up against Jesqellan's forehead, chanting sibilantly in some ancient tongue. He rolled his hands around and around it and fingered the chain lovingly, the way a tailor experiences an exceptional fabric.

"Do not worry, my friend. I will not tell you your own future today." His burn-scarred face held a permanent tightness that was accentuated when he smiled, an effort that looked as though it pained him, though in truth it did not any longer. The "accident" had occurred long before Jesqellan's time. The man who had thrown the oil lamp was long since gone; trampled by three runaway horses just outside Revelin not six weeks later, exactly how Trevile had described the event just prior to being hit with the lamp. Trevile had forgiven the poor sod. After all, he had been shocked, and it wasn't as if his reaction was a complete surprise to Trevile.

The ancient man's eyes glittered as he released the contents of his hand, splashing it onto the table, and Jesqellan jumped in his hard wooden chair.

"A little nervous, are we?" the old man wheezed.

Jesqellan ignored him and took a keen interest in the *very* unusual wire mesh lamp that hung just above the Diviner's left shoulder.

The long silver chain strewed itself over the table, moulding itself into the uneven surface in a bizarre pattern of loops and angles. The tiny chain links sparkled red in the firelight, reflecting in Trevile's bright eyes. Whenever he released the chain, the Diviner pored with delight over the story the links were about to tell. Jesqellan found his enjoyment unnerving; he loved foretelling a man's death as much as predicting when he'd meet his true love.

Jesqellan shuddered. At least the dangers of his own method of magic were unambiguous, indisputable. But fortune-telling was useless. Why would anyone want to know the future? It wasn't as if you could escape it; no matter how hard a person tried to avoid a thing, it always found a way to come about. Oh, certainly some would argue that it was nice to know beforehand so you could prepare. But Jesqellan's view remained: No matter what your behaviour, the event would take place anyway. This old geezer's stories always haunted Jesqellan for weeks afterward. The mage tried to appear relaxed and failed. In an effort to stop the bouncing of his right knee, he planted his heels firmly on the stone floor.

"It is for your whole party that I read, not for you alone," Trevile whispered. "Oh! When you leave the city, you will be one fewer."

"Not a remarkable piece of news," Jesqellan said dryly. "We've known all along that Valrayker would not be leaving with us."

"Ah! Is it something more *diverting* you would like to know?" He leaned forward eagerly, peering more closely at the links that laid out people's lives before him.

Jesqellan regretted his comment.

"Your number will decrease again before you reach your destination."

Jesqellan adopted a nonchalant air. Really, this information meant nothing to him.

"Hmm, this is most interesting," Trevile enunciated sibilantly. "There is one in your party who is not what they seem. Hmm, but the link is in shadow, I cannot tell more about the one. There is no intention of deceit, I believe. You see? That link there, it is fallen into this knife gouge in the table and is on a rakish angle."

Jesqellan suddenly found that the conversation at the table behind him was rather absorbing, as was the view of the girl who delivered tankards of ale to the two long-haired Deathgrips over against the far wall who intensely studied a piece of scroll.

"There are two among you who will grow in authority, gain superiority, though in different ways. Someone . . . is more powerful than you. You must take care that—"

Jesqellan sliced the air with his hand. "Don't tell me about myself; I don't want to know."

Trevile was patronisingly amused. "Very well. But that which I would have foretold is long away. You need not trouble yourself about it." And he gathered up the chain in his hand again, rolling it around and caressing it lovingly. "I will talk to you about something else." He released the chain again with less of a thrust behind it this time.

Glancing up at his companion, he said, "I watched you all ride into the city today."

"Oh yes?"

"There is one I have not seen before. A woman."

"Yes, that is Kyer."

"Yes. Kyer." The Diviner took a perfunctory glance at his chain. "Her aura is green. Very dark."

"Is that so?" Jesqellan fidgeted in his chair. "What is the significance of that?"

"She is young," he said idly, leaving Jesqellan uncertain how the comment related to the question. But Trevile was not finished. "She has considerable strength and courage. Which she needs." He lowered his nasal voice, and Jesqellan had to lean forward to hear him. "She has brought danger to your party. She will bring more. The girl is in grave danger herself, directly and indirectly, from multiple origins. She will make errors in her trust." He ran his finger along the chain, following its twists and curves. At one point, the chain developed a tiny fold, and the Diviner tapped the table next to it. He whispered. "She is soon to generate a bitterly vengeful enemy."

Jesqellan stared at him, frozen, through a long-held breath, then, "I must go." He got up, knocking over his chair and garnering much more attention than he wished. He had hoped to have a brief discussion with Trevile then leave him to find one of his other wizard acquaintances to trade stories and boast about his quick progress with the particularly difficult beast summoning spell. But not this time. He was far too uneasy after Trevile's little horror report. The mage adopted a determinedly steady gait that carried him between chairs, tables, and magic users, gripping his staff before him like an amulet. The door flew open with a wave of his hand, and he stepped out into the warm evening air, gasping it in, the smoke from inside wafting out after him.

He walked the streets of Shael for quite some time, seeking an elusive calm.

Seven

Acting on Impulse

O nce in the foyer, leaving the party in the great hall behind, Kyer changed her mind. The glow from the torches and candelabra on tables and corbels gave the entrance hall a shadowy warmth. The sounds from the hall were several notches more subdued out here. Her agitation was instantly calmer. Although the day had been long, it wasn't really sleep she required but fresh air. Her head needed to be cleared of the noise and music, the wine and the smoke before she would be ready to retire. The Lady Alon Maer looked down encouragingly from her portrait. Kyer greeted her with a nod before passing underneath. Pulling open the huge front door, she stepped past the sentries who stood at attention and out into the inner ward of the castle.

Her mood already considerably improved, she followed the path away from the door. The torchlight faded behind her; ahead, the flagstone path was a meandering river into shadow. The lateness of the hour meant that those people who weren't at the feast were either in their quarters or on duty. Three soldiers left the barracks and headed toward the gate, but in her dark colours, they missed her. She needed this alone time; the constant company of her travelling companions after so long on her own was something to get used to. She could still hear the music from the hall through the high windows, but it did not intrude on the stillness and serenity of the castle yard. The evening air was uncommonly warm despite the clarity of the sky, and Kyer felt no need for her cloak. She was glad because getting it would mean having to go all the way back to her room.

She circumnavigated the inner ward and decided she was still not ready to retire, so she made her way to one of the towers with designs on seeing what the city looked like from above. She wandered to the southwest tower. The short-bearded guard at the door stopped her.

"May I help you?" he asked.

"I want to walk along the battlements. How far do I have to climb?"

He stepped back to open the door for her, his sword hilt knocking gently against the heavy wood.

"It's on the third level," he directed, "but there will be three doors. The one in the centre is the tower entrance, and the other is to the south wing. The one you want is the door on the right."

"Thanks." She began the long, dizzying climb up the circular staircase, grateful for the rope along the wall to hold on to. *Too damn many stairs.* When she reached the third level, she paused to catch her breath. He had said the door on the left was the south wing, and she felt just a little proud for guessing that this was the tower nearest her room. Saving it for later, she opened the right-hand door, breathing a sigh of relief at choosing the correct one. She was on the southwest battlement, at the front of the castle. It overlooked the outer ward and the gate to the city. She jumped at the voice in the darkness.

"Who comes?"

Kyer turned swiftly to find the owner of the voice. She could barely see him in the shadows. "Kyer Halidan. I'm a guest of his lordship."

The thick-necked sentry took a step closer and peered into the darkness to get a better look at her. "Ah, so you're the woman who arrived with Lord Valrayker this afternoon."

"That would be me." *Word travels fast.*

She took her leave of him and crossed the parapet to an embrasure. This was a perfect vantage point to view the city. And what a view! The stars frosted the sky with no more than a slit of a moon to upstage them. Beyond the outer curtain of the castle, Shael at night was spread out before her like a vast relief map, dark in some areas, others dotted with tiny lights of lamps lining the streets. Glimmers of lamp and firelight spilled out from what Kyer concluded must be taverns. The stars shimmered on the surface of the river that groped its shadowy arm through the south end of the city. She could just make out the gatehouse of the city wall in the distance and wondered what it must be like to be lord of such a place. *Three* such places! Imagine being Kien Bartheylen and standing in this spot, surveying *his* land, *his* city. She breathed deeply of the sweet air. What pride he must feel to plant his feet on the parapet of *his* castle and gaze out over it all. And he had two others. *What if all this were mine?*

The door of the gatehouse to her right opened and someone emerged, but she didn't bother to see who it was. She didn't know anyone, anyway. The footsteps approached. And stopped.

"I thought you were going to bed."

"I changed my mind," she replied. "After riding all day and sitting all evening, I needed a walk more than sleep."

Sir Fredric joined her at the wall.

"What do you think of Shael?" the captain asked. "I guess I should ask you if you've been here before."

"No, I haven't. It's pretty impressive."

"Would you like me to show you around tomorrow?"

"Don't you have to work during the day?" Kyer asked.

"In my position, I can easily have someone else fill my place for the afternoon if I choose. Besides, it is one of my duties to ensure the happiness of Lord Kien's guests."

As the final trace of Asp Moon appeared at his ear from behind the gatehouse, she regarded him with a new perspective: it seemed that the fresh air had taken his edge off. Much as his suggestion appealed to her, she had already been promised a tour. "Actually, Derry made the same offer earlier, so thanks, but I should take him up first."

"Would you not prefer to be led by someone who lives here and is therefore more acquainted with all the goings-on in the city?"

"Perhaps you can show me anything that Derry misses," she proposed as a compromise, puzzled that it was so important to him.

"Well, if that is what you'd prefer . . ."

"Yes, it is," she said, peeved.

After a time, he asked, "How did you meet Lord Valrayker?"

"We met in a tavern. I shared a bottle of wine with him, and he introduced himself." Her duel with Simon was nobody's business.

"And he asked you to join him, just like that?"

"It wasn't that simple. How long have you worked for Kien?"

He bought into her abrupt change of direction. "I've been captain of the guard for eight years." His voice sounded nonchalant, but she could not miss the odd sidelong glance to check for her reaction. She remained politely focussed but not enthralled. "Before that, I served on the guard itself for ten years, proving my worth to Lord Kien as well as the governors who have served him. And from the time I was ten, I worked as a squire. I have been involved in the protection of Shael in both a minor and major capacity for most of my life."

"I doubt there are many who could say that."

"A few, perhaps. Your friend Derry, now, he hasn't been in Lord Valrayker's service nearly that long."

It struck her that Sir Fredric wanted her to be more impressed with him than she was with Derry. And though she had not been on the best of terms with Derry all evening, she had known him a week, during which he had earned her loyalty as a friend. "That's true," Kyer conceded, turning back to the view of the city below. "But consider that he's about—what, ten years younger than you? And he's Valrayker's captain, your equal. I don't believe that Valrayker's standards are any lower than Kien's."

Sir Fredric's body stiffened at her words. "Far be it from me to speak ill of someone who is, as you put it, my *equal*." Kyer noticed his emphasis on this last word. "But young Derry has a lot to learn, and there's a reason why he has not yet been knighted. I don't doubt that it will follow one day, but it will be a long time coming." His tone became almost fatherly. "You have known Derry for a week, and I'm sure his professional behaviour has been impressive to you in that time."

If it had been daylight, Sir Fredric may have been insulted by the grimace he would have seen on Kyer's face. "It's true," she reasoned. "Though deeds mean more to me than an appearance of competence. Truth is, had you been with us this last week, you may have had an opportunity to impress me as much as Derry has."

Sir Fredric said nothing for a moment. When he spoke again, it was with the determined, calm tone one uses after counting to ten. "Well, as I was not with you on your travels, I cannot guess what transpired. I shall have to take your word for it."

She'd pushed him to his limit, and Kyer decided it was time to end the exchange. With an easy manner, she said, "Listen, I'm the first one to say that Derry takes life far too seriously. And yes, he is young for a captain, but his youth shouldn't be held against him when he does so much to prove that he's worthy of the position."

A truce had been called, and Sir Fredric accepted it with good grace, relaxing and recovering his friendly side again. "That may be so, Kyer. It's only that I've never had the pleasure of working closely with him, I suppose. Now what of yourself? Do you wish to be knighted one day?"

Kyer laughed. "Whoa! One thing at a time. I only just joined Valrayker. I have no thought at all about a knighthood."

"Surely you've dreamed about becoming a knight someday. Most young warriors do."

"Do they? I suppose someday that might be appealing. But I've never had any thought about dedicating myself to any one person or cause. Right now I'm content to work for Valrayker on this one mission. After that, I'll be open to other possibilities."

"I'm curious. After all, you yourself said that Valrayker's standards are as high as Kien's. How did you find favour with the duke?"

Bloody persistent on this point, isn't he? Kyer pierced him with a look of challenge. "Perhaps while I'm here, I'll have the opportunity to show you. And at the same time, you can demonstrate to me why you deserve to be captain of the guard."

His face was silhouetted against the splash of silvery stars. The shadows softened his features and reduced the aging effect of the scars and wrinkles that experience had given him. Never mind that he was about fourteen years her senior. He was pleasing to her eye. He regarded her with the same intensity as when they first laid eyes on each other at the city gate, and she liked it as much now as she did then. She allowed the turn of her lip to beckon. His eyes glowed like embers in the night. He leaned down and kissed her.

She was not even mildly surprised and did not resist. She couldn't be certain, but Kyer had the feeling that this move was not part of a natural progression for him; he had made up his mind to prove something to her. But she was content to go along with it. What harm could it do? He was arrogant but attractive enough. Admittedly, this very thing had crossed her mind several times since that moment at the gate.

Stillness surrounded them. The guard at the door to the tower must be there, but he was motionless. Even the breeze was hushed.

"I don't know what to make of you, Kyer. You are unlike any other woman. You don't behave or speak like other women, and I'm having a hard time figuring out how to—to react to you." He brushed the back of her hair with his fingers. "On top of that, you're a personal guest of Kien's, and I would be defying my duty as his captain to treat you disrespectfully. But I find I . . . can't help it."

His callused fingers on her cheek and the back of her neck sent a tingling to the small of her back. "Nobody is accusing you of disrespect," she replied. "Do you have to tell Kien everything you do in your spare time?"

"Of course not."

Her head tilted slyly. "Well, I'm not inclined to tell him."

His reaction was immediate.

"Come." He did not take her hand but walked to the tower door. She followed. The guard saluted his captain as he passed. Kyer nodded to the guard and began the long climb down the steps. Before opening the door on the ground, Fredric turned, grabbing her where she stood on the bottom step, and kissed her hard, as if making sure this was still the plan. She let him know, in no uncertain terms, that it was.

Sir Fredric opened the door. The guard snapped to attention upon recognizing his commander, but no words were exchanged. Fredric led Kyer across the lawn to the building that housed the barracks.

They hurried up the steps and slipped into Fredric's room. He closed the shutters and lit some candles, a lamp, and a fire to take the chill off. She removed her weapon belt, unlaced her waistcoat, and was draped on his bed in only tunic and breeches before he had even finished puttering. She watched him with a coy half smile as he took off his sword, mantle, mail coat, and other pieces of dress armour that he wore for the banquet. She chuckled.

"What's so funny?" he said.

"Nothing, really. It's only that there seems to be at least one drawback to being captain. I'm apt to be sound asleep here by the time you've finished with all that."

"Well, I guess I'd just have to wake you up again, wouldn't I?"

She feigned weariness and closed her eyes. He wouldn't stand for that. Finishing speedily, he pounced on her, and she stifled a squeal.

"I am sure it will be worth the wait, my dear." He kissed her neck.

"You let me be the judge of that, Great Sir Fredric."

"Never mind the 'Sir' nonsense, all right?"

"Yes sir, Sir Fredric, sir!"

Her insolence was vanquished rapidly with his lips on hers. Then they travelled to her neck, her ear. His short beard rubbed her skin with pleasant roughness. As his hands moved around her body, he soon found her medallion and inquired about it, caressing the violet gem in its centre.

"Family heirloom," she whispered and changed the subject by pulling the laces on his breeches. He rolled over onto his back.

"Who are you, Kyer?" he breathed.

She said nothing but began to draw his tunic out of his trousers.

"You enter this city, a woman fighter, working for Valrayker, no less, and when I asked him, even *he* said he doesn't know anything about you." He tickled her back with the end of her braid.

"No more than he needs to. It must be very disconcerting." She ran her hands up under his tunic and toyed with the curls on his chest. "To be in such a position of responsibility, yet unable to learn everything you think you ought to know about a person. Look at it this way: If I were a man, all that you already know would be enough for you, but since I'm a woman, there *must* be something strange going on.

"You know," she said, "you ought to be a bit more wary." Her hands continued their work.

"Of what, you little upstart?" he scoffed with a grin as he flipped her over on her back and took the upper position himself. "Look at you: fresh faced, hardly a mark on you! Do you really mean to tell me how to do my duty?"

"Oh, incidentally, speaking of that . . ."

"Speaking of what?"

"Well, you said before that it's occasionally one of your duties to make sure the duke's guests are happy. I just wanted to know if I'm a duty or a pleasure."

"Oh, you are most definitely a pleasure." He brought his face down close to hers. The sweet aroma of wine was still on his breath.

"Good because I was a bit concerned that you would have to go provide the same service for each of my colleagues."

He laughed and kissed her. "You're the only one I'm interested in giving pleasure to at the moment."

"Ah, very good." She sighed. "Mind you, that brings us back to where we were before."

"Where were we before?" He blinked in bewilderment.

"I mentioned that you ought to be a little bit more wary of who you associate with." Her fingers inside his tunic came across the familiar smoothness of a long, wide scar on his upper arm.

"Oh, yes. And why was that again?"

"Like you said yourself,"—from inside, she pushed the sleeve down, forcing his arm out of it—"nobody really knows much about me. It's possible that I've told everyone the truth, that I was bored of living in a tiny village and along came Valrayker to rescue me from monotony. But maybe . . ." She pulled his tunic off over his head and brought her voice down to a whisper. "Just maybe I have some deep, dark secret reason why I travelled south to find Valrayker. How do you know I'm not working for Dregor, trying to get information from you?" She grinned wickedly.

He was startled but then he caught on.

"Well, you're making an awful lot of assumptions, young lady." He traced his finger down her cheek. "How do you know this isn't a setup? Maybe Valrayker and Kien have suspicions about that very thing and asked me to get information from *you*?"

"Then I won't say another word. I will reveal nothing."

"Hmm, that's too bad." He kissed her throat. "There are a few things I was really hoping you would reveal." His hand caressed her breast through the soft linen of her tunic.

She breathed in sharply. "You can just forget that, now."

"Oh, well then, maybe I'll have to resort to more . . . drastic measures," he whispered in her ear. Reaching his hand up under his pillow, he pulled forth a dagger and laid it so the hilt nestled between her breasts and its cold steel touched her throat.

Her senses stirred mercilessly. "Mmm." Her breath quivered. "I've never made love at knifepoint before." She clutched his body. There would be no stopping now.

"Have you decided whether or not you're working for the enemy?" he asked when the kiss was over.

"What difference does it make at this point?" she hissed, her hand reaching inside his breeches.

He let out a gasp. "So we can choose whether we're going to make love or if I'm going to kill you." He was trying to smile, but the rest of his body wouldn't allow it.

"Decision's already been made," she managed to say. "We're definitely making love. We can decide about killing later." She took the knife and let it fall to the floor.

Kyer awoke with a shiver. The fire had died, welcoming back the chill. They were covered with nothing more than the linen sheet. It was still dark. *Good.* She slid out from under the sheet, adjusted it, and drew the blankets up over Fredric before groping around for her clothes.

Fredric's arm reached out from under the covers and brushed her shoulder. "Where're you going?" he asked sleepily.

"It wouldn't be a good idea for me to still be here when the sun comes up."

He drew her to him. "I suppose not. Promise me you'll come again?"

She kissed him fully but patted his cheek. "I'm not foolish enough to make any promises at this time of the night. But I'll see you later."

"Oh, all right," he grumbled childishly and rolled over. She dressed and slipped out the door, now wishing she had her cloak; it was too early in the year for the warmth of the day to survive the chill of the night. She walked briskly across the lawn to the tower she had climbed to reach the battlement. The guard opened the door wordlessly.

When she reached the third level, she paused to get her bearings. *The one in the middle is the tower door.* Convinced that her choice was correct, she opened the door on the left, revealing Janak—much more of Janak than she ever wished to see—exiting the garderobe to return to his room. His open-mouthed horror transformed into a deep scowl.

He slammed his door, and she hurried along to her own tiny apartment and undressed again. The one thing she had to do before she could crawl into the blankets was to find in the bottom of a saddlebag a muslin pouch that contained the serrated leaves of a powerful herb. Drawing out three tiny leaves, she put them in her mouth and chewed them, shuddering at the unpleasant taste. She chased them down with a sip of water and got quickly into bed, glad that the herb's only major side effect was drowsiness. Thankful she wasn't expected to awaken with the dawn, she sank into sleep.

Kyer awoke in the morning feeling well rested and energetic, despite her late night. She dressed, in her own clothes this time, and opened her door to find a bundle resting outside. It was her freshly laundered tunics and underthings, cleaner than she had seen them in weeks. Dropping them in the chest, she went out. A petite, dark-haired servant greeted her at the top of the stairs.

The girl curtsied. "I am to escort you to the breakfast room, miss."

The breakfast room turned out to be the same room in which they had met Kien the day before. When she entered, a cry went up within.

"Here she is at last!" Kien waved her to an empty chair. "Shall we tell her what her punishment is for sleeping late?"

"Punishment?" said Kyer with playful scepticism. "If I'd known there would be punishment, I'd have been much more determined to find discomfort in my accommodations."

"My, how skilfully she hides her trepidation by casually throwing in a compliment," Kien said to Valrayker with mock amazement. "As a reward for your cleverness, you will avoid the pillory this time, but mark you! I will not be so forgiving next time."

Kyer grinned and sat. The room had been rearranged to accommodate a table for the meal. Most of the others had finished eating, but Phennil was helping himself to another heaping plateful of potatoes pan-fried with tomatoes. Kyer wondered how many had preceded it. She filled her bowl with bread, cheese, and some fresh fruit, while Derry poured her some watered wine.

"We all decided that the last two to join us would have to start off the training in the field today." Valrayker's grey eyes laughed. "You'll notice who is yet missing; he will be your opponent."

Kyer looked around and finally realized who the lucky fellow would be. "Janak. How lovely," she said cheerfully. "I didn't even miss him until you pointed out that he wasn't here." She took a bite of a peach and had to slurp the juice off her hand and wrist. "I'm sure he'll welcome the opportunity to put me in my place."

"And he will make the most of it, you know."

"Without a doubt. But I'll give it my best. Incidentally, Valrayker, I'm ready for that discussion you promised, whenever you are."

"Excellent. Perhaps later today, then."

Kyer inquired after Jesqellan's visit to the guildhouse. He straightened. "Fine," he grunted, hardly making eye contact with her. "Fine."

Great. She tried to surmise how she'd offended him.

Janak entered the room amid a chorus of hurrahs. Only the presence of Kien Bartheylen stayed his tongue from a doubtless nasty reply. Upon hearing of his "punishment," he merely glared at his opponent with wild satisfaction.

"I'll be there," he growled. "Will *you*?"

"Wouldn't miss it. I'm in a tizzy with anticipation." Kyer was not overconfident. She was well aware of the dwarf's skill and had no intention of taking him lightly. But there was no way she would let him see that she was nervous. He would likely best her, but she hoped she would not make it easy for him.

"I'm surprised to see you up this early," he said sarcastically as he sat in the last vacant chair, which chanced to be right across from her. "You were out much later than the rest of us." He seemed pleased to drop hints that might provoke a scandal. She paid no heed to the curious glances that turned her way.

"That's true." She calmly spread butter on her bread. "So what's your excuse for getting up later than I did?" Without waiting for an answer, she added, "Were you warm enough?"

"Of course," he answered gruffly.

"Oh, good. I was worried you might have caught a chill." She gave him a look of concern, which made him glower, though he carried it no further.

"Dunvehran, may I have a word?" Derry said as the rest of the group filed out to the practice field. Kien politely exited as well.

"Of course," Valrayker said, adjusting his tone and demeanour to match the use of his formal name.

"I wonder if I might speak to you about Kyer," Derry began. "I know her fighting is impressive, I have witnessed it myself, but my concern lies with her . . . outspokenness."

Dunvehran's eyebrows went up, but he remained still.

"She demonstrated her . . . relaxed attitude here this morning, which adds to—perhaps further illustrates my point of view. But I am referring specifically to her introduction to Lord Kien yesterday."

"Ah, yes."

"I know he did not appear to be offended by her comments," Derry went on, "but still, I cannot help but doubt her readiness for a mission such as the one before us. Is it wise for us to have in our party a person who does not know how to conduct herself in situations where diplomacy is required? It may prove detrimental." Listening to himself, his words sounded overwrought, and he wondered briefly why Kyer's comment had bothered him so much. But he said nothing more.

Dunvehran regarded him, thoughtfully massaging a knuckle. "I agree," he said carefully, "though I am not sure that we have yet seen a lack of diplomacy, but rather a refreshing directness."

Derry shrugged.

"Are you of the opinion that she should be left out of this mission?"

"I'm not sure," Derry replied with a sigh. "She's very young. We're crossing enemy lines. Will she bear up to all that is expected of her? It is a concern; that is all."

"I know someone else who continually feels his abilities are questioned because of his youth. She is not so much younger than yourself. Besides, we do not know of all she has experienced."

Derry took a preparatory breath. "May I speak frankly?"

"You may always be frank with me, Derry."

"I must confess I have been asking myself this past week how you would think that we would be a suitable team." Derry had trouble meeting his lord's eye. "It's not that I doubt you, exactly, it's only that she seems so . . . *wild* and . . . *unrefined*. We are not alike at all."

"I don't actually agree with you there," Dunvehran said, and Derry looked up. "I think you share quite a few traits, in fact. Though I did not suggest that you should work together because you are alike. It's often the differences between companions that make them stronger together." Dunvehran leaned forward. "A good leader will seek out a person's strengths and nurture them. The weaknesses often solve themselves. And Derry," he added, "she did study the *wæpnian*."

Derry raised his eyebrows; this was the first he'd heard of that.

"Though she is still not flawless, that ought to count for something."

Derry tipped his head to the side. "Yes, I grant you that, the discipline and all, in her fighting perhaps. But she seems to take no situation seriously. She always has some witty comment to throw in, whether or not it is appropriate—"

"I think you know that is an exaggeration on your part. She takes a good many things seriously. Besides, there are often times when a witty comment is the perfect solution to a problem. Perhaps . . . it is possible that you take things too seriously?"

Derry's heart dropped. "I have to uphold my position."

"And you do. Know that you always have my confidence."

Derry raised his head, as if needing to feel worthy of that confidence.

"Don't be too hasty to judge others, lad." Dunvehran put a hand on Derry's shoulder. "If you accept and respect the ways in which people are different from yourself, you may find that you can learn something from them."

"From Kyer?"

Dunvehran nodded. "Whether you like it or not."

Kyer gazed around her, a little overwhelmed, at all the weaponry there was to choose from in the armoury. Short swords like her old one all the way up to a massive greatsword. Clubs, maces, morning stars, battle axes, lances, pikes, halberds, and every conceivable kind of hand weapon. Short bows, longbows, light and heavy crossbows. It was the hugest collection of deadly devices she had ever seen, even if they were blunted for practice. She felt suddenly small and rather green.

"Pretty amazing, hunh?" said a cheerful voice at her side. "Lots to choose from."

"Too much."

"And just think," Phennil went on, "this is only the practice weaponry. Just wait until you see the real armoury. It's unbelievable! Why, there must be ten times as much stuff in there as there is in here. So what are you going to use? I'm partial to the longbow myself, as you probably know, and it's an excellent distance weapon, but I also like to practice my up-close combat. I need to work on my sword arm. I generally use a bastard. You do too, right?" The elf picked up a four-foot cut-and-thrust weapon with a handle allowing for both a one- and two-handed grip.

"Yes," was all she managed to say before he spoke again, but this time she listened carefully, for he had lowered his voice.

"Now listen, Valrayker likes us to practice with different types of weapons, so that we learn how each one is used. That way we learn how to defend against all types. But look at old sourpuss over there," the elf gestured to where Janak was intently eyeing the battle axe collection. "He'll choose a battle axe as close as possible to the one he always uses. He doesn't see this as a chance to train, but a chance to show you up. He's been dying to do that since the night we left Wanaka. I don't know what his problem is, but that's Janak, all right. So my suggestion would be that you find a sword as close to your own as possible. Don't try to fight him with something unfamiliar, or he'll beat you in no time. He may beat you anyway but that's all right. Just don't let him do it without working up a sweat, okay?"

Though she would never have believed that Valrayker would have an idiot in his party, Phennil's endless chatter gave one the first impression that he was a scatter-brained fool. And his perpetually good-natured disposition masked any ability to detect a disagreeable quality in anyone. Kyer had a new respect for him now that he was unveiled as a shrewd and cunning observer. She found a bastard sword of similar weight and length to her own, just as Valrayker entered with Derry.

"Are we ready?" the duke asked with a hint of eagerness in his voice.

Out on the field, the opponents faced each other. She had known Janak was large, but his size truly struck her now: hardly shorter than she, with arms as thick as her thighs and legs like tree trunks. And he had to have been at least twice her weight. She swallowed. They crossed weapons and bowed in the customary agreement of goodwill, though the grimace on Janak's face suggested to Kyer that his gesture was not heartfelt.

She focussed her concentration inward, blocking out the observers on the sidelines: the curious castle soldiers who had time enough to watch Lord Valrayker's people in action, especially the woman; the other members of the party, who, all but Derry, had never seen her fight; Valrayker, who would be waiting to critique her later; and even Kien, yes, she was fully aware of his presence up on the parapet, watching the activities on the field, waiting for . . . For what? For her to prove to him that Valrayker had made a good choice.

Breathing deeply, she allowed them all to fade away while she scanned the ground, as she had done a week before in the yard of the Burnished Blade. But even that event was forgotten as her senses and reflexes sharpened. There was no sound in her head. No sound but Brendow's voice, running through her mind like a mantra, every instruction he had ever given her, every word of encouragement, every warning. Then she was ready.

She looked directly into Janak's eyes, and even he faltered at her emotionless face and her deep, green eyes that showed not a hint of fear. He was doubly confused a half second later when she gave him a slow, pleasant smile. Was this the same woman he had growled at during breakfast?

She swung and he suddenly awoke to the clang of his battle axe blocking a ferocious attempt at his lead arm. They were off.

"You sure have caused a lot of trouble on this trip," he accused.

"Maybe." She just about caught him in his right tree trunk.

"I hope you don't expect us to fight your battles for you."

"Nope. I don't." *Clang!* She redirected his swipe to her left arm. "Why would I?"

"You're a girl," he sneered.

"Yup," she agreed, not lending any more meaning to his statement than it warranted.

A slash toward his shoulder, a cut near her leg. A few moves later, he came out with his next flurry of verbal attacks.

"Rumour has it you're considered good looking," he said sarcastically.

"That so?" she said with feigned delight. "Thanks, Janak."

"I didn't start it," he grunted. "I've seen better-looking humans lying dead on the battlefield."

"Neat." She was concentrating too hard to take his brow-beating seriously. "Well, I've never seen—" *clang* "—an uglier dwarf." A bead of sweat trickled down the side of her face.

He swung harder for lack of a retort. The stillness between crashes of metal was broken only by their panting. As if the match had been choreographed, they stepped away from each other, Kyer exhaling long and slow. Then they engaged again. He took the opportunity to change the subject.

"Pretty simplistic moves," he puffed. "Shouldn't expect more from a girl."

She parried his axe handily with a *Braemar* block. "Working well enough on you," she retorted breathlessly, glad this was just a training match. The dwarf was as deadly as she had been warned. His battle axe was heavier than her sword, and he swung it with unerring speed. Now with every swing there was a grunt of exertion from each participant. She cried out as he clipped her shoulder. *Shit!* A gasp went up from the growing crowd and instantly subsided. *Focus.* She pulled her mind inward again.

"Nice one," she said sincerely, calming her breaths. *Good thing his blade is only as sharp as his wit, or he'd have sliced my arm off.* She pivoted on the balls of her feet and, muscles straining, thrust his weapon away and countered with a sweeping *Sharlan* blow to his midriff. He didn't expect the move and though he tried to dodge it, she did snag him, her sword scratching a silvery line in his armour. "Hooray for the breastplate, hunh?"

He was not as gleeful about this observation as she and changed his tack again, trying deviously to shake her concentration.

"Slept with every officer in Shael yet?"

She exhaled fully. "Whoa! We get to go all the way to Nennia together. Better save some insults for the road."

Grinning wickedly, he dodged her backhand strike and, lunging, managed to poke her in the chest with the blunt curve. He took a step back and steadied himself. Kyer welcomed the chance to inhale.

Suddenly he darted forward, his hands separated on the shaft of the axe, and knocked her sword upward. It described an arc over her head, but she stayed with it in a one-handed *Penning* manoeuvre, spinning around and clapping him on the back of his helm with the flat edge.

"Ooh, fancy," she said. "You got elf blood in you?" She could feel fatigue setting in. Dwarves were renowned for their stamina, and she was only being realistic in admitting that she would have to give in soon.

The dwarf sneered. "Stupid."

"Oh, excellent comeback." She lashed forward again.

With a *Svelke* twist, she locked her sword behind the outer curve of his blade. The opponents stood their ground, her comparatively slight, yet muscular form unwavering in the shadow of his Dwarven bulk. His breath was hot on her face. Their eyes at the same level, he glared at her, while she returned the gaze coolly.

"Well, I'm tired," she announced. "And I'm ending this match before you decide to kill me." She gave him a shove and wrenched her weapon free.

"Giving up so soon?" the surly dwarf taunted. "Afraid you'll lose?"

"Knock it off, Janak," she replied, bored of his little game, and swallowed to moisten her dry throat. Panting, she added, "Listen, I have no idea why, nor do I really care, but you've clearly made up your mind to hate me."

The dwarf made a grunting noise.

"Well, let me just assure you of one thing, my friend. You may not care to do the same for me, but I'll watch *your* back because you're part of Valrayker's *chosen* team, as am I. Outside of that, go ahead and think whatever you want about me; I'm equally resolved to disregard you completely." She pivoted and walked away and felt him staring at her back as sharp as the point of a knife.

The audience applauded and cheered. Kyer took several even breaths as she approached them and had all but caught her breath by the time she reached her friends. Several people clapped her on the shoulder, Derry said, "Well done," and Phennil pumped her hand.

"I was worried there, I must confess." Excitement glittered in the elf's eyes. "But you gave him a run for his money; that's a fact. You were right to stop when you did, though."

"He's stronger than I am, without a doubt," Kyer conceded, glancing at Valrayker, who listened with interest. "But it was a good, challenging match. I'd do it again if someone could guarantee that he wouldn't really chop my head off."

Valrayker nodded with a satisfied gleam. "Excellent. Have yourself a rest and meet me back here after lunch. Who shall we see next? How about Phennil and Derry? Come on, lads."

Janak stalked away, brushing off all congratulations offered to him.

The sessions over for now, Kyer headed back to the castle with Derry for the midday meal. Derry was particularly quiet. It was not uncommon for him to have little to say, but this silence had more depth. Kyer had the sense that the man was . . . observing her. They walked side by side along the path, aiming for the door that accessed the rear passage to the main floor of the castle. They both reached for the door handle and stopped. After the slightest hesitation, they looked at each other. Kyer recognized Derry's instinct to open doors for ladies and at the same time knew he had arrested his habitual action for her sake. He was too polite to provoke her, and Kyer knew it was the wrong time to prove a point. She let her hand drop.

They walked wordlessly along the dim passageway, the only sounds their footfalls and the slight clink of Derry's armour. They became aware of approaching voices farther on around the corner and, after a few paces, could make out the words.

"He said it was so easy. Melted her with a single kiss, and she was all over him, he said."

"Valrayker's new friend? On their first night here!"

Kyer and Derry stopped in their tracks at the mention of Valrayker's name. Kyer's heart tightened.

"Sir Fredric said she was one of the best he's ever had."

Derry looked at Kyer in confusion, as if desperate for her to tell him they weren't talking about her. But she couldn't hide the truth.

"Aidan's breath! Valrayker's got good taste, then, has he?"

"So has Sir Fredric." Their laughter reverberated down the echoey tunnel. Derry's confusion became disbelief, and Kyer stared straight ahead, her face like cold stone. The two young men emerged from around the corner and recognized them. The laughter ceased. They looked to be in their early twenties, old enough to know that their futures in the castle guard could be very short if these two wished it. The tension in the tight corridor was like heavy air before a storm. After an interminable stillness, Kyer spoke.

"I won't pretend we didn't hear every word that just passed between you. Where did you get this information?" she said with remarkable calm.

The young men glanced at each other uncertainly.

Her voice rose only slightly. "Answer me."

"Uh," the taller one cleared his throat. "It was—well, Sir Fredric was telling Sergeant Laity, miss, and I happened to be nearby."

"So you were eavesdropping," she clarified.

"No, miss! Sir Fredric knew I was there."

"I see. And how many others have heard this little tale?"

"Not many, miss," he assured her. "Sir Fredric told me not to tell anyone."

"I see," she said again. Her eyes snapped pointedly over to his friend. "And what else did your friend here not tell you?"

She watched him squirm as he took in her sword hilt, the cuts and slashes in her armour, and the sturdiness with which she carried herself. She watched it dawn on him that she was not to be trifled with.

"Well—you see," he stammered, embarrassed to repeat the words. "Sir Fredric said you told him you would show him how you found favour with his lordship, and . . . well, there has been a lot of talk—you know, about why Lord Valrayker would have a woman in his group, see. And Sir Fredric said you probably . . . went . . . with his lordship as well."

Kyer's breath came in short puffs of outrage. *That bastard!* To not only tell people they had slept together, which was bad enough, but to deliberately misinterpret her words and spread rumours about her and *Valrayker*? Insufferable! Seething, she itched to draw her sword. Instead she clenched and unclenched her fists. "Where is he now?" she asked slowly, her voice grinding like iron on stone. She stared into the shadows between them in an effort to maintain control.

"I believe he is on the west battlement," one of them said, she didn't care who. Stabbing them each with one final glare, she pushed past them.

She practically ran. Why would he do such a thing, boast carelessly to his friends about his association with her? How many others had he told? And what would Valrayker do when he found out? Which he surely would. Shame shuddered through her. She should have trusted her gut feeling that he was not good enough for her, she who had always prided herself on her judgement of character and selective tastes in men. Barely seeing through the sea of red, she ploughed through the door and stalked across the foyer of the castle, her boot heels tolling her anger.

Derry was aghast. Not that she had slept with Fredric. No, it was the other issue that gnawed at him. How dare that d—ed Fredric insinuate that Dunvehran, of all people, would select his members based on—on—physical relations! Derry was well aware that his lord had been rather . . . well known, but to add a woman to his party because she— No, it just wasn't possible. Was it? Surely Kyer Halidan was not the soul mate Dunvehran had hoped one day to find. She was much too—

Derry had been asking himself what else Kyer had done in Wanaka apart from killing Ronav's man. How else she had impressed him? After his discussion with Dunvehran this morning, he had resolved to be more open minded to Kyer's personality, but now . . . Suddenly he could read dual meanings into many of the things Valrayker had said about Kyer, and into all the little looks and sidelong glances his lord had shared with her over the past week, even the extra attention she had paid him as he entered the hall for the banquet last night. He felt as if he'd just swallowed an ingot of lead. *This is ridiculous.* He gave his head a shake. *Dunvehran would* never *do such a thing.* And what did Derry care who Dunvehran slept with? He pressed on, hoping to catch up with her.

He entered the foyer of the castle and followed the echo of her rushing footsteps across the hall and out the front door.

Eight

A Flurry of Consequences

Fredric Heyland awoke earlier than he usually arose wearing a smug grin. He idled through his morning preparations and allowed himself a second cup of tea, all the while congratulating himself for his triumph.

That little chit of a woman had really put him off in the great hall. Sir Fredric Heyland was not accustomed to being ignored. When he spoke, others listened. When he said something witty, people laughed. When he asked a question, he received an answer. Those were the rules. Especially with women. Women didn't argue with him; they drooled over him. They did not speak forwardly to him, and they absolutely did not *correct* him. He had earned the right to those expectations through years of devoted service to Kien Bartheylen. And yet that Kyer woman had broken every last one of those rules. And more.

When they'd first laid eyes on each other at the gate, Fredric thought she might have been enticed. But after dinner . . . Fredric wondered if that upstart Derry Moraunt had badmouthed him. *No, he's so* good, *he wouldn't dream of it.* But still, experience had taught Fredric that women would be taken with him. They routinely engaged in civil hostilities toward each other while competing for his attention. And those lucky enough to sit on either side of him glared triumphantly at their friends and nastily at each other. *Oh, but she's above them all.* Fredric chuckled in mild disgust as he trimmed a couple more hairs from his beard. Even if she had decent skill with a sword, her biggest trouble was that she was green and learning from the wrong people. Pompous Derry Moraunt, captain to an exiled duke. She thought Derry was his *equal*? Laughable.

There she'd been, out on the parapet, as if waiting for him. The starlight and fresh air had softened the roughness around her edges, and she actually looked . . . pretty. It hadn't really been his plan to seduce her, but he always enjoyed a challenge. *It was all too easy once I began it.* Women were powerless to resist his charm.

Fredric was certain he'd impressed the little thing. And himself? Fredric sighed contentedly as he drew a wet comb through his wavy red hair. In spite of her youth and inexperience, he'd enjoyed her immensely. Aside from the smooth skin, well-defined muscles—*very pleasant on a woman,* he concluded —firm breasts that fit in his hands with no wasted flesh, deep eyes that virtually screamed their longing for him. Her lips, her tongue, her teeth . . . Aside from all of her physical attributes was the simple fact that she worked for Lord Valrayker. *The first human woman Vally's ever had working for him, and I overcame her on her first night in Shael.*

The smug grin appeared again. Such a triumph was meant to be boasted.

Fredric emerged from his room whistling in the early sunlight.

"Lovely morning, Captain," said the guard at the tower door, smiling at him.

Fredric stopped. "Did you finally get laid by a woman last night, Cleal, or did you screw your dog again?"

The guard's face fell, and his salute faltered. "Sir?" he asked tremulously.

Fredric laughed and cuffed the man so he stumbled. "Show some strength of footing, Cleal, or I'll think you sit down to piss." The captain merrily flung open the door and took the tower steps two at a time, still chuckling. *Ah, the privileges of the highest-ranking officer in the Shael guard.* He needed to remind his men of their place.

Kyer was another such person who wouldn't suffer from being put in her place. Her opinion of herself was far too high. He'd love to see how she bore up to a little humiliation. Prattling, after all, was a socially unacceptable offence. He burst out onto the parapet. He strutted over to the wall and beckoned to Sergeant Laity. With a wink to the young guard who stood nearby, Fredric said. "Guess who I spent the evening with last night?"

Kyer raced up the same tower steps she had climbed last night. *How ironic that I should find him in the same place.* She surged through the door at the top of the stairs, and the guard there was nearly knocked over by her voice.

"Where's Fredric?"

The poor startled fellow didn't have time to answer because she had seen the man she sought, surrounded by about twenty of his men. She strode over.

"Good morning, you arrogant, deluded son of a whore!" she called gaily, and there was shocked silence as the onlookers waited for their captain's response to this unexpected arrival.

Fredric hesitated, a startled look on his face, then chuckled lightly as he approached her. He extended his hand.

"Hello, uh, Kyer, is it? I trust you are happy with your accommodations?"

Bastard! "You seem surprised to see me. Is it because you figured I would sit in my room, pining for your company or because you didn't expect me to have the nerve to confront you about this?"

She didn't accept his hand, and he put it on her shoulder, to draw her toward the gatehouse, but she shrugged it away. "Would you care to speak in private?" he suggested in an earnest whisper.

"Funny that you're so concerned about *privacy* all of a sudden." She smiled prettily. "Am I embarrassing you?"

"Kyer, you can't just come up here and interrupt my work—"

"Oh, can't I?" She put a clenched hand on her hip. Her voice chilled to ice. "You will listen to me." The breeze whistled through the crenellations. He stood his ground, but the quiver in his brow betrayed his misgivings. He had no idea what she was about to say, but he'd realized, too late, that Kyer was dangerous.

"You'd better be careful of what you say," he said tentatively. "Word can travel pretty quickly around here—"

"So I've learned."

"—and you wouldn't want Lord Valrayker to hear that you have behaved . . . inappropriately . . . for a warrior of his." Fredric's eyes were like slits as he tried to convince her to back down.

"Oh, don't you worry about me," she said with a smirk. "Valrayker likes us to do what we believe is right. And if he finds out? Well, all I can say is that I will never regret what I'm doing now as much as I regret sleeping with you last night."

The soldiers were aghast at her outspokenness.

"Let's just get one thing straight here," she continued. "I made a *choice* to go with you last night. In favour of a little romp, I *decided* to disregard my gut feeling that beneath your pretty face you were repulsive and not worthy of my company. If you think you overpowered me in some way, you have a really vivid imagination. And though I'm delighted to learn that it will go down in the annals of history that I was one of the best you've ever had, I'm insincerely sorry that I can't say the same of you."

The men stifled laughter, and Fredric looked as if he had been walloped.

She began to turn but stopped. "Oh, and one more thing: This delicious little rumour you've begun about me and Valrayker?" She shook her head in disgust. "You deserve to lose your knighthood for defaming the character of one of the greatest men Rydris has ever known. You aren't even worth my spit."

She strode to the door with her head up but stopped dead in her tracks, shocked to see Derry standing there. With an inaudible groan of dismay, she brushed past him and fled down the stairs. His impassive face told her nothing, but she could guess what he was thinking. She had slept with Fredric Heyland, whom Derry did not like. She now knew why, but that didn't change what had already happened. Confronting Fredric was something she was certain Derry would disapprove of.

By the time she reached the bottom of the stairs and blew out into the yard, most of her anger had subsided. But there was also a strong message from her conscience that she deserved what she was getting today.

Fredric stood dumbfounded on the battlement. His men avoided eye contact with each other and began to invent duties to perform. Derry stepped forward from the doorway where he had stopped to listen to Kyer's words. He didn't know where to put his hands. Finally one rested on the back of his neck.

"Kyer did not want the circumstances of her flight from Wanaka to be discussed openly because she preferred to avoid drawing any extra attention to herself. But since that is no longer relevant, I will tell you, if only to dispel this myth about Valrayker." He still harboured his own doubts about the subject but kept that part to himself.

"Ever heard of Ronav Malachite?" he asked redundantly, knowing full well that every man present would have heard the infamous name. "One of

Ronav's men had the honour of meeting Kyer in a tavern in Wanaka. He was less than polite to her, and by the end of the brief rendezvous, the man lay dead in the yard. It was that confrontation Valrayker witnessed, and that is why Kyer is now travelling with us. That reason and no other."

Fredric's body was limp.

Derry turned to go, but Fredric stopped him with one more desperate attempt to save face. "One man?" he scoffed with a trembling voice. "Surely you don't believe that was enough to convince him."

Beneath Derry's glare, the other captain lost several inches in height.

"It doesn't matter what I believed at the time. But I know he was right. In the week it took us to get here, Kyer has been pursued by more of Ronav's men, and her courage has impacted us all. On the very night we left Wanaka, she and I were attacked by four men. She single-handedly killed two of them and wounded another. She studied the *wæpnian,* you know."

Fredric's face went grey.

"Her wounds she has borne without complaint, and any fear she may have does not deter her from her commitment to my Lord Valrayker. She is a valiant warrior, and she," Derry gazed levelly at Fredric, "already has my utmost respect." He walked away, letting the humiliated man find his own interpretation of Derry's last comment.

As the door closed behind him, he heard Fredric hollering impatiently at his men to "Quit staring and get to work!"

As he descended the stairs, Derry analysed his feelings, hopeful that with his speech he had convinced himself the rumour had no basis in fact. He himself had just said Kyer was a valiant fighter and had every right to be there. He believed it and should have dismissed his troubled thoughts easily but couldn't get the subject out of his head. Even after her vehement words to Fredric. Why was there still a nagging doubt connected with it? *If only it weren't possible!*

Kyer was famished and heaped her plate with stewed pork and dumplings. If Valrayker had heard the story being circulated, he showed no sign of it. Her logical side told her that the duke would not be bothered by what she did in her spare time. Her concern was more that his good opinion of her might be soured by her poor choice. She was draining her second glass of wine when Derry walked in.

Valrayker had been watching her with amusement. "Kyer, the wine is meant to be savoured, not guzzled."

She smiled, feeling somewhat more relaxed now, thanks to the wine, but it was with some unease that she watched Derry move to his seat. He hadn't followed directly after her, so what had he been up to? His face was unreadable. He didn't look at her for the entire meal. She'd definitely made it into his bad books.

"I'll see you out on the field, then, Valrayker?" she asked as she rose to leave.

"I'll be there in a few minutes," the dark elf responded and she left.

Out in the yard she heard her name. It was Derry. She stopped by the cherry tree so he could catch up with her, though she braced herself, certain he was about to upbraid her for her behaviour. Before he had a chance to speak, she turned to him. "Well, go ahead and say it. I know you want to."

"Say what?" Derry looked as if she'd caught him in a lie.

"'I told you so.'"

"Why would I say that?" He seemed confused.

"Oh, come on. From the moment we saw him at the front gate, I knew you didn't like him, and now I know you have good reason. Don't try to tell me you aren't all smug that I found out."

"But I'm not," Derry insisted. "I have to say I am indeed glad that you found out, but I regret dreadfully the way you had to learn it."

"Why didn't you just tell me?" she demanded.

"I couldn't do that," Derry said gently. "It wasn't my place, nor would it be proper. You must understand that."

Kyer sighed and sat heavily on the bench at the side of the path. "Yes, I do. You believe in chivalry, and if you spread evil tales about Fredric, you would be no better than he is." It suddenly dawned on her. "*That* is why you sounded so bitter about his knighthood: You aren't so much jealous of him as you are indignant that he was seen by Kien to be worthy of the honour. He doesn't deserve it because he doesn't obey the code of chivalry."

"That's right." He sighed. "He is always on his best behaviour when Kien is around, and nobody tells Kien because—well, a number of reasons, I suppose." He ran a hand through his blond hair. "They might be afraid of repercussions. Or maybe they don't understand or care what the code of chivalry means either. Or perhaps they do, and that is what prevents them, like myself." He reached up and plucked a newly sprouted leaf off the cherry tree.

"And of course, the honour guard was just to impress Val."

"Keep Val thinking highly of Fredric, yes."

Her chin cupped in her hands, she thought back to the ribbing Derry had received from the knight after dinner and how she had felt that his conduct was unbecoming to a man of his rank. She kicked herself again and again for not heeding her instincts.

"Kyer." Derry's voice was hesitant.

"Uh hunh?" She had practically forgotten he was there.

"I have to ask you . . ."

"What?"

"Well, I hope you don't mind my asking, but I *need* to know. Is it . . . true?"

"Is what true? Did I sleep with Fredric? Yes, I slept with Fredric. You heard what I said to him. I may as well shout it out, I suppose, since the rest of the population of Shael Castle is going to know soon, if they don't already." She kicked a pebble onto the path. "Boy, a castle is just as bad as living in a tiny village, if not worse."

"No, that isn't what I meant," Derry said, apparently fascinated by the activities of a beetle in the grass. "I apologize for my forwardness. I was referring to what they were saying about . . . you and Dunvehran. I mean, does your relationship with him . . . extend that far?"

She stared at him. "I'm astonished that you, of all people, would entertain such a thought."

He shifted uneasily. "I simply need to know for certain."

She looked him in the eye. "Derry, I think you know the answer to that question. It isn't any of your business, frankly, but since it's so important to you: No, I did not sleep with Valrayker. Honestly, why in all levels of hell would I sleep with Fredric Heyland if I had Valrayker for a lover?"

"I never thought of that."

She looked at him squarely. "Tell me you didn't really believe that. After all that's gone on this week?"

Derry breathed a sigh and relaxed his shoulders. "You're right. I knew it couldn't be true that he would ask you along because of . . . that. You've proven your worth." Derry rushed on, the words tumbling out. "But I need to be aware of all things relating to this company and my lord. It is for his protection, which is my utmost responsibility. And I prefer to have straightforward answers from the people involved rather than deal in speculation and supposition." She could have pointed out his resemblance to Phennil, but she didn't. He joined her on the bench. "You understand that, don't you?"

"I suppose so. And now I just ride it out, I guess," she said to the flagstone path. "The worst must be over."

"You already did more than anyone else has ever done," Derry said stiffly.

"Okay, here it comes," she said, preparing for the flood of scolding.

"What? I was only going to say that I was alarmed that you might do something foolish, but then I heard what you said to him. I have to tell you, I admire you." She looked at him sceptically, but he was gazing at the gardener who was pruning the hydrangeas. "For doing the very thing that I have never had the courage to do."

"Nonsense," she said. "It has nothing to do with courage. You choose to conduct yourself by the code of chivalry because that's what you believe in. I have no ambition to become a knight, so it matters less to me what people think. What matters to me is what *I* think, and I couldn't let him make a fool out of me."

"And hopefully by the time we come back, it will all be forgotten."

"Let's hope so." She brightened. "And now I must go meet Valrayker."

Val was right, Derry thought. There was plenty he could learn from Kyer. The lead in his belly melted away, and he all but forgot about it. He walked back to the castle feeling quite tall.

She lay on her back on the edge of the practice field, studying the cloud formations, and imagined how Valrayker would react to her escapade. Would he want to discuss it right here and now? A shadow cut off the glare of the sun, and she turned her head toward it.

"You sure do like your wine," the dark elf's silhouette said. She could tell by his voice that his eyes were smiling.

"Yes, I do, as a matter of fact."

He gestured to her supine position. "So are you drunk?"

"No!" she laughed. "Will you cut it out now?"

"Then get up, you lazy lout, and let's get on with it."

She got to her feet and brushed herself off, not making eye contact.

"Why don't we start by having you show me what happened the night we left Wanaka," he suggested. "I'll be your opponents. Tell me what you want me to do."

Kyer sent her mind back to the night of the battle. "It was dark and pouring rain so hard, we couldn't see very well. Water was everywhere. I kept slipping in the mud." She paused, frustrated that she wasn't explaining well. "The first man was there, and the other arrived about there." She tried to sort out the details, but everything seemed fuzzy in her mind.

Valrayker watched her thoughtfully and finally interrupted. "You're not focussed." It was an observation, not an accusation. "What's on your mind?"

She shrugged. "I'm just . . . a little preoccupied. Maybe we should try this later."

"Anything I can help with?" he ventured.

"No. I think there's nothing more to be done at this point."

"Care to tell me about it? It's what I'm here for, you know, not just the wine." He winked.

She hesitated. This was the first time since leaving Brendow that she had been so comfortable with someone, and after so long trusting no one, it was refreshing. Mostly, she realized, she had to learn to trust her own instincts about people. The observation applied both to Valrayker and Fredric. She was beginning to understand why Derry felt the way he did about this man, but it still felt too soon.

"Someone betrayed a confidence, and it didn't go over well with me; that's all."

"What have you done about it?" He leaned thoughtfully on his five-foot sword, *Ondrædan*. The sun reflected red sparkles from the ruby in the pommel.

"The only thing I knew to do. I confronted him and set him straight." She squinted up onto the outer wall, where there was scarcely a sign of activity apart from the guard walking on his rounds. Which one of the windows above the wall was her room? "Maybe I should have shown more restraint, but I don't like to let people get away with that kind of thing."

"I've noticed that about you." He chuckled.

"I'm too impulsive sometimes," she admitted, as much to herself as to him.

"Maybe." He cocked his head to one side. "Let me ask you this: Do you feel you did the right thing this time?"

"Yes, I do. He was completely out of line, and there was no way I could let that go."

"Good, then." Valrayker nodded. "But you're right: if you know you tend to act impulsively, it's all the more important that you take a pause before you act. Some situations are best handled by walking away. You can bring a lot more woe on yourself if you just react without thinking."

Her face grew warm, and she looked away from him as renewed guilt seeped in. She felt again the jarring vibration up her arm as her sword ploughed through Simon's body and crunched in the dirt beneath him— "It sounds as if you're speaking from experience."

"You could say that." The dark elf shrugged. "An accomplished warrior is not just skilled at the art of fighting, but also at the art of knowing when not to."

"I hate to back down." She shook her head. "I can't just let the other person win."

"Unless it's Janak," Valrayker suggested with a chuckle.

Kyer rolled her eyes. "That's different."

"Hmm," he said. "Maybe." His tone told her she should think about that. "Sometimes everyone wins if the conflict is avoided," he went on, though his half smile and softened eyebrows suggested that he knew what she meant. "Just make sure you think about the difference between the two before you act—at least when you have time," he added, his eyes twinkling.

She sighed, wrestling with the notion of opening up to him further. "That's a tall order. How long did it take you to learn that?"

"Oh, only about four hundred fifty years, but I'm a quick study."

She returned his smile and appreciated his confiding in her. From that point, it was easier to put aside her cares and concentrate on the lesson.

They began again. She explained where the two men were and what each was doing. They went through the fight in slow motion; Valrayker made comments and observations throughout. He reminded her about how to make use of the fighting conditions, to turn them to her advantage, rather than negatively affecting her. They discussed ways to throw off one opponent to deal with the other and to read her opponent's body language, so she could anticipate his moves, as well as be aware of her own indicators and eliminate them.

"Now, when you were fighting Simon, you didn't rely solely on defence. You were more in control of the situation."

Kyer's knees and elbows went rigid. "It feels very strange to continue on a first-name basis with a man I killed," she said softly.

Valrayker rested his hands on his pommel. "Why do you think that is?"

She considered the question. "I suppose because it would be easier to kill if nobody had a name." He waited while she tried to put her thought into words. "A life is not to be taken lightly. Any life." She was definitely blushing now and couldn't meet his eyes, sure that he had judged her and found her wanting.

"You're right, Kyer," he said gravely. "We do not seek to kill. The necessity comes to us. If it were the other way around, we would be no better than Dregor." She nodded and gritted her teeth against emotion. "All the more reason to try to prevent our own life from being taken lightly."

Kyer's gaze wandered across the field, and she forced words between her lips. "I didn't really mean to kill him," she confessed.

To her surprise, he replied, "I know." After a beat, he added, "It was automatic, right?"

"I couldn't believe it when he used that knife." The hatred and outrage gushed out. This was the first time she'd talked about the incident. "And it was his *second* cheat! I was letting him off. I'd already started to walk away, that should've been the end of it, but the bastard—" She cut herself off. "People don't cheat in practice," she finished. The words sounded childish to her ears.

Valrayker shook his head. "No, Kyer, they don't. And I'm afraid it won't be the last time you kill out of passion. But neither can you put your own life at risk for fear of killing for the wrong reason. Only experience will teach you the difference. And Kyer." He waited until she was regarding him squarely. "Your instinct there was right. Simon would have killed you."

She pressed her lips together and nodded to him gratefully with not the slightest regret for opening up. She truly understood Derry's feelings now. "Thanks, Val."

The lesson continued for a short while longer. Then Val summarized.

"Keep your opponent off balance by continually surprising him. Don't allow him to get set and take initiative; keep him moving. Get within his measure, and fight smarter. Your footwork is excellent, the mark of a deadly swordsman. Combined with your speed and coordination, you can outmanoeuvre almost anyone, even those with greater reach or strength than yourself, and you're certain to fight a lot of those."

Kyer looked at him thoughtfully. "You sound a lot like Brendow when you talk about this stuff."

"Your trainer?" he said noncommittally. "That's funny. Just similar experiences, I guess."

Kyer felt exhilarated by more than just the training, and as they walked off the field together, she was much more at ease. The dark elf seemed to understand her, just the way Brendow always did. She felt—she thought about it a moment—a sort of kinship with him.

Valrayker walked through the castle to the inner ward, lost in thought. His newest recruit was a continuing source of curiosity. As he learned more about her, he sorted through his appraisals. Did they support his suspicions? She certainly reminded him of— He stepped out the door and was blindsided by Phennil, breathless with excitement.

"Oh, sorry, Val!"

"Is there a fire or something?" Valrayker asked, rubbing his tingling elbow where it had bashed into the heavy wood.

"Oh, I was heading to get something to eat," the younger elf said, picking himself up and carrying on as if nothing had happened. "Isn't it amazing about Kyer? After all these years of Sir Fredric's games and storytelling and getting away with it because no one is willing to stand up to him, it's our Kyer who brings him to his knees on her first day in the city. She's proving herself to be the wrong person to cross. I can't imagine people actually *believing* that you and she slept together! Not that she isn't attractive or anything, but it's obviously completely unnecessary. I mean, none of us saw her fight Ronav's man, but not only do we have your word to take for it, but her personality speaks volumes about her character. And I know Derry was blown away by her skill against the other four men." Phennil finally paused when he became aware of Valrayker's vacant stare. "What?"

"What, by all that is precious, are you talking about, you utterly ridiculous elf?" Valrayker said with exasperation, though not without affection.

"Oh. I guess you hadn't heard, then."

"Why, no, now that you mention it, I hadn't heard," the older elf replied, good-humouredly drawing Phennil along with him to the bench alongside the path. He pushed the young fellow onto it. "Now," he demanded politely, "I think you should tell me about this. Only slower. If you can."

The dark elf listened while Phennil imparted a most interesting tale with a lot of detail, for Phennil paid close attention and, much as when he was firing arrows, he had a flair for accuracy. Valrayker's mood became dark, then darker still. The darkness was dotted with surprise and even amusement. He felt a twitch at the corner of his mouth as Phennil spoke of the way Kyer *confronted Fredric and set him straight.*

"She's certainly not intimidated easily, is she, sir?" the fair-haired elf said.

"No, she is not that," the dark one acknowledged and nodded thoughtfully. "Thank you, Phennil, for sharing this with me. I think it's time for a chat." Valrayker strode away.

He stepped along the path, considering where he might find Kien's captain. It was no wonder Kyer's concentration had been off. "Betrayed a confidence," indeed! That was an understatement. He was pleased with the way Kyer had dealt with the situation. Yes, she definitely had a few traits that reminded him of himself: a young adventurer, eager to experience life and make things happen. He had to smile. When he recalled the concerns his young captain had expressed only this morning . . . Yes, the two fighters would definitely have a positive effect on one another.

But what struck him the most was her statement about the taking of a life. Such wise words from such a young person! He had met countless soldiers of far more advanced years who had finally come to understand that, and still others who never learned it at all. There again was that inner quality he had spoken of. *I must finish my discussion with Kien.* For she also reminded Val of some other people. What else had Brendow taught her?

Valrayker saw Sir Fredric from across the lawn and hailed him. The knight hesitated but the duke knew the younger man wouldn't dare ignore him. He sauntered over, presenting a cheerful yet respectful curiosity.

"Join me, Sir Fredric." Valrayker's voice was friendly, but his face, solemn. Valrayker stood in the middle of the ward, where there was no danger of any unwelcome ears hiding behind doorways and windows. "I have heard some disturbing reports that concern you, that you have been engaging in some behaviour that is unbecoming to a man of your station. I can't imagine these reports to be true."

Sir Fredric shifted and looked around. "Of course not, sir. You have my word that I would never intentionally treat someone with disrespect."

"That is not the story being circulated, Sir Fredric."

"Who told you?"

"I am not required to reveal my source to you *Sir* Fredric." His eyes locked coldly with the captain's.

"I have nothing but contempt for those who engage in gossip," Sir Fredric said.

"Don't be a coward, Fredric," the dark elf warned, dispelling any notion of Fredric's that he might be fooled. "Live up to the responsibility of your actions. Do not try to shift the focus from yourself by placing blame on others. I *will* have to speak to Kien about this, you know."

The captain nodded but still refused to look directly at Valrayker.

"It may not go well for you. But your situation will not be improved by denying your guilt. Allow me to impart some advice since you clearly need it. Tell the truth to your lord, and you will be treated fairly. If not, Kien will not be merciful."

Nine
A Day of Reckoning

"**A**t last!" Jesqellan exclaimed. "I sent Borograd in there half an hour ago to find you."

"You did not expect me to waste half a pint of ale, did you? Why did you not come in yourself if it was so important?" Mykret spoke dryly but with a smirk on his upper lip, as if he already knew the answer.

"I had a run-in with Trevile only last night," Jesqellan replied irritably. "He has a dark elf-like way of lurking in there, where one cannot see him until he wants to be seen. I didn't want to risk it." The two headed along Harwood Road toward the river.

"He likes speaking to you because he knows it frightens you."

"It does not *frighten* me," Jesqellan snapped. "I just find the nasal quality of his voice to be unpleasantly discordant."

"You are a source of entertainment to him. He hardly ever approaches me anymore."

"I shouldn't think there'd be much point," the bald man grumbled moodily.

"Starling's?"

"Of course." The vast difference in their heights made them an odd-looking pair as they walked the last few paces. Mykret stooped under the door frame after his friend. They squinted into the dimness of the tavern and found themselves a comfortable spot in a booth in the back corner. Their orders were promptly taken by a dark-robed girl who floated noiselessly to the bar to fill their requests.

The proprietor of Starling's had found his establishment was attractive to magic users and did his best to accommodate them. Accordingly, the windows were covered with oiled sheepskin to keep out the afternoon sun. These mysterious folk preferred the gloom; perhaps it inspired their conversation. The place was lit by only the single candle on each table and two or three behind the bar. The only food offered at Starling's was what could sit all day in the one and only pot over the fire, so there was soup or stew, never both. Sometimes bread was available but only if someone had bothered to fetch some from the bakery. The patrons didn't mind. They did not come for the food, as a rule. They came for the tavern's own special brew that helped mages reach their deeper selves, to find clarity, to enhance the broadness of their minds.

"How's that spell coming? The one you were telling me about last time?" Mykret asked, settling into his cushiony seat.

"Oh, the beast summoner?" Jesqellan said casually. "Or the tunnelling?"

Mykret looked impressed, as well he should. "I was thinking of the former."

"Ah, yes, the latter is my newest undertaking. But the summoner. . .? Passably, passably. As well as can be expected what with my recent reconnection with Valrayker. I haven't quite mastered the third step yet."

"Step three already?" his friend replied, nodding in awe. "That's pretty good for only three months. But then, you were always one for speed."

The girl set their tankards before them.

Jesqellan cocked his head in an attempt at modesty. "Though it cannot be said that I sacrifice quality for quickness. No, Mykret, my training as a shaman with my people gave me the ability to achieve a depth of concentration that is difficult for others to reach. That is why I am able to learn as quickly as I am. Not to mention my ability to block out distractions during stressful situations so that the spells can be performed as instantaneously as is necessary amid battle."

"Which is why you are a battle mage, while I am a mere Perceptor." Mykret hooked a long tendril of brown, wavy hair behind his ear. "Now what is it you want me to do for you?"

Jesqellan's eyebrows went up. "I thought you were not in the habit of using your talents on old friends."

"It takes no special skill to know that you have something to ask me, Jesqellan," the other replied. "That is simple observation, like any lay person uses. What is it?"

Jesqellan lowered his voice and glanced over his shoulder. "There is a new member in Valrayker's party. A woman. I have reason to believe that she is not being completely forthright with us and may not have our best interests at heart. I would be grateful if you would . . . do what you can to learn what her intentions are."

Mykret's face darkened. "This has something to do with your discussion with Trevile. That is your 'reason to believe,' yes?"

Jesqellan nodded. There was no point in lying to a Perceptor, especially one who had known him for fifteen years. "It is only that I have sensed magic emanating from her since we first met, and though it could just be residuals from a certain item she won off an opponent, I have my doubts that that is all, and now that Trevile . . ." He trailed off.

Mykret regarded him objectively. "Has she done anything to cause you to distrust her?"

Jesqellan hesitated. "Well, no."

"Then the only reason you wish to learn more about her is because of Trevile?"

"He believes she will bring danger to the party! If I can give Valrayker good reason, he might pull her from the group, and trouble will be avoided."

His friend's face did not change. Jesqellan knew he was lying to himself, but if he could at least postpone problems until later—he was thinking only of the success of Valrayker's mission. "We have an important mission before us," he explained sternly.

His companion swirled the pale liquid around in his tankard. "Jesqellan, you ask me to do something that is against my code of ethics. Yes, there *is* a code of ethics among Perceptors. If you had yourself witnessed any extraordinary behaviour on the part of this woman, or if Valrayker had sent you to me in an official capacity, I might be able to help you. But as it is . . . I cannot go around reading people's minds without just cause. I have the ability, of course. It does not take extra effort on my part to turn it on and off, any more than your body is weakened dramatically by a simple clumsiness spell. But can you imagine what position I would be in if I used my skill continually? I would not be trusted in any society. The only friend I would have would be they who must judge a person's guilt or innocence. Such a skill as mine can be just as much of a curse as it is a blessing, my friend. Would you still keep company with me if I had not sworn to you that I would not read your mind unless you asked me to?"

Jesqellan sighed and shook his head.

"You are still reacting to the discomfort Trevile gave you. My advice is this: wait until you return from your journey," Mykret said. "If at that time you have your own reason to think this woman is of concern to yourself or to Valrayker, come to me, and I will reconsider. In the meantime, if you still want it now, I suggest you go find another Perceptor, perhaps from across the river, where ethics are less prevalent."

Kyer drooled over the hundreds of volumes that filled the shelves in the modestly sized library. It was on the second floor, on the windowless side, for it was up against the inner castle wall, but was made warm and pleasant by an ever-present fire in the grate and the decorations. A portrait of Kien himself oversaw from above the slate mantel, and a life-sized statue of an old elf stood in the corner near it. Armchairs waited here and there, next to handy side tables, and brightly coloured braided rugs warmed the stone floor. But most inviting were the bookcases that lined the walls. A lightweight ladder stood nearby for accessing the higher shelves.

Already Kyer looked forward to a return visit to Shael so she could read all the volumes that snagged her attention. *Bartheylen* was predictably a family history, whereas *Coming of Ages* looked like the story of the southern duchies, how they had been divided originally, and how they were being united under Kien's rule. Some histories of Equart interested her, as did *Heath and Its Peoples,* the history of her home duchy. Shelf upon shelf of fictional stories would have occupied her for weeks. Most of the books were in the Rydrish tongue, but there were many in Elvish and High Elvish.

Then she found the section in the darkest corner of the library. Here were a few volumes so dusty, they couldn't have been touched for decades. The titles were barely readable, but they beckoned to her because they were in Dark Elvish. Kyer had never beheld any written form of Dark Elvish that had not been penned by Brendow.

Contrary to Derry's claim that Valrayker was the only one, there were three people left in Rydris who could read, write, or speak this language. That she was one of them was not a thing she was ready to confide in Valrayker. Brendow had made it clear she must never reveal her knowledge to anyone. The Dark Elves, her trainer had told her, were extremely protective of their secrets. Their language was a key to their very identity; her speaking it could be interpreted as the ultimate violation, subject to what consequences Brendow was not willing to guess.

"Why do you speak it then?" Kyer had asked, careful not to sound impertinent.

Brendow had been unwilling to explain beyond his having "special permission," for reasons he would not share. Kyer had further inferred that if she revealed *her* knowledge, it would follow that *his* identity and whereabouts could be traced, and she respected him too much to risk that.

What would Valrayker do if he found out? Maybe he would have to kill her. The thought unsettled her. This, however, was an opportunity not to be missed. A chance to learn more about dark elves, where they came from, where they had lived, what had become of them! She moved the ladder over to that corner and climbed up to the second shelf from the top. She gently pulled *Crendesh Ferrulann,* or *Hidden Wonders,* off the shelf and tucked it carefully under her arm as she climbed back down. She set the heavy book on a table and moved the ladder so anyone coming in might not see at once which section she had been to. She lit a lamp and curled up in an armchair.

The book in her lap, she carefully lifted the cover and turned it back, the handwritten pages squeaking with age, protesting the unfamiliar movement like atrophied muscles. Eagerly Kyer read about the northern caves in which the Dark Elven people had once made their homes; the crystal palaces that glowed deep beneath the earth from whence much of their riches had come; the immense, carved-out halls of stone that could only be equalled by those of the dwarves, except for the minute delicacy of detail for which the dwarves were not known. And the caves had other properties as well . . .

Kyer was lost in the wonders described and had no awareness of the passage of time. A soft "ahem" startled her, and she slammed the book shut with a bang. Derry stood in the doorway.

She exhaled loudly. "You scared the hell out of me." She hoped her surprise hid her guilt.

"Your teachers must have found you to be a studious pupil."

"Nope. She called me 'fractious' and threw a five-pound doorstop at me."

"Goodness! Were you hurt badly?"

Kyer grinned. "No. To her great vexation, I caught it. She nearly lost her mind, she was so sick of me being mouthy and knowing more than she did."

Derry smiled. "I'm sure Fredric understands her point of view."

A surprised laugh escaped her. Was that evidence of a sense of humour?

"What were you so engrossed in?" he asked.

"Oh, just a boring old history of Heath," she lied, stretching languorously. At least Derry wouldn't be able to make out the title of the book in the dim light. "Is it time for supper yet?"

"Not yet. Actually, I have been looking all over for you. We are both wanted in the hall in a few minutes." His gaze wandered and, to her dismay, landed over her shoulder, somewhere up high.

Alarmed, she stood up, hoping to draw his attention. "I'll be right there. I just have to put this away."

He nodded, paused as if to say something more, then departed.

Shit! She was sure he had just seen the empty place on the shelf where *Crendesh Ferrulann* ought to have been. She hastily moved the ladder back and replaced the book, assuring herself that it was far too dark in this corner for him to have seen the gap between the volumes. Probably he was not familiar enough with Kien's library to know what section that was. She purposefully leaned the ladder up against the shelf that held the history of Heath and pulled it out, wiped the dust off it so it looked as if it had been used recently, and replaced it.

She blew out the lamp and rushed out.

Less than two hours after his talk with Valrayker, Sir Fredric was summoned to the great hall, where he was met with a gathering that dismayed him. Each footfall was painfully audible as he walked the full length of the room. Dread swelled in his heart with each step. Valrayker looked at him with the same warning in his eyes as when they last spoke. Derry was next to his lord, wearing typical Derry pomposity. Kyer, too, was there with her head held straight and her eyes focussed on some indeterminable point in the air. The anger in her face had been replaced with something that resembled indifference, and Fredric couldn't understand how he ever found her attractive. Sergeant Laity and Usher Tompkin were also there, as well as two of the younger lads from the guard. Of all those present in the room, only the sight of one gave him pause.

Kien Bartheylen wore cold sternness like a panther wears its black. The duke was seated at the far end of the hall, his fingers stroking the arms of his chair. After his conversation with Valrayker, Fredric had still been of a mind to try to talk his way out of this difficulty. To at least minimise his own guilt in the affair by pointing out the folly of his men in passing such a foolish tale along, and even hinting at Kyer's lack of discretion. But he saw that look. Valrayker was right. Kien could be ruthless. Far better to be truthful and be dealt more minor consequences than to be seen as a liar and suffer the ultimate wrath of his lord.

⚜

Kyer avoided eye contact with Fredric as he strode into the hall, but she watched him. She watched the way he held his head and gazed around him, like a cocky teenager who is used to getting away with everything. Did he have any idea how angry Kien was? Kyer could see it, and she'd known him less than twenty-four hours.

Fredric bowed. "My Lord Bartheylen."

Kien moved in his chair. "Sir Fredric. Do you know of what you are accused?"

"Yes, My Lord, I believe I do."

Kyer managed to not roll her eyes. *He believes he does.* No, Kyer was pretty sure Fredric hadn't a clue how much trouble he was in.

"I have spoken to the others present about their knowledge of these vile rumours being circulated. You are the captain of my guard and a knight of my banner. Speak now on your own behalf. What do you know of this, and what is your part in it?"

Fredric took a deep breath and spoke with the same ceremonial voice he'd used to greet them upon their arrival at the gate.

"My Lord Kien." He bowed. "I deeply regret that it is true. A delightful evening spent with your guest Kyer has been debased by my ill-considered decision to relate our ... private business to a friend when an apparently untrustworthy younger man was nearby."

"You are their captain," said Kien flatly, ignoring the vain attempt to shift the blame, "and as such are responsible for their behaviour as well as your own. Your actions have not been worthy of your station or of your men."

"Yes, My Lord."

"I would also question your prudence, given your choice to discuss private business of this particular nature even with a friend, let alone when another person was near."

"Yes, My Lord. I humbly apologize to Kyer." Fredric bowed to her.

False humility. But Kyer nodded in return.

"You are gracious, Kyer," Kien said, "considering the indignity you have suffered. I apologize for your treatment in my home. Your first day in Shael has not been as much to your liking as I would have hoped."

"Perhaps not, My Lord. But what's done is done; I am willing to put this behind us."

Kien's stern frown remained fixed on her. She didn't flinch. Fredric had settled into his position, relaxing. Did he think it was over? He was wrong.

The duke placed his eye on his captain again. "Now what of the part of the story that suggests a slur on the character of Lord Valrayker?"

Blood rushed up Fredric's neck and coated his face. "A mere jest, sir," he said with a hint of desperation. "There has been much speculation amongst the men about Kyer's presence in his lordship's party. It was an ill-considered attempt at humour; I didn't dream anyone would take the notion seriously and never intended it to be spread around like the pox." He glanced at the two young soldiers—the unfortunate pair who had met Kyer and Derry in the passageway.

Kyer had to commend his performance. He almost had her convinced that he'd meant it as a joke. Fredric faced the duke of Equart. "Lord Valrayker, I know it to be untrue, and I sincerely regret such a flippant remark." His bow was a silent plea.

"Well said, Sir Fredric. Thank you for both the explanation and the apology." Val's tone was sincere, but Kyer picked up on his sarcasm and had to stare at the stone floor and clench her teeth to keep from smiling.

"That will do, Sir Fredric. Your story matches those of the others present in this room, and I thank you for your honesty. However, there is one other piece in the history that you have not volunteered, and it is the part that disturbs me the most: I am told this is not the first time you have shamed or degraded those around you. And that you have threatened repercussions for anyone who dared inform your superiors of your behaviour. Is this, like the other stories, true?"

Fredric's sudden pallor and widened eyes within a head that looked too heavy for him to hold up anymore, told her he was unprepared for this. Kyer watched him wrestle with his reactions: Would he feign indignation? Claim he was falsely accused? His eyes darted around at the soldiers present. At last he looked only defeated. His voice sounded like chalk. "Yes, My Lord." No excuses, no talking his way out of it. No denying it.

Kien's face was grave. He drummed his fingers on the arm of the chair and rubbed his chin with the other hand. "You have humiliated your men. You have treated women with a deplorable lack of respect. You have flagrantly abused your authority."

"Yes, My Lord." His shoulders sagged but his teeth were clenched.

"Have you anything more to say?"

Fredric took a moment then straightened. "Only, My Lord, that I have erred, and I admit my guilt. I beg of you to remember that I have served you —fervently—since I was a child. I am sorry, My Lord Kien." There. He had cleaned his slate. "It will never, ever happen again."

Kyer actually believed him.

The air hung thick and soundless. Kien's jaw was tight, and a vein in his forehead pulsed more and more persistently as his brow furrowed. Kyer was awed by the duke's self-control, for the stiffness of his body, the whiteness of his knuckles, and the emotions that passed across his face told her Kien could have struck at Fredric like a cobra if his years and wisdom had not taught him restraint.

Kien finally honoured Sir Fredric again with his gaze. "I must admit to the shame I feel at my unawareness of these goings-on." Kien's words tumbled out matter-of-factly, contrary to the emotion he held in check. "You were ... a paragon. Or so I believed. And yet I learn that all this while, your ... *ignominious* behaviour has become commonplace at Shael Castle. Behind my back."

Grasping the arms of the chair, he slowly pushed himself to standing, and Fredric took an involuntary step backward.

"Draw your sword, Sir Fredric," the duke said.

Fredric paled but obeyed. He held the hilt in both hands, and Kyer saw the trepidation in his stance as he tried to be ready for whatever Kien had in mind.

"What is suitable atonement for all your wrongdoings?" Kien ruminated aloud. And suddenly there was a tremendous *crash* as his own greatsword—Kyer hadn't even seen him draw it—clashed with Fredric's, and the knight circled slowly, his weapon locked with his lord's, sweat beading on his forehead and his own death in his eyes. Kien, by contrast, remained stolid. He loomed over Fredric as though the knight were no more than a youth.

The ring of the steel reverberated through the hall and shuddered through Kyer's bones. Only when the echo had ended and the silence became expectantly palpable did he speak again, his voice as cold as the stone floor.

"Perhaps I shall give you the opportunity to decide your own fate," Kien suggested reasonably. "Shall I challenge you to a duel?"

Fredric's voice trembled. "My Lord?" he pleaded.

"If you win, you will have proven your worth. If you lose . . ." Kien stopped circling and chuckled humourlessly. "If you lose, you'll be dead."

Fredric may as well slit his own throat as agree to a duel with Kien Bartheylen. The knight breathed an inaudible sigh of intense relief as Kien withdrew his greatsword and placed its point on the floor. His huge hands rested on the guard.

"It is true that you have served me for over twenty-five years," he said, finally responding to Fredric's words. "And in that time, my standards, the expectations I hold of all my men, ought to have become habitual, ingrained. Instead, you have cast a shadow over this household, this city, this duchy. By association, you have tarnished *my* good name. It is unforgivable."

He stared down at Fredric. Kyer dreaded knowing what he was thinking.

"You have abused the power entrusted to you as my captain. As a result, my only option is to remove you from that power.

"Fredric Heyland." He spoke what sounded to Kyer like a memorised speech, one saved for just this sort of rare occasion. "You are dismissed from the guard of Shael Castle. You are no longer its captain. I hereby relieve you of your knighthood. All items marked with the symbol of Shae Duchy you will forfeit, and you will leave this castle and this city at once, taking only what you can manage on your horse and on your back. You may live anywhere you choose in this duchy, except the city of Shael. Please give me your sword at once: I no longer require its services in your hand." He turned to where the other men stood. "Usher Tompkin. I hereby appoint you captain of the guard of Shael Castle. May you serve it well."

Fredric's face was grey.

Kyer hoped she would never find herself on Kien's bad side.

Fredric had not bargained for this at all. He had thought he might be reprimanded, put in the stocks for a short time, suspended even. But to have his knighthood removed, his captaincy . . . He opened his mouth to speak but could find no words of remonstrance. His gaze locked on the weapon in his hand. The sword his lord had given him had been his constant companion for eight years; to part with it would be like cutting off his arm. Fredric gritted his teeth and swallowed hard. Kneeling, he laid the precious item gently at the feet of Kien Bartheylen, the small clunk of the hilt on the stone startling in the stillness. Then he turned and walked unseeing out of the great hall, a shamed man, never to be welcome in that fair place again.

Fredric Heyland packed his horse and rode out through the gates of the castle he had loved and proudly defended for nearly thirty years. Twenty-four hours after meeting Kyer for the first time, he had lost everything that mattered in his life. His lord, Kien Bartheylen, whom Fredric had served with devotion for so long, had sentenced him to the worst fate imaginable.

He resented his men for allowing the stories to be passed on, he was furious at whoever it was who told Valrayker, and he was angry even with himself for his actions. But more than anything, he hated Kyer Halidan.

Con joined the entry queue at the Sunset Gate along with several others: a few merchants, a coachful of tourists, and a passel of performers. He had put on a hat with a brim but nothing more to alter his appearance; he relied on being just another one of the crowd. He didn't avoid eye contact with the guard, but neither did he maintain it, allowing his gaze to peer into the city as if he were unable to contain his excitement. When asked his purpose, he replied, "Comin' in to meet my girl in time for the festival."

Funny. He wasn't even lying. He passed through into Shael unmolested.

Ten

The Springrites Festival

That evening's meal was a quiet one. Kien did not join them, and Valrayker made only a brief appearance. There was little to no conversation, and no one mentioned Fredric's name.

Kien's words to Fredric had shocked Kyer. She had told Fredric he deserved to lose his knighthood, but she had said it for effect. At first Kyer thought that Kien had treated his captain harshly, that his exile from the city ought to have a time limit, perhaps. But she began to understand why the duke was unforgiving. The more she thought about it, the more Kyer realized that Kien was right: Fredric had rejected all those things he had vowed to uphold, to protect, and to serve. How many other people had he hurt? How long would it have gone on if she herself had not caused it to be brought into the open?

And that is where she faltered. There was one person Kyer had completely forgotten in the heat of the moment. Acadia.

Fredric was Acadia's brother. In the aftermath of her impetuousness, Kyer recognized that she may have inadvertently caused the steward a great deal of pain. Kyer avoided eye contact with Acadia for the rest of that day.

The next morning, the scouts had still not returned. Valrayker told them that the previous day's events merited a break from training. Besides, it was the eve of the new year and a time for celebration, not work. So Kyer approached Derry to take him up on his offer of a tour of the city. Tucked under one arm and concealed under her cloak next to her sword, Kyer carried the chest containing the armlet, which used to belong to Simon Diduck.

The city had undergone a transformation since Kyer's parade to the castle the day before yesterday. From the top of the hill, the view below was awash with colour: flags, streamers, and flowers represented every hue and shade bursting from the soil at this time of year. Kyer and Derry plunged into the sea of merriment that was the Springrites Festival. The blur of activity in the square could have consumed the market in Paterak twenty times over. There were the usual stalls and vendors, plus stages and booths had been erected for musicians, dancers, and magicians all in flamboyantly decorated costumes who performed with an intensity that rivalled a battle. The singing, shouting, and steady stream of laughter surrounded them. In the fresh, clear morning, joy and happiness sparkled and were infectious. Kyer's troubles of yesterday were obliterated, the mission ahead of them set aside.

"This is nothing," Derry told her. "We'll come back in the evening, and you'll see what Springrites really means to these people."

For now, she and Derry squeezed single file through the throng, Kyer clutching the little box, careful not to let Derry get too far ahead of her. They chose not to linger in the market itself since Derry didn't trust the quality of medicinal items sold by transient merchants and preferred to fill his physicking kit from reputable shops with which he was familiar. They left the square to rove up and down the streets, music following wherever they went as buskers with flutes, whistles, tambourines, drums, pipes, and fiddles danced on virtually every street corner.

Accustomed to low-level buildings, Kyer felt tiny next to Shael's gargantuan structures of four or five storeys. With no room for outward expansion within the walls, the city had to expand in an upward direction. Additions to many of the buildings represented a myriad of styles: a jumble of timber, brick, wattle and daub, stone and plaster, all thrown together in a patchwork of beams, angles, and gargoyles. Residents inhabited apartment rooms and worked either below their homes or in separate quarters. Some houses had three storeys above ground and steps leading downward from ground level to cellar spaces. They even boasted tiny gardens with space for a few vegetables or a chicken run.

They went south toward the river and crested the arc in the bridge so Kyer could glimpse the south side: the dark side, where the sun did not reach. Though the river itself was in full sunlight, the far bank was under the heavy shadow of the mighty wall. A few of the buildings stretched vainly sunward, but most did not bother and remained low and dark, like slinking black cats stretched out along the roadside. Their fur was the deep green moss that perpetually clung like parasites to everything that could not walk away, in itself more animal than plant life. Kyer and Derry did not cross to the other side of the bridge.

Eventually they arrived outside an apothecary's shop.

"This is where I like to restock my kit." Derry reached for the door and lowered his voice. "Ulf is a little odd, nervous—maybe it comes from working so closely with pretty strange herbs—but he's knowledgeable, and he has better quality selection than the other place."

"Would he know what this is?" Kyer indicated the chest. "And is he trustworthy enough to take it?"

Derry nodded. "Yes he has some alchemical knowledge. Just let him know who you are, and he won't dare be anything but completely honest with you."

The shop smelled of a pungent blend of herbs and spices and incense, behind which skulked mildew and fungus. Ulf, the apothecary, was helping another customer. While they awaited his attention, Derry moved among the floor-to-ceiling shelves, selecting items for his physicking kit. He told her a bit about each item he needed: which were parts of her favourite salve, which drew out poison, which reduced pain. "Ulf and his son go and find the plants themselves, dry them or extract whatever they need. The other fellow often buys from travelling sellers, and who knows where they came from?"

Once Derry had paid for his collection, Kyer placed the chest on the counter.

The thin-necked man bobbed his head at it. "I don't buy; I sell," he said shortly.

"Good thing I don't want to sell it to you, then," she replied. "I acquired this chest." She lifted the lid. "And I want to know what this device is."

The old man frowned at the contents of the box and raised an eyebrow at it distrustfully. He squinted at her, closing the lid with caution.

"Where did you say you got this?"

"I didn't. I won it."

The apothecary glanced at Derry then back at Kyer, as if he doubted they could possibly be associated with each other.

"Is there a problem?" Kyer said innocently. "I could take it elsewhere if you're unnerved by the task."

The man hastily opened the chest again. "Oh, not at all. It isn't that. It will require some time—a few days, perhaps. Identifying unfamiliar magical devices requires caution."

She nodded. "I am about to embark on a journey for Lord Bartheylen and Lord Valrayker." She paused for the fellow to blanch slightly. "You won't mind hanging on to this for a week or two until I get back, then, will you? Excellent. Good day." She held the door open for Derry and got a glimpse of the unsettled apothecary gingerly picking up the chest and secreting it away in his back room.

Con stepped out from the side of the building and fell in step behind them again.

Kyer, Derry knew, was not one to conceal her emotions easily. He watched, therefore, for her reactions to the sights he showed her. From the tree-lined streets to his description of the city's postal service, the pleasure and awe shone so plainly on her face, it fairly sparkled, and his own excitement fed on this. He shared with her stories of his own experiences in his visits to the city, things he hadn't shared with anyone else: the time he'd had a run-in with a goblin in a seedy tavern on the dark side of the river; the purchase of a new pouch, which was shortly thereafter stolen, thankfully still empty; how the beauty of the singing during the winter solstice on his very first visit to Shael had made tears roll freely down his cheeks. Derry eyed her sidelong. She seemed to be studying him, yet it didn't cause him discomfort. He somehow knew his secrets were safe with Kyer. She may not have shared the same passions, but neither would she laugh at him or mock him to his friends. With some surprise, it occurred to him that the only other person he felt this comfortable with was Valrayker.

Still, it was with some hesitancy that he took her to one of the places in the city that was most special to him. In the northwest quadrant of the city was the temple district, where they passed shrines erected to several of the deities. As Kyer stood by that of Felviona, the goddess of pleasure, Derry watched an irrepressible grin open on her face. Kyer, in turn, watched the tiny fountains on the shrine bubble like laughter, bringing the mirthful marble face of the statue to life. Derry laughed as Kyer contorted her body, in an effort to imitate the goddess's pose, her torso twisted and arms reaching over her head.

"Pity I don't have my sketch book with me," he said.

Kyer laughed and it occurred to Derry that the goddess had influenced the mood.

"Where's the shrine to Guerrin?" Kyer asked as they moved on.

"About a ten-minute walk from here. Would you like to see it?"

She shrugged. "God of War and Battle... I guess he's supposed to be, you know, my patron god, or something, and I just wondered . . ."

"Wondered what?"

She chuckled as if dismissing the thought. "That's nice." She pointed at a granite statue of Kien himself, surrounded by a grove of maples. She had deftly changed the subject.

"Yes." Derry felt a pang of disappointment. He'd opened up to her. Wasn't it customary for her to do the same?

Then they arrived at the place he'd wanted to show her.

Derry stopped before a low building with a peaked slate roof. The double doors were of a light-coloured wood and had been carved with elegant, interlocked circles. His moment of disappointment made him tentative. "This is my favourite temple," he said.

She smiled. With scepticism? With encouragement? The captain couldn't quite tell, but he pressed on.

"The circles on the doors denote the interconnectedness of all things in the world." He watched her think through and identify each of the statues of all eight gods and goddesses that stood in between the pillars at the top of the steps. Derry indicated the statue of Aidan, to the left of the door. Emboldened by her interest, he went on.

"Since I first laid eyes on that particular depiction of her, I loved it," he said. "See the look in her eye? There is lifelike caring and love in that eye. *This* is what I think she would really look like."

Kyer didn't say anything. Somewhat embarrassed, he needed to clarify.

"I guess there's a part of me that hopes they are real. I have a hard time . . . trusting the gods." He felt a familiar tightness in his chest and a memory of a dark night in Equart flashed across his mind.

"What do you mean?"

He hesitated, choosing his words. "The clerics tell us they are truly a part of our world and tell us how to worship them. But the gods don't seem to ever get involved." He paused. She would either understand or she wouldn't. "I hope I don't offend you."

She said nothing for a moment. Was she tactfully telling him she wasn't interested?

"What I was meaning to say before," she said finally, "was that I wondered if—if Guerrin might pay more *attention* here in the city. I haven't decided about them either. I always felt like I had to manage on my own. I wondered if I'd feel . . . *something* from him here. Because I don't back in Hreth." Then she quickly added. "It's a nice temple, though."

"Yes, it's nice to come here and sit inside and feel peaceful."

The doors opened and a crowd of worshippers poured out, threatening to knock the two observers off the steps. "Except at new year," Derry finished.

They headed back toward the main road. "Fredric offered me a tour of the city," Kyer said. "I turned him down because you had offered first." She looked up at him. "I think the things he would have shown me would have been, by comparison, soulless."

He smiled.

"We're going to come back tonight, right?" she said.

"If you wish."

"I think I'd like to see the party in full swing."

It was some time past noon, and their stomachs began to summon their attention. Derry led her to a tavern he knew of.

The Harvest Moon was a popular place. Right on a corner, it was visible from several directions, and a good many people had noticed it today. Derry and Kyer squeezed inside past a mass of other patrons and crammed in against the wall to wait for seats. A girl passed with a large tray of beverages, looking hot and harassed, her hair escaping her braids. Another carried plates of food that left a wake of delicious aromas. An elven fiddler sat in the corner at the end of the bar, next to the empty fireplace. The crowd called him by name and yelled out requests for songs.

"Play tha' one—tha' one with the shailor on the island, hazh a bear in it," slurred one individual who had started his evening revelry much earlier than was considered typical. But the musician knew what he meant and obliged immediately.

Finally two stools became vacant at the end of the bar farthest from the entertainer. Kyer took the seat on the end and Derry the next one. They ordered ale and Derry raised his mug.

"To—" Derry stopped, uncertain. "Friends?"

She smiled. "To friends," she agreed.

Derry sipped and felt pleasantly warm. He lowered his mug to see Kyer continuing to drink. And drink. He couldn't help but grin, and when she finally plunked her tankard on the bar again, she noticed his amusement.

"You're not enjoying that at all, are you?" he said.

"Nope, it's pretty hideous." She took a few more large swallows

"Wait until you taste the food."

"Yeah, it all looks positively indigestible." Her gaze followed a trayful of meals passing her on its way to a far table. Derry's mouth watered as the aroma flowed around his head. His light breakfast of a pear and some milk was but a distant memory.

Shepherd's pie was the special of the day. Derry found that the lamb was chopped instead of minced, so the fact that it was cooked to perfection could not escape him. It melted on his tongue, and its juices mingled delicately with the potato; the flavour of neither was overpowered. A hint of rosemary —

Suddenly next to him, Kyer flung herself onto the floor.

She landed right in the path of a server whose tray dumped over, heaping Kyer with half-empty bowls, dirty plates, and tankards with foam still clinging to the rims. The crash drew the attention of practically everyone in the place, apart from those caught up in the music, who demanded the song continue.

Derry stared, open mouthed, as amid the server's babbled apologies and exclamations, Kyer finally hauled herself to her feet. In her right hand was a dagger, its tip darkened with a spot of blood. Her left arm clutched a yelping heap of colour. At first instinct, Derry thought it might be a wayward child, but when she pulled it out from under her cloak, it was a fully grown halfling.

He was dressed in a canary-yellow tunic with a scarlet cravat and tall boots that matched his moss-green cape. The top of his curly head didn't even reach Kyer's armpit, and his eyes were narrow with uncertainty, as if he were concocting a way to get out of his predicament. A shallow cut in his right cheek indicated where her dagger had evidently made contact. He abruptly let go of her money pouch and raised his hands, palms out. The money pouch, still attached to her belt, dropped back into place.

"I know what you were after. Don't try to pretend you were polishing my boots." Kyer sneered at him.

Derry was more or less poised to help her, but he didn't think she would need it.

"Dear lady," the halfling said grandly, bowing deeply. "Are you in town for the festival?"

Kyer gaped at him in bewilderment at his contradictory demeanour. "No," she corrected him carefully. "I am in town because I am a guest of Lord Bartheylen."

The halfling's eyes widened at the mention of the duke's name, but his dignified manner did not change. "I do apologize for confusing you with someone else," he said with a sweep of his cape. Kyer grabbed it and tugged him back.

The proprietor of the tavern arrived then and stood, red faced, next to the bar.

"What's the trouble?" he barked. He turned sharply to the horrified waitress. "Maia, what have you done?"

"It wasn't her fault," Kyer said sourly, not taking her eyes off the halfling. "I got in her way while preventing my money from being stolen by this outrageous pickpocket of yours."

The proprietor immediately flushed with ire and embarrassment and shouted incensed obscenities at the halfling. The little fellow quailed in spite of his strange gentlemanly behaviour and tried to shrink away, decreasing his already minimal stature. Kyer assured her host that she would take care of it and sheathed the dagger, drawing her sword instead. The proprietor murmured apologies for such a thing occurring in his establishment, while Kyer instructed the halfling to aid the waitress in cleaning up the mess. She sat on her stool and continued her meal while occasionally prodding the halfling when it looked as if he were letting the girl do too much of the work.

When the area was tidy again, Kyer went about the crowded room, halfling in tow, and asked at each table if anyone was missing anything. She ordered him to return stolen items and apologize. Only when every one of his pockets was empty did Kyer order him to leave the place. He did so at the fastest trot ever used by one of his kind.

Derry had all but finished his pie when she returned to sit next to him. The proprietor bustled over.

"Please accept your meals on the house with my thanks for what you have done."

Kyer and Derry nodded their thanks and cleaned the last morsels from their plates. Soon after, they made room for more hungry patrons by vacating the inn. Derry held his tongue until they were several blocks down the street.

"You know, being in your company is never going to make me drowsy."

Con watched the young man and woman cross the street. No point in wasting any more time today; he knew where to find her tonight.

"I am reluctant to agree with you." Kien stalked the length of his antechamber. "It is her home village; she has a right to know it has been flattened."

"Yes," Valrayker repeated with patient vehemence from his wing-backed chair. "But think about it: What is the first thing she would do?"

"Go back, of course," Kien said.

"And how wise would that be under the circumstances?"

"But only if you are right in your suspicions."

Val shrugged. "Granted. But I don't believe in coincidences. And the timing is significant. I haven't received any kind of message, so I have to assume that for some reason, Bren d'Athlan has had her under his wing."

"And that he sent her away?"

"*Just* before the village was attacked." Valrayker tapped the arms of the chair with his fingertips. "It could even be that my sword, that she herself *is* the message."

"And how will you find out? It's rather delicate."

"Quite. I shall have to . . . bide my time and observe."

"By then it will be too late for her to do anything about the trouble in Hreth."

"Kien." Valrayker's voice was low. "Even if I'm wrong, it's already too late for that."

The high elf stared at him with cold fire in his grey eyes. He resumed his pacing. "Why can't you just ask her?"

Valrayker looked at his friend as if he had asked him to dance a polka.

With a deep sigh, Kien rooted himself in the middle of the room, hands clasped behind him. "Very well, old friend. We will say nothing."

When Kyer announced during supper that she and Derry would be going into the city for the evening's festivities, Phennil asked if he could join them. Derry was silent but Kyer said, "Sure." To exclude the elf seemed wrong, despite him not being Derry's favourite companion. Shortly after the meal, the trio walked down the flagstone path. Kyer noticed an extra body following them. It was Valrayker.

"Can I come too?" He sounded as eager as a six-year-old.

"Of course," Derry said.

Kyer said, "I thought you and Kien would have all kinds of important stuff to discuss."

"Nah, we don't need to spend every waking moment together. Besides, I'm on holidays now that you all are almost ready to go."

It crossed her mind that she, Derry, and Phennil weren't simply people who worked for him; they were also his friends. The glance over his shoulder at the north gate of the city was proof that his mind was not completely off his worries, but he made a good show of it.

The sun was setting in brilliant reds, oranges, pinks, and purples as the little party emerged from the castle gate. They paused on the hill and gazed at the breathtaking spectacle that stretched halfway toward them across the sky. Wordlessly they watched as the colours deepened to violet and sapphire and retreated, drawing in on themselves, sinking into the horizon. Behind them the expanse of indigo was dotted with the first stars, and finally it faded to blackness in the east. Her feet rooted to the path, Kyer could not have turned away if she wanted to. The faint sounds of revelry below did not interrupt the scene but enhanced it, providing the music to welcome the stars. Every one of them breathed a sigh as the last of the magical colours dived down below the edge of the world. As if in response, a light breeze whisked around the edges of their cloaks and sailed upward to greet the coming night.

Phennil was, not surprisingly, the first to find words. This time, though, he spoke with quiet reverence. "Wow. That was stunning. Where I come from, you're so secluded in the trees that you don't see that kind of thing. Out and about the Guarded Realm, though, you get to experience the Sky Spirits. Now *that* is truly something to see!"

They continued down the hill, each one depositing those swift moments in a memory to be treasured again later.

Con rubbed his chest as he watched the girl and her friends descend the hill. She walked by him, five sword lengths away from where he sat on the step at the edge of the square. Tonight, in all the crowd, there would be an opportunity to separate her from the rest. He waited a decent interval then fell in a few paces behind them.

There was such a hubbub in the square, Kyer doubted anyone had even noticed the sunset. Kyer had thought it busy earlier in the day; now there was not just a crowd of people but hordes of revellers pushing to get a better view of the performers. She was glad she'd left all but a few coins in her room, just in case another halfling should come along and be lower profile than the last. More than once she was heavily jostled and saved from falling only by the closeness of the person she was knocked into. People shoved to make way for the parade of jugglers on stilts with lanterns and drums.

Torches on tall posts sputtered overhead, illuminating what the eclipsed new moon did not. The huge lanterns carried by masked creatures made the wild-looking fanged and tusked face coverings exaggerated and grotesque. The angular shadows dripped off them in the way that spit and foam would on the real thing. Over to Kyer's right, a group of drummers carried on a musical conversation, large, deeply resonating drums responding to the comments of shallow, higher-pitched ones. Off to the left, a vigorous trio of singers step-danced and belted out rousing harmonies, accompanied by fiddle and flute. Up ahead on one of the stages, a brave rogue dressed in nothing but a tattered loincloth danced lewdly and gulped flaming torches the way Kyer had often attacked a hunk of meat on a skewer.

With the new Swan Moon came the Rydris new year. Springrites was the official end of winter, the beginning of spring, embodied by the mating of animals, the start of new growth, new life. Further to that, conception of a child during Springrites was a blessing, meaning an easy pregnancy and a long and healthy life for the child. Kyer couldn't help but notice that much of the entertainment was *inspiring* to that goal. It was a celebration of every kind of love. Some couples were so deeply inspired, they couldn't wait until they got home; one couple found a sorry excuse for privacy up against an ale vendor's booth, and another was tucked in behind one of the stages.

Business boomed for ale and spirit vendors. They were spaced at regular intervals throughout the square, so as the last drop of one cup was drained, there was always more to hand. Even at this early hour, a few men and women were completely soused but continued to drink and meander through the crowds, barely able to stay on their feet. Derry steered Kyer around a pool of muck where someone had had to purge himself before heading back for more.

The group was suddenly overtaken by a parade of dancers, pipers, and drummers. Four men held up long poles on which lanterns were suspended from hooks, forming a rectangular moving stage area around the performers. The women were clad in strips of brown and green cloth that barely concealed their most interesting areas. Their hair was dyed strange colours with ribbons woven through it. It was as wild as their dancing, hopping, jigging, undulating. The men had painted their torsos and faces, and some wore masks to look like fantastical bears, deer, birds, and fish. They had torn old trousers to knee-length shreds and danced barefoot, kicking their knees up to nearly shoulder height. Kyer clapped in time with the music, and her face ached from grinning.

Con wove through the throng, his left hand making itself comfortable on the hilt of his dagger. There she was. Just ahead. Oblivious. A few more steps, and he could—

One of the dancers grabbed Kyer by the arm and pulled her into the dance, holding her body close to his and whirling around and around until she was dizzy and laughing so uncontrollably, she could hardly keep on her feet. The music reeled and the dancers chased it. Her very male partner smelled of body paint, spirits, and sweat. She breathed deeply, intoxicated by it. She was seized with an understanding of why Springrites could be so appealing.

Phennil and Valrayker had been similarly accosted, the former showing up his partner with his nimble feet. Only Derry was spared, but as she went around, Kyer caught a glimpse of his mirthful smile as he clapped along. Amid a cheering crowd, she tipped her head back and laughed, hooting and hollering along with her partner until it finally ended and she was released, staggering, over to Derry.

"Whoa there!" He laughed as he steadied her until her head stopped spinning. The man who had held her so seductively beckoned to her with an inviting leer, but she waved her rejection, and he moved on.

The two elves returned, Phennil looking cheerful and in control as if nothing had happened, whereas Valrayker said, "I think I'm going to puke." But he didn't. They stumbled, laughing, along to the next performance.

Con cursed as his mark was surrounded by her friends again. *Patience,* he told himself. *The right time will present itself.* Ah. Up ahead the group had stopped again.

The friends neared another stage, where a small figure was juggling a club, a clay bowl, and an egg while singing "When My Love Comes Home Again" in a hearty voice.

Kyer grabbed Derry's arm in disbelief and pointed at the halfling from the Harvest Moon. The cut was still visible on his cheek.

Derry said, "He appears to be a much better juggler than he is a pickpocket."

When the song was over, the little fellow swung the club around and clutched it under one arm, then caught first the bowl then the egg, which he cracked into it.

"Anyone hungry?" he offered, eyes spanning his cheering audience until they rested on Kyer. She began to clap in spite of herself. He bowed and reached into his vest.

Con's grin overtook the half of his face that functioned. All eyes were on the halfling. No one would notice the sudden departure of one of the crowd. The knife came up, still concealed, ready to fit neatly into the small of her back. *Quick now.*

The halfling pulled out a bouquet of dried flowers and tossed it to Kyer with a grandiose gesture. She caught it, completely befuddled. How was she supposed to react when given flowers by a strange creature who had tried to steal money from her not eight hours prior?

And before she knew it, he was there in front of her, to the amazement of all her companions. Down on one knee, he barely reached her hip, but he took her hand and kissed it.

Con melted back into the crowd, breathing heavily. He nearly hadn't checked himself in time. Had he been one instant sooner, the eyes of all would have followed the halfling to rest on him as well as the girl.

"Dear lady, I am your humble servant," the preposterous fellow orated. "Skimnoddle is my name, and I would like—nay, I *must* tell you how utterly enchanting you are. You are indeed the most beautiful, bewitching creature I have ever laid eyes on, and if I may beg but one kiss from those sweet lips, I would be the most gratified—nay!—*honoured* halfling in all of Rydris!"

Kyer was too befuddled to even laugh. Her jaw gaped unattractively. Derry looked stern; Phennil, confused; and Valrayker, pleased as punch with the little man.

Skimnoddle didn't stop there. "You are speechless. Perhaps you think I have forgotten the events of this afternoon? Nay! I assure you I have thought of nothing else these seven hours and twenty-six minutes! When you released me and I first beheld your exquisite countenance, I was dazzled by your resplendence. You are, in short—and I know not how to put it more accurately—*pulchritudinous*!"

It could not be borne. Kyer finally gasped out a laugh and shook her head in bafflement. "I don't even know what that means! What is the *matter* with you? Get up, for gods' sake."

He did so, with a hand on his heart. "If it would please the lady, I will do it!"

"Okay, you know what?" Kyer slapped a hand on her forehead. "I don't know what you've been drinking, but you are by far the most outlandish person I have ever met. I want you to go away from me now. And stay away." She pushed the flowers into his hands and turned on her heel, leaving him crying, "Refused! Denied! Repudiated!" to her back as she pushed her way through the crowd. Soon she became aware of Derry's tall figure alongside her.

When they reached the outskirts of the square, where the crowd was thinner, she paused for him to catch up. "I've had enough," she said. "I'm going back to the castle. You don't have to cut your evening short on my account, though." He assured her that he, too, had seen plenty of revelry for one night, and they started up the hill.

"I think I need a nice, quiet glass of wine. Would you care to join me?"

He said nothing, responding with a nod, but his silence held an undercurrent of subdued amusement. Finally, when they reached the gate, Derry murmured, "Like I said, never a dull moment."

She managed to not slug him.

Con leaned breathlessly against a booth and rubbed the numbness surrounding the scar on his face. He decided to call it a night. He was too desperate. *Wait for it. She will come to you.*

Several hours and as many cups of wine each later, Kyer let the last drops of nectar linger on her tongue. She closed her eyes and sighed deeply.

"Do you suppose it's time for bed?"

She opened her eyes to find Derry watching her, his lips parted.

The clarity in his blue eyes startled her, and the smile that played on her mouth melted away. Wordlessly they rose and she broke the eye contact. They reached the door at the same time, both extended their hands. A slight hesitation as they looked at each other. A small smile passed between them, and Derry let his hand drop.

She passed through the door, and just as she turned to approach the entrance to the stairs, Kyer was startled by a voice from above.

"Kyer." It was Acadia. Kyer hesitated. The steward's cloaked figure floated down the stairs, saying nothing more until she reached them. Kyer, confused by the abrupt switch from one mood to another, was particularly entranced by the candelabra on the table. It held five candles.

"Good evening, Acadia. You're up late," Derry said with a bow.

"Yes, I—couldn't sleep. Kyer, I am in need of a walk. Please, would you walk with me?"

Kyer nodded. *Now's as good a time as any to talk this out.* She said good night to Derry over her shoulder. With a short bow, he turned away.

The two young women went out the door and stepped slowly along the path. The night was still, the noise from the festival checked by the high walls. Kyer was glad she had her cloak. They walked in fresh, cool silence for a while.

"You are very fortunate—to have Derry in your party," Acadia said finally.

"Yes. He's a good man." She was curious about the depth of Acadia's feeling for her friend. But this wasn't what the fair-haired woman wanted to speak to her about.

"Kyer, I—" She took a breath. "I feel awkward even approaching you about this, but you probably know why I want to speak with you."

"I suppose I do." Kyer kept her eyes ahead on the path.

"I wanted you to know that I do not harbour any resentment toward you."

Kyer stopped by the bench under the cherry tree. "You don't? I wouldn't blame you if you did. It's my fault Fredric's gone." The scent of blossoms wafted down.

"That's where I think you're wrong," her companion said in the tone of one who is used to speaking and being listened to. "It's Fredric's fault he's gone, Kyer. He has been guilty of more than one indiscretion; you aren't the only victim of his . . . insensitivity." Her quelled vehemence told Kyer that Acadia spoke on full authority. "It took many years of ill behaviour to arrive at such a result," the steward continued. "If his only mistake was to talk of his relations with you, then Kien would never have reacted as strongly as he did."

"But I was the one who caused it all to come out. I meant only to let him know he couldn't get away with treating me like that. I had no idea it would go so far."

Acadia spoke firmly. "I've thought of nothing else since Usher told me all about it yesterday. It may take some time, but I believe that most people will not censure you for your involvement in this but thank you."

"But he's your brother!" Kyer exclaimed. "You may never see him again. How can you not hate me?"

"Do you want me to?" Acadia asked thoughtfully.

"No, of course not." Kyer was faintly pleased that her companion would speak so pointedly. "Just the opposite, in fact. I suppose I was worried that you would," she admitted to the leaves above her head. "I . . . don't have many friends."

"Neither have I." Acadia sat with a heavy sigh. "Have you any brothers or sisters, Kyer?"

Kyer shook her head then said, "No," because she realized Acadia wouldn't see her gesture in the darkness.

"Fredric left home before I was born. He was twelve. I lived at home with our parents until I was fifteen. So I was an only child as well. When Mother and Father died, I came here to the castle. Fredric was here; he was my only family. I think he felt that he ought to play the part of Father for me. But I didn't *know* him. He's more like a distant uncle than what I imagine a brother ought to be. And we haven't always been on . . . the best of terms. Sometimes I felt I was in his way, an inconvenience. He would criticise me just as easily as he did his men. He even tried to make me believe I was given the position of steward because he's captain."

"But that's ridiculous," Kyer said automatically. "You're perfect for the job."

"Thank you. It was only recently that I found myself able to accept that." The darkness seemed to reveal the bitterness she would otherwise have concealed. "Do you know what I wanted to be? I've never told anyone else. I was once an apprentice healer. I was perfect for that job too. Even more so."

Kyer sat down at the other end of the bench. "What happened?"

"My parents were taken with fever the winter after Fredric was made captain. I tried . . . everything." Her voice tightened. "I was with them day and night. I used compresses. I gave them broths and ointments. I nearly exhausted myself with energy transference. But I couldn't save them." A sob escaped and was hastily dampened. "For the first two months I was here, Fredric didn't say a word to me. For years, I believed it was my fault our parents were dead."

Kyer tried to think of something to say, but consoling was not her strength.

Acadia took a breath and puffed it out. "But you're a warrior." She adopted a cheerful tone, and her words tumbled out like a brook. "You don't want to hear about all that. I only wanted you to be aware that you needn't be concerned that you've hurt me by your part in Fredric's dismissal."

"I'm glad of that. But I don't—"

"In fact." Acadia rose. "Let me be the first." She extended her hand. "Thank you."

Kyer shook her hand awkwardly and did not know what to say. "You're welcome" seemed inappropriate, somehow.

The scouts arrived the next day. After a short meeting with them, Valrayker pronounced the all-clear. There followed a day of hurried preparation, leaving no room for getting to know anyone from the duke's other teams. Kyer caught sight of a female elf, very pale and austere, with the typical disdain of a snow elf, just before the latter withdrew to keep entirely to herself.

Kyer had few preparations for the last minute, so she picked up her leather cuirass from the armoury, where its small gashes had been repaired. She asked Phennil to go into the city to fetch the few things she needed. She had had enough of the sights and experiences of Shael and was reluctant to risk running into Skimnoddle the halfling again. Ever. The elf was more than willing to oblige.

Phennil left the general store loving the world. He grinned at passersby and said hello to anyone who would make eye contact with him. He would ride this wave of pride and self-satisfaction for days, and if it continued to carry him this high off the ground all the way to Nennia, it would be an easy journey indeed. His instinct upon first glance at the other customer had been to mistrust him. The odd paralysis on one side of the man's face made him look gargoylish. But when Phennil noticed the long scar, he reproached himself for judging a man's character based on facial damage. The poor fellow had been wounded. Did he deserve to be shunned for the rest of his days? And once the elf had got past his initial reaction, he had found the man to be quite chatty. *What an amiable chap!* Phennil grinned again, and a woman peered over her shoulder at him as she passed. He was certain he had not even looked startled when the man smiled with only half of his face as they bade each other good day.

Kien gave them each a vial of healing potion as a farewell gift. "Not to heal injuries, but to prevent them. It always seems that the only time I am injured is when I do not have any healing potion on hand," he joked. "If it weren't impractical, I would fill your saddlebags with them!"

Just after dawn, they made their farewells to Governor Lyndon and Acadia in the foyer. The young woman was pleasant and genuinely sorry to see them go. Kyer observed a peace about her that she had not seen before, even heard her laugh. *She truly seems to be fine.* She shook the fair woman's hand and sincerely wished her well.

Kien and Valrayker accompanied them to the castle gates and watched as the party took the secluded road around to the right of the wall. The distant sounds of the Springrites revelry underscored the departure, and Kyer turned to give a final wave to the two dukes. *Now the waiting began for them.* The horses went around the northeast tower, and the castle entrance was out of sight.

The northern High Gate was much less travelled than the others—a more suitable exit for a group setting out on a mission for the dukes of Equart and Shae. The guards stood at attention as the group of five passed through the gate. This time Kyer did not turn but looked at the road ahead. Her first mission had now begun.

Eleven

What a Beautiful Morning

Kyer couldn't imagine anything going wrong on such a beautiful morning.

They were two days out of Shael, and Swan Moon was waxing, awakening the new year with it. The clearing in which they were camped was about two furlongs from the road, nestled up against a hillock and surrounded by paper birch trees. She had the last watch of the night, waiting for the sun to hurry up and rise. She found the peace and solitude of the watch restful, allowing her to meditate and reflect. She looked up through the still leaves; a thin veil of early-morning cloud deprived her of the joy and wonder of the stars. But no matter, all was calm. She continued her methodical movement around the camp, stepping over Phennil's outflung arm. The rhythmic breathing of her friends, the occasional soft snore, Derry rolling over again as if dreaming he was cross. She neither saw nor heard anything that could not be attributed to the activities of the local wildlife. Everything was as it should be. Strange, then, that she should feel so nervously expectant.

She paused her steps to stroke Trig's neck. Her companion nickered, his breath warm and smelling like sweet grass. Still, she could not shake the restlessness. The darkness in the camp was thinning, so she dismissed her nerves in favour of making breakfast. Between short walks around the camp to look and to listen, she put a pot of water and oats on the fire and collected bits and pieces of foodstuffs from each person's saddlebags to create a thick porridge: some wrinkled but sweet apples, two pears, and some spices that Phennil always carried with him.

While the porridge cooked, she rolled up her bedroll then brushed and braided her hair. She served herself a cupful of the mess and carried it around with her to eat it while she continued her watch. The sun was making its presence known, but the freshness of the air still made her shiver. The hot food lifted the chill. Usually her cooking left a lot to be desired, but this actually tasted very good. She toyed with the idea of tossing a handful of dirt into it so the rest of them wouldn't come to expect it from her.

The sun's early rays were winning the war over possession of the camp. They shone through the trees onto dewdrops, turning the area into a fairyland of sparkles. It was truly a beautiful morning. Jesqellan was the first to stir, and she wordlessly indicated that he should help himself to breakfast. She took off her armour, slung her weapon belt over her shoulder, and followed a short path with natural steps created by tree roots that led down to the rocky edge of the river. A low waterfall tumbled over the wall of jagged stone a dozen or so paces upstream. Downstream, the water disappeared around the bend of the hillock by the camp.

Her boots left shallow imprints in the sand at the edge of the stream. The spring melt had packed it down hard, and it was moist but not muddy. Across the stream, massive willow trees perched precariously on the steep embankment, their branches cascading into the water. More birches and firs beyond the willows came alive with birds and squirrels who loudly expounded on their own enjoyment of the morning. The very air carried the scent of spring and the fresh spray. At the foot of the waterfall was a good-sized waterhole, but only a snow elf would enjoy such a plunge at this time of year. Instead, Kyer found a suitable spot next to a pool about the size of a washtub and crouched down in the frosty-fresh spray, placing her belt next to her.

She dipped her hands in the pool of fresh, clear water and splashed it up on her face, the cool liquid bracing as it trickled down her neck. Her medallion escaped from her tunic and swung down, annoyingly in her way. She drew the chain over her head, folded it around the medallion, and tucked it into her pocket, where it was secure enough to not fall out. The rush of water tumbled over the falls and splashed around over the rocks, and she found herself humming as she repeated the action several times. She felt . . . happy. It had been a long time since she'd felt this way. *Correction: I've never really felt this way.* She took one final splash of water on her face and began to shake the water off her hands. Her eyes were shut, and her ears, full of the sound of the running water.

A force pushed the back of her head, dunking her face-first into the frigid water. Her gasp of surprise was her only intake of breath as she toppled forward. Instinct stifled her scream, so she didn't inhale water. Blood freezing in the cold, her frantic attempts to pull herself up were checked by the large hand that gripped her hair and held her under the terrible glacial silence. Panic tightened her chest. Her limbs flailed, thrashed, useless, unable to reach or grab or kick or fight or— Her right arm was wrenched behind her back. A yank on her hair hauled her up, coughing and spluttering, lungs sucking in precious air. Before a single thought could form in her drenched mind, her other arm was pinned to her side as a hand clamped over her mouth. A muted *shring* of metal and a splash told her what became of her sword.

He was not a small man. And he smelled worse than Phennil.

He gripped her like a steer about to be branded. She gasped short, sharp breaths. *My ribs are about to cave in.* Though she kicked furiously, she only made him stumble as he hefted her several hurried paces along the stream. Her heart clunked against her chest. All she saw were the willows on the far bank and the sky. With a grunt of effort, her assailant flung her over the withers of a horse, in the lap of the man in the saddle.

Mid-moan, she arrested the sound as the point of the rider's knife touched her throat. They obviously wanted her alive, but she dared not call his bluff. Before she had a chance to take one full, deep, glorious breath, they started to move, and wind was knocked out of her as the horse's withers dug into her gut. Pain wracked her. Kyer couldn't tell where they were headed. She blinked water out of her eyes as they splashed through it and heard several other horses join them. She grunted with throbbing breaths as the horse climbed the grassy bench on the opposite bank of the stream.

Jesqellan watched Kyer descend the path to the river. He'd filled his cup with porridge, and stood at the head of the path where he could still see her. The others were in various stages of waking. In the gaps between trees, he saw Kyer select a pool and kneel down.

"Now whose turn is it to sneak a look at her while she's bathing?" Phennil called from the fire where he dished up his own breakfast.

Jesqellan did not turn his head. "I am certain Kyer will find comfort in knowing that *one* of us is looking out for her, bearing in mind that she has been relentlessly pursued since the day we left Wanaka." He told himself that Trevile's foreboding words had nothing whatever to do with his decision to stand here.

"Well, sure. I was just kidding." The elf sounded sheepish.

Not a moment later, a thudding sound from the west side of the camp jerked Jesqellan's attention away from his charge. His and Phennil's eyes met just as Phennil sharply called out.

"Intruder!"

The company moved as one, scrambling for weapons. Phennil dropped his cup to snatch his bow and Jesqellan calmly hastened back toward the camp. No woodland creature Jesqellan was familiar with made a sound like that. A low growl came from behind the hillock.

"Ogre!" Janak yelled as it appeared, crashing into the camp. There was no time to take a breath. It was upon them.

The knife had been removed from her throat; still, there was nothing she could do but gasp for breaths. Bouncing like a piece of game they had hunted down, she pushed herself up with her elbows to relieve the jolting and the rhythmic knocking against her gut. Her captor walloped her in the back. She groaned. Her short breaths exited with strangled moans, and her body ached more and more with each jarring bump. It was like a hundred kicks to her belly.

Finally—Kyer had no idea how much time had passed—they reined in and stopped. She choked dusty air in and soon felt a shove and landed hard on the ground. She curled up, lungs heaving. Her rib cage ached from jostling, her neck throbbed, and her whole body felt stiff as a tree branch. Two men grabbed her and tied her hands behind her back and her feet together. Perversely she wondered where they thought she would go if they left her untied. She wore no armour, for which she cursed herself, and her sword was at the bottom of a pool. More cursing. She hadn't been wearing a weapon belt, so their quick search included just her trouser legs and boots, which rewarded them with her boot knife. Still more cursing. There was nothing for it but to wait and see what was in store for her. She didn't think for a moment that it would be much fun. Shifting, she took a look at the company.

She'd had a pretty strong suspicion of who her riding companion was, and she celebrated her correct deduction. Eight men heartily congratulated themselves. They were rough-looking men, burly, unshaven, *dirty*. The lap she had just disembarked was the very lap she had briefly occupied the night they left Wanaka. It and the scarred face belonged to Ronav's man. When she'd stabbed him, only the left side of his mouth had opened. The other had appeared tight and still, as if the muscles were frozen.

"How's the chest wound healing up?" The words escaped her mouth automatically.

Wiping sweat off his horse, he stopped mid stroke. Her heart hammered in her throat as she met his eyes. "Whoops, was that out loud?" she said.

The scarred man's nostrils tightened in visible hatred. "The Highness said he wanted you alive, but he didn't say he wanted you undamaged." He hauled her up by the front of her tunic, and she gasped with the pain in her stomach. "There's plenty o' things I could do to you where you'd still be able to talk after."

She cringed away from his touch and the stench of his hot breath. He shook her violently so her teeth knocked together then thrust her to the ground. She curled up, suppressing a moan. Fear was a useless emotion; Kyer pressed it down into her belly. Anger drifted into its place.

"Yep, she made it easy for us this time, eh, Con?" a barrel-chested fellow said as he wiped sweat off his horse. He might have been the one who'd accosted her at the stream.

"Finally," said another. "Who'd a' thought it would be so hard to pick up a girl?"

Con barked at his men to shut it. He did his task with brisk, sharp movements, and Kyer stared with horrified fascination at the jagged scar that ran from his jaw to up past his temple. His right eyebrow and the corner of his mouth drooped. Kyer surmised that her previous escape had given Con two wounds, the greater of them not from where she had stabbed him.

Finished with his mount, he shot a glare at her and went to join his comrades. He removed a small sack from a pocket and took a pinch of some kind of leaf or fungus, rolling it expertly in another small leaf. Soon the pungent, mouldy smell of *solawid* shared the air with the grass and clover. Kyer wondered if this was a celebratory smoke or one to get him through.

The one who had spoken first looked over at her as she lay on the dusty grass and clover. She stared back at him. He laughed.

"Look at you, all trussed up, a pig ready for slaugh'er." He sauntered over to her. "Quite a bit different from when you escaped from Con before. You were so cocksure o' yourself."

She looked at the huge man as levelly as she could from the ground. "I got away, though, didn't I?" Her voice was hoarse. "And you weren't even there. Or else you'd be dead."

His facial features tightened, and he looked ready to kick her. He crouched down next to her. "You've done it now, 'aven't you?" he said contemptuously. "Going off on your own like that this morning, you played right into our 'ands." She agreed with him but didn't say so. He grinned. "We didn't even need our secret weapon. But we used it anyway, and now your unsuspecting friends 'ave probably been disembowelled." He left her with that and walked away.

Kyer's mind teemed with curiosity about this secret weapon, and her fear rebelled against the force that held it at bay. She tried to suppress her imagination. It was nothing her friends couldn't handle. He was bluffing, hoping to undermine her confidence. She didn't know where she was but deduced that the horses had come out of the river on the west side. There were no trees in sight.

An idea struck her, and she idly rubbed her foot in the dry dirt among tufted grass, a clue for Phennil. Almost instantly, she was startled by the thud of a knife sticking in the ground at her foot. She paled and looked cautiously for its owner. A tall, skinny fellow sidled over. "Con says to tell you that if you try anything like that again, he'll cut your foot right off."

She nodded. "Gotcha."

After only a short break to rest and water the horses, they were riding again. She still had to ride with Con, though this time he allowed Kyer to sit up, which made breathing easier. But that was where the positive side ended. With no stirrups for her feet, she was steadied only by Con's arm. Worse, her hands were bound behind her back. She held her hands as high up her back as she could to avoid positioning them neatly in his crotch, but his chain mail dug at her knuckles. The sun climbed higher behind them. Gophers ducked into their holes ahead. She cringed against Con's arm around her middle and wracked her brain. The sun continued its steady ascent, heedless of what transpired beneath it, and the prisoner grew hot and dusty. She blinked dust out of her eyes, and shook insects away from her mouth. The river water had long since evaporated out of her tunic, and now it clung to her back with sweat. Midday was fast approaching, and not a single idea for escape had come to her.

Eventually her arms ached, and she lowered them as far as she dared, avoiding contact. But the jostling worked against her.

"Good idea," said her companion, the *solawid* taking full effect. "Pleasure me as we ride." He cupped her breast.

"Not likely." She squirmed, trying to shrink away from his hand.

"I *said*"—he clutched her throat in his fingers—"pleasure me."

She coughed and choked, but an idea finally struck her. Her eyes watered and she gasped for breath through her nose. He rocked against her fist. She punched down into his crotch, and while he cried out and instinctively cringed to protect himself, he also released his grip. She flung her head back and smashed his face, and he screamed in pain and anger.

Kyer braced herself against an impact and plunged over the side of the horse. With a painful thud, she hit the ground but scrambled to her feet and ran, stumbling over the uneven grass. Her hands still bound behind her back, keeping her balance was tricky. She heard the cries behind her, the thumping of hooves approaching. Two horses came up alongside her, heading her off, and she tried to dodge. Running feet neared. She ran harder. This wasn't about getting away; it was about not being cowed. *Eight to one.* As Con's full weight pounded her into the ground, she noted, with some dismay, that there was still no sign of horses following them from the east. Fear and frustration simmered.

Con grabbed her hair in his fist and slammed the side of her face into the ground. It was hard packed and hurt like hell. Her ear rang, but the grass saved her from a broken jaw. "Nice try," he said, roughly rolling her over. Con's ruddy face was so close to hers that a bead of his sweat now trickled down her cheek. The blood that flowed from his nose and mouth did not douse the murder burning in his eyes.

Kyer lay flat on her back, looking to where eight grown men surrounded her, poised to arrest any attempt at escape.

In the schoolyard, eight to one was different. She was a trained fighter and they weren't. That's why it had taken a gang of eight to bring her down. And in spite of the girls running to tell the teacher, the bitch stayed indoors and made no move to help her.

She was on her own. *Fine.*

The schoolboys beat her up pretty good, but they suffered a good deal of damage themselves. She knew they wouldn't kill her; they wouldn't dare. And when it was over, they looked as much of a mess as she did. They had to support each other, but she, Kyer Halidan, walked home alone. And unlike her, they had to live with the knowledge that they may have won the fight, but they still hadn't defeated her, even at eight to one.

"Eight to one," she whispered, seething with fury. "Congratulations."

Con smacked her across the face. "I'll give you eight to one," he hollered and began to unbuckle his belt. She kicked at him, her face hot with the sun and anger. The tall one who passed on Con's warning earlier grabbed Con by the arm and pulled him back. Con shook him off with a growling, "Get off me, Gyles." But Barrel-Chest joined in to restrain him.

"The Highness said not yet," Gyles yelled, Con fighting him. "Later. *After.*"

The brute finally heard but didn't break eye contact with his target. "All right, then. You don't want to ride with me? Rope!" Con untied her hands as someone tossed him a rope.

Kyer's mind raced to keep up with Con's plan. When he yanked her arms over her head and tied them again with the longer rope, she began to get an inkling, and the fear mutated into something that twisted inside her. Kyer swallowed hard, meeting his gaze evenly, but said nothing.

"Con, what are you doing?" Gyles's tone held a warning.

Con ignored him. "You'd rather run, bitch? Then run." He fastened the other end of the rope to his saddle.

This was not good. Frantically Kyer grabbed at the rope. If he was going to drag her, she wanted the rope in her hand, not just around her wrists. Con slung himself onto his mount. She scrabbled to her feet. Surely she could postpone the inevitable. She squinted over the plain back in the direction from which they had come. *Please . . .*

⁘

"You two distract it!" Derry cried. He ploughed off to the right into the birch grove, hoping to get in behind the monster.

An arrow zinged across the clearing from Phennil's bow and stuck neatly into the creature's upper arm. With a claw, the beast flicked it away as Janak flung himself straight into the ogre's path. Matching the creature's murderous howl with one of his own, he levelled a chop at the ragged fur covering its legs. Janak had a moment of perverse pleasure as he felt the dwarf-forged steel slice into the ogre's left thigh and lodge into solid bone. A trifle slower but with no less determination, the behemoth swung its knobby club at the dwarf, intent on batting him aside like a corn stalk. The stout warrior felt something clip his left shoulder. Then a tremendous blow hammered into his head, and the world went black.

Phennil's second arrow merely tagged the beast's ear and whizzed off. Dismayed to see Janak go down, the elf tossed his bow aside and dashed in to engage the ogre with his sword. He checked his approach and gasped as the ogre drew a blade and flung it, point down, at Janak's motionless form. Furious at the beast, Phennil chopped at his outstretched arm.

Jesqellan positioned himself on the opposite side of the fire pit and calmed himself in preparation to cast a spell.

Derry clutched the grip of his bastard sword, feeling the tiny rings on the mail gloves bite into his knuckles as he wound through the birches. Through the trees, he saw the ogre swing its club straight down at Phennil.

The ogre's club pounded into the ground as the elf danced aside. The beast felt the sting of a sword in its right arm. As it turned to face the swordsman, its left leg buckled, the dwarf's blade still protruding from it. Phennil triumphantly stepped in for the kill. With his blade nearly behind him, he began a long, circular sweep to sever the ogre's head from its shoulders. But the ogre, grunting with pain and anger, shifted its bulk and swung its club hard to the right. Phennil's eyes widened as the club came around, and he hastily altered his move to parry. He successfully reduced the strength of the attack and, as a result, did not die. It clunked him in the breastplate and sent him head over heels across the camp. His sword flew from his hands and hurtled through the air in an arc that fairly twinkled as it reflected the morning sunlight. It landed in the bushes several paces away. Phennil lay surrounded by underbrush, desperately sucking in air, and wondered if he'd ever breathe again.

The ogre pushed itself to its feet, yanking the battle axe out of its thigh. Fresh blood streamed out of the wound and fell in fat drops on the scrubby ground. The beast peered about for another victim. Across the fire, Jesqellan fervently articulated the last words of the chant, summoning the energy from his staff into himself. As he completed the spell, power surged through his arm, pulling him forward to send lightning leaping from his fingers. It blasted the ogre full in the abdomen.

The ogre went berserk, enraged by the searing electricity. Casting aside the club, it ignored its burned flesh and charged like a maddened bull, scattering hot coals and burning sticks on its way to the sorcerer.

At that moment, Derry finally burst from the trees, emerging right behind the ogre. Fuelled by his rage, he struck instantly, severing its left arm at the elbow. The creature turned awkwardly, snarling and grasping with its good arm. Frothy saliva dripped from the yellowed fangs, and Derry smelled the sharp, sweaty tang of fear. He brought his sword down in a precise attack and split the beast from neck to sternum. Gobbets of blood splattered his armour and face as the ogre fell.

Across the carcass stood Jesqellan, looking strained, his features taut and pinched. Electric air sizzled around them, raising the hair on their arms.

Derry panted slowly. "Where in hell did that come from?"

Jesqellan lowered his staff. Suddenly his eyes flashed wide. "Kyer." He wheeled around and tore off down the path, Derry close on his heels.

A moan from behind him halted Derry's pursuit. He hesitated at the top of the path, the momentum of his desire urging him forward. Peering through the trees and willing a glimpse of his friend to appear, his duty as captain did fierce battle with that of physicker-adept. The more skilled trade won out. Duty to the wounded was more immediate. He fetched his kit, cursing, yet surprised at himself for forgetting—and wishing to ignore—that cardinal rule.

Phennil was merely winded and soon regained his breath. He had a lump on the back of his head, a result of his spectacular landing, and a few bruises. Janak, however, was in more serious condition. Derry sent Phennil to help Jesqellan. He set to work examining the dwarf's head wound. In spite of himself, his mind was not on his task.

Jesqellan plunged his hand into the frigid pool and pulled out Kyer's sword. Trevile's withered face passed through his mind, and he reluctantly recognized that the party had decreased in number.

"This ogre made no random appearance," Jesqellan said. He dropped Kyer's sword and belt next to the captain. "They knew we were here."

Phennil was silent.

Derry, still kneeling next to Janak's motionless form, finished tying the cloth bandage around the wounded dwarf's head then wiped his hands. He picked up Kyer's sword and slowly wiped it dry too. "I suppose she gave them a golden opportunity by going down there on her own."

"I was looking out for her." Jesqellan sounded defensive.

"Of course," the captain reassured him. "You could do nothing more when they were equipped with such a distraction."

"Their camp was two furlongs beyond that hillock," Jesqellan pointed. "Downwind."

"Jesqellan found traces of a burned scroll in the fire pit," Phennil put in. "He says it was a single-use beast summoning spell, and I found where it must have arrived, the abrupt indentations in the dirt. I tracked the group about fifty paces downstream, where they left the river on the far bank. I couldn't tell how many, but I'd say eight to ten horses."

Derry imagined Kyer alone against ten men, and his heart lurched. Why did the elf have to give so damn much detail? Phennil was still speaking.

"I tracked them some distance—they've not made any effort to cover their trail—and they seem to be headed due west. It shouldn't be hard at all to—"

"Thank you. I have a very clear picture," Derry snapped. Janak shifted, groaning, and the captain turned his guilt-ridden attention to the wounded dwarf.

"Then I've done my job." Phennil quietly walked away. Derry scolded himself; the elf was no more to blame than Jesqellan.

"Captain?" Jesqellan said in an undertone.

Derry shook his head. "I know, I know. But why can he not simply make a brief report and be done with it? Why does it have to be an oration?"

"Captain." Jesqellan crouched next to him and picked up Kyer's sword and sheath where Derry had set it. "This is hard on all of us."

A growl came from the supine dwarf. "Why can't I see out of my left eye?"

A violent tug and Kyer ran to keep the rope slack. Con looked back at her and kicked the horse harder. Enraged, she ran faster, peering out through half-closed eyes. The dust stirred up by the horse's hooves pricked at her skin and infiltrated her lungs. She uttered barely a sound, but inwardly she screamed. *I can't do it. I can't keep up!* Con laughed at her effort and kicked the horse. Kyer gripped the rope as it yanked her off her feet. She squeezed her eyes shut against the dust and the impact. She hugged her head as best she could to protect it, but the hard-packed ground was merciless. Thuds reverberated right through her.

It wasn't more than a dozen hacking breaths before Kyer heard shouting and the horse stopped. More shouts among the men, but Kyer cared only that they'd stopped. She heard words like "chief," "bargaining tools," and "reward" and shuddered, but her immediate situation was more pressing. Gasping and coughing, she took inventory of her body. Her sore head wasn't the worst of it. Her arms ached but were still attached. Scrapes stung on her face and her belly where her tunic had ripped. Rope burn on her hands was better than having them sliced right off at the wrists. Bruising on her hips and knees for certain, but a bit of bending told her nothing was broken. Maybe a cracked rib. She lay there, panting and sweating and cursing her stupidity.

Footsteps. *Oh, what now?* Gyles appeared.

"You ride with me now."

"Anything would be an improvement," she muttered.

He pointed the knife at her. "Watch yourself. I'm no more your friend than he is; I just don't hate you as much. Yet."

Gyles cut the excess rope, leaving her hands tied in front, and lifted her up onto his horse. She raised her eyes to find Con still glaring at her as if he would just as soon slash her to ribbons here and now.

Gyles steadied her with one arm. He held her tightly but without hurting her. Already she was glad of the change in companions.

After a while, she asked, "How long a ride is it?"

"We'll be there after dark." After a pause, he said, not unpleasantly. "So what's your name?"

"You didn't bring me along to make friends. I'll speak to your chief. If I feel like it."

Gyles chuckled. "Oh, you'll speak to him all right."

Kyer said not a word but held her head high. She'd regained control for now. A burning curiosity gnawed at her. "Why'd you make Con stop dragging me?"

He grunted. "The Highness would prefer to interview a live subject than a dead one."

"Hmph." There was still time. Derry would never leave her to an unknown fate. Soon, very soon now, she would see dust billowing in the east. She and her captors had travelled almost due west the entire day, concentrating more on speed than throwing pursuers off their path. Phennil was an expert tracker, and surely Jesqellan knew some sort of spell that could —*Jesqellan!* She silenced a gasp of dismay. *He won't ride a horse.* He walked quickly but never as quickly as these men had been riding all day. A twinge of doubt crept up her neck.

For the first time today, it crossed her mind that perhaps Ronav planned to be finished with her before her friends caught up with them. How could they possibly catch up? The precariousness of her situation sank in. Ahead, a dark line of conifers edged the distant horizon as far as she could see in either direction: the foothills of the Tarmigon Mountains. She swallowed hard and craned her neck to see behind them, but all she could glimpse beyond the horsemen was wide open plain. Empty plain.

"Don't bother watching out for your precious friends, my girl," her companion said, guessing her purpose. "We left them plenty to keep them busy so they'll not even be thinking about coming after you. If they aren't dead, that is."

Kyer tried to sound casual. "Oh yeah, what is this 'secret weapon' I heard about?"

"An ogre."

Fighting the fear back down into submission, she said, "Only one?"

"Even if they survive, by the time they find which way we've gone, you'll be dead. Or worse: still alive."

Kyer held her head up higher.

"I understand you're pretty new to the group," Gyles said casually. "How can you be sure you're worth the effort it'll take them to find you?"

"Of course I am," she scoffed. But the bastard's words struck a nerve. Was he right? What were Valrayker's instructions to Derry? Perhaps the mission was more important than a new recruit whose usefulness was untried.

Finally she was forced to concede that Derry and the others may never find her.

She was on her own. *Fine.*

Twelve

A Vanishing Act

For two hours, Janak lay still, waiting for Phennil and Jesqellan to return from their search for the trail of Kyer's captors. They had ridden for a painful half hour in which Janak's head became addled with dizziness before the elf lost the trail and they were forced to stop. Derry had stayed with Janak, whose inner rage simmered at being treated like a powerless wretch.

Janak had asked for one of Kien's healing potions, but Derry refused, saying the risk was too great of the magic simply fixing the eye in its damaged position without actually solving the underlying problem. That would prevent a Healer from ever being able to mend it. So the dwarf lay on his bed, simmering with emotion. The ogre-inflicted pain peened in his head, and his left eye throbbed. The physicker's special brew eased his head a little, but it did nothing for the dull ache that had settled just below his ribs.

It was a cold, leaden ache, an icy fist around his heart that squeezed each time Janak opened his eyes and could see with only one. With the other, he saw nothing but changes in light. From his propped position, Janak had watched Derry move around the camp, trying to keep busy, and his mind flitted about like a slow-motion passing of his life before his eyes. The exhilaration of a well-timed swipe with his battle axe; the warm, well-measured handshake of Lord Valrayker, with gratitude and congratulations in his grey eyes just as ingenuous and unaffected as his words; the breathtaking beauty of Rael e'Fallen as she sang "Awaken" in the Heath Concert Hall—surely it was directed right to him; Kyer Halidan's fierce determination and the strength of the blows he countered with sweat trickling down his back... What bloody good was a one-eyed fighter? Janak's desire to snatch up his battle axe and strike something with unparalleled ferocity was almost more than he could withstand.

When the two finally returned, and Jesqellan said, "Nothing," his voice held a note of despair that Janak had known of him only once before. That time Janak had shared in his grief. This time the dwarf felt quite differently.

As Phennil gave the details, Janak gazed up at him, straining to see more than shadows out of his left eye. But the pain intensified as he stared, and soon he had to close it.

It did not stop his meditating on revenge.

As long as Derry had known Phennil, the elf had never been less sanguine in either body or voice. As he reported the condition of the trail, it was as if he were reporting the destruction of his home town.

The earth, Phennil said, was hard-packed and the light gusts of wind had ravaged many signs of the horses' passing. The dust shifted continually, and even dismounting to check more closely had yielded nothing. The frustrated tracker had been forced to admit defeat when he saw the herd of antelope roaming the plain. The trail was obliterated. He was foiled.

"We could carry on west," Phennil said doubtfully, "but we have no way of knowing if we're on the right track. We could end up miles away and never find her."

Derry squinted in the tree-filtered sunlight, desperate for some sort of direction. Precious time was already lost, and the sun did not slow its crawl across the sky. His fear for Kyer redoubled, his imagination roiling like floodwaters. Helpless she was not—Derry, of all people, knew—but even she had limits. Ten men and no weapon. Ronav Malachite, a man whose hunger for greatness made him ruthless, waited at the end of her road. Kyer would not be meek. He would beat her, bloody her, even kill her. Derry pictured her dark gaze scrutinizing him on the stairs the night they met, her laugh as she told a joke at supper last night. *Is that the last time—?*

The compulsion to leap onto Donnagill's back and pursue her was so strong that the restraint made him feel sick to his stomach. Derry glanced sidelong at Janak, rubbed his head, and cursed violently. The others waited tentatively for orders. A stone sat within kicking distance, taunting him. Derry clenched his teeth and pulled his gaze away from it.

Janak lay there silently, uncaring, wallowing in his own selfish world of self-pity. Yet . . . he was here and Kyer was not. And the dwarf's left eye was filled with a pool of blood. Derry gave in.

"Let's go northwest to Stoney Hill. We've got to get Janak to a healer. Mayhap we'll learn something of Ronav's whereabouts so we'll know where to go." Not quite under his breath, he added, "We've got to find her. We can't just leave her to—" recognizing his men were waiting for him, Derry gestured, and they hastened to pack up camp. He remembered something and called, "Phennil."

The elf approached him, looking like a chastened child.

"Phennil, I apologize for my impatience earlier. You were doing your job, doing it well. It was selfish of me to forget how this would affect us all."

The elf nodded, but the expression on his face did not transform into relief. Instead he paled. He opened his mouth to speak, hesitated, and tried again. "Captain, I—" He breathed deeply and straightened. Derry had to look up. "This is all my fault."

"No, Phennil, don't think that—"

"*Yes*, it is. See, there was this man with a lopsided face in the general store in Shael when I was buying Kyer's supplies. He asked all sorts of questions; I thought he was just being friendly. I . . . well, I told him."

Derry stared at him, his heart plummeting. "What did you tell him?"

"He said it looked like I was prepping for a journey. I said we were heading north, looking for some information for Valrayker. I think I even told him we'd be leaving the next day."

Jesqellan sighed heavily.

Derry glared at the idiot elf and wondered why he'd spoken to Valrayker about *Kyer's* suitability in the group. "Did you mention Nennia?"

"No, I definitely didn't. Derry, I'm sorry. I thought I was being charitable! He seemed so friendly, and you have no idea how proud it makes me to be able to say I work for Val—"

"It makes you *proud*." Derry hadn't felt this kind of wrench to his gut since they'd told him his sisters had gone missing. His breath came out in a slow hiss. "Brilliant, Phennil." The elf flinched as though he'd threatened to hit him.

"I'm sorry!"

The words squeezed out between taut lips. "Just hope Kyer's still alive for you tell her that." Derry walked away before he yielded to the urge to wallop him.

Derry had hoped to reach Stoney Hill by mid-afternoon, but circumstances did not allow it. He had never been so close to losing control. Janak could not ride for more than an hour before the pressure in his eye became too much. The ogre's club had also caused bouts of dizziness, and he needed frequent rests. Derry had suggested a litter, but the cantankerous dwarf had refused "to be toted like some gelded, mewling infant." Derry conceded that even with the stops, riding was faster than it would be to carry over twenty stone of Dwarven bulk.

They had briefly discussed Jesqellan's healing spell but dismissed it almost immediately for the same reason as for the healing potion. The mage could not be certain he would have enough control over the spell to simply relieve some of the dwarf's pain without doing permanent damage.

The sun brushed the tops of the Tarmigon Mountains far to their left, and they slogged through dogwood and willow-dotted marshland in search of a decent path. Phennil rode in ashamed silence at the rear of the party, and Derry did not have the strength to ask him to take the lead. His feet were soaked, he had a stabbing pain in his belly from not eating much that day, and his head ached. Yet he must not complain; somewhere in the west, Kyer was in the hands of the enemy.

"Captain." It was the first time Derry had heard Phennil's voice since the morning; it must be important. He called a halt and looked past Jesqellan and Janak to where Phennil sat astride Leoht, peering into the trees.

"Hmm?"

"Do you smell that?"

Derry was surprised Phennil could smell anything over his own odour but sniffed the air himself. It took him a moment, but then he detected it. *As if we haven't problems enough.*

"We're downwind of him, or he'd be after us already." Derry dismounted. "You go check it out while I get Janak down."

Phennil obliged, bow in hand.

"What the devil is it?" the dwarf said.

"Keep your voice down. Their hearing isn't anything to boast about, but he'll hear you if you rail on." Derry and Jesqellan lowered Janak to the ground, where the dwarf grasped the cinch strap for support.

"What is it, Captain?" Jesqellan asked in subdued tones.

"A bloody fen troll."

Janak let out a growl. "Get my axe and I'll be on him!"

"You'll do no such thing." Derry grabbed Janak's arm, but the dwarf flung him off, whacking him in the shoulder. Janak stumbled but found the straps holding his battle axe in place.

"Whoa there, Janak," Jesqellan said, also trying to restrain him.

"I'm not a gods-be-damned *horse*; don't you *whoa* me! I'm a fighter and I'm going to fight."

"You do and you'll never fight again," Derry said, working with Jesqellan to pinion the dwarf's tree-limb arms.

"Then it'll be my final showdown." He kicked Derry, who yelled and toppled into the muck.

"Jesqellan, do something."

A few muttered words and a flash later, Janak lay still, his right arm and leg in a puddle of murky water. He was too heavy for the two of them to drag him out of it, so they left him. His good eye screamed silently at them, but his mouth, frozen mid-yell, couldn't voice his outrage.

"I apologize, Janak, but you left us no option." Derry unsheathed his sword, and Jesqellan followed him toward the trees.

"How long?" Derry asked.

Jesqellan shrugged. "Maybe a quarter of an hour."

"I had no idea we had so many halfwits in the company."

Jesqellan began a cross reply, but Phennil came running out of the willows. "He's only a youth but a hungry one," he said, not even a little out of breath. "I could hear you all hollering, and so could he. He's confused 'cause I fired an arrow at a tree behind him and he doesn't know which way to go, but he'll find us soon enough." His enthusiasm for the challenge had loosened his tongue again.

"How far?" Derry asked.

"About two hundred paces beyond that big willow there," Phennil pointed, his eyes stabbing back and forth into the shadowy shrub brush.

"Can't we just skirt around the area and avoid him?" Jesqellan put in.

"Not likely," Derry said. "He's heard us already, and the instant he catches our scent, he'll follow us relentlessly until he tastes flesh, no matter where we go."

"Could we draw it out somehow?" offered Jesqellan.

Derry thought rapidly. "Phennil, you get back in beyond him and drive him toward us. Jesqellan, you and I'll have to be thorough. They only take a few seconds to begin regeneration. You'll need to finish him off."

Phennil led them into the willows. They picked their way slowly, striving for noiselessness. Ten minutes later, Phennil held up his hand for them to stop, his keen eyes scanning the shadows ahead.

"It's behind that large maple," he whispered. "We're downwind. Wait here and I'll go flush him out." In seconds, Phennil had disappeared.

"What if it charges Phennil instead?" muttered Jesqellan.

"I hope he runs fast," Derry replied.

They spread out and Derry crouched low in the grasses, his arse dipping into water. He heard the twang of Phennil's bow—three times in such quick succession, they were all but simultaneous. There was a loud grunt then a bellow as the troll staggered backwards into his view, three shafts jutting out of its short, dense hair. It crouched beside the maple and pulled them from its midsection. More arrows whipped past the troll, and some thudded into the tree. Its eyes darted wildly around, thinking there were several archers attacking, and tipped its snout to the air.

Finally the troll found a scent. It lumbered toward Phennil, who dashed across the soggy ground in the direction of Jesqellan, then dropped behind the brush, out of its sight. Derry's heartbeat rushed as the troll came straight at them. In search of the elf, the monster passed the humans and pulled up, astonished, as their scent reached it. Derry stepped out from the brush and attacked. The troll swiped with one arm and clopped Derry a good one on the same shoulder Janak had hit. Crossly, Derry swept at it again. In the meantime, Phennil charged from behind. Both man and elf struck solid blows then dropped to the ground. The stunned troll had only a moment to be confused. Flailing its horns at the twilit sky, its wounds had no time to regenerate before it was hit with a ball of fire two feet in diameter—the only weapon that would terminate it. Derry crawled away as the troll turned into a living torch. It cried out in horror but fell and sank into the boggy ground, a burned and very dead husk.

Shoulder aching, and soaking from top to bottom, Derry made his way back to the horses, where Janak was just coming out of the spell that had frozen him in place. He flexed his hands and feet, and though he could move his jaw, it was stiff and the lips and tongue were not quite ready for speech. It didn't stop him trying.

"Waw yoo hink e kawfee?" He shook his shoulders, loosening them.

Jesqellan and Phennil came up, both soaked to the skin from lying low in the marsh.

"What was I thinking in stopping you?" Derry clarified, impatiently cleaning his sword. "Like it or not, Janak, even injured, you're more useful to us alive than dead. I can't have you throwing yourself away just to prove you're still capable of it. We'll get through this. All of us."

Phennil said nothing and cleaned off the few arrows he'd retrieved. The heads were blunted, but at least two of the shafts would be reusable. He returned those to his arrow bag. The others would be kindling. Janak pointed at him but spoke to Derry.

"You blem him fer all 'iss. He 'id sumpin' dumb." He shook his head and managed to roll onto his side. "Naw his faul'. *Hers*." He pushed his knees up and pushed himself to standing. Derry didn't help him but slammed his sword into its sheath. Janak pushed through the stiffness to form words. "I said... aw along... 'hat she had no place... in 'hiss company. I said she was nuffing... but trouble." He blew through his lips, stretched his mouth and carried on. "What use is she to us? Her problems have become *my* problems. It's her own damn fault she got took, and if I never fight again, it'll be her damn fault too." He clutched his saddle, vibrating from his effort.

Derry felt as if he were the one who'd been hit by a freeze spell: hand on Donnagill's flank, head on his hand, numb throughout, as if filled with cotton wool. In one short day, he'd lost control of everything. Despair was an insidious poison, breaking down company morale like termites destroying a house from the inside. Derry was the captain. He knew if he did not take command now and counteract the poison, they would fall apart. The mission would fail.

Failure was not an option. But they had to find Kyer first. If they didn't, Derry would not be able to face Dunvehran, no matter how much success they might have in Nennia.

"I'm going to presume you are joking," Derry said quietly, "because if I do not, I will likely kill you myself." He looked around at them all, staring at him expectantly. "Let's move. We are going to Stoney Hill. Now let's get the hell out of this muck."

⚔

Kyer had long since stopped peering behind her. The sun was setting behind the mountain in front of them as they finally reached the first of the trees that embraced the foothills. A couple of hours later, with darkness settled around them, they came upon a cabin built up against the side of the hill. With trees all around, the house resembled that of a trapper. Though she could not see a chimney in the dark, the smell of smoke and roasting meat reminded Kyer that her porridge was a distant memory. The horses drew up alongside the house, and the men tied them to the trees, alongside several others. There was no stable or corral to be seen. Gyles dismounted, pulling her down with him, not shoving her to the ground, Con style. She checked an impulse to thank him for his gentlemanly behaviour, mainly because her teeth would have chattered if her jaw weren't clamped shut. Night seeped through her tunic.

Trembling just a little, with the chill or nerves, she waited for someone to tell her what to do. Con glanced at her then cocked his head at Gyles and a heavyset man called Tobb. Con swaggered on ahead. Kyer was given a shove that nearly knocked her down, but she didn't give them the pleasure of seeing her fall. She caught herself and kept her footing.

"My, she's a proud one, ain't she?" Tobb said.

"We'll see how long that lasts," said Gyles.

He's bluffing. She stepped over the threshold as directed. The house was deceptively small on the outside; it was actually set into the hillside so the front room was just an entryway into a banquet hall. Kyer's heart sank when she saw the gathering before her. The party that had come to fetch her was about a one-quarter contingent. The odds against her stacked higher.

Two or three pots simmered on the large fire in the centre of the room, cooking whatever cabbagey-smelling dishes would accompany the fat pig that turned on the spit, cranked by a small boy. The fire sucked away the chill of outdoors, the smoke rose obediently twenty feet up to a hole in a ceiling she could barely see. A few torches clung to the walls like oversized stick insects, adding their pitchy smoke and feeble light to that of the fire. The men helped themselves to tankards of beer from a massive keg. Gyles and Tobb stopped Kyer, hands still tied in front, at the end of a trestle table, and they sat down to await orders.

Con approached a low dais at the far end of the room, set apart from the rest of the circle. Chief Ronav was draped on an excessively grandiose chair. A woman handed him a bowl, and he pinched her rump as she moved away. It didn't faze her. Ronav dug into his meal as Con spoke to him, hooking his thumb in Kyer's direction.

Kyer stood waiting, her eyes never leaving the chief. "Nice place," she remarked to her guards approvingly. "Cosy atmosphere."

"Righ' plucky, ain't you?" Tobb said.

Con signalled to her guards, and the two men rose to grab her arms. They led her across the room to stand in front of the chief then left her. The chief ignored her as he finished slurping up the last of his dinner. She raised her eyebrows with indignation. *Trying to unnerve me.* His dark hair was thinning on top and his skin looked sallow, as if he didn't get enough sun. The way he sat, she couldn't guess at his height, but his long legs led her to believe he was fairly tall. His robes had once been fancy and stylish but were worn, with faded colours, some vestige of class he was trying to cling to. They were too large for him, as if he'd removed them from some lord whose life he'd taken while pillaging his lands and household and raping his women. Ronav had thin, soft-looking lips that brought to Kyer's mind a repellent youth who had tried to kiss her when she was fourteen, and she wondered what attribute he possessed that had raised him up to such a level. To her mind, it couldn't be a natural leadership quality. Setting his bowl aside, he finally appraised her expectantly through pale, steely eyes.

She stared right back at him. This was his party; let him speak first. At any rate, she didn't know what he wanted. Her heart beat on her ribs like it was trying to escape. After a time, he finally spoke with a voice that was filled with authority but softened by a smooth charm.

"So this is the little girl who has eluded us for so long."

Kyer knew he was trying to rankle her and didn't oblige him.

"Con," he called, "she doesn't look at all as fierce as you led us to believe."

Con glared at him.

"I have been looking forward to meeting this fearsome warrior." Ronav chuckled then turned his oily smile at Kyer. "Do you know who I am?"

"Ronav Malachite," she said in a clear, confident voice.

"Ah, my reputation precedes me, I see."

"As does mine, it would seem."

"Indeed. Yet you have the advantage, my dear, for I do not know who you are. It seems rude to not properly address you, a guest in my house."

"My name is Kyer Halidan."

"And where are you from?"

"That hardly matters since my actions have nothing to do with you prior to the incident in Wanaka." She hoped her heart beat was not visible.

"Ah, yes, the *incident* in Wanaka," he said, a hint of acerbity sneaking out from behind the charm. "But we will get to that later."

Con joined them, leaning against the back of Ronav's chair to stare at Kyer with triumphant hatred.

"You have created quite a stir amongst my council, you know," Ronav continued with a glance up at his right-hand man.

A lofty name for a bunch of bandits. Kyer watched him blankly.

"You must really be something special. A young girl, yet you are personally responsible for the deaths of four of my men."

"Your men attacked me, so I killed them. What exactly did you expect?"

"Nothing less from such a surprisingly skilled fighter as yourself."

Con grunted.

If he's trying to swell my head to win me over, it's not working.

"I am extremely upset that Simon was killed. Do you know what that means, my dear girl? That means you have angered me. And if you choose not to cooperate with me, you will not have a pleasant time here. You must not think that you will be treated with the respect that is usually due a gifted fighter like yourself."

Kyer looked at him levelly. "I would never expect it of you."

Con, at least, picked up on her subtle gibe. He stepped forward and gave her the back of his brawny hand across the mouth.

With the sudden taste of blood, she staggered but kept her footing.

A crash of glass from the other side of the hall was followed by a cheer. The rest of the hall continued their party, oblivious to the goings-on at the front of the room.

"That looked like it felt good, Con," Ronav said. "You see what I mean, Kyer Halidan. My men and I are not to be trifled with.

"So now," he said, lowering his voice, "what have you done with my property?"

She considered the question. If he meant the cart, she hadn't touched it. He probably meant the chest. But rules were rules. The chest had been in Simon's possession and was, therefore, now her property, regardless of who had paid for it. If Ronav were a reasonable individual, she might be more open to negotiation. "I know nothing of your property."

"There were some goods that Simon was bringing to me."

"Your cart is in the hands of Wanaka's sheriff now."

"I don't mean the cart. There was a small box. You know what I'm talking about."

"Oh. You mean the armband?" She slurred over her rapidly swelling lip. "I left it in Shael, with an apothecary. It's mine now, so I want to know what it is."

Ronav looked unimpressed. His nostrils flared. "Never mind. As you say, by rules of combat, it *belongs* to you." He pursed his fishy lips, which made her shudder because he'd agreed too readily and she didn't know what he was thinking.

"What is it you know about our plans?"

She shook her head. "Nothing."

Con backhanded her again. She felt blood trickling down her chin.

"Liar." Ronav shifted in his seat and drummed his fingers on the arm of the chair. "What do you *know*?" he repeated, more insistently.

She exhaled impatiently. "Listen, I'd never even heard of you when Con said your name. Sorry, but you're just not as notorious as you'd like to think."

Con kneed her in the gut so her stomach rammed into her lungs, and she doubled over, gasping. Her knees hit the stone floor with a jolt that sent sharp pain up her back. Fear escaped its confines then, and she began to tremble. She got shakily to her feet.

"Look," she said hoarsely, pleading in her voice in spite of her effort to contain her fear. "I'd've thought nothing of it, except that ever since I killed Simon, your men keep attacking me. Why couldn't you have just let it go?"

"Why did you kill him?"

Kyer sighed. "I was enjoying a beer, and he demanded I go to bed with him, so I challenged him. What would you have done in my position?"

"You expect me to believe that?"

"No, I don't. He cheated, all right? It was a legal duel, all public and proper. He drew early, *and* flung a knife after there was an obvious winner. So I killed him."

"You are one of Valrayker's puppets, and you expect me to believe that you did not kill my man under his orders?"

"Believe whatever you want. Yes, Valrayker was there, but I didn't even know who he was until afterward. Actually, it was as a result of that fight that Valrayker asked me to join him. Simon died for a worthy cause." She cried out as Con hit her again. Ears ringing, she found herself on the floor.

"My dear Kyer, please tell me what you are doing for Valrayker." He licked a drop of spittle from the corner of his mouth. "Where has he sent you?" Ronav prodded, his voice insipidly quiet. "What is required of you?"

On all fours, she spoke over a swollen lip. "It has nothing to do with you."

"How do you know?" he asked casually.

It struck her that it may very well have everything to do with him.

"Look at her," Con remarked with a sneer. "Spoutin' off comments, brassy as hell until I hits her, and when it matters, she finally thinks to hold her tongue."

"Hmm. Maybe she likes it," Ronav said, his index finger drawing thoughtful circles around his clean-shaven chin. "You know? Rather than demand the return of my property, I shall simply have to regain their value from you. You don't mind paying a small sum, now do you? But you have no money. No matter. You are a worthy warrior, so we will take it out of that worth."

Hope leaped into her heart. He saw her as an asset! Working for him would give her a chance—

Ronav cocked his head, and suddenly the whole room moved as if he'd suggested a dance.

Con yelled, *"Post!"* and hauled her to her feet. He stank like stale *solawid* and rotting teeth. Kyer looked at Ronav's self-satisfied gaze with confusion and stumbled as Con wrenched her around and dragged her to the centre of the room. The men were positioning a tall post, braced at the foot, with an iron ring driven into it. She tried to wriggle away, but Con only held her tighter. Fear tasted like bile in her throat. Protest would be in vain. As would divulging information now. These men no longer cared about her mission. Within seconds, her arms were above her head and tied to the ring. Someone yanked her tunic up, baring her back. Her head now covered, she couldn't even strain her neck around to see what they were doing. She had a feeling she already knew.

The reality of her complete and utter helplessness finally hit her like a waterfall. Her friends were not coming. She was in a room full of brutal men. How could she have thought she could possibly defend herself? *Fool.*

She heard the snap of a whip, and searing pain clawed at her skin. She screamed. *One.* Again the lash cracked against her. *Two.* And again. *Three.* Was that Ronav's voice counting? Or her own? *Four. Five. Six.* Each time she cried out, the men cheered. She clenched her jaw until her teeth felt like they might break. *Don't satisfy them!* She felt her own warm blood trickling. She tried to brace herself, but every muscle in her body seized with each *snap*, and she sagged with agony, her arms wanting to wrench from her shoulders. The wielder of the whip varied the tempo of his cracks, not allowing her to achieve any kind of rhythm with her breathing. A close-mouthed scream escaped. She had lost count. What a fool. Why couldn't she have kept her mouth shut? Maybe they'd have thrown her in a cell somewhere, but perhaps it wouldn't have come to this. *Crack!* Her body slammed against the post as she lost her footing. Blood streamed down her back now. It was impossible not to cry out.

"Do you suppose she'd face me with such boldness now?" Ronav asked the room at large. "Such a fearsome warrior, sobbing like an infant!"

The cheering, jeering, and laughter continued as if she were the star of a comedic play.

His voice softly oozed. "Valrayker will be disappointed in you for being so . . . weak. What a waste of his time."

From somewhere deep down, she felt a determination simmer, and she planted her feet more firmly.

"Was that twenty?" Ronav cooed in the back of her mind. "And yet she still looks so bold, so sturdy. Let's have another ten."

Crack! Searing, burning, scorching. The smell of her own blood and sweat. And fear. The men's voices had distorted into a ringing and buzzing in her ears. Kyer sobbed in spite of herself, and her tears stung the gashes on her face. Her wrists bled from twisting against the ropes. She had been too cocky. Gyles had warned her, and she'd brushed him off. In her mind, she heard Brendow's voice. *Show all opponents the respect of never underestimating them.* Even Brendow seemed to be laughing at her. He'd spent countless hours training her . . . for this? What a waste of his time. Sobs gusted out of her with each lash. She was beyond pain, beyond agony.

The eight boys who'd attacked her in the schoolyard took a second run at her. Only they were no longer boys, just a few weeks ago. Still not as trained as she but bigger, stronger, and drunkenly intent on getting their own back. On her way home. Tired from an intense training session. Relaxed after a few drinks with her mates. They'd ambushed her in the lane. With her sword in hand, she was not helpless. Her medallion flaring with the warmth of the fear she wrestled under control, she drew and with the advantage of being in a crowded space between buildings, made quick work of them. She killed none of them but left them hurting. One week later, she left Hreth.

With her sword in hand, she was not helpless.

Ronav's voice, the cheers of his men, were a buzzing in her head. She was on her own.

They would kill her. Derry and the others were headed north; she was just not worth the effort. The mission was more important. If she died now, nobody would miss her. *Just let it end.*

She gave in and drooped against the post.

Cheers erupted and they seemed like echoes all around her and within her, as if she were in a vast cave. She felt a yank, and her hands were free from the iron ring. She slipped and crumpled ungracefully to the floor. She struggled to pull her tunic down, though it sent flames of pain through her body. Her eyes flickered open, and she watched her blood stir up the dirt, blend with it, and form a muddy whorl. Her eyes closed. Voices and clapping and cheering buzzed around her head like flies. Ronav's voice stood out, a solo amid the cacophony.

"So, young warrior, do you have anything to say now?"

Her breaths came short and ragged.

An agonizing wallop to her side like a blow with a tree trunk. Con's boot. She rolled over, moaning, arms still clenched to her head. She hadn't the strength to kick or struggle. Fine. Ronav had won. There was nothing more they could do to her now.

Ronav's voice again. "She is still beautiful, do you not think so?"

Kyer craned her neck so she could see her enemy. He shifted to a more comfortable position, glancing over at his man. "The trouble with flogging is that the wounds, even after they have healed, remain hidden." His voice was like a serpent's, and the way he alternated sidelong looks at her and at Con froze what was left of her blood. "The other danger here is that even after she has healed," he leaned forward slightly, "she will still be a *nuisance*. Still able to wield a sword, still able to attack, to kill." There was an uproar of cheering as the demons clambered over each other like snarling wolves to get closer.

Con stepped forward, his half grin leering down at her.

Ronav urged him on in a sing-song voice. "What do you suppose we could do about that?"

Her eyes welled and she curled up tighter on her side. Her back felt like she'd been branded a hundred times.

"To render her virtually useless."

No. Con sank onto his knees, straddling her bloody form. She clutched her arms to herself, but he forcibly pushed her onto her back. She screamed, arching her spine to lift the lacerations, not completely covered by her tunic, off the ground. He shoved her down, and the dirt on the floor drove its grit into her wounds. Con grabbed her right arm.

"Hold her," he growled and Gyles and Tobb happily obliged, one grabbed her left arm and the other pinned her right shoulder down. Struggling brought only agony, so she lay still.

Con caressed her hand and she yanked, desperate to get it away from him. But he clutched it, and the pain sent a new dread to every muscle. She tried to kick, but he sat on her. "You're mine now. To throw in a room down below where I can take you whenever I want." He leaned down to her, his fetid skin and breath too close. "You'll never see the light of day again." She turned her head from side to side, trying to avoid him, but he grabbed her face in one big, filthy hand and thrust his tongue into her mouth. She gagged.

He backhanded her without restraint. A new cut formed over a swollen bruise.

He took her thumb in his fingers. "And you'll soon be useless to anyone but me."

By the gods . . . No! He was right. She would be able to wield no weapon, to hold nothing at all. Not even a beggar's tin cup. Useless. Dread cranked each muscle as taut as a crossbow.

Somewhere Kyer could hear Ronav's despicable chuckle.

Con drew a knife from somewhere and turned it over where she could see it. Kyer wriggled and struggled, despite the torturous gashes on her back. Con slammed her hand on the ground, fingers together, but her thumb neatly separated. Kyer screamed in rage. Tears streamed down her cheeks and into her hair.

But something had caught Con's attention. He was staring—not at her, but down around her hip. A whole new fear seized her as she remembered what she had tucked into her pocket.

The chain had slipped out onto the floor. She squirmed as if that would prevent his fingertips from grasping it. He lifted the chain, and despair was a dagger in her heart as she felt the medallion slide out of the pocket. She stiffened and struggled some more. *No! No, not that!* "No!" she cried.

He lifted it and it swung gently, tantalizingly above her.

"Well, well, what have we here?" he said. A hush descended on the room. His greedy eyes flashed with the recognition of value. Such an unusual metal, such a large violet jewel in the centre. To him, it was wealth . . . and power over her.

To Kyer, it was her lifeline. The one and only connection with her past. A single clue to her identity. As precious to her as her arm. As the thumb that made it a sword arm.

A growl forced itself out of her throat. She skewered him with an enraged glare.

He scoffed at her. He held it up to show his comrades his treasure. He reached with his other thumb and index finger to touch the large jewel that centred the medallion.

The blood rushing through her ears blocked the sound of the room. *"You will not have it!"*

A surprising thing happened.

A small explosion threw Con backwards, screaming in terror and pain. Kyer's guards jumped back. The medallion fell onto her belly, and she snatched it. It was hot but did not burn her hand. She pushed herself onto her side and up onto one elbow to witness the spectacular display. Con was hurled to the ground, and his body was licked by tongues of fire. Though he was no longer touching it, bolts of lightning shot from the jewel in the medallion and leaped for him as if they had been aimed at their last enemy in the world and were intent on retribution. The crowd of men scrambled back; some even fled in horror. Ronav struggled out of his chair and crouched behind it to shield himself from the sight of the lightning jolting through Con's body. The bolts visibly outlined every bone and muscle, and as they died down, Con's blackened body lay like a charred log in the fire. The nauseating stench of burned flesh took her breath away.

She was free from her captors for a moment. Now was her chance to run. But they'd left her barely able to pathetically drag herself across the ground. She sobbed with terror.

I've got to get out of here, to find Derry.

A shimmer of light, unnoticed by anyone but herself, seemed to shudder through, not the earth, but the very air she breathed. It formed the shape of an archway and was no more than a brief, quiet glow. Kyer drew the medallion's chain over her head. She dug her fingernails into the edge of a stone, dragging herself into a desperate crawl. No sooner had the shimmer appeared than it was gone . . . and Kyer with it.

⊰⊱

Far in the northern wastelands of Rydris, someone stirred. "Oh, now that is interesting."

⊰⊱

Con's body still sparked. His charred eyes were open, blackened, and sucked dry, and even in death, his expression was frozen in utter horror. His screams still echoed throughout the hall. The men had been struck dumb in those few short seconds. When the sound finally died away, no one knew what to do. Even Ronav, their esteemed leader, had nothing to say as he peered out from behind his chair. They were afraid to touch Con, lest he should crumble to cinders before their eyes.

The silence was splintered by a cry.

"She's gone!" Gyles was pointing to where Kyer had lain.

That got them moving. A few ran to the door, and others were happy to escape the scene and see if she had gone elsewhere in the caverns off the main hall. They quickly realized they had somehow lost her again. She could not have run far or fast in her physical state. There was no evidence of her going into the yard, and all the horses were still there. There was no sign whatsoever that she had even moved from that spot where smatterings of blood smeared the floor. She had vanished. They all gathered and looked at Ronav expectantly. His face was stricken. The hush was deadly. Ronav let out a scream of fury that quaked through the hall and into the caverns beyond.

"Idiot!" he shrieked. He bashed his hip on the chair as he stepped around it. He kicked Con's body with all his force, scattering ashes everywhere so they fell through the air like black snowflakes. Charred bone skittered across the floor. Ronav's men screamed and feverishly brushed off the ashes of their dead comrade.

Jesqellan had been on watch for about an hour. He paused in his rounds next to Kyer's horse, within the aura of the animal's warmth. The others slept uneasily, disturbed by their imaginations. They'd found their way out of the marshes but had had to stop several times to rest. Janak was in considerable discomfort with his eye, and Jesqellan himself had turned an ankle in the wetland. The going had been slower than ploughing through snowdrifts, and Jesqellan had watched Derry's inner battle play out on his face before he finally called a halt for the night, with the heaviest of spirits. Jesqellan's ankle pain had eased, but he still treated it tenderly. He reached up and combed the silky mane of Kyer's horse, rewakening a memory of thicker fur entwined in his fingers; feeling the love emanating from her body as he ran his hand through fur that smoothed into soft skin when she changed form—he lifted his hand from the horse's hair. That decade-old memory might bring a smile to his lips, but it would not help him stay focussed here and now.

He stroked the horse's neck. Did the beast wonder where his rider was? Did he feel, the way most of them did, it seemed, something was missing? Kyer had a presence that filled empty spaces like water poured into a jug of pebbles. However new to the group she was, with her, the company felt . . .

complete. Trevile had predicted her abduction; there had been nothing in his chain-reading to suggest her return.

Jesqellan stroked Trig's neck, feeling tired. There hardly was a point to keeping watch.

A tremor buckled his knees. It was followed instantly by a quiet shuffle and a moaning sound from the other side of the fire. "Intruder!" he cried, alerting the others, and dashed across the clearing, his hand raised.

A split second after the shimmering had appeared, it was gone, and Kyer found herself lying in the dirt on the edge of the light of a campfire. Whose, she hadn't a clue, so she instinctively grabbed for her only weapon, her boot dagger, and quickly remembered it had been taken. She winced and tried to stifle a moan. A warning cry erupted, and she knew her presence had been detected. *I can't . . . I can't do this.* Silhouetted figures were coming at her, a sword, a nocked arrow pointed at her.

"Please." She managed only a whisper. "Please—"

Thirteen
Mystified Mage

Jesqellan lowered his hand. He had been poised with a particularly devastating spell and stopped himself just in time to avoid frying Kyer. The others rushed toward her, but he held back. Her hair, dishevelled like a tumbleweed, was wet and plastered to the side of her face. In the firelight, her eyes showed terror yet something else too: like a buck awaiting the final arrow. Goddess Helke, but she was a frightful mess! Phennil stepped aside and puked. There was no sign of a horse; there had been no sound of her approach. Kyer could hardly move at all, let alone walk. It was as if she had appeared out of nowhere at all. Was he the only one who had felt the tremor? While the others asked what had befallen her and where she had been, Jesqellan couldn't help but think, *How did you get here?*

Derry recovered right away and started giving orders, which the others hurried to carry out. "I'm going to lift you, Kyer, and it's going to hurt." She did not respond but growled like a wounded dog as he picked her up as gently as he could and carried her over to her blankets. He laid her down, on her side, as carefully as if she were an infant, and indeed, as soon as he'd placed her, she let go all she must have been withholding all that endless day.

Sobs spewed out in gushes, her body shook, and Derry did the only thing he knew to do. He placed his hand gently on her hair and caressed it the way he used to with Amber or Lily when his little sisters needed comforting.

Derry glanced up at the others. They were sitting or standing, looking away.

At length, her sobs subsided. Derry waited a time, letting her know he was there, not abandoning her, but neither pressuring her. Finally he whispered, "I'd like to tend you now. May I?"

She nodded.

Janak tossed some more fuel on the fire then came and crouched nearby, watching Kyer with eyes like the firelight.

"Jesqellan, Phennil, stay on hand to assist me," Derry said. "Janak, go lie down. Now. There will be no questions tonight," he added unequivocally.

Derry plied his trade long into the night, checking for broken bones, cleaning still-wet blood, stitching, bandaging. Lumps and bruises disfigured her face. Her right eye was swollen and blackened. Her lip was doubled. A bulge on the left side of her head was a deep shade of purple, and a gash on her right cheek oozed fluid. Her back—*Guerrin's fire*—her back was a bloody pudding of lacerations. Kyer was uncomplaining, apart from a few uncontrollable winces. It was as if nothing he could do came close to relieving what she'd gone through that day. And although she was in bad shape, he thanked Aidan repeatedly that she was back.

She spoke only five words: "Just don't touch the gem."

Phennil couldn't watch as Derry physicked Kyer. He did as Derry asked but found ways to keep his eyes averted. Shame clutched him like a winter chill. What had she gone through all day, and he didn't have the strength to look? Phennil saw the look of grim determination on Derry's face and wondered what else the captain was hiding. And there was Janak over there, staring up at the stars and staying out of it altogether. Without a thought, Phennil stepped over to the dwarf.

"If your problems are *her* fault, who's to blame for *hers*?"

Long after Derry had gone to bed and Phennil had taken watch, Jesqellan could not sleep. Kyer's reappearance had stunned him. He was frustrated at his inability to explain it. There was a spell—a powerful one. He had felt its tremor, and he still felt the vestiges of its energy. The only one he could think of that remotely fit these circumstances was the Gate spell. But it had two rules: either the wizard had to be able to see their target location, or they had to visualise it accurately from a memory of being there before. Who in Ronav's band of rogues was a strong enough wizard to have mastered a spell that he, Jesqellan à Boldaran, a highly trained battle mage, hadn't nearly the power to learn? And even so, why would this person choose to release the prisoner right from under the chief's thumb? And how? How could he know where her friends were?

Unless . . . Maybe the mage who teleported her also had a locator spell. It was the only explanation he could think of. Yet if Ronav had such a powerful wizard working for him . . . *We could be in trouble.*

Puzzled, he considered the medallion around her neck. It radiated magic, like a fading perfume. At the very least, her medallion explained the faint smell of magic Jesqellan had detected on her all along. He finally slept but not before he heard Trevile saying that there was one in their party who was not what he seemed. *Or she.*

Ronav fled from the hall amid the shrieks and cries and plunged into the darkness of the passageway. He had to get to his room, where he'd find comfort, relief from the panic into which he was descending.

Once he had found himself again, he would think about what to say to Golgathaur.

Torches were few and far between in these tunnels, supplies scarce in these times of preparation. As the light of one died out behind, he had to dash a few paces in pitch black before the dim glow of the next torch gave assurance that he was still alive. He gulped in the light as it intensified and glanced nervously around, watching for those horrible creatures with the beady eyes that liked to sneak up on people in the dark and bite and sting. The mere thought of darkness brought back all-too-vivid memories of the time he'd spent in Dregor's dungeon. He had never been afraid of the dark before then.

He'd been lucky. Lord Dregor did not often dole out second chances. But Ronav had provided information that proved to be useful in the fall of Equart City, thanks to his previous relations with Kien and Valrayker, and Dregor had conceded a need for informers and suppliers who could operate within enemy territories.

He watched his feet carefully to avoid tripping over the few rocks that jutted out of the stone floor. The creators of the inner mountain hideout had been unable to smooth down every sharp edge; some rocks were more stubborn than others. Or perhaps they just didn't have time to complete the project before that particular tribe of dwarves was attacked and wiped out by Dregor's army of orcs and goblins. But that was before Ronav's time. Dregor had done significant damage to these duchies further south in previous centuries, but since the ascendancy of Kien Bartheylen, his efforts had been thwarted. His lordship had had plenty of time to regroup, and now, three years past the fall of Equart, he was gathering his forces to begin the move south again. Ronav cursed Simon for getting himself killed and slapped his hand on the wall to emphasise it. Without the goods and the information, the young fool's journey had been for naught. What did that damned girl know of Simon's business?

And what had she done with his armlet? She said she had left it in Shael. His footsteps slowed in his despair. That device was vital to his plan. It had been extremely expensive. *Damn it.* It wasn't fair that Kien Bartheylen had risen to such power and he had not. Kien was damned good with a sword, but Ronav was clever. So why had Kien gained power and he had not?

And now he had had a taste of such power and respect, though on a much more limited scale and at a large price. He wanted more. But he needed that armband if he were to succeed to Kien's throne. And beyond. *A device to eliminate fear.*

Ronav stumbled blindly past the openings that led into the kitchens, the meeting room, and the on-duty guards' office. Just past the point where the tunnel began to make its descent into the caverns below, he veered off, with a gasp of relief, into the well-lit passage on the right. His passage. He was the chief; he deserved some extra light to guide him to his own quarters. The gloriously bright and soundless tunnel was far away from the screams and cries of the men he had left behind. The downward slope he left only served to remind him that there was an empty cell far below that ought to have been occupied by a young snippet of a girl who was far too big for the breeches she wore. Mouthy bitch. She had to be some kind of witch, that was all there was to it. Where the hell had she got to? And what the *hell* was he going to tell Golgathaur?

Grabbing the candle from the bracket outside his room, he held it up to the burning ember of the torch that hung across the hall until its own tiny flame flared. Then he fumbled with the latch on his door. He burst into the room and quickly lit every candle and lamp he could find, everything that could eliminate darkness and shadow and the demons that accompanied them. He built a fire in the grate to suck the chill out of the cold stone walls and floor. Then, with quivering hands, he poured himself a drink of the pale yellow liquid that never failed to incinerate his nerves. Desperately he leaned down and licked up the trickle that had escaped when the trembling bottle had missed the cup. Setting the bottle back on the table, he took a deep breath before turning to move into his wooden armchair.

He gasped in shock and let the cup fall from his hand, the precious fluid spread into the cracks and disappeared into the shiny floor. But he had forgotten it already.

A pair of tall, black boots, crossed at the ankles, rested on his footstool. Attached to them was a pair of long legs in black trousers, above which was a torso, hands clasped on its trim midriff as its elbows rested comfortably on the arms of Ronav's chair. His face, its unnatural pallor highlighted by the contrasting dark hair, was all innocence.

"You seem surprised to see me," he said, a puff of heliotrope wafting from him.

"Golgathaur!" Ronav spurted. "You're early."

"Why whatever is the matter, Ronav?" His concern was certainly feigned. "You seem all in a tizzy." He gestured, inviting the shaken man to sit in his own other, less appealing, armchair.

"Nothing," Ronav said unconvincingly, sitting in the chair and crossing his legs with an attempt at nonchalance. "Nothing is the matter. Everything is perfectly under control."

A silence ensued, relaxing for one man, disquieting for the other, though he tried admirably to regain the composure he had not actually felt since just before Kyer Halidan had opened her mouth for the first time.

"What does a man have to do to get a drink around here?" Golgathaur said, startling Ronav again. Golgathaur could have produced his own beverage with a snap of his fingers if he so chose, but Ronav didn't remind him. The last drop of liquor from that bottle fell into Golgathaur's cup, leaving none for Ronav. But he dared not say a word aloud. He would have to fetch more tomorrow.

"Now how fares this latest scheme of yours?" the ... wizard? Or whatever he was, asked in a tone that suggested he already knew the answer.

Ronav said nothing. He hadn't had time to prepare a speech.

"Well, I will tell you what I have already surmised," Golgathaur continued, "since you don't seem to have found the courage to tell me yourself. You have not been successful in your venture."

Ronav stared at him.

"You should not wonder that I have guessed it, which I see that I have. You see, if the bird were in hand, you would have no reason to be so distressed at my early arrival."

"I had her, sir; she was here. Up in my hall. Con brought her in this evening."

"And you lost her again already? So soon?"

"It wasn't—she—" he blubbered. "I *had* her!"

"And during her brief visit, did you manage to collect the information as you promised?"

Ronav faltered. He had no news that would gain himself favour with Golgathaur and certainly not with Lord Dregor himself.

"Just tell me, Ronav. I can find out quite as easily from someone else if I so choose. The fact is that I'm enjoying my drink and I'm quite comfortably seated. Besides, you give me such delight with your company that I hesitate to leave. But I will if I have to. And Dregor doesn't like to hear stories that aren't from the horse's mouth, as it were. You are the horse. Speak, my good fellow."

Ronav sighed. "I had her," he said again, but this time he was just tired. "Con and a few others took her this morning from the place where she was camped with the rest of Valrayker's men. I asked her some questions. Things became a little ... heated."

Golgathaur snorted. "What did she tell you?"

Ronav squirmed.

"Did she give you any answers at all?" Golgathaur pressed. "What reason did she give for killing your man in the village?"

"She told me some cocked-up story about him insulting her," he blurted. "It was nonsense. She was completely uncooperative. She refused to speak about what she's doing for Valrayker, where they are headed, what their instructions are— I tried everything in my power to make her talk. I was patient with her . . . and polite. I complimented her, as any man would do to a beautiful woman, only he would expect to be treated with more respect in return. I was forceful when that got me nowhere."

"Did you beat her?"

"Yes! Beat her, even flogged her. Well, Con did. He deserved it; she'd eluded him for so long."

"And still it produced no results?"

"None whatsoever. She had an amulet of some kind. Con touched it and it flared up and he was burned to death!" Ronav had reached shrieking pitch. He hesitated. "Then she disappeared."

Silence.

"Disappeared?"

"Yes."

"Just vanished. Into thin air." Golgathaur's voice was quiet.

"Yes," Ronav insisted. "Vanished like a bleedin' Cymrion! My men looked everywhere. She was practically immobile; there was no way she could have run. I don't know what happened to her." There. It was out. He had now but to wait to learn what his fate would be.

"And you say she had an amulet?"

"Yes, some trinket in her pocket. I didn't see it very well."

Silence. Golgathaur chewed on his tongue. "You do know that I shall have to report this to his lordship."

Ronav fell to his knees. He made no effort to mask the shaking whine in his voice. "Please, Golgathaur! Give me another chance. It wasn't my fault. She just disappeared. What was I to do? I can find her again. We'll tie her up next time. I'll find out everything you want me to."

"That is what you said last time. You promised that you would take full responsibility for this girl, this child, you said, if I did not tell Dregor about her. You wanted to take care of it, capture her, find out all you could, so that you could gain instant gratification from him with your prowess as an agent. You have failed, Ronav."

Ronav shrank as he nodded. He withered into a heap on the cold floor.

"I can't just let this go," the wizard continued. "Young girls who go around vanishing into thin air are, I am certain, of some interest to my lord Dregor. Whether or not the rest of the information that you failed to obtain is important, that much I have to share with him."

Ronav nodded wordlessly.

"Now you say she had an amulet?" Golgathaur repeated.

Ronav nodded again. "It had a gem in the centre." He was exhausted. He shrank beneath Golgathaur's contemptuous smirk, which confirmed his self-analysis as a snivelling lump.

Golgathaur rose. He shook his head. "A girl," he chuckled. "Did you find out her name, at least?"

"Kyer Halidan." Ronav spit the name out as if it were bad fish on his tongue.

"I am going now to report this to his lordship. I will return shortly." With that, Golgathaur nodded and was gone. Into thin air.

Ronav snapped. There was altogether too much vanishing going on today. He let out a sob. Lamp in hand, he burst from his room and fled up the passageway to fetch some more of his precious liquid. He knew he didn't have much time before Dregor's lieutenant would return to take him away. He felt his throat constrict with terror. He tried to breathe and calm himself so he would not appear the fool in front of his men. Again. *Damn that girl.* This was all her fault. She had stood there so coolly in front of him, making sarcastic comments, refusing to answer to him. *If I ever find her, I will kill her for what she has done to me.*

He repelled the recognition that he hated her because she showed so much more courage than he had ever felt in his life.

He stalked into the office where four men sat at the table, visibly shaken, staring into their cups. No words passed between them. They hardly noticed when their chief availed himself of a full bottle and left the room.

Ronav opened the bottle immediately and guzzled from it, leaning against the outside of the office door. He dreaded returning to his room but knew he must. Golgathaur would find him no matter where he was, and he would far rather be taken from there, where it wouldn't be witnessed by anyone. Bad enough that they had seen him cower behind his chair as Con burned. It would be worse if they saw him quake as Golgathaur made him go through that awful shimmering doorway into Dregor's vast, shiny obsidian hall. *Just not the dungeon again. Please!* He took another draught to stop the trembling. Placing one foot in front of the other, he made it back to his room.

His hand trembled on the door handle for an eternity before he managed to forget why he was afraid to open it. Only then could he turn the handle.

Empty. Golgathaur was nowhere in sight. And suddenly Ronav wished that he had been there, sitting patiently in his armchair, with that smirk on his frighteningly intelligent face and that ever-present glint in his eye. Ronav hated him and feared him because of what he knew he was capable of and even more so because of what he *imagined* him to be capable of. Ronav wished the wizard had been there to greet him upon his return because now he'd have to wait.

More than two hours later, Ronav lay sprawled on his cot in the corner. Many of the candles had burned themselves out, and the fire was low. The two-thirds of the bottle he had consumed had resigned him to his inevitable fate. He jumped when Golgathaur reappeared, but he was no longer afraid. He was even beyond despair, relieved that it was time to go. Time to get it over with. He sat up unsteadily, his head whirling.

Golgathaur stood with his arms folded across his chest, his hair brushing the ceiling. "Well! I see you have prepared yourself." He smirked. "I am sorry to disappoint you."

Ronav looked up at him with droopy eyes. "Hunh?"

"You can go to sleep now."

"Wha'? What're you talkin' 'bout?"

Golgathaur was clearly tickled by his own tactics. "He doesn't want you. I told him your whole sordid tale about this girl, Kyer, and your reasons for withholding the information from him. He was extremely fascinated by the part about her vanishing act but didn't much care about the rest of it. He said that was all he needed to know and returned to his meditation as peacefully as ever. You're off the hook, Ronav."

Ronav continued to stare, slack jawed, at Lord Dregor's lieutenant. Golgathaur gently pried the bottle from his hand and set it on the side table. With the end of a finger, he tipped Ronav over onto the bed. The stunned man's eyes were still open as Golgathaur said, "Sweet dreams," and, carrying some floral fragrance with him, exited the same mysterious way he always did.

At the end of the next day, Ronav was lying peacefully on his bedroll in their camp a half-day's ride north of his headquarters. He could not believe his good fortune. Somehow, he had managed to avoid another encounter with Dregor, and he was certain it had had something to do with the way he had explained it all so eloquently to Golgathaur. His other worry was solved too, that of who should be his right-hand man now that Con was—had been —was gone. The first logical choice was Gyles, but Ronav had always been unimpressed with the swordwork of that fellow, though he was loyal and had worked hard for him.

But the man who had arrived this morning was perfect. He had been brought in from outside while Ronav, his massive headache relieved by the herbal tea, shouted out orders to his company as they packed up to leave. The newcomer had watched with such a high-and-mighty attitude that Ronav had dared him to accompany them. He went by the name of Hunter. Ronav was satisfied with him by the end of the day; at least, he would try him out, on a probationary basis, perhaps until the end of this task. If the stranger succeeded, he would definitely be given the position. His swordwork had been impressive to say the least, and he had a couple of other things that Con had lacked: good looks and charm. Very useful tools, both of those, especially where a woman was concerned. Ronav was looking forward to a long and happy relationship with his new assistant and was certain to receive praise from Dregor for his choice.

Kyer awoke with no sense of how much time had passed. She felt numb throughout, as if it emanated from deep within her and spread outward to the tips of her fingers and toes. She lay on her side, body curled with knees up, one hand by her cheek. Eyes felt heavy, thick; opening them was like pressing them against her sockets. In her line of vision: blankets, grass, dirt, fire pit. Also, her own swollen cheek. Smells of dirt, wool, and something else, something ... clean masking something filthy. No pain. No nothing. Memories of a nightmare stirred, but blue sky and morning birdsongs seemed to dissipate any association of badness. Shuffling and whispers drifted into her attention.

"You saw how it was," a voice said in a subdued tone. It was vaguely familiar. "She was immobile; she couldn't crawl, let alone walk any distance. No horse." There was a murmured response, but she couldn't make out words. The whispering went on, and Kyer felt urgency, close to panic in the timbre. "And where are we? I don't even know where we are, so how could she? I'm telling you, there's something wicked at play."

The other voice responded again; in contrast to the first speaker, it sounded like warm water, with calm and relief. Then soft footfalls approached and a shadow knelt down beside her. A hand warmed her forehead, and she tilted her head to see who it belonged to. She saw concern through caring blue eyes below pale hair. He half-smiled at her.

"Kyer?" She was sure this was the source of the calm murmurings. "Are you in there?"

It came to her then. "Derry." Her voice was hoarse and dry, and it hurt a little to speak.

Picking up on her cue, he brought a cup to her lips and cradled her head to help her take a sip. It was warm and soothing, tasting of berries and spices.

"I don't want to pressure you. Are you ready to talk about it?"

What did he mean? *Talk about it?* "'Bout what?"

His face fell and a glimmer of alarm flashed through his limpid eyes and was gone again. "Let me know; that's all." He moved out of her line of sight.

She continued to stare at her blankets and the ground and the fire pit until a short time later, a tingling sensation came over her back, changing rapidly into stinging. When she was small, Kyer had burned her fingers in the steam from the teakettle. This was akin to that experience, with the difference that it was not localized to a small area. Her neck, shoulders, all the way down her back to her bottom sizzled like hot oil. Her body ached in places that had never ached before. She gritted her teeth but soon had to call out.

"Derry, whatever you gave me ran out."

The vague, cloudy memories of what she had gone through yesterday sharpened from nightmarish shadows into vivid, unobstructed reality. The places that didn't sting throbbed. She closed her eyes and exhaled deeply.

Derry knelt behind her with his kit. "I need to check things over, and then I'll decide what to do next. All right?"

Kyer sucked in air and flexed her fingers and toes. "Just make it go away."

She braced herself as Derry uncovered the scene and made his assessment. He worked silently, and Kyer sensed a hesitancy. It would do no good to pretend she didn't understand it.

"I *had* forgotten," she whispered. "But I remember now."

He said nothing but the silence was full of expectation. She heard the *pop* of a jar lid. She winced as he dabbed on salve. "Sorry, my hands are a bit cold."

Kyer laughed cheerlessly. "I don't think your hands being cold is something I could ever complain about."

His chuckle sounded both sheepish and relieved. "I guess you've been through much worse discomfort."

"Discomfort doesn't begin to cover it." She sensed that he was digging for more. "Look, if it's all the same to you, I'd rather not talk about it, okay?" Shuffling sounds told her the others had gathered around.

"Well, all right. But—"

"All you need to know is I didn't tell them anything. And Con is dead." Should she perform the wine ritual? She didn't know if she was responsible for Con's death.

Phennil's feet and legs blocked her view of the fire pit. He crouched low. "Hey, Kyer," he said gently, apologetically, even. "Who was he? What happened to him?"

She fingered the medallion and saw again, even with open eyes, the sparks and fire. It turned out she was ready to speak about it. In a faltering voice, she tried to describe it: his corpse, still in human shape, blacker than coal, shards of fire and electricity trailing throughout it like dying embers; the jet of lightning that spewed out of the gem on her medallion, a mere trinket in a previous life; Con's weight pressing against her body, suddenly hurtling into the air and coming to a dead stop fifteen feet away. The nauseating odour of burning flesh. And the low chuckle of Ronav, swelling, building on itself until it grew to a fever pitch, piercing her like a shaft of ice.

"If they'd given me a sword, I could have—" She shook her head. "Even he didn't deserve to die like that." She decided against the ritual.

Jesqellan asked if he could examine the medallion. She held up the chain so he could scrutinize the device without touching it. He shook his head. "I have never seen anything like it. It could be an energy cell. What happened then?" His voice sounded curious but seemed to be hiding something. "Who sent you here?"

"Um. Sent me?"

The mage prodded. "Yes. How did you get here?"

"I . . . well . . . I don't know. I remember a door." She closed her eyes and tried to remember.

"A door? Yes?"

"Jesqellan?" Derry said.

"Wait," the mage said.

"It was . . . well, it *seemed* like a door. It wasn't there and then it was. Made of . . . I don't know . . . *light*. Pale light. Small, shimmery, faint. Hardly there at all, really."

"And?" the mage insisted.

His tone was startlingly similar to that of Ronav Malachite, the renewed memory of whom brought bile into her throat and made her quiver uncontrollably. She craned her neck around to glare at the mage. "Guerrin's fire, Jesqellan, next time you're lying on the stone floor, surrounded by filthy enemies, bleeding, beaten, flogged, nearly mutilated, with the body of your captor smouldering before you, and something resembling a doorway appears next to you, you tell me what *you* would do. *I* fucking-well crawled through it."

The flames licking the wood in the fire was the only sound within the shocked silence. Kyer shut her eyes so she didn't have to see Phennil gawking at her.

After a moment Derry said, "I'm sure there's a logical—"

"I don't care how she got here," Phennil piped up. "Only that she's back."

Jesqellan grunted. "Makes sense, considering it was your fault they took her."

Kyer's eyes snapped open. "What the bloody hell do you mean by that?"

Phennil, his face crimson and voice tight, told her about the man with the scarred face who'd spoken to him in Shael. "His appearance put me off, but I – he seemed so friendly."

Kyer listened to the elf's story, her eyes welling up. She reached out and took his hand. "Phennil, don't be troubled. You've punished yourself for this, I can tell. And maybe you helped him along. But Con had been after me for two weeks. It was only a matter of time."

Phennil gestured with his arm. "But they did . . . all this!"

"*Not* your fault," she insisted. "Forget it. It's over. Con is dead and that's that."

Derry, finished with his treatments, covered her with her blankets. "You're a generous person, Kyer. More so than—others." He squeezed her shoulder and moved away.

Kyer realized then that one voice had been missing from the entire exchange. She raised her head and looked around. When her gaze rested on Janak, his head wrapped up like a bloody name day present, another memory returned to her. "The ogre." At their surprised faces, she added, "My new friends told me about their secret weapon."

Janak's good eye stared at her for a moment. She read some deep emotion in it but couldn't tell what it was. He turned away and she was glad of it.

Derry stitched the cuts on Kyer's face, and some on her back. He trimmed off threads of skin that were unlikely to reattach, applied his medicated salve, and bound the wounds. Finally, he gave her a healing potion to speed her recovery. He then left with Janak on the half-day ride to Stoney Hill so the dwarf could be examined by a healer. Even as physicker-adept, there were limits to Derry's abilities. A healer had other powers that Derry did not have at his disposal.

A light rain fell as Kyer lay on her bed, feeling useless and restless, watching Phennil care for Trig as well as Leoht. She was not sorry to see the dwarf go. He'd been surly and silent, and when their eyes connected, albeit unintentionally, his good eye pierced her like Derry's needle from within all his bushy hair. She could not read him but felt the sting of his gaze as if he'd spoken aloud his hatred for her. Plus, the worry that had taken root while Gyles's strong arm held her had germinated: the worry that she was not of value to the group, that Janak's wounds were too pressing for them to bother with her, and the fear that if the mystifying door hadn't appeared and somehow brought her here, she would still be a prisoner of Ronav Malachite.

The drizzle continued all that day. Kyer dozed off and woke up to dim light and a drop of moisture on her cheek. At first she thought it was night already, but then she realized she was in a sort of tunnel. Several pieces of equipment, a saddle, and saddlebags were piled in a row next to her. It wasn't a tunnel; someone had erected a makeshift tent by resting a blanket on top of the pile and extending it down to the ground next to her. It had been there long enough to become saturated with rainwater, and she could see another drop of water gather and grow. It dropped on her face, and she wriggled out of her blankets to peek out of the tent. It was the first time she'd made any significant movements, and she was as stiff as if she were petrified wood. Phennil sat huddled in his cloak next to a tiny fire. A small animal pelt was stretched over the fire and secured to three sticks a couple of feet up, barely protecting the fire from the mizzle.

"Thanks," Kyer said.

Phennil looked up and grinned at her. "It was the least I could do. Sleep well?"

"Fine." Kyer grunted just a little as she struggled her way out.

"Can I—," Phennil began.

"No thanks." She stung and ached but much less severely. In her slow progress, she knocked against one of the rocks that held her shelter on the ground, and it fell inwards.

"Hungry?" Phennil asked.

Kyer fetched her own cloak, slowly, slowly, from her saddlebag and joined Phennil at the fire, seating herself slowly, slowly. She sat so the cloak rested on her shoulders but did not cling to the bandages on her back. The stinging made her wince and she pressed her lips together. Phennil handed her a cup.

"It's the tea Derry had me make for you. It's for the pain, he said. I made it awhile ago so it's probably cold, but I wanted to be sure it was ready when you woke up."

She nodded, and its cool temperature allowed her to drink it quickly. "With any luck it'll start to work faster."

Phennil handed her the piece of meat he had just finished roasting. "Fox," he said. "It's not bad. And his skin is helping keep our fire going so we can cook him. He's a pretty obliging creature, all 'round."

Kyer took one bite and instantly recalled how long it had been since she'd eaten. Porridge the morning she was taken. Two days ago? Three? This was the first time she wasn't turned off at the thought of food. No wonder she felt faint. "This is fantastic."

"Glad you think so. I've had better myself. Squirrel is quite tasty, actually. Raccoon is kind of tough if you don't cook it slowly, but it tastes good too. Groundhog, opossum . . . I've eaten most everything."

"Anything'll do if there's nothing else around. I thought you were a vegetarian?"

He grinned sidelong at her. "Anything'll do if there's nothing else around."

A companionable silence followed while she ate, and he skewered another hunk of fox meat. He tossed some sticks onto the fire, which smoked in protest at their dampness.

"Where's Jesqellan?"

"We've been taking turns all day hunting for wood and food. See, we didn't ever intend to stop here so long."

"Sorry."

He smiled sardonically. "I'm the one that's sorry."

"Phennil—"

"No, really. When I saw what they did to you . . . Regardless of my stupidity in Shael, we should have protected you better." His pitch rose even as her self-worth descended. "We should have been on the lookout all the time. What kind of company are we that doesn't look out for each other?

Everyone's so busy competing, looking for ways to find fault with each other, instead—"

Jesqellan padded into view, and Kyer noticed that not only had the rain stopped but darkness was drifting over their camp as swiftly as the smoke was rising.

"I imagined it would be different; that's all," Phennil finished, looking up at the mage and the scant sticks and leaves he'd gathered. Kyer guessed it was not a topic Phennil had broached with Jesqellan.

The elf handed her another piece of meat and she brooded. All this time, she had thought she didn't need protecting. And it had used to be true. But she was no longer in her home town, contending with schoolyard altercations. Not even six weeks since leaving her humble farming village, and she was living her dream, working as a warrior for her greatest hero. It was real. Life would not be easy from now on. Six weeks in the real world, and she'd already garnered some true enemies. She glanced at Phennil. *And maybe true friends?*

Yes, Phennil, she thought. *I, too, imagined it would be different.*

Fourteen
Nennia

Derry and Janak returned mid-morning the next day, bringing supplies with them. Through her own swollen eye, she saw Janak struggle with a buckle as he affixed his battle axe to his saddle. According to a low-voiced Derry, the healer had done what she could, but he would likely never see properly out of his left eye. Nothing more than shadows.

Derry sat next to Kyer and called Jesqellan over.

"What can you do to help Kyer feel well enough to ride?"

Kyer wanted to protest but bit back her pride. It would be days before she would be able to ride without significant pain if she did not accept help. Those days meant precious time to their mission.

"May I see?" Jesqellan gestured to Kyer, and she exposed her back to him. He and Derry assessed it together.

"I see swelling and redness, some oozing," Derry said. "All normal at this stage. Ordinarily it would take several days for this stage of healing."

Jesqellan nodded. "I can speed that up a bit, but I will need some time to recover myself, afterward."

"Of course," Derry said. "Better that you take that time now so that you are fully recuperated by the time we are set to leave."

Jesqellan prepared himself, drinking a lot of water, and meditating for several minutes, while Kyer gingerly lay on her side on her bedroll, head on a ball of clothing, her bare back revealed. Her broken rib was still far too painful to lie on her front. The mage knelt at her side.

"Lie still and try to relax. Let yourself go completely limp. Derry and Phennil? Please stay at her head and feet, just in case."

"In case of what?" Phennil said, placing himself at her feet.

"In case she moves suddenly. It's important that she be still."

Jesqellan rolled up the sleeves of his robe. Kyer closed her eyes and concentrated on being limp and still. Relaxation was hard to achieve, and several times she had to breathe the tension out of her legs and arms.

She felt the warmth of Jesqellan's hands, not touching, but hovering above her lacerated skin, and her muscles contracted with the fear of his touch.

"Shh," he whispered reassuringly. She breathed and let go.

He murmured words she couldn't understand, and after a moment she felt, not *pain*, exactly, but an odd sort of tightening that played on the edge of burning. A low growl escaped her throat, and Derry's hands pressed gently on her upper arm and her head, Phennil's on her legs. Movement from the mage told her he was not focusing the energy from his hands on one localized spot but that he was shifting their position. The sensation was very like when as a child she had painted herself with mud and it had dried, making the skin feel shrunken. A tugging inside her torso that took her breath away seemed to be consistent with her rib knitting itself.

Finally, Jesqellan's body seemed to shake, and Derry's voice said, "Enough," and the sensation stopped. The mage flopped to the ground next to her, a constricted scream trying to pierce its way through a closed throat. Derry leapt up and Kyer opened her eyes to see him and Phennil hefting their companion over to his bedroll. Kyer realized that whatever Jesqellan had done for her had not resulted in mere exhaustion in himself.

A quick analysis of her own condition told her she was not completely healed, but she hadn't expected that. The pain of her wounds had lessened, had changed. It felt . . . shallower, somehow. A light pressing on her side revealed a much improved broken rib.

Soon Derry returned, kneeling next to her to observe and offer his impressions.

"The wounds have scabbed over," he said, "and the oozing has stopped. I would say he has bought you a few days of sub-cutaneous healing. I think you will find that you can probably put on a shirt without it rubbing too painfully, and in another day or two you will be able to ride. At least for short stints."

"Enough to get on our way?"

He nodded. "I believe so."

Kyer's gaze slipped over to where the mage was prostrate on his bed. "At what cost?"

Derry, sat back on his heels. "It's a spell that we choose to use only when absolutely necessary. He has literally taken on a few days of your pain. You could say your loss of pain is his gain. With him out of commission for a time, we needed to do this in a place where Phennil and I could easily keep watch."

Guilt wracked her innards enough to replace the pain she had given away. "What about Janak?"

Derry shook his head. "We chose to help you because there is nothing more to be done for him. He can ride, where you could not. No spell of Jesqellan's can change what has happened to Janak."

For a couple more days, they stayed put so both Kyer and Jesqellan could recover. Kyer showed her gratitude by focussing every iota of energy she had into healing. They had a mission to carry out, and she was acutely aware of holding them up. Derry continued to apply his salve, which kept the surface of her skin from stinging when she put on a shirt. A healing potion would accelerate the process.

At last, the captain determined that the two invalids were fit for travel, and the mage was quite recovered, so they began to pack up. Kyer, her joints and muscles stiff and aching, moved carefully through her preparations. There wasn't much to do. The rain had dissuaded her from leaving items lying around, so her saddlebags were already packed. She'd been immobile, so little had been disturbed; only her spare tunic and wool sweater had been removed. Her bloodied and torn tunic she'd added to the meagre supply of sticks for the fire. She replaced her stolen boot knife with the dagger Jesqellan had given her in Paterak.

The dwarf tried to shove his rolled-up cloak behind his saddle, missed, and dropped it, cursing under his breath. Without thinking, Kyer hastened over and, with a hiss of pain from the sudden movement, picked up the bundle even as Janak bent down to grab it. She handed it to him.

"I'm . . . really sorry."

He snatched the garment out of her hand. "Yes. As soon as I'm able to wield a weapon again, if ever, I know what I'm going to do with it." With that, he gave her his back.

Cheeks aflame, barely seeing, Kyer went and, with Phennil's help, hoisted her saddlebags onto Trig.

If all went well, they ought to have arrived yesterday, Valrayker surmised. He was trying to read, sitting on one of the velvet-upholstered armchairs in Kien's library, but was distracted by so many things on his mind. One of Valrayker's teams had arrived from the northwest to report on the success of the task he had set them. There were rumours of bands of orcs sighted just on the northeast corner of Ballin, but recent experience had taught the dukes not to trust these reports. Twice now, an overeager scout from Ballin had reported the sight of an unfamiliar army, and in fact it was one of Kien's own patrols, protecting the borders. All the same, every time he heard such a tale, it was unnerving. He awaited the return of his other team for a more accurate picture.

Valrayker also felt some concern for Kien, who was awaiting a message from Bartheylen Castle, two duchies away. Kien's wife, Alon Maer, had been prevented from coming to Shael by an illness. Kien was expecting word as to her condition and had hoped to receive news well before this time. It caused him no trivial amount of vexation. Naturally, Kien's concern for his wife became Val's own; the two Bartheylens were the only people Valrayker thought of as family; any true relations were gone.

The dark elf had thought to come into the library and read to prevent his mind from dwelling on those subjects. He'd pulled an old favourite off the high shelf and blown the dust off it as he sat down. But it was impossible to concentrate. His long legs could not find a comfortable position. Sitting straight was out of the question and sideways with his legs flung over the side made the arm of the chair dig into his back. The floor was an option, but it was chilly. Maybe it was his choice of material. It just wasn't gripping enough to pull him in and away from his troubles. He closed it and climbed back up the ladder to return it to its place on the shelf. He would try another. He slid *Crendesh Ferrulann* out of its slot on the high shelf and inhaled to blow the dust off the book. He stopped mid-breath. Something was odd.

Crendesh Ferrulann was dust-free. The book he'd tried first was from the same shelf, and it had been topped by a snowy layer. These ancient volumes had sat in this library for countless years. He had read *Crendesh Ferrulann* before, but that was long before his exile from Equart, before Derry was even part of the castle guard. He examined it carefully, comparing it to all the other leather-bound works, noting the way the dust clung to the organic material on their spines as well as the tops. *How strange.* He was the only one in the duchy who would be interested in this book, let alone able to read it.

One other fleeting thought occurred to him. "What are the chances . . . ?"

But he did not have time to dwell on it because Acadia appeared in the doorway and said, "Val, Piper asked me to summon Kien. I am taking the liberty of assuming you will wish to be with Kien when he receives the message."

Val interpreted this last as Acadia also believing, in the astute fashion that made her an invaluable Steward, that just as he would wish to be with Kien, Kien would wish him to be there. Involving Piper, the castle mage, meant it was probably more than just a message; it was more likely the Healer herself wishing to speak directly to Kien. The energy and organization necessary to complete such a spell was no small feat. Whatever the message was, it was critically important.

Valrayker thanked her from his rung and replaced the book.

The dark elf noiselessly entered the tiny room at the top of the tower, where Piper stood still as a statue, hands raised before her as if she were pushing the wall away. Her eyes were closed, and her stocky form was awash in light from a hundred vanilla- and cinnamon-scented candles randomly placed around the walls, the counter, the floor. Before her was a panel of dark glass, flanked by windows on either side that looked out eastward over the expanse of Shae's patchwork field and forest. The light of the mid-morning sun front-lit the mage's concentrated features and highlighted the grey veins in her brown hair. Val found himself a spot to stand in the space, mindful of the candles, and waited.

A moment later a servant arrived with a tray laden with sticky buns, flaky pastries, a dish of honey, a covered plate that smelled suspiciously of grilled venison, a pot of tea and an earthenware wine jug. She skirted expertly around the candles and set the tray down on the one counter space clearly reserved for it. With a nod to Valrayker she exited just as silently as she had performed her task.

Not long after, Kien rushed in with Acadia close on his heels. The high elf looked about to burst with questions, but checked himself, illustrating the wisdom he had learned in all his years as duke by respecting the power the mage was mustering for a difficult spell.

Valrayker admired his friend's patience and self-control.

Acadia sat on the stool in one angle of the hexagonal room, ready to deal with any aftermath. She poured herself some wine.

Valrayker also helped himself to a cup of wine, pouring one for his friend as well, though he refused it. He took a sip just as a quiet sigh startled them all amid the soundlessness.

"Ready." The mage relaxed her obelisk stance. "It will be time very soon." She rolled her shoulders and shook out her hands. "You will want to stand here, my Lord."

Kien stood where she had been, while Piper stepped aside and placed herself in front of the window to the left of the dark glass wall. Valrayker moved forward so he could see well.

"It's time." She placed her hand on the top corner of the glass and a soft glow emanated from the previously opaque surface. It brightened and a form began to take shape, eventually coming into focus as shoulders and a dark head.

"Roman," Kien said. The woman in the glass bowed. "Thank you to Piper here, and Cweivin there, for making this possible. For their sakes we won't waste words."

"My Lord Kien," the Prime Healer at Bartheylan Castle said, "and Valrayker as well," she added with a bow to the dark elf. "The news I have for you is both happy and sad, and I do not know, now that I stand before you, which I ought to first make known to you."

"Begin with the former, and I shall endeavour to stay my reaction until I have heard both. I shall hope that the joy of the first may be the stronger and hearten me for the second."

"Let it be so, my lord. My Lady Alon Maer, as you know, was ill when you departed Bartheylen Castle. Shortly thereafter it was determined that she is with child, my lord."

Kien's light-coloured face took on a glow that Valrayker recognized as joy and delight. But his friend did as promised and did not alter his mood. Indeed, there was a furrow in his brow as he braced himself for the second part of the message. It came directly.

"The other, my lord, is this: her illness took a different turn these five weeks ago." Valrayker watched Kien's complexion cloud with an ashen pallor as the Prime continued in the compassionate yet matter-of-fact tone of her profession. "We have waited rather than inform you at once because we wanted to have something to tell you. At first we did not know what to make of it. My lady did not suffer from the normal sickness that accompanies her condition but was unusually fatigued yet unable to sleep. Over the weeks she became delirious and spoke wildly of rampant infestations of rats and locusts then of coming tempests and enemy attacks." The woman had obviously witnessed this herself, for she spoke with an ever-deepening crease in her forehead. The pitch of her voice rose. "She eats but cries out in pain, and instead of gaining weight, she is losing it. We simply--" her voice caught, "--do not know what it is, only that this illness is quite separate from the pregnancy, and we fear that serious harm will come to the child if my lady is not cured soon." A sigh escaped her throat. "But we do not know how to cure her."

She fought back a strangled sound, and looked at Kien in anguish. "She cries out for you, my lord. So plaintive, I cannot erase it from my memory. I wish I had more I could tell you."

Kien needed no hand to steady him. He bore the news with the stoicism for which he had always been admired. To any outsider, he may have appeared unmoved and uncaring. He finally took a drink of the wine Valrayker had set near him and cleared his throat.

"Thank you, Roman, for bringing this to me with such forthrightness. By the goddess, I hardly know what to do."

Val said, "You must go to her, of course."

Kien nodded. "You're right of course. Roman, I will be there as soon as I can."

The Prime bowed her head in thanks, and stepped away. Piper tapped the glass again to break the spell, then with a gasp she crossed the room and fell on the food. Acadia rose and placed the stool, guiding the mage's body onto it, even as she crammed sticky bun ravenously into her mouth. Acadia kindly spread honey onto a pastry and Piper nodded her thanks as she replenished her depleted energy.

"You must go immediately," Val said.

Kien gulped his wine. "Yes, of course. But you, will you wait here for your company?"

"Yes, and I will be of whatever assistance I can to Lyndon in your absence."

Kien sighed, running a hand through his steel-grey hair and resting it on his forehead. "There can't be a cure if the disease is not known," he said darkly.

Valrayker put a hand on his friend's shoulder.

"I can't lose her," the high elf said in a whisper. "She is everything to me."

"I know."

"A child! I never dared to hope . . . But now—" Kien could not finish the thought aloud.

Then Piper's voice interrupted with a word as soft as a breath. "Kayme."

Val put a hand on her back. "What did you say?"

Piper turned around. "You must ask Kayme. He will know."

Valrayker's throat tightened with dread. But he knew Piper was right. Their only hope was Kayme. The most powerful wizard in all of Rydris.

That first day of travel was difficult for Kyer. She dismounted frequently to walk off stiffness, and it surprised her that the healing potion accelerated the mending at the site of her wounds but didn't actually make her feel much better. After travelling only a few hours, she was done in, and Derry called a halt. She slid down Trig's sleek body, inhaling the smell of him and taking strength from it. She didn't let go but leaned against his shoulder, possessed by an all-consuming weariness. She hated holding them up but knew that Nennia was not going anywhere. Better to rest now and at least be of some use when they got there.

Each day, her condition improved. Having a mission to focus on was the best medicine. Ronav and Con appeared less and less in her dreams, and the camaraderie among *most* of her friends allowed her to force the horrifying memories into rapid retreat. By the fourth day, she was able to ride all day, still fatigued by the time they made camp, but her aches had eased and her dizziness subsided. She was even able to go through her slow-motion swordwork routine. Though twinges of pain stopped her short once in a while, it felt good, energizing, as the blood pumped and awakened those muscles. When she caught Janak watching her, she was glad he couldn't see the flush that rushed up her neck. Would he think she was flaunting her recovery?

Phennil led them through the narrow western tip of Deerwood Forest. The air was still, and only a few jays and starlings played and tormented one another in the budding branches of the birch trees. A ground squirrel darted across Kyer's path, a badger disdainfully ambled aside, and a woodchuck fled as they approached. The hooves plodded on the spongy ground. They broke out of the forest in the early afternoon, where the sun god, Dima, spent just as much time hiding as he did showing his fiery face. Only a few hours ahead was the enemy-occupied Equart. They would have to proceed with caution from here, alert for border patrols. The village of Nennia was perhaps another two days beyond the border.

They crossed the imaginary line into enemy territory as the shadows neared their longest with not a patrol in sight. Kyer braced herself for a sudden sense of foreboding, the feeling that they were being watched, or a confrontation by a band of orcs. Instead, the lowering sun stretched its sweeping arm across land that quite astonished Kyer. Buttercups, bluebells, and purple cowslips brought the meadow to vivid life with colour. She had unconsciously feared that nothing would grow in land that was occupied by Dregor. Fields of tall foxtail and brome grasses brushed against their legs. The spikelets were nearly up to Jesqellan's armpits, and he had to use his staff to wave it aside and open a path for himself.

As the sun dipped, they descended a hill into a dusk-dimmed valley and were confronted with stands of cattails and bulrushes. Jesqellan cried out in surprise as he and the horses suddenly found themselves ankle deep in water. A startled flock of herons rose into the air in a deafening beating of wings, and the horses reared up in alarm. The mage narrowly missed being knocked into the marshy water by Janak's horse as he regained control.

"I want to thank our tracker for seeing the water before it reached my nether regions," Jesqellan said dryly.

"I'm sorry!" Phennil cried. "It came out of nowhere."

Janak added, "Too bad our *tracker's* skills did not do us the service of noticing the water before we walked into it."

Derry sighed. "Just get us out of here, Phennil."

Kyer cast Phennil what she hoped was an encouraging glance, but his eye roll clearly said, *I've messed up again,* as he turned them away from the marsh.

<hr />

At midday two days later, the village of Nennia lay below them like a ghost town. Through the thin fog, the only movement Kyer could see was a stream running eastward, cradling the village like a caring arm. It appeared to need as much care as it could get. Even from the hill, they could tell by the weathered, grey buildings that neglect had taken its toll.

"Not much to look at," said Janak as though their journey were a waste of effort. His vision in his good eye had improved enough to make out details, particularly in bright light.

"It troubles me that it has come to such a state as this," Jesqellan said.

Kyer shared his dismay. "Where are the people?"

"We will have to go in and find that out." Derry crouched down and indicated that the others should join him. "And to that end, we must still proceed with caution."

A contingent of five warriors was liable to arouse suspicion; it would be better to send in a couple of scouts disguised as common travellers.

Jesqellan was an easy first choice, as he could relay a message back to the others telepathically. Derry, in his armour, could draw too much attention. Kyer might have been the logical second choice if not for the bruises still on her face.

"Why not Phennil?" Kyer said. "His hair and hood will hide his ears."

Janak grunted. "The *tenderfoot* has a lot to say for someone who's done nothing since she joined this group but make trouble for the rest of us."

Her sword was pointing at Janak so fast, he fell on his backside. "Don't expect me to cut you any slack just because you're a cripple."

"Easy!" Derry's voice sliced through the tension. "Easy."

Alarm burned in Janak's eyes. She lowered her sword and shifted her gaze to the eastern horizon.

"Let me just point out," Derry said, "that we are in enemy territory."

One of the horses stamped the soft ground.

"Phennil is not a bad choice, indeed," said Jesqellan.

Derry was not convinced. He glanced at the elf. "My concern is your concentration and discretion."

Kyer flung out her arm. "I suppose in all your years as Valrayker's captain you've never made a single mistake?"

Phennil stifled a gasp. Derry stared at her, his blue eyes stormy. A squirrel shuffled on a tree branch.

Jesqellan said, "Perhaps we—"

"All right, then," the captain's eyes didn't leave Kyer's. "Phennil will go in with Jesqellan. But his loyalties will be given away if anyone finds out he's an elf, so he had better not let them. Understood?"

Kyer tried to hold his gaze but weakened and turned away.

"Yessir," Phennil said.

Phennil's feet slipped on dew as he and Jesqellan descended the hill through the afternoon haze. Phennil felt edgy and restless, his head never still as he glanced around, looking for . . . whatever it was they were looking for. His keen eyes were suspicious and watchful as they darted around underneath his hood. Upon entering the village, though, his nerves settled and sank into something more resembling sorrow at what his eyes beheld.

Dilapidated houses were little more than broken-down boards and logs. Weeds grew in window boxes, and dandelions were the only wildflowers bold enough to show any colour. The whole village blended with the cloudy skies that enveloped it.

"People actually *live* here?" Phennil whispered to Jesqellan.

"No," the mage responded gravely. "They exist."

For there was evidence of people living there, though they had yet to lay eyes on a person. Smoke trailed upward out of a crumbling chimney. The watery smell of someone's midday meal wafted around them. A shop sign creaked on its hook, and there were footprints in the dust on the porch.

Both elf and mage jumped at the sound of a voice.

"Oh," sighed a woman in a dreary wool dress that looked much like a sack. "You're late for the event too." She spoke slowly, as though exhausted. "I had to find my other shoe, you see." She gestured lazily to her mismatched pair of worn boots. Her gaze turned along the dirt road, and her feet began to follow it. She hadn't noticed they were strangers.

The two friends exchanged a look of curiosity. "Event?" They went after her.

They reached the square, where what looked to be the entire population of the village had gathered around a raised platform built of stone and timber. The woman melted into the crowd.

The companions needn't have worried about drawing attention to themselves. No one paid them any heed whatsoever. Phennil had the feeling that Derry could have ridden his warhorse directly up onto the platform and no one would have batted an eye.

Jesqellan motioned for Phennil to follow him, and they moved back toward an unkempt house, careful to avoid the piles of cow dung and a broken milking stool. Phennil climbed agilely into a leafless cherry tree by the house to get a better view.

Phennil noticed at the far end of the square, behind the platform, a clumsily erected scaffold, at the top of which hung a large bell with a rope dangling from it. He pointed it out to Jesqellan. "Suppose that's to remind them when to eat?" he said, only half joking. He drummed his fingers on the tree limb, waiting along with the villagers for whatever it was they were expecting.

He saw movement across the square. Two tall, thin men escorted a girl through the crowd. A path opened before them as the people politely allowed her to pass. They hoisted the girl up onto the platform. She could not have been more than fifteen and, judging by the size of her belly, was within days of giving birth. One of the tall men stood next to her. He raised his hand for silence, which was not difficult to achieve; there was little noise before.

"This girl is not coupled!" he cried in a clear voice. "She must be punished."

The crowd erupted in a sudden furore that nearly knocked Phennil out of the tree. Waving fists and shouting, yelling, shrieking words of sheer hatred when seconds ago they were like statues in a museum. "Whore!" "Witch!" "Scum!" were a few of the words that reached Phennil's horrified ears. The crowd had switched from noiseless apathy to an instant frenzy. Then it stopped as abruptly as it had begun. The man had raised his hand again.

"Jesqellan, what are we going to do?" Phennil whispered frantically.

The mage looked up at the elf, perplexed. "These are Valrayker's people."

The man on the platform had walked to the edge. Phennil pulled off his hood as he reached for the bow on his back.

"She must be punished!" the man shouted again. "Magistrate, the first move is your right!" He jumped down off the platform, leaving the girl standing there trembling, alone and bewildered. She did not say a word as a salt-and-pepper-haired man in the front row raised his hand, which gripped a fist-sized jagged stone. He pulled his arm back and aimed his throw.

But before it thrust forward to release the missile, the magistrate cried out and dropped to the dirt, an arrow jutting out of his shoulder. The crowd was shocked. No one looked around for the source of the arrow. They just stared at each other dumbly. Then mayhem broke out.

People panicked and ran in all directions, screaming wildly. Stones that had been intended for the girl were now thrown at each other, pieces of furniture were pulled out from under cloaks and used as weapons in a sudden brawl that put the lowest-class tavern to shame.

Phennil didn't have time to congratulate himself on the accuracy of his shot. He slithered out of the tree and fought his way through the throng of madness, shielding his head with his arm and dodging blows. Weapons flailed, making occasional contact, drawing blood in a few instances. He ducked out of the trajectory of a flying soup ladle. He hadn't intended to start a riot, but at least they weren't throwing stones at the girl. "Go home!" he hollered at people as he pushed his way through. Some listened and began to move away, while others looked to the voice for a new target. Their reflexes were slow, though, and he was already past. A woman was dashed to the mud by a carpet-beater to her back, and two men fell over her, leaving three of them in danger of being trampled. A red-faced teenage boy wrestled with the rope another man was tightening around his neck. Phennil snatched the chair leg out of the boy's clutch, cracked it against the man's hand to loosen his hold, and ripped the rope away from him.

Just before Phennil reached the platform where the poor girl stood, shaking and forgotten, he heard the bell. Its low, sonorous tone resonated through the square and had a most marvellous effect on the chaos. Phennil looked about in amazement as every man, woman, and child who had been screaming and brandishing a weapon stopped. Arms lowered and they began to move peacefully out of the square.

Gathering his senses, Phennil scrambled up onto the platform. He ignored the girl and raced across to the other side. The bell rope still swung back and forth. The bell swayed. But whoever had rung it was gone.

Fifteen
Nightmare of a Sleeping Village

Kyer swung her sword through her warm up patterns, pleased that her shoulders were finally loosening up. The muscles on her back, on the other hand . . . She was grateful for the pain transference Jesqellan had done, because she couldn't imagine how she would feel right now if he hadn't. Her muscles throbbed, the searing agony on the surface had eased to constant stinging, and occasional twinges shot down her legs. Her rib felt merely bruised, though, so she managed a small celebration. There was no way she was not going to be ready to use her sword if called upon.

Out of the corner of her eye, she saw Derry approach and a spate of embarrassment rushed through her. Her reaction to his doubt of Phennil had been a little over the top, and she couldn't explain why. Maybe because she knew how hard the elf tried to make a good impression, how desperately he wanted to make up for his earlier mistakes, and how that would never happen if his leader did not believe him capable of it. Perhaps she understood the elf because she shared his feelings.

She felt less guilty about her outburst at Janak. His vitriol was getting awfully tired.

As if reading her mind Derry said, "Janak is not the group's spokesman, you know."

Kyer paused mid-swing. Staring at the tip of her sword, the working of her legs as she held the position gave her a feeling of sturdiness. She nodded once, his point taken. She continued the sword's movement into the next stance. "Phennil wouldn't make so many mistakes if you didn't expect him to."

The captain exhaled. "You sure don't make it easy—" He stopped, and the suddenness of it drew her attention. He was staring at the rocky outcropping behind her wearing a puzzled frown.

She relaxed her stance wondering if he'd seen a poisonous creature over her shoulder. "What?" Then she realized he was listening.

"A message from Jesqellan." He hastened over to Donnagill, calling to Janak, who got to his feet with surprising agility. "We have to go into the village."

He flew up onto the warhorse's back and rode down the hill in a thunder of hooves, as the distant sound of a bell echoed off the low clouds. Kyer leapt onto Trig's back, his auburn sheen vibrant in spite of the filtered light. Janak followed close behind.

They slowed their horses to a walk and ambled down the main village road in stunned silence. The village was like any other including her own, if every village was inhabited by close to lifeless people who did not care about thriving. Kyer's gaze followed the villagers as they wandered along the roads, tired looking, detached. A few of the women were in various stages of pregnancy. The dazed faces did not alter even slightly at the sight of a warhorse ridden by a man in plate mail, a very ominous-looking dwarf, nor a battered woman with a bastard sword at her side. If Valrayker himself had come parading through the village, Kyer figured these people wouldn't have turned a glance.

Kyer drew up into the square, stunned to see a dozen or more wounded villagers lying scattered in the mud. Derry had already slid from his horse. He grabbed his kit and hurried over to examine a woman whose shirt was smeared with blood.

Jesqellan's hands rested on the shoulders of a middle-aged woman. He was peering into her eyes and whispering. Phennil waved from the raised platform, where he sat cradling a heavily pregnant girl.

Kyer dismounted and joined him. "Something in the water or what?"

Phennil looked at her quizzically.

"All the pregnant women." She shook her head dismissively. "Never mind. What happened?"

Jesqellan stopped another villager and stared intently into his eyes, whispering his incantation.

"They said she had to be *punished*," Phennil said with a frown, "but I daresay they would have killed her if I hadn't . . . turned their attention elsewhere." He described the scene in detail, including his well-placed arrow to the magistrate's shoulder and the villagers' response to the ringing of the bell. "It was sickening. The magistrate himself was about to throw the first stone."

Jesqellan let the young man go, stood in the centre of the square, arms out, palms up, and chanted.

Kyer touched the girl's arm. "Are you all right?"

"All I can get out of her is that her name is Emma. Here, Kyer you're a woman. Maybe she'll talk to you. She sure isn't talking to me."

"Hey! Do I look like an expert on--? Oh never mind."

Phennil left Kyer with the girl while he went to prioritise the wounded for treatment.

"Emma," Kyer ventured. The girl didn't respond. Phennil might as well have handed her a bowl full of wheat and told her to bake something.

"Captain," Jesqellan called. "I have done a sense magic spell on several of the villagers and looked for magic in the air around this area."

"Anything?" Derry gave a final tug on a bandage, dismissing that patient.

The mage shook his head. "It's not magic, whatever it is that's causing this madness."

"Not magic." Derry sat back on his heels. "In a way I'm relieved, because I was worried it *was* magical, and then we'd be up against something none of us but you has knowledge of."

Phennil led the next patient over--a youth with blood oozing through his dark curls.

"Conversely," Derry went on, soaking his cloth in a pail of water, "I am disappointed, because now we have to search for a way that some adversary could so dramatically affect the entire population of a village. This is not half a dozen people; it's," he looked around the square with uncharacteristic helplessness, "*everyone.*"

"Is it in fact intentional?" Jesqellan said. "Perhaps we should not assume that it is not, some sort of illness."

Phennil picked up the water pail. "I don't think so," he said hesitantly, as he carried it to the well. "Getting ready to throw rocks at her? The rioting? The reaction to the bell? Why is there even a bell--?" He stopped as if realizing he somehow shouldn't be speaking.

Derry dabbed at the boy's head. "You're right, Phennil," he said, with a glance at Kyer. "I have a hard time believing any of this is inadvertent."

Phennil looked pleased as he filled the pail.

Janak eyed the buildings that outlined the square. "Maybe we should talk to some people. Dazed or not, someone must know something."

"Maybe that magistrate," Jesqellan agreed. "Or one of those other fellows that gave the orders."

Derry agreed that it was a good idea and the two went off to find the magistrate, after getting directions from an old man in the form of a vague wave.

Finished with the boy, Derry moved on to a woman whose arm hung limply at her side.

Kyer turned back to Emma, giving her a little shake on the arm. The girl's gaze rested on her, lost focus, and wandered away. Kyer looked right into her eyes. "Who told them to do this?"

There was a flicker in Emma's eyes, and she strayed again. Kyer was baffled and getting frustrated. "I'm here to help you. Who is the father?" she asked sternly. "You can tell me."

"I—I can't—tell."

Kyer couldn't guess whether it was a secret or the girl simply didn't know. She frowned, completely out of her element. "Listen, let's, uh, get a drink of water." Standing, she hooked her elbows underneath the girl's armpits and raised her to her feet and helped her down off the platform. She led the girl over to the nearby well and drew up a bucketful, splashing it on Emma's face. She encouraged her to cup her hands and take a drink.

"Better now? Where do you live? Shall I take you home?"

"All right."

"Do you live with your parents?" Kyer went on, following in the direction Emma pointed.

Emma drew herself up with subdued pride and said, "My father is magistrate of the village." She looked up at Kyer with delighted eyes.

Kyer stopped dead in her tracks. *Shit.* She swung Emma around. "On second thought, let's just go back and join my friends again for a minute or two." Propping Emma against the platform, Kyer went over to Derry. The woman whose arm he had just put in a sling wandered off, murmuring, "Such a *nice* young man!"

"We can't take her home," Kyer said in a reasonable tone that belied her rage. "Her father is the one who wanted to hurl the first stone." Kyer looked around helplessly. "What the *hell* is going on around here?"

Derry applied salve to the forehead of a light-haired youth. "This is quite a different story from what Valrayker told us at the Twisting Pine," he agreed.

"Dev did say that the villagers had become unemotional," Phennil put in, as he tore a cloth into strips for Derry to use.

"Well, it's gone farther than that now," Kyer fumed.

"Yes," said Derry calmly. "But we cannot allow our own emotions to get out of hand and overcompensate for the villagers' lack thereof."

"He was about to throw a *rock* at his own *daughter*, Derry."

"That detail was not lost on me, Kyer. But Valrayker sent us up here to find out what is happening and to help these people if we can. Losing our minds will not help them."

Kyer knew Derry was right, and clenched her teeth, trying to be sensible again. "Can we assume Dregor is behind this?"

"I think it's safe to assume that Dregor is behind pretty much every bit of evil or nastiness we ever lay eyes on." Phennil smiled wryly.

"But why this?" Kyer shook her head. She looked over her shoulder at the very pregnant girl who sat on the steps of the platform, picking off splinters of wood from the edge, wearing a contented smile. "She's forgotten all about it already."

Kyer took the girl to the one and only inn and took her pick of all the musty-smelling rooms. The proprietor could not say how long it had been since his last guest, though he didn't seem to be bothered by it. Judging by the stale air and the carpet of dust over all the shabby furniture, it had to have been several months since anyone had set foot in this room. Kyer brushed aside cobwebs, plucked a spider's egg sack off the pillow, and shook the moth-eaten blanket out the window before laying it over the mildew-stained straw tick.

She left the windows wide open in the vain hope that the still air outside would relieve the staleness of the room and left Emma resting on the bed while she went back to the hilltop to fetch the party's belongings. By the time she returned, Emma was gone.

Jesqellan and Janak eventually found the magistrate's house after knocking on several wrong doors. The magistrate of Nennia was one Peter Dillon. He invited them in with more cheer than Jesqellan expected of someone who, not all that long ago, had an arrow protruding from his shoulder. But Derry did good work. He seemed to be moving well, given that his right arm was in a sling.

"We work for Va—the duke," Jesqellan said.

"Ah, he must be very busy, since he just arrived in town."

Jesqellan shot a glance at Janak. "I—beg your pardon?"

"Or else he would have come himself again. Like yesterday."

"Yes . . . of course," Jesqellan said, sitting next to Janak on the sofa.

"I expect you have another message for me?" Dillon said eagerly.

"What kind of message were you expecting?" Janak asked.

"Well, you know, the laws and things."

"What sorts of messages has he given you?" Janak pressed.

The man's wife entered with tea and biscuits for their guests and laid the tray out on a low table. She turned to them with a curious smile. "You're both very short."

"Uh," Janak leaned forward. "You perceive that we are sitting down?"

"Yes, please do." She left the room.

The two friends exchanged a bemused look.

Dillon went through the motions of pouring tea, although it was plain from the outset that the pot was, in fact, empty.

As Dillon returned to his chair, Janak lifted his cup, flipped it upside down and peered into it. Jesqellan gave him a sharp elbow in the ribs. Janak glared at him as if to say, *Don't blame me!*

Aloud the dwarf announced, "Mine is far too hot to drink at this time."

"Ahem," Jesqellan said.

"My wife is always happy to please the duke's men," the magistrate said.

"Yes, well, certainly." The mage composed himself. "But what of these messages?" He eyed the biscuits with suspicion and didn't take one.

With much prompting they managed to piece together the story of how, for many months, the magistrate had been receiving messages from someone calling himself "the duke," delivered orally by an emissary. At the start it had been instructions to build a simple item, for instance, a specific kind of box. Then they were told to take it apart. There were instructions regarding harvesting of crops. In the autumn a curfew was imposed, whereby it had been unlawful to be outside after sundown. The punishment was for the culprit to be chained on top of the platform in the square for the night, exposed to the elements and whatever else might find him there. Then no visiting was permitted at all, except from the duke's emissaries. But after a time, the duke abolished that law. Instead, it was permissible to steal bread.

"It was chaotic around here for that one." The man said. "People running about at all hours, damaging windows and doors. It got so that people would just leave leftover bread out on the doorstep to avoid the trouble. It was quite a time."

"Sounds like a real hootenanny," Janak agreed.

Jesqellan ignored him. "Can you give us an example of one of these messages?"

"Certainly. He has me repeat them to be sure I get them right. The most recent one was just yesterday, delivered by the duke himself." He pushed himself to his feet again and grasped his slinged hand with his left in a formal attitude.

Dillon spoke with authority. "It is unlawful to be with child without marriage vows. Punishment: Public stoning." He turned to them. "The villagers agreed to it without question."

Jesqellan had seen at least ten young pregnant women since entering Nennia, and hoped with his whole heart they had put a permanent halt to the practice of "punishing them".

"I beg your pardon, but uh, what is this duke's name?" Jesqellan asked.

Dillon cocked his head to one side. His face went blank. "I . . . It's . . . Well, it's just the duke."

"How does the bell fit in?" Janak demanded.

"The bell? It summons us. And it sends us home."

"Who rings it?" Jesqellan asked.

Just then the door opened and the pregnant girl walked into the house. The truth struck him, and his stomach lurched. Janak found his voice first.

"She's your *daughter*?"

Jesqellan suddenly wondered how so many young women had become pregnant. Dillon had mentioned something about visits from the duke's emissaries. His blood froze.

The magistrate glanced up and held out his hand in greeting. He pulled her close and kissed her lightly on the cheek. He sat before her and placed his palms on her belly and caressed it.

"I can feel him kicking," he said. Then, remembering his manners, he said, "Sit down, my darling. You must take care of my little one in there."

The daughter obeyed, lowering herself awkwardly into the ash wood rocker by the fire. "Yes, Papa," she said.

Janak leapt to his feet.

Jesqellan put a restraining hand on his arm, fearful of the dwarf's intentions. "Well, thank you for the . . . tea. We must be off."

"Don't wanna keep the duke waiting," Janak added.

Beneath the heavy cloud cover, Derry felt hemmed in. The stillness of the village was spooky. It was as if everyone had been sucked back into their homes after the brawl. Standing at the crest of the hill overlooking an evergreen wood, Derry took long, deep breaths, but his lungs were tight and would not expand. He couldn't keep his mind from the possibility of having to tell Valrayker they had been unable to resolve the villagers' situation. He imagined the discouragement his lord would feel, the sorrow for his people.

Derry had stepped away for a few solitary moments to think. Soon he would be required to give his company some form of direction. He breathed the heavy air, bracing himself against admitting defeat before he'd begun. A few steps down the hill took him to a circle of nine statues: The gods and goddesses, all carved out of obsidian, the weeds grown up to knee height around their bases. They stood facing one another, as if in conference. *Discussing a way you can help me?* He asked with little faith.

Sure enough, Kyer and Phennil ambled toward him along the ridge of the hill. The black stone figures remained motionless and unhelpful. But Derry knew in his heart that it was with himself he felt frustration, not with the divine ones. Why should they aid him when he had taken no steps on his own to discover how this strange condition was afflicting everyone in Nennia? With a strange sense of trepidation, he stepped into the circle of stone creations. *Will you give me a clue? A place to start?*

The rest of the world fell silent around him.

Derry studied them with admiration. Dima, the sun god; Guerrin, god of fire and war; Aidan, goddess of life; Therys; Coaldor; and the rest. These were wondrous representations—some of the best Derry had seen. This Aidan cradled a sheaf of wheat in one arm, and with the other hand held the *Spirarus*, the flower that breathes life into all living things. She was even more lifelike than the statue he had shown Kyer in Shael. He couldn't take his eyes off them, drawn by their power and mystery. The statues seemed to speak to him. His doubt of them wavered.

His gaze rested on the statue of Dionne, the water goddess. Her hair flowed in wavy ringlets from her head the way a stream gurgles forth from a spring. He followed the hair down her sleek body, past the hands, rippled like the surface of a lake when a pebble has been tossed in. Nestled in her arms was the *huisqe*, the mythical creature resembling part fish, part cloud. Her finlike feet were together as though she were about to dive . . .

Derry stared at the statue. Dionne. Goddess of water.

"That's it!" he yelled just as Kyer and Phennil stepped up.

"Captain?"

Derry was too excited and relieved to feel embarrassed. "Phennil, go to the inn and ask if we can borrow some pots and pans."

"Hunh?"

"I'm serious! Please."

The elf obediently trotted back up the hill, but Kyer was looking at him quizzically.

"The water," Derry explained eagerly, leaving the circle of statues. "It's so obvious."

Her bruised face lit up. "You think someone's contaminated the well."

"Yes!" Without even thinking, he flung his arms around her. She let out a hiss of surprise and pain. He let go instantly. "I'm sorry."

"It's—" She wasn't looking at him. "I'm fine."

He backed off, heat flaring on his face. "I guess . . . I'll need Jesqellan's help with this."

They hurried up the hill.

⁘⎯⎯⎯⎯⎯⎯

Kyer and Phennil sat up on the platform. Jesqellan and Janak had returned, and the dwarf hacked off a corner of the platform to make a fire at the edge of the square. The mage drew a bucketful of water from the well and distributed it among the pots and saucepans they borrowed from the inn. Derry laid out various herbs and fungi that they would add to the water to test it. He and the mage crouched by the fire, their heads together in earnest discussion. The mage dropped bits of stuff into the water, a pinch here and a pinch there. Kyer fidgeted, pulling at splinters of wood the same way Emma had done earlier. Her body simmered like one of the saucepans, with a mixture of uselessness and impatience, with a pinch of hope added.

Soon Janak joined them, standing off to one side awkwardly. *As if he doesn't want anyone to think he's with us,* Kyer thought with amusement. The dwarf told them about his and Jesqellan's visit with the magistrate, the laws, the horrific announcement he'd demonstrated, and the appearance of the man's daughter. He seemed to *need* to talk about it.

"And it's worse," he went on. "It looks like the magistrate isn't just *her* father."

Kyer added a pinch of nausea to her concoction, and Phennil murmured, "That's horrible."

"And he even told us that the duke himself is in town," Janak finished. "I'm dying to find out who does a good Valrayker impersonation."

"There's some sort of conditioning going on," Kyer said. "They started with simple instructions. Probably as a test."

"Build a box, take it apart," Janak said.

"They separated folks from each other, maybe so they couldn't discuss anything?" Phennil said.

"Then the directions became more complicated, and they added punishments," Kyer said.

"Someone told them the girl's pregnancy was wrong," Janak put in. "Someone told them to start throwing rocks at her."

Kyer picked up his point. "But they didn't get to throw their stones at Emma; they reacted instead to the arrow. They went mad and then someone rang the bell."

"What worries me is that if someone got them all riled up and then nobody rang the bell to tell them to stop . . ." Phennil began.

"They'd likely beat the daylights out of each other, and they'd all be dead," Janak said. "One village destroyed by Dregor without so much as the lifting of a finger by a single orc."

Kyer bit her tongue and swallowed bile, horrified at the irony that there really might be something in the water. "I guess as long as people drink from the well, they'll be affected, without any awareness of it." She turned this over and over in her mind. It led somewhere, if she could only pinpoint it.

"Dregor could easily use the same treatment on other villages and towns, maybe even cities, and eventually have complete control," Phennil added, his voice strained.

"Oh come on, it would never go that far, " Janak growled.

They looked at each other grimly.

"I'm thirsty," said Phennil.

Kyer looked over at Derry and Jesqellan, stirring, smelling. She was aware of a few pairs of eyes peering out at them from behind tattered curtains in the low buildings that surrounded the square. *Watching the proceedings,* she observed.

"Listen." Kyer straightened. "Like you said, *somebody* is feeding them these instructions. Wouldn't it make sense that whoever was causing this would want to be present to oversee it? And if so, wouldn't it also make sense that *they* would want to be near a fresh water source?" They looked at her blankly. "There's a stream down there," she said, pointing. "And for that matter, if it's the well water that's poisoned, wouldn't it stand to reason that *anyone* who happened to live by the stream wouldn't be affected?

"Remember Val mentioning Carver? The man who spoke to Dev and seemed to still have his wits about him? He was aware enough to tell the scout what he had noticed," she said. "Do you suppose *he* rang the bell?"

Ronav clasped his hands on his belly and observed his new Right Hand man appraisingly.

Hunter tipped his chair so the back rested on the wall of the cottage. "Doesn't it bother you that things didn't go as planned?"

Ronav shook his head. "The result was interesting, all the same." He gave his new Right Hand a smirk. "How did you enjoy your first day as duke?"

Hunter's face looked impassive. He was about to answer when the cottage door was flung open.

"Chief, it's Valrayker's company that stopped it." He looked at Ronav, his face stricken with distress. "They're doing some sorts of tests on the well water. And, Chief . . . *she's* with them!"

Ronav felt a moment's panic but contained it. Hunter's knuckles were white where they clutched his liquor cup. It was up to Ronav to keep control.

He shrugged dismissively. "We're not dealing with amateurs, after all. Lord Valrayker doesn't take on imbeciles."

"What do we do?" Richie asked. "The others are cracking. They think she's a witch."

Ronav could relate. "Perhaps she is." He looked at his Right Hand. "I haven't shared with you the story of our little guest we had recently. It was the day before you arrived." He chuckled. "She's one of Valrayker's playthings, you know, and I had a need for a chat with her. She caused us some trouble." He suppressed a shudder, sipping his drink. "She has a pendant with a jewel on it."

Hunter blinked but was still.

"A very peculiar thing," Ronav went on. "My man Con was quite taken with her, of course—she's a rather pretty treat—and was fascinated by the pendant. He touched the jewel, and a very peculiar thing happened." He heard his pitch rising and wiped his suddenly sweating palms on his shirt but regained his nerves. "It exploded and killed him." The scene was so vivid in his memory! The man's screams echoed around the chamber.

"Peculiar indeed." Hunter drained his cup and poured again.

"So do we attack, Chief?" Richie said, clearly hoping the answer would be "No."

The wheels turned in the chief's mind, and a smile formed on his lips. "There will be no need. We have one more experiment to perform."

Richie leaned against the cottage door frame, relieved.

Ronav looked at his Right Hand man. "You, Sir Duke, have new orders to deliver. And you must not be seen by them."

Hunter shrugged. "I have no wish to be."

The horses had been waiting patiently for some attention, so Phennil, Janak, and Kyer stabled them at the inn. Soon after, the trio stood on the north hill overlooking the stream. It was more like a creek. Kyer had never studied Equart geography but she imagined this was a tributary to the north flowing river along which they had travelled to get here. It cradled the hill on which the village perched, and disappeared into some trees around the bend. A few cottages were scattered along it, a few sheep and cows wandering between them. Kyer was glad to be doing something productive instead of feeling helpless and restless.

They descended the slope to the right and investigated the first cottage. They walked through the wide open door. The braided area rug in the front room was saturated with water; the result of gaping holes in the thatch roof. At the second cottage, goats had the run of the house, and it looked as if the human residents had left right in the middle of dinner.

At the third home, the fence had collapsed from lack of maintenance, and a few sheep wandered around aimlessly. Something made Phennil take a closer look. He waved the other two over.

"This fence was very well made. Look how sturdily this corner was built. The joint doesn't even wiggle." He demonstrated. Moving farther along the fencing as it lay nestled in the dirt he pointed out dents caused by a wide-headed hammer. The horizontal portions had not deteriorated. They had been smashed.

"Somebody wanted to make life pretty difficult for this farmer," Kyer said.

"Here's another place where the fence looks like it was kicked down," Janak leaned over a section a few paces farther along. "This indentation in the dry mud looks like a boot heel where it was stomped on."

Phennil said, "You're right. You'll make a decent tracker even with only one eye—" He bit back the words and looked at the dwarf in alarm.

Janak stood like a monolith and Kyer's fingers twitched, ready to draw her sword in Phennil's defence. Then the dwarf shocked her. "Then you'll be out of a job and could take up poetry."

Kyer allowed herself a breath and relaxed her hand. She hesitantly played along. "Just promise never to share it with any of us."

The elf grinned ruefully. Kyer moved to go around to the back of the house. She didn't know what to make of the dwarf's response. Perhaps he had been so affected by the plight of the villagers that he had summoned some compassion. She chose to accept it, but not count on it.

There was a stone outbuilding behind the house, sturdy, with a solid door and shutters on the windows. They were latched from the inside. Within, the darkness was barely lifted by the grey light from outside. Something crunched under Kyer's boot as she stepped across the even dirt ground to open the shutters. Phennil and Janak stood in the doorway.

Once the window was open, she could see what was spread all over the floor: chunks of flat stone surrounded by smaller bits and a great deal of dust. Grains of wheat and corn were scattered about, and a couple of broken wooden rods, useless for anything more than fuel.

"A grindstone?" Kyer asked, puzzled.

"That's what it looks like," Phennil agreed. "Or a small rotary quern?"

There was no mistaking that it had been purposefully smashed. No piece of the contraption was salvageable.

Kyer walked around to the front door of the house, Phennil close on her heels. She tried the door. Unlike the others, this one was locked. She and Phennil exchanged a puzzled glance. Janak hung on the path behind them.

There was no answer to Phennil's light tap on the door. Kyer peered in the window and saw a rather disturbing silhouette.

"Uh-oh."

"Hello?" Phennil urgently rapped again. "Is anyone there?"

Finally a voice came from the other side of the door. "Who are you?" it demanded. It sounded very young.

"We're here to help," Kyer said. "We work for the duke." Would such a young person know who the duke was?

"Papa's duke or the other one?" Suspicion was strong in the voice.

"As far as I know, there's only one duke," Kyer said, "and that's Valrayker."

After a moment, they heard a click, and the door handle moved. A small face peeked out through the crack and eyed them from within a fringe of dark curls. The door opened wider, revealing a girl of about six years. She gripped a large knife in both hands.

Phennil got down on one knee, keeping a respectful distance from the knife. "Hey there," he said quietly. "My name's Phennil and this is my friend Kyer. That, back there, is Janak. What's your name?"

"Sasha Carver."

Kyer caught her breath. *Carver.*

"Papa says Lord Valrayker's the real duke, not the other man."

"Your papa's right." Phennil nodded sombrely.

"What other man?" Kyer said.

Sasha looked at Phennil, puzzled. "What are you? You look different."

Phennil grinned. "I'm an elf."

The girl's eyes grew wide. "I didn't never meet a elf before! Papa says no elf would ever work for the fake duke."

Phennil nodded. "He's right."

The knife slowly lowered. Sasha looked openly at Kyer. "Your face looks funny."

Kyer smiled stiffly, having forgotten the yellowish bruises that must make her look a bit hideous still. "I . . . had an accident." Kyer was struck by the child's awareness. This girl was decidedly not in the same sleepy state as the rest of the village. "Where's your papa right now?"

"He's—right here. But he's—" Sasha turned her head around to look at him. She opened the door a bit more, and Phennil entered, followed by Kyer. The grey light from outside revealed a horrific sight, and Kyer stifled a gasp. Phennil bit his lower lip.

Sasha's papa was half propped up by a wooden chair, his head and arms dangling at awkward angles. A pool of blood was drying all around him, and Kyer realized that Sasha's apron and dress were splotched with rust-brown patches that must have come from this source. The man had been stabbed repeatedly in the chest, and as if to punctuate his death, his assailant had planted a knife straight through his throat. The lifeless eyes were open, still showing the terror of his final moments. Kyer felt hot rage sizzle inside her.

"By the Gods, little one, how did this happen?" Phennil whispered.

Kyer fought back the nauseating mass of fury and sorrow.

"It was the other duke. I didn't see them. I was in my hiding spot. Want to see?"

They nodded and for a moment Kyer was worried by the girl's lack of concern. But this wasn't the same as the sleepwalkers up the hill. Sasha was in shock. A darkening in the doorway told her that Janak had approached. Sasha led them into the pantry and set her knife on a shelf then pointed to the tiny cupboard door in the corner. She opened the door and squeezed in. "I always hide here when the men come. They were talking to Papa, and they sounded cross. Papa said he liked the real duke best, and they yelled and there was bumping and then the men went away. It was so quiet." Her lip began to quiver, and her voice dropped to a whisper. "Papa always said wait until he calls me to come out, but—he didn't call me." Tears overflowed from her eyes and spilled down her round cheeks. "I waited and waited, ever such a long time, but he didn't call. I got hungry." She turned her sweet face up to Kyer. "So I came out. And found him."

Shit, Kyer thought.

Phennil took Sasha's hand and patted it. "It's good that you came out and that we found you. Come on out of there now. We'll take you with us."

Sasha shook her head, and bits of her brown hair stuck to her tear-dampened cheeks. "I don't want to leave Papa."

Phennil drew her out of the cupboard and held her close, stroking the back of her head. "We need to get you out of here in case the men come back. I'm really sorry, but you can't help your Papa now, my dear. How about—" He looked desperately over at Kyer. "You stay with Kyer . . ."

Kyer nodded.

"And Janak and I will tend to your papa? All right?"

Sasha pulled back and looked at him with rounded brown eyes. She nodded. Phennil ruffled the child's hair.

"Where did the men come from?" Janak surprised them from the doorway of the pantry.

"They live in the temple. Just over in the woods." Sasha pointed. "We haven't been allowed to go there in a long time."

Phennil turned to them. "We'd better go check out the temple."

The dwarf nodded.

Kyer's hand moved to loosen her sword; then she glanced at Sasha. "You two go on, and I'll take her up to Derry." They wordlessly agreed and made their way out of the house.

Kyer felt wooden but thought of the child's father rapidly cooling in the other room. She crouched. "Come on, Sasha. I'll take you up into the village to meet my other friends."

"What about Papa?"

"We'll come back and tend to him; I promise. Right now we have to leave here."

Sasha nodded. "Wait, I have to get Arrow." She ran from the room.

A moment later, she returned and held an object out to Kyer: an extraordinarily beautiful gryphon, like those that guarded the towers at Shael Castle, but carved out of dark wood. It was in a sitting position, and from its bottom to the top of its head was about the size of Kyer's hand. Its wings were partially folded in the back.

"Papa made him for me. His name is Arrow. He will help take care of me."

Her papa made him. *Carver.* Kyer's mouth went dry. "Yes, he will." She took Sasha's hand, and to Kyer's surprise, Sasha put her arms around her neck. After an instant's hesitation, Kyer put her arms around her and stood up, lifting the girl. Kyer winced, and ignored the sharpness and stinging inflicted by even the slight extra weight. Sasha, oblivious, held her tight and exhaled deeply, as if realizing the truth of what had happened. Kyer carried her out the front door and away from the house. A few sheep bleated forlornly.

The woods were on their right as they ascended the hill to the main village.

"That's where the men live," Sasha said, pointing.

Kyer nodded. "Phennil and Janak have gone to see if they can find them."

"Do you really know the true duke?" the little girl asked.

"Yes, he's . . . a very good friend. I only just—"

She was interrupted by a sound from the woods, a cry and a ring of steel.

"Uh-oh," she said, stopping. "Sasha." She set the child down. "I have to go. I think my friends are in trouble. But I'm going to give you some instructions. Can you follow them?"

The child nodded.

Kyer hated to send her on her own, but there was nothing for it. "Good girl. Now, up in the square—you know the square?"

Another nod.

"Excellent. Up there is a tall man with blond hair. He's wearing chain mail and armour. Do you know what that means?"

She nodded again.

"You're amazing. Now that man is my friend. He is Lord Valrayker's *best friend*, okay?"

The girl's eyes widened.

"Go to him and tell him that Kyer sent you to him. Can you remember that?"

"Yup," Sasha said.

Kyer gave her a hug and sent her up the hill, trusting the child to tell Derry everything about where she had gone and why. Then she went to the woods.

Sixteen

Revelations

"Wait a minute! Don't lift it yet!" Jesqellan put a hand on Derry's arm just as the captain was about to remove the pot of water from the fire. Derry withdrew his hand and watched the mage's eyes, bright with excitement as he tried to retrieve some distant memory. Jesqellan wafted the steam toward himself, breathing it in.

Derry had spent the last hour like an alchemist's apprentice, helping the mage pour portions of water, adding herbs and powders, stirring, sniffing, even tasting. He was tired and his stomach was nagging at him for sustenance. More than anything the strain of worry had gripped every muscle in his body with sharp talons, and he wondered how long they would carry on with this futile exercise. Now, a sudden hope was renewed at Jesqellan's outburst, and his heart rushed the blood through his body with regained fervour.

"Yes," the mage said. "I think that's it."

"What's it?"

"It nearly escaped me because I couldn't identify the smell, but then I remembered a brief warning by one instructor I had long ago. The steam has a bitter, almost metallic aroma, which leads me to believe there is amorin present in the water." Derry had heard of it but didn't know its properties. Jesqellan explained. "On its own, it would merely dull the judgement, similarly to alcohol, though more intense. But added to that is a hint of . . ." He squinted in thought. "Cinnamony basil, which I believe is pequille. It would intensify the results of the amorin; I am certain of it. This could account for the villagers' state of belief and acceptance of simple statements they would normally discount. This mixture would, I fear, make one quite susceptible to outside influence. The power of suggestion would become very strong."

"Which is certainly what we're dealing with here, taken to the extreme," Derry said. But a nagging doubt remained. "The one thing that bothers me is that doesn't account for the dulling of emotions, the lack of fear or concern about what is happening."

"Hmph," the mage agreed.

"All I can think is that there must be still another substance working on them. From another source, perhaps." Derry frowned, dismayed by the implications.

"That could very well be." Jesqellan's nose wrinkled. "Another drug or concoction with the effect of an antidepressant, something that removes concern, that makes the victim feel as if all is right with the world. It's quite possible. And very clever."

"How do we find out what it is?" Derry replaced herbs and fungi to their respective pouches. "And in the meantime, we know to avoid the well water, but what else do we avoid so that we don't fall victim to this . . . mess?"

Jesqellan met his gaze. "Good question."

"The best we can do . . ." Derry sighed and rubbed the back of his neck. "Eat or drink nothing that we didn't bring ourselves, for now."

Jesqellan stared at the experiment area, littered with pouches and vials, tweezers and tongs. "What do we do at this point?"

"We cover the well, for one thing," Derry said. "And we'll set a watch—" His attention was diverted by the sight of a small child running toward them.

"My name is Sasha," she said breathlessly. "Kyer sent me to you. Are you really the duke's *best friend*?"

The magistrate's wife opened the door to the handsome young duke. He brushed past her into the front room, where Emma rocked gently and her father sang to her.

"New instructions, Dillon," the duke said brusquely.

The magistrate ambled to his feet. "How may I serve you, Your Lordship?"

"Kill the strangers at dawn."

Janak waited several trees away while Phennil slid stealthily toward the stone building. The front door was ajar, and pushing it open, the elf found himself in a dark, closet-sized entryway, a cloakroom perhaps. With his ear to the inner door, Phennil could make out several voices and thought perhaps the two of them would be unwise to pursue this on their own. He soundlessly waved Janak to stay back, and slunk out to make an equally stealthy retreat.

All at once, he heard Janak cry out and whirled around to see two men rushing toward him. They had seen Phennil at the same time as the dwarf had seen them returning to the temple. Janak had already snatched his battle axe from its hanger and attacked. Phennil drew his sword. Hearing the commotion, four other men piled out of the building and entered the fray. Phennil dashed around a tree to get closer to Janak and to keep their opponents from surrounding them.

Cursing their ill luck and timing, Phennil fought back the desire to turn tail. He wasn't useless with his sword—his elven agility gave him a bit of an advantage—but with three-to-one odds, his energy might flag before his opponents'. And with Janak's poor eye... Phennil did not like their chances. A clip on his right arm was turned by his chain mail, and as he ducked to avoid a blade to the neck, he said to himself,

I hope Kyer thinks to come back before we're dead.

Kyer pelted through the trees, keeping her body low. She darted from tree to tree to avoid exposing herself before she could size up the situation. How many opponents? How best to use her advantage?

She watched Janak's first swing miss, his monocular vision troubling him. At the same time, Phennil caught a blade in the shoulder and was knocked sideways and slammed into a tree. Then Janak's axe made contact with the top of a head with a horrible crunch. The fellow never had a chance to give a dying murmur. Kyer drew her sword and steadied her breathing. Surrounded by three men, the half-blind Janak had taken to spinning in a counter-clockwise direction, his axe blade shearing through the air with a whistling sound. The elf confounded his opponents by shinnying up the tree as nimbly as a squirrel in spite of the dark trickle down his arm. When one challenger tried to follow, Phennil made easy work of slamming his sword onto the head as it rose, and Kyer silently cheered. He stabbed the blade into a branch of the tree and drew his bow.

Janak's enemies had backed off to a safer distance and were making ready to strike if the dwarf should become dizzy. Mere seconds after her arrival, Kyer chose her man and stepped into the clearing, poking at his legs to get his attention. He whirled about to see the newcomer, and his face went pale with surprise.

Sword clenched with both hands, Kyer stepped up to him and brought her sword down with a cracking thud onto his shoulder. More bones splintered as she twisted it free. Janak made a sudden jump, flipping his axe over to the other side and began to unwind, this time sweeping it up and down, making it difficult for them to get in closer. One man backed away from the blade, unaware of what was behind him. Kyer tapped him on the shoulder. He turned and gasped.

"Hello," she said evenly, raising her weapon. A feint to his sword arm, along with the element of surprise threw him off balance. He put in a vain effort to get back in line and took a swipe at her, but she easily blocked him, and his weapon was still down when she raised hers and cleaved his midriff. He fell with a gurgling cry.

All sound ceased. The clearing had taken on an eerie darkness, as the cloudy mid-afternoon light tried to dodge the trees. Kyer wiped her blade and sheathed it. All at once she felt the unmistakable sensation of eyes boring into her back. She wheeled around. Peering into the shadows, hand on her hilt, she stepped cautiously forward. *Someone is there.*

"Kyer!" Janak's voice from behind her.

Startled, she whirled again to see the dwarf standing beneath a tree on the far side of the clearing. Phennil's semi-conscious form was draped over a branch. Six bodies lay around the clearing. With one more backward glance into the shadows, Kyer shuddered as the presence seemed to fade. Recovering herself, she hastened over to help the dwarf.

Phennil's blood plopped drop by drop onto the face of a dead man below whose neck was pierced with one of Phennil's arrows. Kyer shinnied up the tree, ignoring the uncomfortable stretching and chafing in her back. A six-point shuriken was deeply embedded in the elf's left shoulder, pinning links of chain mail into his flesh. Knees clutching her own branch, she gently dislodged the elf from his perch and let him slowly tumble down to Janak, who barely slumped under his weight.

When she joined them on the forest floor, Kyer removed the throwing star and bound the wound with a sleeve off one of the dead men. Janak put Phennil's sword through his belt and slung the bow across his back. Then together they hoisted the elf onto their shoulders. Kyer looked once more into the darkness on the far side of the clearing. She saw no one, but she knew someone was there.

They were halfway up the hill when Derry met them. He had asked Sasha a few pertinent questions about what was happening and where and left her with Jesqellan. He took a portion of their burden, and they raced to the inn.

"There's someone else down there," Kyer said. "We've got to find out who it is."

"They will have to wait," Derry said.

Jesqellan followed with the last of the pots, and Sasha carried Derry's kit. Concerned that the sight of the injury would be frightening for her, Derry sent Sasha upstairs to fetch blankets. Kyer and Janak laid the elf on a bench. Derry knelt next to him to examine the wound.

"Who is the child?" Derry asked, peeling off Phennil's mail.

"We went looking for Carver," Kyer said. "We found him, all right. Half falling off a chair in his own front room with a knife through his throat."

Derry swore under his breath.

"I hate the people who did this, Derry. All of this." Her voice sounded detached. "If I ever figure out who's behind it, I will kill him."

The captain halted his procedure and glared at her. "You will do nothing of the kind."

"I bloody well—"

"No!" Derry said harshly. "You think you feel angry about it? What about Valrayker? These are his people. These crimes are in Valrayker's jurisdiction, and Valrayker is the one who will pass judgement. If we discover those responsible, we will *take them to him*. Do you understand me?"

Kyer's chest heaved and she didn't speak. Her gaze was locked on some point beyond his elbow, and he wondered what she saw.

"Kyer." Derry grabbed her shoulder until she met his eyes. "Promise me you will not take this into your own hands. *Promise*."

Kyer's eyes were as dark as the woods. She shrugged off his hand, and he released it. "All right," she said. "I promise."

He turned back to his task. "Will you please go get some water?"

She still sounded remote. "I'll have to go to the stream." She went out.

Derry looked over his shoulder to where Janak still stood next to him. The last thing he wanted to hear was a comment from Janak right now.

He redirected the dwarf's attention to Phennil. "What happened here?"

"Six men in the woods," Janak said. "The wee one told us they were there, and we took them by surprise."

"Did you take care of them all?"

"All that were there."

"Too bad you didn't keep one alive for questioning."

"It was over rather quick."

"Any idea who they were?"

"None," said the dwarf.

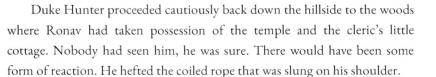

Duke Hunter proceeded cautiously back down the hillside to the woods where Ronav had taken possession of the temple and the cleric's little cottage. Nobody had seen him, he was sure. There would have been some form of reaction. He hefted the coiled rope that was slung on his shoulder.

It was true that he had no wish to be seen by Valrayker's party. Not that he was afraid of an encounter with one of them; of course not, although that would bring on its own set of . . . complications. No, it was more that he felt like an outsider, being so new to Ronav's company. This experiment in Nennia, though clever and having great potential for use in other villages and towns, was Ronav's baby. Hunter didn't feel like fighting Valrayker's people in its defence.

He passed the temple and tripped over something in the clearing. Squinting through the dim light, he discovered the first body. As his eyes adjusted, he peered around. Several more. Had they got *everybody*? He shook his head in disbelief. Proceeding to the stone house in the gloom of the trees, he flung open the door, half expecting the place to be empty.

Ronav sat up and Hunter was impressed by the casual greeting. If the chief had been shaken by what had happened outside, he gave no sign.

"Well?"

"What happened here?" Hunter shrugged the rope off his shoulder onto the floor.

Ronav poured himself a tumbler of liquor with a steady hand. "Someone told them we were here. A few of Valrayker's people paid a visit."

"But not to you?"

Ronav waved a hand dismissively. "I have other men. I am needed to see the task through. And yourself?"

"I have done my part. It is in motion."

"Excellent." Ronav smiled with satisfaction. "I'd like you to return to headquarters and get some replacements for those lowlifes. Bring along Misty and Juggler if they have returned from their errand."

"Suits me. I prefer to let you bask in the glory of your own success," Hunter said dryly. "I will leave immediately. I don't want to be caught up in the excitement of the morning."

The heavy clouds that had surrounded the village all day descended to nestle in among the dilapidated dwellings, and evening fell hard. Kyer felt the fog without and within. Its damp chilled her soul. Some villagers were milling about the still-uncovered well, and she rushed over.

"No." She pushed them away with very little resistance. A pregnant woman already had a bucketful, and Kyer dumped it out. "I'm sorry but the well's off limits until further notice. You'll have to go down to the stream." There were half-hearted mumbles of protest, but she steered each person away with a small push. "Off you go, down the hill to the river." She cut the bucket from the well's winch with her dagger. That would confound them.

On her way to the stream, she paused at the top of the hill and gazed down into the murk that concealed the woods. Someone was there. Promise or no promise, she would find out. The fog settled deeper, without and within.

Derry cleaned out the mess that was Phennil's shoulder using water from a flask. *What's taking her so long?* He reminded himself that Kyer would have to go all the way down the far bank to the stream and back.

"Can I help?" The girl's quiet voice startled Derry out of his frustration. She held out a blanket and pillow. He smiled at her and held up Phennil's head so she could thrust the pillow beneath it. He had been unnecessarily concerned about shielding her from the sight of Phennil's wounds; she proved to be an asset. As she handed him items from his kit or dabbed blood that seeped out, he was reminded of an earlier time in his life. He cast aside those mixed emotions with a shake of his head.

"Here." Janak crouched beside him with a bottle in hand. "Found some liquor behind the bar. Thought it might be useful."

Once the worst was over, Derry poured some of it into Phennil. The elf coughed and gasped.

"Lie still, you fool. I can't see what I'm doing," said Derry.

Finally the door opened and Kyer walked in, weighed down by the full pail.

"At last," Derry said. She didn't speed up. "Don't hurry or anything."

"Okay." She ambled over and put the bucket down, either missing or ignoring his sarcasm. "I'm going back out to cover the well."

Derry glared at her back, feeling frustrated. Isolated. Earlier in the day, she had been so impassioned. Now she seemed to have detached herself. He hoped she'd snap out of it soon. Things were not quite right when Kyer wasn't herself.

A glance showed him that Janak, too, was glaring after her.

Derry was too tired to deal with him. He wished the dwarf would cut it out, or at least he hoped Kyer was unaware of his scrutiny. All he needed was for those two to break into yet another fight.

"Weren't there some dead people to take care of?" Derry said, startling Janak.

The dwarf harrumphed. "Yeah. Come on, Jesqellan." Each with a lantern, they slipped out into the murk.

In spite of the presence of the child, Derry was alone again.

Kyer absently covered the well with boards from the platform. She went back inside and ate some food. When Sasha's head began to nod, Kyer took her to the room she had prepared for Emma. Sasha curled up on the bed, and Kyer closed the shutters she'd left open hours before. The mist's fingers had crept in and touched everything in the room with their cold dampness. The tendrils curled into Kyer's heart. One warm spot was impenetrable, that place where her feelings for Sasha and her father resided. But the tiny spot where those responsible lurked, *that* spot was numbed like frostbite.

Her bedroll was dry, and she unfolded it to spread across the both of them. Kyer was asleep too soon to know whether Sasha tossed and turned or not. She was completely unaware when the child left the room shortly before dawn and did not return for half an hour.

⋅⋅⋅

A second poison.

Consumed by that conundrum, Derry had slept badly. His body felt so tired, he didn't even notice the hard floor beneath him, but the eventful day hadn't been a strong enough soporific.

Jesqellan knew of no antidote for the herbal cocktail and surmised that the effect would simply have to wear off. Nor had the mage any idea of how else the concoction might have affected the general health of the villagers. They might be ill for years to come. All Derry could hope for was that even after continual absorption of tainted water for so many months, the poison might be flushed out by drinking large quantities of fresh water from the stream. There was no telling how long that would take, especially considering that there had to be a second ingredient involved in the full treatment.

Now at the pale, diffuse sunrise, the idea of the water seemed obvious, and he could think of nothing else that made as much sense. *We must have missed something in the water, that's all*, he thought, dejected. Since he was awake anyway, he might as well go for a walk and see if anything came to him. Yesterday his walk had carried him to the Circle of Divinity, as he had come to think of it. He would go there again.

There was no guessing the hour, for the fog was still densely packed around them. The mist clung to his hair and week's growth of beard. He pulled his cloak around him against the chill and walked more briskly. The village still slept, and his footfalls sounded thunderously loud. Reaching the top of the hill, he let his gaze rest on the woods down below, where the battle had taken place yesterday, and a lump rose in his throat. *At least we've stopped them from hurting any more innocent people*, he told himself.

Still, it had to have been many months since the poison was introduced, and he mourned the villagers' loss of so much of their lives. He despised the men who had brought it about and felt grim, unchivalrous satisfaction that they'd paid with the balance of their own lives.

It had pained him to let Sasha help with Phennil last night. He wouldn't have dreamed of turning down her offer to help; she needed companionship more than anything right now. Her bright eyes and eager grin brought back more than one memory that ought to have been happy but were accompanied by too much sorrow. For Sasha reminded him dreadfully of his own beloved sisters, Amber and Lily. Childhood was happy, and as he grew up, both girls had looked up to their brother as an important figure, a young man about to enter the service of Lord Valrayker. Lily, the smallest, was ten years younger than he and had the same playful spirit and eagerness to learn as little Sasha. Amber had been more serious, like himself, yet was able to keep Lily from feeling disheartened when Derry's duties prevented his coming home as frequently as he would have liked. The two girls played music and sang together and had always brought joy to the home.

He had tried to persuade his family to move into the city so he could be closer to them, but they had refused, saying it would be nicer for Derry to take a sojourn into the country during his leave. Besides, his father was the miller and did a good business. What did Equart City need with another miller?

About a year after he joined the Equart Guard, Derry was looking forward to some days off to visit his family. A messenger arrived at Equart Castle to tell Derry there had been an epidemic in his family's village. Most of the village was wiped out. Derry's mother and father were dead. There was no word about Amber and Lily. He rushed to the village to inquire after them, but no one knew what had become of them. As of now, he hadn't seen or heard of his sisters in six years. If they were still alive, they would be eighteen and sixteen years old. He heard the echo of their singing as he stood on the mist-dampened hillside.

Nennia was much like his boyhood home, and the affliction of this village was all too similar to the pestilence that had obliterated his family. There had been nothing he could do to prevent their deaths. *Of course if anyone dies here,* he told himself, *it's murder.* Here, at least, if he were clever enough, he might forestall further loss of life. *If* he could solve the final puzzle.

With a deep breath, he stepped within the Circle of Divinity. He closed his eyes and begged the cold, lifeless figures of stone to offer him guidance. Again the world took on a strange, light hush. He waited. But maybe it was too cold. Maybe it was too wet or too early in the day. They were still. Mute. Silent as death.

An ache of despondency flowed with Derry's blood, soaking into him like the mist. He had been foolish to think that they had spoken to him. It was as he had thought all along. The water idea had come from his own knowledge and experience. That was all. Yet . . . He turned back to Dionne and stared at her. What had he noticed yesterday? Her feet poised to leap. He looked around at the others. All of their feet were hidden by overgrown grasses. The weeds surrounding Dionne had been ripped off.

The faintest glimmer of hope sparked deep down under his dejection. He looked around from one statue to the next, his feet shifting, rotating his body in the centre of the circle.

He turned once. Nothing. He turned a second time, frowning with concern. He began a third rotation and started to lose heart. He had moved on to the figure of Therys when something jolted in his brain. Turning back, he wondered that he had not seen it before. That he had not noticed it yesterday, even. Aidan, the goddess of life and fertility, held the *Spirarus* in one hand, and in the other, she cradled a *sheaf of wheat*. A sheaf of wheat that was incongruous to the rest of the statue, to all the statues. "Dirt," Derry whispered. The deep blackness of every other figure was untarnished by dust and speckled only by the last fall of rain. But the sheaf in Aidan's arm was topped by a sprinkling of fresh, dark dirt, like cinnamon on top of a cake.

Now what did it mean? Did it mean anything? It had to. Then Derry, the miller's son, felt the dawn: from wheat comes flour, and apart from water, the other staple of a villager's diet was bread.

There was no mill in Nennia. It was coming from outside. If the poison were a powder, it would be no difficult task to add it to the wheat during milling, so it would already be present before the flour was put into sacks and delivered. Wherever it was coming from, the miller must have struck a bargain with someone.

He raced back to the inn.

Several villagers stood around the platform in the centre of the square, and Derry wondered in passing why they would be out and about so early in such weather.

He burst through the door of the inn to see Janak thrusting a hunk of bread into his mouth. "Where did you get that?"

"My pfack. Where'd you fink?" the dwarf said through the bread, and a good many more crumbs found themselves nesting in his beard.

"The other poison—it's in the flour," Derry said, catching his breath.

"Good thinking, Derry," said Phennil, who, apart from his bound shoulder, was back to normal this morning.

"I feel like we ought to have thought of that," Kyer added.

"Well, we won't know for certain until I can check it. I'm not sure how to do that. Any ideas, Jesqellan?"

The mage was about to answer when some voices outside turned all their heads. There was a fumbling and a pounding on the door, and Emma burst through, water dripping from under her dress, forming an expanding pool. She clutched her belly, groaning.

"Help me!" she cried in a panic-stricken whimper.

Chairs tipped over as they all flew to their feet.

"By the Goddess, the baby!" Jesqellan cried.

Derry rushed to her, fighting his fear as if he were attacking an orc. Supporting her under the arms, the physicker-adept assisted her to the chair that Kyer drew out. This was a healer's job, not his. Desperately banishing the frenzy of terrifying pictures of complicated childbirths, he pulled himself together.

"I need clean cloths, blankets, pillows, and—damn it, *water*." He coaxed Emma to the front edge of the chair and looked over his shoulder for the pail. Sasha brought it over. It was half empty. "Sasha, you'd better go upstairs to your room. Somebody get me more water!"

Phennil tucked a pillow behind Emma's back, and Janak spread a blanket on the floor.

A horrifying sound began to rise in Emma's throat. "Is somebody getting water?" Derry yelled.

Then he heard what had already stopped the others in their tracks. The yelling from outside in the square was building in an alarming way.

Jesqellan opened the door. "By the Wolf Spirit," he whispered.

Phennil joined him at the door. "That looks way too much like yesterday."

"Death to the strangers!" a voice cried with rage. The roar of the approaching crowd all but drowned out the sound of Emma's scream of pain.

"Bring your weapons!" Jesqellan cried.

There was a flurry of movement all around him as Derry tried to hold Emma's attention. "Breathe with me!" he demanded in a hoarse whisper, and he made his breaths steady. The pounding on the door distracted him.

"Captain!"

Derry looked up and was startled at the alarm in Jesqellan's eyes. The mage was leaning, pressing his body against the door. "We have to get to the bell," Jesqellan said. "These people don't know what they're doing. We must try not to harm them."

But they're trying to kill us, Derry thought. Emma's fingers pinched Derry's forearms as she growled.

The captain's gaze went from the sweat on Emma's forehead back to his company. Phennil was wrestling to get his mail on over his wounded shoulder, with help from a worried-looking Kyer, whose colourfully bruised face was still pinched with pain from the hell she had gone through only days before. Janak, battle axe in hand, stared at Derry out of only one good eye.

One strange girl and her baby versus his entire company. All they had to do was ring the bell. *What would Dunvehran do?*

It all seemed impossible.

Emma's frightened eyes were no longer focussed as Derry pulled away from her and stood up. He flinched with the twisting in his gut but grabbed his weapon and put her out of his mind.

Seventeen

Madness

Kyer pressed herself against the building. The throng of people closed in.

"Defend yourselves but do not kill," Derry ordered. "Spread them out. Phennil—"

"On it, Captain."

The crowd surged and the company plunged in, fanning out in an effort to change their focus, distract them, so Phennil could get to the bell.

"Death to the strangers!" came the cry again. "Kill them!"

"Go home!" Derry returned as he pressed forward, dodging blows and slapping legs with the flat of his blade. If he could locate the one giving the order to kill, he might be able to take control of the situation.

Janak flung himself into the crowd. The villagers had knives, heavy sticks, rocks, pots and pans, anything they could get their hands on to use as weapons. He used the side of his axe to push people and knock them over, for the most part successful at keeping his blade from contact. Less success at avoiding their weapons. He cursed his bad eye and wiped blood off his forehead. It was exceedingly difficult to defend himself without hurting anyone.

Phennil darted around to the left of the crowd, trying the most direct route to the bell. When a heavy blow took him on his already wounded shoulder, pain shot down to his knees and he wilted, dropping his bow. Regaining his footing, he turned to his assailant, astonished to recognize the first dazed woman they'd met on their way into Nennia. She was again raising her weapon, a heavy clay urn.

"Not fair!" Phennil swerved away from the blow. "I'm not allowed to kill you." Picking up his bow from the muddy ground, he struck her in the back of the neck with it, and she fell to the mud.

"Death! Kill them!" came the cry again, this time from up on the platform. Derry went in pursuit, thankful that the villagers' weapons were no match for his armour. *A new dent, though.* He reached the platform, but the man had jumped down into the crowd, and Derry lost him.

Jesqellan wove through the throng, knocking weapons to the ground and racking his mind for a useful spell. He wrestled an axe out of someone's hand and threw a smoke bomb over the square. The effect was not at all what he had expected. Instead of calming their rage, it sent the crazed villagers into a fury.

A woman climbed up onto the remains of the platform, shrieking. "Dragons! Dragons are attacking!"

Others joined in the cry. The smoky mist swirled around as the frenzied people ran in all directions, flailing their makeshift weapons savagely and screaming.

A light rain started to fall. Kyer kept her back to the inn, so she couldn't be surrounded. She watched the others move into the crowd and draw the villagers' attention. She picked up a couple of rocks and tossed them at two of the people coming at her, putting them off. Through the rain and the smoke, Kyer could hardly make out her friends' positions anymore. But she had no time to search for them. A woman hefted a large rock and flung it at Kyer's head.

Derry peered past a woman in a black dress. *There he is.* He surged forward and grabbed the man, who looked up at him in terror and screamed.

"Kill! Kill! The strangers!"

Derry twisted him around and put his hand over the man's mouth. Pain shot into his hand as the man bit him and Derry recoiled.

"Death!" his assailant cried, brandishing a rusty short sword.

Don't make me do this. Derry whisked rain off his face and drew.

Phennil climbed onto the platform where the dragon woman was pulling stones from the pockets of her skirts and winging them into the crowd. She had a very good arm. He arrested her actions by hauling her down, but others picked up her rocks from the ground and threw them back to the platform. One of the rocks caught the elf on the ear as it whizzed by, which confirmed his suspicion that this was not where he wanted to be. The dragon woman clambered to her feet with a knitting needle in her hand. Phennil screamed as she drove it into his shoulder wound. He ploughed a fist into her face, and she plummeted backwards. Then he fell to his knees.

The stone wall bruised Kyer's elbow as she stepped back against it. A man came at her with a club, and she kicked him in the groin, sending him down. A woman with an iron pot banged it on her own head, and it rolled up against the wall of the inn near Kyer's feet. The woman staggered off. A tall, thin man had a coiled rope and was trying to throw it around her. She dodged but he rewound it and tossed again. It was an impressive trick, but this was not the time to admire it. He was getting more accurate with each try. As the rope came down the third time, she caught it with her sword and pulled back and down, the keen edge of her blade slicing right through the rope. Cursing, the man jumped on her, knocking her into the side of the stone building. Her sword flew from her hand, and she was winded. They slid to the ground, the man on top of her. The partially healed lacerations on her back seared and snatched air from her lungs. He pushed himself up to a sitting position. He tried to grab her head to pound it into the ground, but gasping for breath, she tilted it out of his way. She drew up her knee, seized the dagger from her boot and embedded the blade in his left thigh. He screamed and grabbed the wound. She pushed him off into the dirt.

The rain pelted down. The turmoil in the square mounted. Jesqellan ran about wildly, casting clumsiness spells and trying to pull people away from each other, but he was on the wrong side of the square, away from the bell. Just like the day before, the villagers fought and flailed like automatons, as if they did not remember why they were fighting, only that they were meant to be angry and to hurt someone. They pitched blows at whoever happened to be nearest. Someone blindsided him and he hurtled against the well. Stars circled his head.

Janak growled in fury as a crazed woman tried to jerk his battle axe from his grasp. He pushed her forehead with the flat of his hand, and it was enough to throw her off balance. Something smashed into the side of the dwarf's head, and he fell, groaning as his assailant stepped on him.

Phennil squeezed his eyes shut on a deep breath and yanked the knitting needle out. A fresh trickle of blood discoloured his armour. He dragged himself to his feet and lurched across the platform. Jumping off the other side, he fell and rolled then crawled over to the crude bell tower. Clutching his shoulder, he struggled up the ladder and clung to it. Wincing with pain, he reached up to grab the rope, only to find his hand grasping at air. Panting, he looked way up to the bell. The rope was gone.

Kyer staggered to her feet and couldn't find her sword where it had fallen from her hand. Leaning against the inn, she tried to catch her breath and looked about the crowd for her weapon. People were everywhere, yelling, panicking, hitting one another. The rain hammered the smoke into the ground. Her attention was diverted by a large man with arms of a blacksmith, setting himself up before her. He held her sword confidently in his enormous hands. Her dagger was stuck in the thin man's leg, out of her reach. *Hurry up, Phennil.* Her eyes met those of the blacksmith, and she felt the blood drain from her face. He was capable of killing her if she didn't act. She leaned down and grabbed the iron pot.

The burly man approached, gripping her sword in both his hands. The pot was ridiculous and insignificant in hers. She braced herself.

Phennil clung to the ladder and looked out over the square, breathing heavily and wondering what to do. It was utter mayhem. At first he couldn't find any of his friends, but at last he made out Jesqellan running about waving his arms until a man drove into him with his shoulder. The mage went headlong into the side of the well and fell to the ground. Janak was nowhere in sight. Derry's sword rang and Kyer— He somehow made it down the ladder with a single idea. Lurching a few paces from the bell tower, he leaned against the house there and nocked an arrow into his bow.

Derry feinted and blocked the man's strike and hoped only to keep him too busy to scream at the crowd. They didn't need more goading; they had gone mad. *Crash!* Derry felt the jolt of the sword's impact run down his arm. *Just defend*, he told himself. *Keep him occupied long enough.* Unidentified objects flew past his head. The man's lightning-fast twist and swipe took Derry by surprise, and his instinctive reaction was a poke at the attacker's forearm. He had obviously been a swordsman at one time. *Hurry up, Phennil!*

Kyer focussed on the blacksmith. *Don't allow him to get set and take initiative; keep him moving*, said Valrayker in her memory. *Combined with your speed and co-ordination, you can outmanoeuvre almost anyone, even those with greater reach or strength than yourself . . .* Her own blade hung above her head and began its descent. She leapt to the side. The blade hit the ground with a thud. The blacksmith, his back now to the inn, didn't bother raising the weapon all the way but swung it around on a horizontal arc. She flattened herself to the ground and felt the rush of air move the hair on her forehead. Kyer flung the pot at the barrel chest. He shifted and it missed him, clanging against the stone wall of the building behind him. He stepped forward and stomped a foot on her belly, pinning her down and taking her breath away. With both hands on the hilt, point downward, he raised her sword and bellowed a war cry. She struggled to roll, to sit up, to kick. No result. Her stare never left the sword tip aimed directly at her.

The bell rang with a weak, *clang clang!* Then, stronger, another *clang clang!* The blacksmith gave his head a shake, stumbled, and let go of her sword. Kyer veered to the right and batted at the weapon as it dropped to the ground. The blade cut through her sleeve and gashed her left forearm. Wincing, she grasped the wound and pushed herself up to see Phennil aim yet another arrow at the bell. He missed the shot. The villagers had not been fully affected by the meagre rings. Kyer snatched up her sword and grabbed the iron pot again. Holding it aloft, she banged it over and over with the hilt of her weapon. The pot rang with a joyful peal, the repetition mimicking the rhythm and timbre of the bell. The blacksmith, his expression transformed from hatred to vague sleepiness, turned abruptly and walked away with evenly paced steps.

Kyer leaned heavily against the inn and watched as all the villagers switched mood and let their weapons fall. They were blind to the carnage for which they had been responsible. She despised them for it. Those who were not injured to the point of immobility turned abruptly from their battles and staggered or drifted toward their homes. The smell of chalky smoke lingered, mingled with the aroma of mud, fear, blood, and hatred. The tall man still lay near her, her dagger jutting out of his thigh. The desire to kick him, to scream at him, gripped her like a vise. She stepped toward him, teeth clenched. *Not his fault.* Instead she drew her dagger gently out, and blood oozed from his leg. "You were about to hammer my head into the ground."

He responded with a glazed stare.

She swiped the dagger across his trousers, leaving a brownish red stripe, and resheathed it in her boot.

She looked over again at Phennil, who smiled weakly and waved. Then he dropped to the ground. She jammed her sword into its scabbard and ran over to him.

⟡

Jesqellan regained his footing and wandered through the debris, stepping over prostrate villagers and assorted household weaponry. He came upon a familiar form. Crouching, he rolled Janak over, and the dwarf groaned.

"Damn. I was hoping I wasn't still here."

"Sorry, old friend."

The mage assisted him to his feet, and together they began attending to the wounded.

⟡

When the bell rang, Derry lowered his sword. He bent, resting his hands on his knees, allowing himself a moment's rest. Reaching down, he gave his worthy opponent a hand up from the mud where Derry's swipe to the back of the knees had placed him. "Go home now, sir," Derry said, unable to keep the pleading from his voice. Never had he been so thankful for a battle to end.

He watched Jesqellan help Janak to his feet. The captain rubbed the back of his head where a lump was forming and examined a small cut on his hand. *Could have been worse.* It was a good thing he—

Emma.

Derry raced back to the inn, nearly tripping over a supine man with a nasty thigh wound. He flung open the door. Physicker-adept though he was, he had never seen so much blood. Mother and babe were heaped in the middle of it. Both were dead, crumpled on the floor in a pool of black and red. Derry surveyed the horrific scene in a daze, impotent, inept. He tasted bile, felt his guts swell, and staggered outside. He vomited into the mass of cobwebs under the window.

He cleared his throat and spat. *Coward.* Steeling himself, he went back inside.

He mustn't hide from it. He must commit the image to memory. He sat on the floor, up against the wall, and stared at the dead girl, white with pain; her tiny babe, blue with suffocation; both, red with blood.

"Can I come out now?"

The physi—*captain* looked up, startled to see little Sasha's face peeking around from the staircase, her eyes wide with fear.

He knew it was all wrong, her being there. She had already seen what she should not. But all he could say was, "You had better go."

She walked past him and went out into the square.

Derry no longer had strength to stem the flow of tears and allowed his grief and anguish to spill over.

⁘

Kyer dragged Phennil to someplace with more light, all the while seething with anger. Someone had planned this. Someone was laughing at the thought of all these people trying to kill each other. *And us.* She laid the elf in the mud and knelt next to him. She found the wound, a bit relieved that it wasn't a new one, though she feared there was even more damage this time. Her only consolation was that they'd managed to stop the mayhem in time.

In time for what? If every soul in the village had survived the battle, she'd have been surprised. Kyer slung Phennil's arm over her shoulder and hoisted him up. How long would it take for the poisons to wear off? Could someone incite them again in the meantime?

Phennil roused enough to walk along. Sprinkled all around were vestiges of the battle. The two stepped over or around pots, a kettle, stones, a tin cup, an axe, a wagon wheel, a bellows.

As they approached the inn, the door opened and Sasha came out, looking all around, her face pale. Then Kyer remembered who else they had left indoors. She darted a glance round the square.

"Where's Derry?" she called to Jesqellan.

The mage shrugged.

"He's inside." Sasha's tone told Kyer that something was very wrong.

"Phennil—?" Kyer asked.

"I need to rest anyway," the elf replied. "Go."

Kyer leaned him against a cart and ran.

She slipped into the inn. The physicker looked up at her with an ashen face. He was using the reddened blanket like a large rag, gathering it around a heaped form.

"Derry, is—is everything all right?"

Her friend looked up at her again, and she knew the answer.

"I made the wrong—" He hesitated then spoke with a low, firm voice, fighting to contain his emotion. "They did not survive."

Kyer stood over him, saw the pain in his eyes, the sorrow and self-blame. She felt her jaw lock in position as she thought about the battlefield dotted with injured people who needed the physicker's care. The faces of the men who had wanted to hurt her, and almost succeeded, then their fixated stares once it was over. And Derry—

Something began to bubble inside her.

"Innocent victims," Derry said. "And I could have—" He pressed his fingertips between his eyes.

A strangled choking sound fluttered through Kyer's throat, startling Derry. She wanted to say something. She tried to but no words came. *So much pain—* Instead she spun around and walked out.

⊹

Hunter pondered his situation as he took a bite of breakfast by a stream. He'd lucked into a decent position, to be sure. Clearly the chief recognized someone of value when he saw him. The rest of the men . . . Well, it was to be expected that respect from them wouldn't be instantaneous.

Was it worth the effort?

Not that he had much choice. Still, he was not bereft of skill or talent, and it would be just as easy to find a similar position—or create one. One that did not put him in line with those sanctimonious bastards of Valrayker's.

Did he really want to align himself with someone? It was too soon. No, he'd go back to Ronav's headquarters and collect the few belongings he'd left there then move on.

Hunter mounted his horse and continued south at a trot, rejuvenated by his new plan.

⊹

Kyer spared a glance for the body-littered square, where Jesqellan, Janak, and even Phennil lifted wounded out of the muck and carried them toward the inn, leaving them outside the door to await Derry's attention. Some revived enough to wander off. A pregnant woman waddled along, one hand using the platform for support.

Kyer frowned. *There are far too many pregnant women in this village.*

Giving little Sasha a quick hug where she hovered at the side of the inn, Kyer strode unswervingly across the square to the hillside with the circle of black stone statues. The woods lay below concealing . . . who? She thought about the reaction of the men she killed in the woods the day before. She'd taken them by surprise, of course. But it was more than surprise. It was more like shock. She had never seen either man before. But *they*, sure as death, had recognized *her*. And there was only one place she could think of where a bunch of ruffians might have seen her before, such that they never expected to see her again.

She stalked down the hillside, her memory taking her back to that particular interchange.

A demand. *"Where has he sent you? What is required of you?"*

Her response while bleeding onto the floor. *"It has nothing to do with you."*

"How do you know?"

Aha.

As she sank into the darkness of the trees, she paused to allow her eyes to adjust. Her footsteps made no sound on the soft forest floor as she approached the clearing where the six men had died yesterday. Barely a trace remained of the skirmish.

She stopped at the place where she'd killed the second man and crouched down. This time she felt no one watching her, but her senses were alive. Someone was there. She knew it like she knew every *wæpnian* movement. Like she knew that Halidan was not her true name. Like she knew that Derry *must not* feel as if he'd failed on this mission. She rose, turning slowly around, and walked toward the woods.

There. At the far end of the clearing, nestled in behind some dense cedars, was a little stone house. She stared at it, ears straining. She hadn't *heard* anything. But a soundless voice inside her head told her who was in that house.

"Ronav!" She yelled into the heavy stillness. "Ronav Malachite, get out here!"

⋅⟨⊱══════⟩⋅

Face-to-face. He was taller than she expected; he had been seated when she saw him before. They stared at each other, mirroring each other's hatred. Ronav's voice was like the ring of steel in the hushed murk. The rain had stopped, and the fog plunged into the valley once more.

"How did you get them to stop?" he said.

"There are other ways to make a bell ring," she replied, "even when the rope's been taken. Nice trick, though, trying to get the villagers to take us out for you."

He gave a small, sarcastic bow. "How did you know it was I?"

Kyer shrugged. "You told me yourself. Only I forgot at the time. Your... entertainment put it out of my mind." She eyed the terrain for obstacles.

He stood very still, smirking. "That was a clever exit. Where did you go?"

"Into thin air," she said mysteriously, and Ronav looked a little uncomfortable.

Grinning, she flexed her fingers. "Who killed Carver? Was it you?"

"No, that was my new deputy. You'd like him; he's much better looking than Con."

"I've learned that looks don't count for much," she said. "So is it Dregor you're trying to impress?"

"Trying? I already have." Ronav shrugged with fake modesty.

"He's that impressed by you taking advantage of a bunch of helpless villagers? His standards must be pretty low." Kyer saw his jaw tighten. "You poison them so they're all half asleep, you rape all their women, you skewer a harmless father, what a threat they pose! Quite a show of prowess for your lord and master."

Ronav floundered. "You have no *idea*—"

"Would you like me to write a testimonial? *Dear Dregor, Ronav Malachite is very brave. He needed just eight men to overpower me when I was without a weapon. Yours tru—*"

"Bitch."

"I get that a lot."

His sabre caught the light as he drew it. "I suppose Valrayker likes that about you."

Kyer laughed as her hand became one with her hilt and released her blade from its confines. "As a matter of fact, I think he does."

Ronav casually waved his sword this way and that, as if testing its balance. "See? We all have our questionable loyalties."

She sneered. "Some more so than others."

"Oh, don't be so sure, my girl."

"Bullshit," she said.

"Is it?"

"I understand your big plan for the future is to overthrow them. Too bad I stole your weapons and your interesting piece of jewellery."

In an instant, Ronav's sword was pointing at her chest, and Kyer reacted swiftly to block it. He began circling and Kyer matched him step for step.

"I needed that device," he said. "You think looks don't count for much? Maybe looks don't but *appearances* do. Your hero and his friend Kien *'Bartheylen'* don't have the noble intentions they pretend to." He lunged and she parried his point, and stepped aside.

Kyer scoffed. "And yours are so much better?" They circled each other in the dim light.

"At least I'm honest."

"Is that what you call it?" Testing his sword skills, she darted forward to slash at his knee, which he dodged, but she noted his imprecise timing.

The pulse in Kyer's temple throbbed, and she gave her head a shake. Her *wæpnian* training took over, and her breathing calmed. The wounds he had inflicted upon her were nothing, ceased to exist in this moment. Ronav must have noticed a change come over her, for alarm dashed across his face.

"If I'm so evil," he said with a grin, "why don't you kill me?"

Kyer held her sword parallel with the ground; her knees were bent; her core, strong. "Derry made me promise I wouldn't kill you. He wants to take you to see Valrayker."

"So you're here as Val's good little knight to make me submit to your will. How quaint."

Calm fury stirred in Kyer's gut. She darted forward, right shoulder flexing as she slashed her blade left to right. He sidestepped and parried. They backed up to the ready position again.

"Emma's dead, you know. She died giving birth this morning."

Ronav feigned a pitiable sigh and shook his head. "How sad."

Kyer's hatred roiled. "I'll bet your mother is proud."

Ronav suddenly flung himself at her, in a deep, forceful lunge. Her point down she knocked his sabre to the left and his momentum threw him off balance. She stumbled slightly, but took advantage of his left side being open and darted in, kicking him in the groin. Ronav tumbled, rolled, and was back on his feet, steadying himself well out of her reach. She moved in again, forcing him closer to a tree. Something else for him to keep track of.

"Who was the father, Ronav? Was it you?"

"No, it was Con." With a touch of pride, he added, "We managed to convince her father that he had done it himself, though."

Kyer stopped moving. His soothing tone brought home to her how twisted and gnarled was this grotesque man's view of right and wrong. That tone had tortured her just a few short nights ago. That twisted view was responsible for all she had endured that night and everything that was behind this mission.

A strange sensation filled her. As she stood rigid, she became the calm eye in the centre of a tornado of fury that swirled in a mass around her. The cold fingers of darkness gripped her fully, wiping out every feeling. Images roared in circular winds. Ronav's silken smile as he praised Con for his fist to Kyer's face. His serpent's voice as he counted lashings and instructed Con to mutilate her. That same man, horror stricken as he cowered behind his chair, watching his comrade burn. The pregnant girl, unable to recall who the father of her child was, oblivious that she did not deserve to die. A little girl's father, petrified in fear, blood seeping from his throat. A village full of innocent people, doomed to destroy each other. Then finally, the howling storm touched down on Derry's face, emotionless no more, weeping as he took the blame for a dead girl and her dead baby.

From somewhere outside herself Kyer saw Ronav standing across from her, watching her transformation with wide eyes and white knuckles, his weight shifting from foot to foot. Energy surged in her gut. Like a cloud of steam, it rose, and a burst of heat blasted straight up into her head.

Someone is about to get what he deserves. That was her last thought as she rushed at him, and he blocked her sword so frantically he nearly dropped his. The crash reverberated off the trees. Not giving him time to recover she danced in and out, drawing him closer, then forcing him back. Some sort of demon possessed her, and her attacks came hard and even. One after another. No time to breathe. To his left hip. To his sword arm. Another overhead. To his thigh. Not trying to hurt him, just tire him out, weaken him. Like a spider playing with its tortured prey.

Ronav flailed. To his credit he tried. She parried every one of his slashes with ease as if he fought like a mere child. He hit the ground more than once as she dodged his sweeps with the agility of an elf. The only contact she allowed him was with her sword.

"I thought—" he panted. "I thought a knight never broke a promise." In desperation, he tried to dodge another slash, but it caught his hand, which bled nicely.

She smiled. "But I'm not a knight, you see. And I don't care."

His eyes were so white!

"Are you ready, Ronav?" She was nonchalant, hardly even breathing heavily. Death was on his face already. She basked in the fear she saw there. "One." She faked to the side then whacked him on his shoulder. Her voice was swallowed by the trees.

His colour went from pallid to ashen as he turned frantically to witness the red ooze seeping from himself.

"Two." Her sword severed his weapon arm. His panic was glorious.

Gripping her hilt, preparing to stab, she paused for the effect it would have on him. Her lips curled upward in a triumphant sneer. "See you in hell." She laughed. "Three."

She had to give him full marks for the way he just stood there, waiting for the end. It must have been quite a sight to see the point of her blade fly toward him, the steel catching what little light reached through the trees. What had gone through his mind at the last, when the tip touched and he felt it skewer him? A pity he couldn't have turned his head to see what it looked like as it exited his back, just underneath his shoulder blade. Was he already dead when she withdrew it? Or had he heard the delightful, moist, bone-snapping, or the sucking noise as his lung collapsed when she jerked it free? And now there he lay in the morning twilight, the deepening mist encircling his pathetic body like the smoke from a funeral pyre. Dead. So dead.

She watched his blood stream in whorls, saw it mixing with the dirt and forming pools of dark reddish brown mud. As his life flowed from him, so did the demon pass from her. Her mind returned from where it had been watching the proceedings from somewhere far above, and a gasp of shock escaped her. Sword falling from her hand, she trembled. It intensified until her whole body shook uncontrollably. Her legs no longer had strength to hold her, and she dropped to the ground. Kneeling in the dirt, only her hands preventing her face from landing there as well, she gasped for air and could not stop shaking.

Then a large set of arms embraced her, and she didn't reject them. The scent of him was familiar, yet she couldn't place it. But he held her close and breathed deeply, and soon she found she could match him. She breathed with him and finally, after what had to be hours, she was calm and was able to see who had lifted her out of her madness.

Janak.

The dwarf's features had softened, showing not distaste, not derision, but compassion.

Kyer felt only shame. "I killed him. He was my enemy . . . and I killed him. It wasn't even in self-defence. I hated him. I sought him out. I waited for him, and I *killed* him." She found Janak's eyes. "I don't ever want to do that again."

"It doesn't feel as good as you think it's going to." His eyes clouded over as if a distant memory had been awakened. "Still," and he was back with her again, "Ronav had altogether too much influence on your life lately. There are not many who could bear what you have borne and yet remain in full possession of themselves." He released her and got to his feet, pulling the forks of his beard back into the preferred position. "I would suggest that you return to the inn and have a cup of ale. Or see if there is any wine. It will do you good. I'll clean up here."

She nodded, rising, and turned to go but stopped. "Janak—"

He gave a warning glare. "Shut up."

Eighteen
Aftermath

J anak did the search of the body on Kyer's behalf and pocketed the few items of value to present to her at some opportune time. He stared at the bastard's corpse and contemplated how to dispose of it. He ran through the options and decided there was just one appropriate method.

Janak picked up the severed arm and pressed it onto the whoreson's belly. He dragged the corpse as far as he could into the woods and let the bastard's legs drop. He wiped his hands on the dead man's jerkin then on the moss. He finally brushed them on his own trousers and walked away. The local wildlife would be happy.

A queue of injured villagers stood or sat outside the inn, leaning against the building, still hoping for treatment from the physicker. Kyer stepped inside. The candle and lamplight was like sunlight compared to the diffused slate grey mist that hung over the village this—was it afternoon? Or still morning? She stood for a moment, blinking, hardly aware of the presence of living beings beyond the door.

"Where have you been?" came a familiar voice, scolding. "And where's Janak?"

She said nothing. The words would not come so easily.

"We could use your help here, you know."

Kyer shut the door and walked across the room to the bar. A keg of ale might normally have been inviting, but she needed something stronger. More immediate effects. She picked a half-full bottle from among the row on the shelf, grabbed a glass, and sat down in a corner booth, her feet up on the bench. She was aware of the surrounding silence and felt several sets of eyes on her, but the sensation was not strong enough to penetrate her mood, and she ignored it. The cork yarded out, she poured, drank, poured again, drank, and soon a heady warmth seeped into the chill of her muscles and mind. She poured yet again and leaned her head back against the wall, eyes shut. There would be no Toast to the Dead today.

Annoyance tremored through Derry's benumbed mind, but he could spare only a moment to observe her. She was not bleeding, unlike the teenage boy with the hunk of pottery jutting out of his forehead. He returned to his work. Jesqellan, at least, hadn't bolted on him. Sasha couldn't be kept away, and once Emma had been wrapped in a sheet and the mess cleaned up—Derry would not let Sasha in the room until that had been done—the child had become a first-rate assistant. She'd also put herself in charge of visiting all the invalids in the rooms upstairs. Even Phennil, his shoulder bound and Jesqellan's healing spell doing its work, was able to help the mage with some of the wounded. The captain was too drained to give much thought to the absent dwarf or the delinquent Kyer.

She'd walked out on him when he needed her most. When had he come to need her, in particular, that much?

Definitely too tired and numb to reflect on that. He put her out of his mind.

All the wounded dealt with at last, the captain sat at a table in the centre of the room and realized how fatigued he was. He could not remember this much activity packed into such a short time since the day he'd gotten Val out of Equart City. Barely twenty-four hours since they'd arrived on the hill above this cursed village. Jesqellan opened a bottle of wine, pouring him a generous cupful. Phennil pulled up a chair after laying a blanket across a napping Sasha, and Jesqellan poured for him too.

"We can't take another one like that, Captain," the mage pointed out. "We're done in."

Derry agreed. "Especially if two of our own people aren't quite with us." He meant Janak and Phennil but had a hard time resisting the temptation to look over at Kyer. He didn't need to. Jesqellan did it for him.

Phennil frowned.

"Perhaps Phennil and I should go talk to Magistrate Dillon," Jesqellan said. "Try to find out if the bastards behind this have sent him another message yet. Or give him one of our own: No more fighting."

"That's an idea," Derry said.

"No need."

Derry turned his head.

Kyer looked so utterly spent. He could not fix on whether she more closely resembled Therys, the goddess of the air, or Coaldor, the god of death. She poured another drink from her bottle and downed it. The alcohol seemed to boost her determination. "No need."

"Do you care to explain?" Derry heard the authoritative tone in his own voice, adopted automatically now that he sensed he was about to hear what Kyer had been up to.

She pushed herself to her feet and stood at attention, looking over Derry's head at the wall beyond. "The perpetrator was Ronav Malachite. I figured it out and went to find him."

Derry had a bad feeling. "And?"

Kyer's voice was calm and strong. "He's dead."

Phennil and Jesqellan exchanged looks.

Derry got to his feet and approached her. "Kyer?" he asked hopefully.

The door opened then clicked shut.

"I killed him, Derry."

A pit opened in Derry's belly. "Kyer? Was it self-defence?"

She clenched her teeth and still did not meet his eyes.

"Was it self-defence, Kyer?" he insisted.

"No, sir." And now she glared at him. "I went down. Called him out. And I killed him. He suffered. I killed him . . . and I enjoyed it."

Derry's heart fell into the pit.

"That's where I went," she pressed, her pitch rising. "I did not go to capture him to bring him before Val for judgement. I went to kill him."

Janak stepped up.

The captain was replete with sadness. "You know what I'm going to have to do now, don't you?"

Kyer looked at him defiantly. "Whatever."

Derry breathed out a long exhale. "Kyer Halidan, I regret that I must—"

"Don't do anything foolish, Captain." Janak warned.

Derry snapped his gaze over to the dwarf.

"We've all had a rough go today, Captain," Janak said. "We've all had to make choices. Tricky ones. It's all about *choices*, Derry."

Derry could not avoid a glance over at the sheet-wrapped form in the corner. His whole body ached. But Janak was right. The dwarf walked away, leaving Derry to look back and forth from the dwarf to Kyer and wonder what had passed between the two of them. He looked into Kyer's dark green eyes and saw that they weren't defiant but troubled. She was experiencing her own pain. No words came to his lips, but he nodded his understanding. Her body sagged. He reached out to touch her. She raised her eyes again and shook her head slowly.

"You didn't kill them, Derry. Not your fault."

He released an involuntary choking sound. *How did she know?*

His body sagged.

Later, they sat in a cosy group feeling, for the first time in ages, serene. The dwarf went to his belongings in the corner and brought a bundle over to their table. He tossed a few daggers down as well as three coin pouches and a quiver of arrows for Phennil. There was also a half-decent pair of wool socks.

"Didn't have a chance to give these to you after we hucked the dead men into the temple last night," he said to Kyer. "Wasn't much of any quality. In the pocket of one of my fellows was this little trinket, though." His eyes gleamed as he held up a polished stone that twirled as it dangled from a chain. "That's pure jade, if I'm not mistaken. It's a beauty. You have my word as a dwarf and a warrior that this was found on the body of one of the men I killed," he added with a look at Kyer, aware that it appeared he had taken the one item of value from the dead men.

Kyer shrugged. "I trust you."

A look of astonishment passed among Derry, Jesqellan, and Phennil. Kyer smiled and lowered her eyes. Janak snorted.

"There was one other thing, Kyer," Janak said. "I found this pouch on Ronav. It was tucked up inside his armour, just under one arm." He handed her a leather pouch. It was padded with sheepskin inside. Kyer pulled from it a vial of a transparent blood-red liquid. She held it up to the firelight and saw that it had a marbled effect, similar to when she'd seen two types of liquor mixed together. She held it up for Jesqellan to examine, and he whistled low. It glowed eerily with the firelight behind it.

"Have an apothecary confirm this," he said, "but I have a suspicion that this is one of the most powerful blends of healing potion available. In fact, not available. Only a very experienced wizard could be a source of such a thing."

Valrayker's company stayed in Nennia for ten days all together.

They buried Ronav's men with all the ceremony that goes into eviscerating chickens. Derry asked what had become of Ronav's body. Kyer didn't know and Janak said nothing. Derry was forced to accept that it had been dealt with as the dwarf had seen fit and to leave it alone. Emma, her babe, and Sasha's father were handled delicately. The company erected a pyre and laid the corpses on it with honour. Derry brought Emma's parents to the lighting ceremony in hopes that they would have some memory of it once they had regained possession of their minds. Jesqellan, the shaman, sang the chants as the fire sent its smoke into the sky, the souls of the departed to be with the gods of their choice.

Sasha showed them the site for the placement of her father's ashes. On the edge of the stream, near their cottage was a flower garden where Sasha's mother's ashes lay. *Sasha Carver* was etched into a stone at one end. They buried the father's in the ground next to that place, encircling the entire area with stones. Janak placed his own contribution himself at the head of the site: a stone that read simply, *Shawn Carver, Loyalty.*

"Shawn and Sasha Carver," Jesqellan spoke softly to the spirits of those who had passed on. "Fear not the welfare of your child. She will be well cared for by friends of the true duke, to whom you remained loyal." For the five of them had agreed that they would not leave her in Nennia. She would return with them to Shael, and a home would be found for her there.

Back at the inn, they ate a light midday meal.

"I can't go with you," Sasha said.

"Why not?" asked Kyer. *What can she possibly think is left for her here?*

"Because there will be no one to tend the statues," she replied with a shrug.

Derry leaned forward so suddenly, he bumped the table, almost spilling all the cups that sat upon it. "What do you mean?" he demanded, then, remembering he was speaking to a child, continued more softly. "What tending do the statues need?"

"Papa told me to pull the weeds at Dionne's feet and to put dirt on Aidan's wheat. I don't know why, but he said it's important. If I go away, there won't be anyone to do it."

Derry leaned back in his chair, the corners of his mouth curled in amusement, but his eyes clouded with grief. "You did that?" He nearly choked on the words.

She nodded. "I went out at night, just like Papa said."

Derry had nothing to say. For some strange reason, he looked as if he might cry.

Kyer made another connection. "Sasha, did your papa have a millstone in a shed that he used to grind corn and wheat?"

The child nodded, her mouth full of egg. Her legs swung back and forth. "We had corn and wheat in the cellar. He used it to make bread. We took a really long drive to another place to get it. But then the men came and broke it all up. So he used a mortar and pestle instead. The bread wasn't as nice after that because he said the grain wasn't ground up enough."

Some time after the visit from Valrayker's messenger, Sasha's father had figured out that both water and flour were contaminated. He had found a way to keep himself and his daughter healthy and had kept a low profile while waiting for help to arrive. His daughter maintained the clues on the statues, in case something happened to him. Leaving the village was not an option for him, for where could he find a safer place in enemy-occupied territory than his own home? And he trusted that help was on the way. They had missed him by less than a day. Kyer's eyes hazed in a swell of emotion, and she hated Ronav more.

Derry leaned over and took the girl's wee hand in his large one. "You have done very well, Sasha. The work you did helped us to discover what was ailing the people in your village, and now everyone is going to get well again. There is no longer a need for you to tend the statues."

"Oh, that's good." She sighed with relief. "I really wanted to come with you."

There was one more burial.

Without an antidote, there was no way to neutralise the poison; a new water source would have to be dug. Kyer, Janak, and Phennil had broken down the stone walls of the old well and filled it in but not all the way to the top. Jesqellan chanted and sang as Derry laid the ashes of Emma and her son in the well and covered them with earth. Phennil planted a fir sapling he had retrieved from the woods, and they filled the dirt around it until it was level with the ground again. Then Kyer and Janak erected a low fence around the area. New life would grow from where life had been laid to rest.

Thus they began the healing of Nennia. Phennil sought information from whomever he could, be it the magistrate or the sheriff or even the baker. He wanted to know where the flour had been sent from so they could stop its production. He also researched where Nennia used to get flour before Ronav's men broke their way into the trade route so Nennia could reestablish trade with its original source. He journeyed away for a few days to bring back some supplies from other villages. Derry and Kyer collected sacks of tainted flour from the villagers and tried to tell the story of what had happened to anyone showing signs of lucidity.

In the meantime, Janak and Jesqellan dug a new well at the other end of the square from the old one. It was far enough away to be out of reach of any contaminated seepage. Progress was slow, however, because of Jesqellan's refusal to pick up a spade. The hole was three feet wide and as many deep, and Janak's back was already sore from the labour, but the mage stood to one side, head tipped skyward, and murmured to himself. His long, delicate fingers alternated between crossing through each other and touching lightly at the tips.

"Your hands would be a lot more useful if you would apply them to the task we have been given," Janak growled at his friend with sarcastic formality.

The mage stopped murmuring and opened his eyes, glaring starkly back at the dwarf in the hole. "Marvellous. You have just destroyed my concentration, and now I shall have to begin again."

"Begin what? I've done a fairly thorough beginning on my own here, and I could use some help."

"You know very well that my hands are my tools—dare I say, my *instruments*—and I would be foolish and destructive indeed to threaten their effectiveness by covering them with blisters and calluses. It would upset the very balance of nature were I to degrade my hands in such a manner."

Janak rolled his eyes as he stuck the spade in the dirt and straightened. "I don't know what rotting maggot-leftovers you are tossing at me, you addlepated, mumbling *magician—*"

"*Magician!*"

"—but I am apt to be finished here before you have even—"

"How dare you insult my craft by speaking of me as nothing but a lowlife player of *tricks*! A delver in *sleight of hand*? Hardly! Do you know how many years it takes to—?"

"At least as many as it will take for you to pick up that damned spade and get busy here."

"If you must know, I happened to be trying to remember a spell I learned a long time ago and haven't used in several years. It takes time to—"

"Apparently."

"—remember how to do it correctly, and if not done correctly, dire consequences will occur."

"As long as the consequence has something to do with this hole being deep enough to reach water, that's all I care about." The dwarf tossed up a spadeful of dirt that hit Jesqellan square in the chest.

The mage stiffened. His jaw jutted out, as he brushed dirt off himself. "You know, for the first time, I can see why people like to have little carved stone versions of you in their gardens," Jesqellan remarked dryly. "Not only can I see that such a creature as yourself might scare away evil spirits, but you do look rather cunning up to your arse in a hole."

Kyer and Derry, heaving a sack of flour onto the platform, saw Jesqellan dashing about, trying to dodge piles of dirt as they were flung at him from the hole. Janak didn't bother with the spade now but threw fistfuls of dirt at the mage, who howled with both rage and laughter.

Silence ensued after a time, but it was broken again by a loud bang and sizeable chunks of dirt falling from the sky and landing all around the hole. Kyer and Derry dropped what they were doing and ran over.

Janak howled obscenities from somewhere down in the hole, which was rather deep all of a sudden. He hurled insults at Jesqellan, who shrugged sheepishly, brushing dirt off his robes.

"I guess I remembered it after all," he said. "One more should do it, but I suppose we ought to get Janak out of there before I try it again."

They had to lower a rope down to the dwarf, who, when he finally emerged, was head to toe in mud and looked more like a goblin as he yelled at the mage, cursing him and his "blasted magic tricks."

"As a matter of fact, it *was* a blasting spell, Janak. Well done, lad!"

Kyer didn't dare laugh, but it was all she could do to suppress it. She bit her tongue until tears came to her eyes.

"Janak, go down to the stream and wash yourself, and Jesqellan, why did you not get him out of there before you cast your spell?" Derry said. "He could have been badly hurt."

"Well, not really. It was just a mild spell. At worst he could have been buried, and then we'd have had to dig him out again."

Derry did not see the humour in this.

"Honestly, Derry, I was quite distracted. I had no thought at all that it would work! How was I to know it would be so effective?" The mage stepped closer to the hole and looked down. "You see? We are close. I'll just do it again, and we'll have our new well. No more digging required. Janak, you can thank me later!"

Janak's steady stream of invectives soared up to them as his filthy, lumbering form descended the hill.

With no new poison being introduced into their bodies, the villagers began to come back to themselves after a week, much to the relief of Kyer and her friends. Derry's concern about long-term effects had not abated, but they did all they could to ensure the welfare of the villagers. The victims began to understand just what had been done to them and could take steps to reestablish themselves.

Kyer put her upbringing to good use, helping a few families with planting and sheep shearing. Derry promised Peter Dillon to send a shipment of supplies, including flour, once they reached Shael. The village cleric spoke with Derry, who told him all he could about what had happened to them all. The cleric promised that he would involve Nennia's healer, and together they would counsel the rest of the villagers to help them through the anger and bitterness they would feel very soon.

Baird, the innkeeper, set himself the task of bringing his establishment back up to its usual standard. He was quite mortified that Lord Valrayker's ambassadors had been staying there amongst filth and negligence and made it up to them by making the place fairly sparkle in short order. One evening, the group returned and were greeted by a cheery fire in a tavern that smelled no longer of dust and mildew but of fresh straw and wood oil. The salty aroma of frying pork sizzled its way from the kitchen. Baird drew them each a pint of ale then uncorked some wine and poured out six cups.

"Nennia will be forever grateful to you for all you have done," he said sincerely. "I drink to you five and to your lord—may he return to his homeland while I still have my youth to be a part of it."

They drank and toasted Baird and all of Nennia, wishing them a speedy recovery.

Once they were satisfied that Nennia would thrive on its own, the company felt their presence was becoming a burden and prepared to leave.

The whole population of Nennia came out to see them off. Some wished they could stay and see the village back on its feet, but Derry reassured them that he would have Lord Valrayker send another group of emissaries in a month or so to see how they were faring. One of the men who had attacked Kyer in the riot came to apologize, saying, "It weren't too gentlemanly."

The storekeeper gave Sasha a kiss.

"Come visit us someday, child, and show us what a grand lady you have become!" Then she pressed something into Sasha's hand and turned away. Sasha opened her palm to see what she had been given. It was a shiny hair clip made of brightly painted wood in the shape of a bow and arrow. The arrow was the sturdy stick that pushed through the bow to hold the clip shut and the hair in place. Sasha showed it to Kyer and Phennil, grinning from ear to ear. Kyer turned it over and saw that carved into it were the initials *SC*. A lump formed in her throat. *I'll tell her about that later.*

Phennil lifted Sasha up onto Leoht's back, and at last they were off. They waved amid a chorus of hurrahs. When they reached the hilltop from which they'd first glimpsed the decrepit village, Kyer turned around for a last look. Already the village showed signs of new life.

⁘

They had been away nearly a month, and spring was in full bloom in the duchy of Shae. The journey was blissfully uneventful, in particular for Kyer, who felt certain that with Ronav dead, his men could no longer have a need to track her. Their spirits were high.

Finally one afternoon, they could see the spire of Shael Castle in the distance. Kyer cheered. "I can't wait to have a bath; I'm sure I'm as rank as Phennil by now."

The good-natured elf stuck his tongue out at her. "Let's enter Shael by the Sunset Gate, Derry," he suggested excitedly, "so Sasha can feel the full effects of the city."

"I would have thought that might be frightening to the child."

"I'm not afraid," Sasha announced, and so it was decided. Rather than going in modestly at the northeast High Gate, they circled around the outer city and made their entrance by the main gate, where Kyer had entered on her arrival. They paraded up the road triumphantly, and Kyer's heart thudded in anticipation of a warm reception and the celebration that would ensue when they told their tale.

The guards at the gate welcomed them, though Kyer sensed a reservation in their hearty demeanour. This was reinforced as they clopped along the road within the walls. Kyer's pleasure at the look of awe on Sasha's face was dampened by a feeling from the citizens of Shael that something was not right. They didn't greet the travellers with anger or unfriendliness, but neither was there even an air of excitement at their arrival. An overtone of greyness hung over the whole city.

"What's going on, do you suppose?" she asked Derry.

"What do you mean?" he said, and she could see that he was beaming beneath his serious exterior at the prospect of reporting to his lord with the good news of their successful venture. She left it alone. Perhaps Shael had not changed; maybe it had been like this when she arrived but she hadn't noticed it, what with her own excitement and apprehension of what was to come. However, Kien's flag no longer flew from the tower.

Acadia met them at the outer castle gate. She was genuinely glad to see them, and this time Kyer was certain of the change in her. She appeared much more at ease and less stilted in her speech than when her brother had been present. She, too, despite her businesslike manner, seemed to be wearing a subtle sign of care in the form of a line across her forehead and a dimness in her eyes. Kyer attributed that to Acadia's observation of Sasha; she most likely guessed the reason for the child's coming to Shael with them.

Kyer felt anew the tremor in her knees upon stepping over the threshold of the keep behind the steward. She could not resist a glance over her shoulder at the Lady Alon Maer, whose congratulatory smile shone down to her. She smiled back.

Valrayker had been informed of his company's arrival, and when Acadia opened the door to Kien's meeting room, he turned from the fireplace and greeted them warmly. He was dressed in casual black with a waistcoat of some shimmery silver fabric. His hair was tied back, so Kyer was able to observe the ancient face that somehow looked more tired and anxious today, now that they had returned, than it had when they left. *Shouldn't it be the other way around?*

"Welcome, my friends. I was beginning to be concerned about what had become of you." He shook them each by the hand. "I have an idea that you must have been successful, or I'm sure I would see heavier eyelids and sadder smiles!"

"You are correct, my lord," Derry affirmed with subdued eagerness. "Though more than one sad smile faced us from the moment we arrived, in fact from the time our journey began." He glanced at Kyer. "We succeeded in doing as you asked."

Valrayker's attention was distracted when he saw a tiny face peering out from behind Kyer's legs. Derry halted his report as the dark elf lowered himself to crouch in front of Kyer and tipped his head to one side.

"Well, well, who have we here?" His voice was kind and playful, his grey eyes sparkling.

"Come on out, Sasha. It's all right," Kyer said.

Phennil crouched down to meet her face and took the child by the hand. "Sasha, this is Lord Valrayker. He is the 'true duke' that your papa spoke of." Turning to the dark elf, he continued. "Valrayker, this is Sasha Carver. We brought her back with us from Nennia. She very much wanted to meet you."

Eyebrows lifting in recognition of the name, Valrayker's assessment of the situation was quick. He stuck out a hand for her to shake and said, "It's a pleasure to meet you." Kyer stood awkwardly between them, her arms folded across her chest, and observed the girl's reaction. Sasha stared at him in awe and did not take his hand. Instead she reached into the pocket of her pinafore and pulled out a rather crumpled, wilted handful of buttercups.

"I picked these just for you," she whispered.

"Well now, wasn't that thoughtful!" Valrayker accepted the bright yellow blooms, picking up the ones that fell to the floor. "It has been a very long time since anyone has given me flowers."

"Who gave them to you before?"

Valrayker chuckled. "It was much too long ago for me to remember!"

"I will bring you some more ones. Better ones that aren't squished."

"I would like that very much."

Kyer knew Sasha had warmed to her father's hero when she stepped out and pulled the gryphon out of her other pocket, thrusting it in his face. "This is Arrow. My papa made him. He brings me good luck. He takes care of me."

Valrayker took the wooden figure and examined it with the arched eyebrows of someone who is impressed. "He's a beauty, all right. Would you like for my friend Acadia to take you and Arrow to look around the castle? I think there might be some other children your age lurking about somewhere."

Sasha's eyes widened and her face broke out into an impish grin. She nodded with enthusiasm.

"Come." Acadia took the child by the hand. "I'll take you to the kitchen first; I bet Cook has some apple turnovers that need a young lady's attention."

"Yes, it's a good idea," Sasha said as they went out. "Arrow's hungry, too, and he's very excited about being in a big castle . . ." The sound of her little voice died away as the door closed behind them.

Valrayker rose, his face now careworn. "Was her father taken from her?" he asked, already knowing the answer. He motioned for them all to be seated and settled himself in his usual armchair by the fire.

"Yes, I'm afraid so," Derry said, taking the reins of the story, though each member of the party contributed anecdotes. When they came to the part about Kyer's capture by Ronav's men, Val looked sharply at Kyer as she described her experience. Though she assured him she was quite recovered, he was not able to turn from her for a moment, his brow furrowed in consternation.

"You suddenly travelled from Ronav's headquarters to wherever it was these fellows were?"

She nodded, shrugging. "I hoped you might be able to shed some light on that one," she admitted.

He continued to stare at her then shook his head. "No, I'm afraid I can't."

Kyer was aware of a twinge of guilt as she realized that for a brief moment she did not believe him. *Can't or won't?* Then the feeling passed.

They carried on with the story of the arrival in Nennia, the riots, the discoveries of the poisonous mixtures, and the slayings of Ronav and his compatriots. Derry here left out certain details, purposely avoiding Kyer's eyes. Valrayker asked questions to fill in gaps that he did not understand but for the most part remained silent, glued to every detail. He reacted with anger, with dismay, with approval. When Phennil told him of the discovery of Sasha and her father, his eyes closed, as if the thought of it pained him. A good many points in the story caused him to raise his hand for a momentary pause while he sorted them and filed them in his memory to be dwelt upon further at another time. Wine and ale were brought to them and later, an evening meal. They told their leader the whole tale.

Val approved wholeheartedly of the plan to send a shipment of supplies right away. Then he rose. Moving around the gathering, he embraced each one in a gesture of thanks for their contributions to saving his village.

"There will be rewards for you all, though I confess I'm not prepared at this time. I've been . . . preoccupied." He filled their cups from the wine decanter on the table and stood staring thoughtfully into the fire. Then he turned, as if remembering they were there. "I congratulate and thank you all." His tone became grave. "Now it is my turn to speak to you of the things that have transpired here in Shael since your departure.

"A week after you left, we received a message from Bartheylen Castle. You will note that Kien is not here to greet you, and he asked me to pass on his regrets. He returned in great haste to Bartheylen Castle upon hearing that Lady Alon Maer has been taken seriously ill."

Kyer's heart jolted and her body stiffened. "How seriously?"

Valrayker's face darkened visibly. "We do not know. The healers could tell us their observations but have drawn no conclusions."

The dread hung in the chamber like the deep resonance of a gong. Kyer's knees were clenched. It was no wonder the mood of the entire city was subdued if people had heard about their lady. They'd had nearly a month to dwell on it.

Valrayker was not finished. "The other part of the problem is that Alon is pregnant. This illness is threatening her life, so of course--" Here he turned away again, and Kyer saw his shoulder blades contract, controlling the emotion that surged.

"There must be *something* we can do!" Kyer spouted hoarsely. "Do the healers not have *any* ideas?"

All five watched their leader.

Valrayker composed himself. "There is one idea."

"Well, let's have it!" Kyer said.

The dark elf contemplated her. "I confess I'm moved by your depth of feeling for a dear friend of mine, though you have never met her."

Kyer frowned away her blush. How could she describe the feelings evoked in her by a mere portrait on the wall? They would never understand why Alon Maer meant so much to her.

Valrayker wandered over to gaze at the map on the wall.

"The Healers at Bartheylen Castle are the best in Rydris. They have employed the full spectrum of their craft, all the ancient arts, their knowledge of spells and charms, all their energy and internal powers and have come up with nothing but minor, temporary remedies. They cannot even come up with a diagnosis, let alone what they need: a cure. The prime healer here in Shael suggested it, and we all agreed that in order to learn exactly what ails Alon, and to discover a cure, if there is one, we need to consult a higher power."

Valrayker turned and looked directly at Jesqellan.

Jesqellan is a higher power? Kyer thought doubtfully. But then she saw the cloud cross over the mage's already dark face.

"You cannot mean that we need to consult Kayme?" Jesqellan murmured, the white of his eyes brightly contrasting with the darkness of his skin.

The dark elf nodded. "The prime can think of no other option."

Kyer looked from one face to another around the room. Nobody seemed happy with the idea. *Who's Kayme?*

"No one has seen or heard from Kayme in *years*!" said Jesqellan. "Why, it has been at least *fifteen years* since I have heard him utter a single sound from his dark tower way up north, and even then it was a three-word declaration, 'I am busy,' that gave us all the strong message that he absolutely does *not* want to be disturbed! One does not just walk up to the tower of the most powerful wizard in Rydris, knock on the door, and ask for a casual favour as if we were asking to borrow some eggs. It just isn't done."

"It's our only hope," Valrayker said, sinking wearily into his chair. "If you don't wish to be a part of it, I won't blame you or bear any grudge against you. It may be that he isn't willing or even able to help us. I'm merely asking you to try."

"I'll go," piped up Kyer without hesitation.

"As will I." Phennil nodded, though his voice was overly brave.

"You know I will," Derry said quietly to his lord.

Janak and Jesqellan said nothing. Janak's jaw was crooked in a thoughtful pose, and the mage sat in moody silence.

"It isn't necessary to make a decision this instant," Valrayker assured them. "The situation is urgent, but I'm also fully aware of the danger you would be heading into. We'll talk further in the morning."

Valrayker sent a messenger into the city and, later that evening, held a private interview in Kien's meeting room.

The next morning, they ate like scavengers of the fare they had so missed while away.

Valrayker entered, whistling. "My, it is good to have you all back again." He dished himself up a liberal helping of blueberries. "I have proceeded with your travel preparations, if only for the benefit of the three who have already committed their involvement." He said this without glancing significantly at anyone. "Further to that, we are expecting one more guest for breakfast." He poured cream over them until they floated.

"Who is it?" Derry asked.

"Your newest travelling companion. I met with him last night, and he has agreed to join the company on this mission. I've discovered him to be an excellent bowman, as well as possessing several other talents that will no doubt be of valuable service to the group. You'll ask yourselves how you managed without him in the past. He's truly a unique find, and I'm very pleased that he accepted with no pressuring on my part."

The others looked around at each other with suppressed excitement. As Kyer knew, Valrayker was able to find suitable members for his company in the oddest of situations, and they were all curious to know who this unexpendable person could be.

The door burst open and Kyer jumped. There was a pause then a rush of movement as a small figure raced over to Kyer in a blur of colour.

"Dear lady, we meet again! And under circumstances such that I cannot adequately express my joy! Travelling companions! To be able to look upon your countenance, to begin each new day with you in my immediate vicinity, and your face to be the last thing I allow to enter my sight before I fall into slumber filled with dreams of you!" Skimnoddle the halfling knelt grandly as he finished his speech, bowing his head.

Kyer was stunned as he placed a hand on his heart and declaimed.

"Such a beauty is Kyer
Shimmering gold lights up her hair
Her eyes, deep green, like shadowed lair
Never was there one so fair
As my lady, my true love, Kyer."

He bowed and hopped onto the seat next to Valrayker, which happened to be opposite her.

Kyer looked daggers at Valrayker. This baffling, annoying creature was to travel with them to visit the most powerful wizard in all of Rydris?

"You'll have to tone down your orations if you are going to gain credibility with this lot," Valrayker murmured to Skimnoddle, who bobbed his head and adjusted his cravat. To the rest of the group, he said, "I believe most of you have met Skimnoddle."

Kyer, intent on her eggs and ham, threw a piercing glance at Valrayker.

The dark elf beamed. Kyer thought he had lost his mind.

Hunter tied his horse outside Ronav's headquarters. He would hustle in, give a brief account of progress in Nennia, find his belongings, and leave again. He stepped over the threshold.

Within moments he was surrounded and staring at the tip of a falchion. He considered it, ascertaining that it was not getting any closer, then lifted his eyes. He met the narrow stare of its owner, the one named Hugh, but whom they thought of as Hew because of his woodcutter style with his enemies.

"Now here's a pretty scenario," Hew said. "You came straight outta nowhere and got yourself in real deep with Chief Ronav, of a sudden. And after one job, now, you're the only one wot comes back. I imagine there's a story there."

Hunter eyed him levelly. "Not much. I've just come back for my things. The others are dead, it's true, but they were in the wrong place at the wrong time."

"I'm sure they were. And where's Ronav?"

"Back in Nennia, overseeing the final stages of the operation. I'm to send up more men. Some people named Misty and Juggler, too if they're here."

Hew lowered his falchion but not his threatening stance. "See here, now. There's another thing we've been wonderin' about."

"Is that a fact?"

"Well an' it is." Hew nodded wisely. "See, we've heard some interestin' rumours lately. To do with Duke Kien Bartheylen and a certain captain he used to have but don't have no more." He didn't give Hunter a chance to react but stepped in. Hew's face was so near to his, the hair on Hunter's forehead moved with his breath. "I've got me eye on you, Hunter. Any sign at all of you being still loyal to that damned elf, and I'll carve your face into the most hideous-looking gargoyle you ever saw. And if you're lucky, you'll die before I can show you your reflection."

"Good thing I'm leaving, then."

Suddenly another voice startled them all.

"We've been a little concerned about the same thing, Hew." Hew swished his falchion in the direction of the voice but nearly dropped it when he saw the tall man who had just appeared out of thin air right behind him. "Loyalty is not a tenuous connection." The extraordinarily tall, pale man stepped into the circle, and the men slunk away to give him room. "So my thought was to come up with a way to keep this man on our side."

A bead of sweat formed on Hunter's brow and he checked the urge to brush it away. He felt bizarrely as though all his clothing had just dropped off him. "No, you see, I'm leaving."

Golgathaur went on as if he hadn't heard. "New things have come to light, though, my friend. Ronav is dead."

Hunter's jaw dropped. "He was alive when I left him," he insisted.

Golgathaur waved a hand. "I know you were not responsible. I watched it happen from my position in the woods. Admittedly, we were tired of Ronav, so we would have found some way to unfortunately lose the poor fellow if the young lady hadn't done it for us. She's a fascinating one, isn't she? I do admire ubiquitousness."

"Kyer Halidan killed Ronav?"

"Yes. Strange, isn't it, that she should be responsible for Ronav's death as well as Con's? Fascinating."

Hunter swore under his breath. She was like a curse that now hung over his head. *That girl gets around.* Hunter felt his guts grind in anticipation of the moment he dreamed of.

Golgathaur clapped his hands together with delight and shot an eager grin at Hunter, as if about to ask a toddler if he'd like some cake. "Now, dear Hunter, would you care to learn of the plan?" Without waiting for a response, he continued. "You have shown such strength of character, not to mention a natural tendency for leadership—"

Not so natural. Hunter thought bitterly. *A whole God-damned lifetime of training.*

"—that I am bestowing upon you—" He turned with a flourish of his black cloak and included the entire company in his announcement. "—the title of chief!" He pumped Hunter's hand. "I just know we're going to be great friends, Chief Hunter."

And as abruptly as he had arrived, Golgathaur was gone, leaving behind stunned silence and a new chief who had virtually no blood left in his face.

Hew glared at him. Hunter clutched the eye contact to conceal his loathing both for his companion and for the position he was now in. How long could he avoid betraying his loyalty to the duke he had loved and served for nearly his entire life?

One day, I am going to kill her, Fredric Heyland vowed.

End of Book One

Dear reader: Reviews go a long way to helping authors reach more readers. If you enjoyed *Gatekeeper's Key,* I would be thrilled if you reviewed it or gave it some stars on Goodreads, or the site where you purchased it. Thank you so much.

For more about me and my books, visit my website,
and subscribe to my
Totally Fantastic Email List
for lots of free stuff and exclusive content
https://kristawallace.com

Turn the page for a sneak peak at the sequel,
Gatekeeper's Deception 1 – Deceiver

Sneak preview

Gatekeeper's Deception 1
Deceiver

One

Whatever It Takes

Kyer leaned forward, her back as rigid as the chair on which she sat, and watched Valrayker. The dark elf chewed the inside of his cheek. There was a slight tremble in his shoulder as he breathed deeply and forced a tight-lipped smile. He was trying to hide it, all right, but she could tell. Beneath that mask of calm the dark elf was distressed. The crackle of the fire challenged the silence in the small chamber. Val stood before her and her four companions with such an uncharacteristically formal attitude, she forgot the full wine cup next to her.

"A week after you left on your mission," Val said, "we received a message from Bartheylen Castle." Kyer made a quick calculation. *Three weeks ago, then.* "You will note that Kien is not here to greet you, and he asked me to pass on his regrets."

Kyer felt like waving her hand to brush the comment aside. Clearly a higher concern took precedence over mere courtesies. But it wasn't her place to dismiss it.

"He returned in great haste to Bartheylen Castle upon hearing that Lady Alon Maer has been taken seriously ill."

Kyer's heart jolted. "How seriously?"

"We do not know. The healers could tell us their observations but have drawn no conclusions. All we know is that it seems her life may be threatened by this illness."

The dread hung in the chamber like the deep resonance of a gong. The group waited.

Valrayker was not finished. "The other part of the problem is that Alon is pregnant. It stands to reason that if her life is in danger, so is that of the child." Here, the dark elf turned away, and Kyer saw his shoulder blades contract, controlling the emotion that surged. She looked around at her friends and frowned with concern at Derry. He looked nearly overcome, with his palm pressed over his mouth. As Val's captain, he had known Kien and Alon Maer for at least half his life.

"There must be *something* we can do," Kyer said. "Do the Healers not have *any* ideas?"

All five watched their leader expectantly.

Valrayker composed himself. "It is true that there is one idea."

"Well, let's have it!" Kyer said.

The dark elf contemplated her. "I confess I'm moved by your depth of feeling for a dear friend of mine, though you have never met her."

Kyer frowned away her blush. They would never understand why Alon Maer meant so much to her.

Valrayker wandered over to gaze at the map on the wall.

"The healers at Bartheylen Castle are the best in Rydris. They have employed the full spectrum of their craft, all the ancient arts, their knowledge of spells and charms, all their energy and internal powers and have come up with nothing but minor, temporary remedies. They cannot even come up with a diagnosis, let alone what they need: a cure. The prime healer here in Shael suggested it, and we all agreed that in order to learn exactly what ails Alon, and to discover a cure, if there is one, we need to consult a higher power."

Valrayker turned and looked directly at Jesqellan.

Jesqellan is a higher power? Kyer thought doubtfully. But then she saw the mage's eyes widen.

"You can't mean that we need to consult Kayme?" Jesqellan murmured, his slackened jaw agape.

The duke nodded gravely. "The prime can think of no other option."

Kyer looked from one troubled face to another around the room. Nobody seemed happy with the idea. *Who's Kayme?*

"No one has seen or heard from Kayme in *years*!" said Jesqellan. "Why, it has been at least *fifteen years* since I have heard him utter a single sound from his dark tower way up north, and even then it was a three-word declaration, 'I am busy,' that gave us all the strong message that he absolutely does *not* want to be disturbed! One does not just walk up to the tower of the most powerful wizard in Rydris, knock on the door, and ask for a casual favour as if we were asking to borrow some eggs. It just isn't done."

"It's our only hope," Valrayker said, sinking wearily into his chair. "If you don't wish to be a part of it, I won't blame you or bear any grudge against you. It may be that he isn't willing or even able to help us. I'm merely asking you to try."

"I'll go," said Kyer without hesitation.

"As will I." Phennil nodded, though the blond wood elf spoke too confidently for Kyer to believe he wasn't afraid.

"You know I will," Captain Derry said quietly to his lord.

Jesqellan stared at the floor and said nothing. Next to him, Janak sat with his jaw crooked in a thoughtful pose and played with his beard.

"It isn't necessary to make a decision this instant," Valrayker assured them. "The situation is urgent, but I'm also fully aware of the danger you would be heading into. We'll talk further in the morning."

Kyer left the chamber as swiftly as decorum allowed. Her teeth felt numb, and no amount of elvish wine had stilled the thudding in her chest. A few hours earlier they had ridden into the city of Shael expecting celebration after their successful mission in the north. Instead she had sensed that a pall had settled over the city. Whatever she had thought the cause might be, she hadn't imagined this.

Derry stayed in the room with his Lord awhile longer, but Phennil, Jesqellan, and Janak followed her into the back of the castle foyer. Kyer gulped fresh air, only now becoming aware of how many hours they had been cooped up in the small chamber. It had been midday when they arrived, and now the torches and candles were lit to fill the shadows that stretched from corner to corner across the stone. The story of how they rescued the people of Nennia had taken several hours. At least two meals had been brought to them as they told their tale.

"I don't mean to sound like I'm complaining or anything," said Phennil with a shake of his blond hair, "but weren't you hoping we'd get to *rest* a bit when we got back here? I suppose we'll have to leave again in a few days."

"Of course." Kyer tried to find a purpose for her hands. "I'd leave now if I could."

Jesqellan clutched the front of his brown, travel-weathered Moabi robes. "Some of us have not yet decided if we will go at all," he said softly. "Some of us are more aware than others of the significance of Valrayker's request."

Phennil's forehead creased with concern at the mage's warning, but Kyer stood her ground. "He needs us to ask a wizard for help. How difficult can that be?"

"My dear girl, Kayme is not just 'a wizard'." Jesqellan narrowed his eyes at Kyer. "I was not exaggerating when I said Kayme is *the most powerful* wizard in all of Rydris. He is arrogant, impatient, and does not like to be disturbed." The black man's voice remained quiet, but its increased intensity betrayed his fear. "Casual favours will not be entertained. And I shudder to think what the price will be for such an interruption."

"This is hardly a casual favour," Kyer said, matching his intensity with no trace of fear. "A person's *life* is at stake."

Jesqellan drew up his entire five-and-a-half foot height. "Many lives are at stake all over Rydris. War does that." He tapped his staff on the stone floor in frustration. "Three years ago, a small party sought his help, and he became so enraged at their temerity they found themselves scattered, separately, to the corners of the continent! No food, no horses, no weapons, nothing. Alone. It took my cousin six months to reach home again, and he very nearly perished." A gusty sigh escaped his lips. "Yes, a life is at stake. Nevertheless, no life is worth the risk of summoning the wrath of Kayme upon myself."

Janak's grunt inserted itself between his two comrades. "I'm deciding nothing until I've slept in a bed for one night." He opened the door to the tower stairs. "Val said an instant decision wasn't necessary—" He darted a backward glance at Kyer, his deadened left eye baleful. "—so, unlike some, I'll not make one." He bumped into the doorframe as he shuffled his dwarven bulk into the stairwell. Jesqellan nodded to Kyer and Phennil and went after him.

Kyer did not follow. Earlier she'd have given almost anything to drag her exhausted, travel-weary body upstairs to her cosy guest room in Shael Castle. Instead, the dark elf's announcement had dispersed her fatigue. There was something she had to do before she would sleep tonight.

Smouldering, she stalked across the stone floor into the shadows of the castle foyer. Granted, she didn't know this Kayme person; perhaps she ought not to be hasty. Would extra consideration change her mind? Janak knew better than the others how she had been affected by her previous hasty actions. He had every right to caution her about her decision making. This time, though, Kyer's impulsive choice was not a reckless one, no matter how it came across to her companions. *I don't need to justify my "instant decision" to any of them.* She hopped up the first few stone steps of the broad staircase that curved its way up to the second floor.

She stopped partway up and turned to face the massive oak doors that both provided and denied entrance to the keep. Raising her gaze above the doors, she beheld there the image she had wanted—no, *needed* to see.

The painted version of Lady Alon Maer stood next to her jet black horse, healthy, dignified, her palm resting on her sword hilt. Beautiful and deadly. How many had she killed? How many of those were duels in which the lady had been forced to make a snap decision? *How many,* Kyer sucked in her breath, *were cold-blooded revenge against the direct order of her superior?*

Kyer had killed six men since coming into contact with Valrayker. Two had been in self-defence during an attack in the woods. Two had been in Nennia, in defence of her friends. The other two had been one-on-one. Face to face. The first was a duel in which a blackguard named Simon had cheated. He would most certainly not have been content to accept his defeat had she left him alive. The other . . . Kyer gripped the balustrade as the tempest of emotion swirled around her again.

In her report to Valrayker, Kyer had admitted to killing Ronav Malachite. She couldn't have avoided telling him. But what she had left out was the manner in which she had killed him. Ronav had made himself her enemy. He had beaten her, flogged her, and very nearly mutilated her. He had done unspeakable things to a village full of innocent people. Oh yes, he deserved to die. And though she had promised Derry she wouldn't take matters into her own hands, she had disobeyed his direct order because *she* wanted to be the one to kill Ronav.

There was no glory in it.

Derry had been angrier with her than she had ever seen him. But eventually he had, she thought, understood why she had done it.

Kyer's vision cleared and she stared at the Lady, a warrior to whom this kind of struggle must not be foreign. Kyer nodded, certain that the Lady's gaze seemed to forgive her. She renewed the vow she had made a short time ago.

"I'll do it alone if I have to."

She was startled by the sound of a throat clearing softly. "You won't have to do it alone, Kyer. Derry and I volunteered, too, remember?"

Phennil's light-footed steps had traced hers. He stood at the bottom of the stairs, eerie and ghostlike in the dim light of a dozen or so half-burned candelabra around the stone walls of the foyer. He looked up at her cautiously, politely not intruding upon her space.

She blinked a few times, and a grim smile finally eased the tautness in her forehead. He took it as an invitation, and leapt, two steps at a time, to join her. Kyer sat and waited for him to ask the question she knew was on his mind—the same question Val had already raised. She braced herself.

"What do you think?" He plopped down next to her. "Will they join us?"

She turned to him, surprised; that was not the question she expected. "Do you doubt it?"

"I don't know. Jesqellan seems awfully hesitant, and Janak—"

"Won't say no to a mission that *I've* said yes to," finished Kyer. "Janak and I . . . we reached an understanding," she said thoughtfully. "I imagine things won't have changed that much." She rested her elbows on her knees.

"What about Jesqellan?"

Kyer's jaw jutted out thoughtfully, and she breathed in the faint odours of coal, wood, and stone. "If I've learned anything about Jesqellan, it's that he needs to know he's useful. He'll know we need him on this mission."

Kyer looked sidelong at her friend. Janak and Jesqellan thought she had been impulsive again. Here was Phennil, in perfect position to suggest the same thing, and he hadn't. Somehow that decided it. Kyer peered up through the darkness to the enormous portrait that was the focal point of the foyer, right above the oaken front doors. The subject of the painting was barely visible in the candlelight, but Kyer knew it by heart. "How well do you know Alon Maer?" The Lady looked down at them out of her exquisitely painted eyes, her pale high elven face surrounded by thick, multihued dark hair.

"I've only met her a couple of times," Phennil admitted. "I think Jesqellan and Janak are both ahead of me." He turned a puzzled eye to Kyer. "But I've met her a couple of times more than you. What made you volunteer? You even beat Derry."

There it was. The question she'd expected.

Kyer didn't answer straight away. Instead she rose and gazed at Alon's portrait with the same admiration she felt the first time she'd seen it. The sword, the marvellous detail of the Lady's leather cuirass that reminded Kyer of her own, unequivocal substantiation of something special Kyer shared with her. The Lady's hand, resting on her hilt, revealing the corded muscles in her wrists and forearms. Kyer clenched and released her fists, sensing her own strength concealed there. This was what Kyer had needed to do before she could retire to bed.

"Phennil," she began, and her throat tightened. "Remember the first time I entered this castle? It was, what, a month ago? And you had to come and get me from this very spot so we could go meet Kien."

Phennil nodded. "I had to call you about three times."

"I have never met another woman who is a swordfighter. A *true* fighter. Soldiers, troopers, yes, but—" She took a deep breath as she considered whether or not to speak her next words. "I studied the *wæpnian*, Phennil, I don't know if you knew that."

He whistled low. "That would explain a few things."

"Back home in Hreth, I used to train with another girl my age, but she didn't take it as seriously as I did. People used to call me a freak and names a lot worse. They'd whisper and stare at me. They'd do everything they could to avoid me." Kyer pointed at the portrait. "She is a warrior, one of the best.

She is—" Kyer's throat caught as she realized what she was about to say, "—*living* proof a woman being a fighter is not freakish." She sat back down. "I have more in common with the Lady Alon Maer than I have ever had with any other woman. That means more to me than I can possibly explain."

Kyer gazed into the wood elf's startlingly blue eyes. "Phennil, I know I have never met her. I never will, if she dies."

To be continued...

Acknowledgements

Thank you to all the people who helped me with this book, in particular Rob Smith, Myst DeVana, Jonathan Lyster, Colleen Condit, Brenda Carre, Jen Landels, Stuart Hollett, Chari Grant, Harold Gross, Stephanie Kwok and editor, Andrea Howe. Paula, John, Edwin, Teresa, Paul, I am so grateful for your support! Shout out to the Original Six (Rob, Doug, Matt, Phil, Brian and Garnet).

Special thanks to Brian Rathbone, who kicked off the whole audio thing, encouraged me, and even helped design my covers.

I could never to do any of this without my family: My husband Matt, who is one of the Best Humans in the whole wide world. My "kids" David and Maggie, who have been dealing with this literally their whole lives (sorry I didn't use your title idea, Boy), and to Heather who joined later, but leapt into the Helpful and Supportive pool with the others.

Who is Krista Wallace?

Krista started out as a singer, studied Theatre and got her degree in Acting at UVic, then eventually added writing to her creative endeavours. She has sung classical, musical theatre, rock, R&B and jazz. She has been the vocalist for FAT Jazz for something like 427 years, and is half of a jazz duo called The Itty Bitty Big Band. She writes primarily fantasy, but dabbles in other genres, in both short and long fiction. Combining all her artistic exploits, she took on audiobook narration, and producing a podcast, [Totally Fantastic Title], which then branched into the production of her own audiobooks. Krista grew up in the Port Coquitlam vortex, and so was naturally pulled back there after her time away.

To be continued...

41466756R00219